LOTTIE CASANOVA

Also by Merle Jones

Mademoiselle
Kingmaker

LOTTIE
CASANOVA

Merle Jones

HEADLINE

'Burlington Bertie From Bow', William Hargreaves. Copyright 1915,
reproduced by permission of EMI Music Publishing Ltd, London
WC2H OEA.

'Happy Days Are Here Again', Milton Ager/Jack Yellen. Copyright
1929, Advanced Music Corp., USA. Reproduced by permission of
Lawrence Wright Music Co Ltd., London WC2H OEA.

British Library Cataloguing in Publication Data

Jones, Merle
Lottie Casanova.
I. Title
823'. 914 [F]

ISBN 0-7472-0225-7

Typeset in 11/11 pt Plantin
by Colset Private Limited, Singapore

Printed and bound in Great Britain by
Richard Clay Ltd, Bungay, Suffolk

HEADLINE BOOK PUBLISHING PLC
Headline House
79 Great Titchfield Street
London W1P 7FN

For Richard Longhurst
Who shares my view that life
is more a music hall act than a cabaret

AUTHOR'S NOTE

Lottie Casanova is a creation of fiction, but 'Ta-ra-ra-boom-de-ay' is one of the real all time great music hall songs. It was popularised, too, by a real Lottie – Lottie Collins – in 1891. Miss Collins, like the fictional Lottie Casanova, found the original song in America, where a bump-and-grind version had been doing the rounds of New Orleans brothels for twenty years before featuring in a forgettable musical called *Tuxedo*. She commissioned an English version of the words from the lyricist B.M. Batchelor.

Lottie's 'abandon dance' was so ferocious that she often fainted in the wings at the Grand, Islington, where she introduced the song in the pantomime, *Dick Whittington*. Between 1892 and 1896 it was the universal popular hit. The song did for Lottie Collins in the end. She was so strongly associated with 'Ta-ra-ra-boom-de-ay' that when the audiences finally tired of it, she, too, went into eclipse. She collapsed and died of a heart attack in 1910, when she was just forty-four years old. Her daughter, Jose Collins, went on to make a much bigger name for herself in music hall.

PART ONE

Overture and Beginners

PROLOGUE
London, 1903

The diamond brooch glittered malevolently on the dressing table. Once a man got to diamonds, you could count off the remainder of the affair in days. Lottie swore under her breath and slammed down the heavy tortoiseshell hairbrush beside the gift. Bastards – all of them, bastards! At the beginning, it was always, 'Just a bite of supper and a glass of bubbly, Lottie . . .' and the next minute, 'Get your drawers off, Lottie, I haven't got all night'. Damn their bloody eyes! Why was she always such a mug?

She picked up the jewel and drew back her arm to fling it at the wall. As she did so, the big central stone sparked with freezing fire. Lottie paused, opened her fingers and looked at it again. Mmm, well, you could hardly call it a *cheap* excuse; and he hadn't been that lovable . . . Lottie relaxed, now holding the trinket at her side, her burst of tears already past. Why should she waste grief on that nobody, when every night she had a thousand lovers unable to get enough of her?

That brought her attention back to this evening. Christ, why was she weeping here when they were already panting for her? Brushing away the last tears, Lottie went back to the dressing table to make up her face. By the time she had finished, Maud was back, ready to help her into her gown. Not that most people would call it a gown, she reflected, stepping into it. Not enough of it for that, really.

Maud pulled it up around her, clucking like a mother hen as she did so. 'If you put on another two pounds, Miss Lottie, you'll 'ave to order another of these frocks. Too much champagne and choclit, that's what it is!'

'Nonsense, Maud, I haven't had a chocolate all week. Anyway, you know I'll sweat it off in twenty minutes out there.'

'Ladies don't sweat, Miss Lottie.'

'And we all know the answer to that one! Come along, now, Maud, do – we've only got a few minutes.'

The woman gave a brisk tug at the boned scarlet satin and it came together across Lottie's back. She breathed in while Maud hooked it in place, then ran her hands down over her ribcage and hips. 'There you are. Nothing wrong with that, is there? Not an ounce in the wrong place.'

'Willpower, Miss Lottie – sheer willpower!'

Lottie stood in front of the cheval glass to check her appearance. The gown barely reached her knees, and the hemline was feathered so that glimpses of her thighs showed as she moved. She intended to move quite a lot. Beneath the skirt, her legs were covered by fine black silk tights, and she wore high-heeled boots of scarlet kid, front-laced to the calf. Her shoulders were bare, and a fichu of glossy black cock feathers emphasised the gown's neckline as it swooped between her breasts. Black stays highlighted her murderously laced waist. Lottie grinned at the devastating vulgarity of her ensemble. Just a few trimmings, and she was ready . . .

She held out her arms, and Maud came forward with the skin-tight black kid gloves which reached almost to her shoulders. They were such a close fit that they had to be worked up her arms before the rows of tiny spherical buttons were fastened at the wrist openings. Then came the hat, a vast red satin cartwheel bedizened with black cock feathers and scarlet ostrich plumes.

As Maud slipped the two long hatpins into place, there was a knock at the door and a youthful voice cried: 'Five minutes, please, Miss Casanova!'

'All right, Maud, here we go again . . . I hope they're ready for me, 'cos I'm bloody well ready for them!' She swayed out through the door, an empress about to receive her myriad lovers.

It was a good house tonight. Lottie could feel them – smell them – waiting beyond the footlights, throbbing with their mounting desire for her. Well, she'd give them their money's worth. The orchestra struck up the introduction to a song that had made Lottie Casanova a synonym for cheerful salacity. Her pulse began to tap out a primitive drumbeat of sexual arousal as she stepped forward into the limelight, her treacherous lover forgotten. She had another lover now, more savage, more exciting, more demanding and more satisfying than him or any other man. She filled her lungs, flung back her magnificent shoulders, and started to sing, a sequence of superficially innocuous words which became dangerous the moment she uttered them:

> 'A smart and stylish girl you see,
> The belle of high society;
> Fond of fun as fond could be
> When it's on the strict QT.
> Not too young and not too old,
> Not too timid, not too bold,
> But just the very thing, I'm told
> That in your arms you'd like to hold!'

And as they strained forward, seeking a closer look at the incomparable legs, she undulated down stage to stand only feet away from the front stalls, turning her back on them and lifting her already short skirt as she swung into the chorus:

> 'Ta-ra-ra BOOM-de-ay,
> Ta-ra-ra boom-de-ay,
> Ta-ra-ra boom-de-ay,
> Ta-ra-ra boom-de-ay . . .'

The audience had seized it now, roaring out the repetitive line again and again as Lottie strutted on the stage, eventually discarding her long tight gloves with an air of such intense eroticism that half the audience imagined she was removing her whole costume.

4

Half an hour later, her gloves gone, her body singing with fulfilled passion, she left them, still howling for more. Suddenly weak, she leaned against a damp brick wall backstage, relaxed for a moment and let her thoughts drift. A random memory struck her. Her first public performance! Quite a long way from tonight. Her dress was high-necked, ankle-length and white, utterly respectable; her face bare of make-up. She was on a makeshift stage in the ballroom, piping out in a childish voice:

'My mother said I never should
Play with the gypsies in the wood . . .'

A trickle of laughter escaped Lottie's lips. 'Oh, Mama,' she said, 'I did, though, didn't I? If only you could see me now! What a long way I've come from Lyonesse . . .'

CHAPTER ONE
Lyonesse, Wiltshire 1895

Nothing ugly was permitted anywhere near Laura Cazenove. A creature of beauty, she expected all about her to conform to her own standards of perfection. This particular summer morning found her seated at an exquisite breakfast table which had been set up on the sunny terrace overlooking the south lake, itself part of a landscape designed generations ago by Capability Brown to improve on nature. Her Irish linen napkin matched the tablecloth. A fragile porcelain breakfast service of translucent white, painted with sprays of pink roses, echoed the delicacy of the linen, and of the lady who used them both. It was unthinkable that such an ethereal being should stoop to the vulgarity of bacon and eggs. Her table was supplied with freshly-baked white rolls, cream and unsalted butter from the home farm, honey from the estate hives and nectarines from the hothouse. Her coffee was finest arabica.

She would not see her husband, Lord Ilchester, until she had finished her meal. He had a lamentable tendency to eat devilled kidneys or cold partridge at this hour of the morning, and to read aloud extracts from *The Times*'s bloodier war reports. Laura Cazenove was privately convinced that the consumption of meat before noon and an interest in military matters were purely masculine pursuits. Gregory had learned long ago that anything which pained his beloved wife would bounce back on him before long. He loved devilled kidneys only a little less than he adored Laura, so abstinence was unthinkable, but he compromised by having them served on a tray in his room. By the time husband and wife exchanged good mornings, he was sated on meat and foreign war news and ready to fit her vision of ideal manhood.

Laura finished her breakfast and summoned a footman by ringing a tiny silver hand bell, elaborately moulded to represent a fairy holding a tulip. Its tone was so muted that the unfortunate servant was forced to lurk behind the french windows in the dining room to await her summons, but in Laura's mind the beauty of the bell overrode such minor inconvenience to others.

Now he had heard the bell, James was free to clear the table. His real name was Benjamin Hardy, but Laura always called footmen James to avoid confusion. She watched him work, glad that he looked so clean and wholesome. She insisted that her personal servants should be free of any visible physical blemish. It was sad enough knowing that suffering existed at all, without having it forcibly drawn to one's attention.

'Thank you, James.' Laura's voice was as lovely as the rest of her. The footman felt less resentful about having to listen for the bell. 'When you have removed the tray, please tell Nanny that I wish to see Miss Charlotte as soon as

7

nursery breakfast is over. Oh – and is His Lordship downstairs yet?'

'Yes, Milady, about half an hour ago. I think he's in the library.'

'In that case, please speak to him before you go to the nursery and ask if he would care to join me here.'

'Very good, Milady.'

Laura rose and moved away from the table to look at a mass of honeysuckle which spread its red and cream glory over a nearby grey stone wall. It would be too unfortunate if she remained seated and James chanced to brush against her as he cleared the breakfast things.

> 'It's the same the 'ole world over,
> It's the pore wot gets the blame.
> It's the rich wot gets the pleasure,
> Ain't it all a bleedin' shame?'

James grinned as the shrill cockney rhyme echoed down the nursery landing. Someone was in for trouble and he knew who.

'Miss Charty, stop it! Stop it this instant! Your mama would have forty fits if she could hear you!'

That was Nanny. The singer desisted abruptly from a reprise of her song. 'I'll do wot I bloody well like and don't fink you can bloody well stop me!' The cockney accent was more obviously faked in speech. In the song it could have been genuine. Nanny was close to hysteria.

'Please, Miss Charlotte! It'll be my job next, if you go on like that. You know young ladies don't use that word.'

'Bloody-bloody-bloody-bloody-bloody! Don't want to be a young lady. All that lah-di-dah nonsense would drive me mad.' The youthful voice was now unmistakably upper class. 'If swearing is all I must do to give up being a lady, I shall learn lots of other bad words and do it all the time.'

As James knocked and peeped round the door he caught a wicked gleam in the girl's eyes. She started again, this time in creditable imitation of her mother's best Lady Bountiful voice: ' "Good afternoon, Lady Margaret, do come and join us in the bloody garden, then you can take the bloody weight off your feet" . . . Oh, goodness!' She saw James and stopped in mid-tantrum, eyes widening until they seemed to swamp her face, hand slapped to her lips as though to stifle the words she was about to utter.

James contrived to look as though he understood nothing of what was going on. Ignoring Charlotte, he spoke directly to Nanny Baxter.

'Her Ladyship says will you bring Miss Charlotte down to her on the south terrace as soon as she's finished breakfast, Mrs Baxter. The master's already with her.'

Nanny looked as though she might collapse in tears any second. She gazed beseechingly at the footman, silently begging him to stay. Even a born rebel like Charlotte Cazenove would think twice before continuing such a display of bad manners in front of a manservant. James understood and felt sorry for Nanny Baxter. The mistress was unlikely to accept that her precious Charty could be so naughty and wayward. If she was ill behaved, it must be the fault of those who were educating her. A demonstration like the one he had just witnessed could lead to Nanny's dismissal. Hardly a cheerful prospect for a woman who had worked all her life for one family.

8

He need not have worried. Charlotte Cazenove was temperamental and outrageous, but she adored Nanny and was not at all fond of her mother. She knew in her heart who would be blamed for her naughtiness and recognised the injustice of the situation. Instantly contrite, she started across the room to Mrs Baxter.

'Oh, Nanny, what a little beast I am! Please forgive me. Of course I shan't disgrace you in front of Mama.' Rebellion surfaced again momentarily. 'But don't think I shall grow up into the sort of milksop she expects! I promise to behave this morning, but after that we shall have to see.'

Nanny sighed with relief. It was more than she had dared hope for a moment ago. 'All right, James, you may tell Her Ladyship that we'll be with her in ten minutes.'

'His name's not James, it's Benjamin. Why d'you call him James just because Mama's too inconsiderate to remember his name?'

Nanny was all flurry again. 'Hush, Miss Charty! If Ben . . . er . . . James . . . doesn't object, I don't see why you should.'

'Don't put any money on that, Nanny. He wants to keep his job, so he'd let Mama call him Monkey-face if he had to. I think it's disgusting!'

The footman decided it was time to intervene. 'Now, Miss Charlotte, you'll only upset Nanny. Don't you worry on my account; I can look after myself.' Just the same, he was touched by the girl's indignation. She seemed to be the only one around here who understood that sort of thing, and she was just a little slip, too.

Still looking mutinous, Charlotte gave up her protest. Nanny sighed with relief. This time the tantrum was really over. She gestured silently at the door, indicating that the footman should leave before the girl was tempted to start again.

'Now let's get you properly dressed. You can't go down to your Mama in that pinafore . . .'

Benjamin Hardy quietly closed the nursery door and nudged his character back into the biddable James. For a minute there, Miss Charlotte had got him feeling as rebellious as she was. Ah, well, dreams were one thing. Reality was four footmen called James, Robert, Thomas and William because that was what footmen had been called in Lady Ilchester's mother's day. And Lady Ilchester paid the wages.

Nanny finished brushing her charge's hair and looked at the girl in wonder, her disquiet fading miraculously as she contemplated her loveliness. At fifteen, Charlotte Cazenove was still a child by the standards of the time. Her personality reflected that immaturity, but physically she was already a woman. At five feet six, she was taller than many girls of her age. She bore a striking resemblance to her mother, with the same jet black hair and wide-set, dark brown eyes that had driven the young men of Laura Cazenove's generation to distraction twenty years before. Her mouth was large, the lips so beautifully sculpted that any hint of grossness was avoided, her nose prominent and straight, balanced by a wide forehead and eyebrows which arched like dark wings above the glowing eyes. It was not a face that would ever be easily forgotten. There was a foreign, exotic look about the Cazenove women, doubly strange in that the families of both Charlotte's parents had been established in England since the Norman Conquest.

Charlotte's body was beginning to ripen deliciously. She was narrow-hipped

9

and had a small waist, its grace exaggerated by a long ribcage. Her breasts were already well rounded but still sufficiently undeveloped to give her silhouette a boyish look.

Although she resembled her mother, the likeness was purely physical. Laura Cazenove lacked the fierce, quick intelligence of her daughter. She mistook sentimentality for sensitivity, and clever conversation for profound intellectual insight. Charlotte had no time for such pretentiousness and half her rebellious tantrums were caused by her mother's determination to stifle the girl's individuality and turn Charlotte into Laura reincarnated. Now, as she fretted under Nanny's hairbrush, Charlotte was already brooding about what her mother might be planning.

'Bet she wants me to learn some soppy poem like *The Lady of Shalott*,' she grumbled. 'All those arty people are coming down from Saturday to Monday. She'll want to show me off, and this morning she'll be planning the campaign!'

'And why shouldn't your mama show you off, you silly child? You're quite lovely, and so like her at the same age it's almost creepy,' said Mrs Baxter. 'Except in temperament, of course. Your mother always had such a sweet, obedient nature, you'd hardly credit it. She'd certainly never have carried on the way you did just now.'

Charlotte scowled into the mirror. 'I'm not sorry about that, Nanny, and don't you imagine I am. I just love you too much to make things horrid for you with her. But I'm not going to be the perfect little lady she wants. I want to live my own life, not drift about being a romantic heroine like Mama. Who wants to be married to one man and have hordes of cow-eyed young fellows mooning around after them? Not me! There must be other ways of getting some excitement.'

Nanny was flustered. 'Now hush – it's very rude to talk so of your mother. She and your papa are a perfect couple. It's only natural that such a lovely lady will have a lot of admirers. When you're grown up and married, with your own children, you'll be just the same. A lady feels neglected if she doesn't get that sort of attention. There's nothing improper about it.'

'That's the trouble – it's all *so* proper!' The girl's tone was frankly scornful, and far more adult than Mrs Baxter regarded as decent. Before the nanny could silence her, she went on: 'What's the point of having lots of admirers like that if you can't be in love with them and . . . well, you know . . .' Her voice tailed off as she realised Mrs Baxter was staring at her, scandalised.

'And where, may I ask, did you find out about such things?'

Charlotte reddened and looked away. 'We – Ivo and me, that is – we were down by the lower lake, over the other side among the trees, last summer, looking for newts, and we heard one of the girls from the village talking to that footman Mama never liked. It sounded, sort of, secret, so we stayed out of sight and crept up . . . and then we saw them and we went on watching.'

Nanny's lips were pursed and her face was sterner than Charlotte had ever seen it. 'And?'

'Well, we needn't have worried about making a noise, because they wouldn't have heard a thunder storm.' Instinctively, Charlotte was almost whispering. 'She was only wearing her shift, and he had his clothes all undone and everything was showing – you know, down there – but it wasn't like Ivo when you used to bathe us when we were little. It was like when we saw Papa's stallion after that little mare and Mama sent us into the house. And he put the girl's hand on him and she was moaning and groaning and saying, "Now, Edgar, now, please, please!"

'Then he sort of wrapped her around him and they both started wriggling about and grunting. It sounds a bit silly now, but then Ivo and I both got quite excited. They were terribly excited themselves, and the wriggling went on and on and they were moaning and crying and then they went all limp and started kissing each other. They didn't do much after that. I think they dozed off. When we thought they wouldn't notice, Ivo and I crept away. We thought they might have been cross if they knew we were watching.'

'Not another word! I'll not stand here and listen to a child talking about such things!' Throughout the account, Mrs Baxter had listened in outraged silence, too shocked to stop her young charge. Now her sense of propriety had overcome embarrassment and she was ready for battle.

'I'll deal with what you said in a minute, young lady, but first, tell me why you should even think of your mama in connection with such an awful situation.'

Charlotte was not quite sure what she had witnessed between the two servants so long ago, but instinctively she knew it was what the young men who visited the house would have liked to do with Mama. She was fairly sure that Mama would not have reciprocated such feelings. It was not in her nature to hide these thoughts from Mrs Baxter.

'When Mama looks at those men, it's like the girl with Edgar before she got all tangled up together with him . . . looking forward to something and wondering what it would be like. But Mama seems to enjoy just wondering and not finding out. And I think that's silly. It's obvious that the servants had much more fun than she does!'

Mrs Baxter had difficulty in keeping her voice steady. She, too, was almost whispering now. 'Miss Charty, if you ever breathe a word of any of this to your parents, I'll not be answerable for the consequences. What you saw was wicked enough, heaven knows, but you weren't to know that. You and your brother were just innocent children. I'm more worried about those terrible things you're saying about your mother. I'll tell you this once and never want to repeat myself.

'Your mama is the loveliest, most virtuous woman who ever lived. She adores your father and he adores her. But there are certain . . . certain appetites which decent women don't have, although men do. Women are complimented when handsome men pay them attention, but both they and the men know it's never going to amount to more than that. Why, the very idea that you should condemn your poor mama for being virtuous! Of course she doesn't wonder what she's missing! It's far more likely that she's trying to think of some way of easing the poor young men's feelings . . .'

Charlotte grinned broadly. 'That's just what I thought, Nanny.'

'Miss Charlotte! If we weren't already late to see your parents, I'd wash your mouth out with soap. As it is, I never want you to refer to this again. Do you understand me?'

Charlotte recognised the desperation, as well as the outrage, in Mrs Baxter's tone, and reluctantly decided to drop the subject. 'Oh, very well. It's all rather silly anyway. I was only trying to tell you why I don't want to be a debutante and a great lady, that's all. You did ask!'

Gregory Cazenove had recently succeeded to the title of Earl of Ilchester when he met Laura Carteret in 1875. They were part of an aristocratic social set who saw themselves as standing outside conventional Victorian high society. They professed a devotion to art, beauty and living well. They believed in sensitivity, in poetry and in true love. The paintings of the Pre-Raphaelites, Tennyson's recycled Arthurian legends, the textiles and decorations of William Morris's Arts and Crafts movement, comprised their ideal. They rejected the hearty philistinism of the English public schools and the flaunting wealth of the new rich with equal fervour, although some of their own fortunes were relatively recently acquired. The men affected soft jackets, flowing cravats and deeply soulful expressions. The women wore loose, softly coloured gowns in sharp contrast to the whalebone and lace favoured by the Prince of Wales's Marlborough House Set. They were criticised for their bohemianism and secretly admired as dashing, cultivated and glamorous.

And it was hard to dispute their glamour. The men were invariably hand-some, the women either beautiful or animated to attractiveness by intelligence and a lively interest in the world. They also displayed the charisma of the unattainable, for this was a circle which it was impossible to penetrate without appropriate qualifications; and the qualifications were a mystery to nobleman and parvenue alike. Beauty and charm appeared to be basics, along with con-spicuous wealth used inconspicuously. In short, the criteria did not fit those of any one social group, and it confused all those it excluded.

Gregory met Laura when this group of kindred souls was first establishing its fellowship. At the time they were yet to be recognised as a clique. They were merely a shifting party of friends and acquaintances who shared various interests rather unusual for their time. Like half the young men in the circle, Gregory fell in love with Laura within a week of meeting her. There was a queue of handsome suitors jostling for her hand, but it was widely accepted that Laura had fallen in love with the man who must remain lost to her.

Edward Challoner was slightly older than his friends, and married. While Laura's infatuation might have been tolerated or even encouraged had she been married herself, it was unthinkable while she was still single. After a few months of despairing prayers that Challoner's wife would be struck by light-ning or galloping consumption, Laura accepted the inevitable and married Gregory Cazenove. Ever since, she had been at the heart of the group, univer-sally admired, regarded as everything a soulful, cultivated beauty should be. Gregory loved her with unceasing devotion. After all, her distaste for sexual love was no great thing; it was a sentiment she shared with many women of her background and delicacy. Her handsome male admirers knew nothing of such coolness, or if they got a hint of it, assumed that Cazenove was the wrong man to awaken Laura's sensuality.

At decent intervals, Laura produced two sons and a daughter, all of them as good-looking as their parents. Together she and Gregory set the style among their friends for pulling down or modifying their ancestral homes to create graceful, aesthetically satisfying settings for their jewel-like lives. The Cazenoves called their new home Lyonesse. They were tempted by Camelot,

12

but it seemed just a little too presumptuous. Lyonesse had just the right Arthurian connotations without a hint of the arrogance that would have claimed the role of King Arthur for Gregory and Guinevere for Laura.

The house was a magnificent creation – light, airy and uncluttered, decorated in fresh pastel tones and simple fabrics at the height of an age which elsewhere glorified the overstuffed sofa, the plush tablecloth and flocked wall-paper. The glorious Capability Brown grounds of the earlier mansion were retained, adding a proper air of antiquity to Wiltshire's newest great house. Today, after twenty years of marriage, Laura Cazenove had everything. Universally adored and imitated, she was also the most profoundly self-centred hypocrite of a generation which virtually invented the type. Luckily for her, only she and her daughter Charlotte were fully aware of the fact – and Laura forgot it whenever she could.

By the time Charlotte joined her parents on the terrace, the morning mail had arrived and had temporarily diverted her mother's attention. Lady Ilchester was crowing with delight over a heavy sheet of handmade writing paper. 'Ah, Charty, there you are at last! Come and listen to this. I asked dear Sibell Grosvenor to send me a copy of this little poem that George wrote when young Percy started riding. It's charming, quite charming.

> 'Heart's Delight is five years old
> And rides an old white pony
> With the easy seat of a rider bold
> By grassy ways and stony . . .
>
> Heart's Delight is five years old
> His face is fresh and sunny
> His English hair just touched with gold
> Amidst a browner honey
> And English eyes of deepest blue
> Whose courage looks you through and through.'

The last two lines brought tears to her eyes and a huskiness to her voice. She blinked a few times to emphasise her deep sensibility and Lord Ilchester squeezed her shoulder supportively.

'Quite delightful, don't you think? I find it heartening that a really *manly* man like George Wyndham is able to express his emotions so freely, without stupid embarrassment. Somehow it sums up all we stand for.'

Charlotte snorted. 'I thought it was like someone pouring syrup in my ear. What's so special about a boy of five thrashing up and down the drive on horseback? Ivo was riding before he was three!'

Laura Cazenove suppressed her irritation with a visible effort. 'Charty, I sometimes wonder whether you resemble me at all in any way but physically. We really must do something about this unseemly cynicism of yours before it becomes offensive! As it happens, that reminds me of why I asked Nanny to send you down. I think it's high time we took your education in hand –' here she turned momentarily to her husband ' – which is why I asked you if you could join us, dearest. It's too important a matter for me to decide alone. Do sit down and I'll tell you what I have in mind.

13

'Charty has a headstrong streak which must come from one of your warrior ancestors –' her silvery laugh removed any possible sting from the remark ' – and I fear it might take her down all sorts of unsuitable paths unless we find a channel for all her . . . er . . . high spirits. I've thought about this for a long time and in the end, I wondered if it might not be for the best if she started joining in some of Ivo's lessons with Mr Farrell. A gentleman's education never harmed a really womanly woman, and did some of our friends a great deal of good. What do you think?'

Lord Ilchester was unsure of what he thought. Had he not been so intoxicated by the tuberose scent his wife always wore and dazzled as always by her early morning radiance, he might have wondered why she had not discussed the matter privately with him before including Charlotte. Now he could hardly do anything else but agree, unless he wanted his daughter to see that her parents were in less than perfect harmony about her future. He dithered momentarily, groping blindly for some objection which did not sound reactionary.

'Hmm, well, have you considered whether it's advisable for a girl of Charty's age to be taught by a man, and such a young man at that? I wasn't aware you were dissatisfied with Miss Horton's capabilities as a governess.'

'Good gracious, of course I'm not! I'm not proposing to dispense with Miss Horton; she will still teach Charlotte singing and embroidery, and I'm not proposing that Mr Farrell takes over with mathematics, either. There's nothing feminine about that. Miss Horton's arithmetic instruction will be perfectly adequate. I was thinking about languages, particularly, and literature. Mr Farrell has such a brilliant mind and Tristram's French and Latin are splendid thanks to him. That's all I'd like him to do with Charty – languages and literature, and some history. I thought that would provide the right challenge to her mental energies without turning her into a bluestocking. You can hardly object to that.'

Gregory Cazenove had a fleeting memory of Ulick Farrell's smouldering eyes and thought he could object with the greatest of ease; but he was at a loss to say why in the presence of his daughter. In fact, he reflected, it would have been damn' difficult to express his opinion to his wife. As a result, he murmured his assent. Laura smiled triumphantly.

'Oh, you are so understanding, my dear! I can only hope Charty is as fortunate in her husband as I have been.' Impulsively she reached out across the table and touched his hand. He flushed with pleasure at the contact, as conscious of her physical magnetism as he had been on the night he met her.

They were so absorbed in their own small flirtation that neither of them noticed Charlotte's reaction. Her mother's suggestion had transformed her sullen expression into one of happy anticipation.

Until now, Ulick Farrell had been an object of distant interest, unapproachable from her nursery or schoolroom prison, striding across the lawns on his long, strong legs, laughing boisterously as he explained something to one of her brothers, or reading romantic poetry to Lady Cazenove in his bewitching baritone voice with its slight caress of Irishness. If extra lessons were the price of closer acquaintance with him, she would co-operate to the best of her ability. Besides, Miss Horton's French accent was execrable and Charlotte really wanted to speak the language well. It fitted in with various half-formed plans of her own.

14

CHAPTER TWO

'Now – isn't – that – a – pretty – sight!' Ulick Farrell uttered the words slowly and deliberately, as if each formed a separate sentence. He spoke them quietly so that the object of his attention was unaware she was observed. He didn't want to frighten her off.

Charlotte was standing on the margin of one of the lakes which stretched away south-west of the house, screened by a belt of young trees. She had discarded her shoes and black cotton stockings and had tucked her white pinafore and petticoats into her drawers, to enable her to wade bare-legged in the water. Had she been ten years old, it would have been merely a charming sight. In a well-developed fifteen-year-old, it was positively erotic. Farrell could hardly believe his luck. As he watched, she muttered an expletive and reached down to adjust her drawers, hiking them well up her thighs. Charlotte had impossibly long, shapely legs, which she appeared to have been exposing to the sunlight in most unladylike fashion, for they were nut brown. Ulick longed to run his hands over them. He could imagine the sensation now . . . downy hairs on the outer and upper surfaces. Nothing but satiny flesh inside, where the friction of flesh on flesh had prevented any growth . . .

Humour, always his saving grace, intervened. Christ, man, he thought, how are you going to keep your mind off her thighs for long enough to teach her Latin? For the hundredth time, he wondered if Charlotte's mother could really be so naive as to entrust a nubile girl of such beauty to his care. Obviously she had been told less about him than he thought before she engaged him to teach her boys.

Farrell was an unusual young man. The second son of a substantial Ascendancy family with large estates in the south-west of Ireland, he had been intended for the Army. At eighteen, his objections to a military future had been so strong that he was sent to Oxford to read Greats. His double first had been matched by a stream of sporting honours, including boxing and rowing blues. His father refused to consider an academic future for the boy and again insisted on the Army. Ulick objected once more – it was rumoured because Fenian sympathies prevented him from supporting the cause of British imperialism – and his father disowned him. Lady Farrell was made of gentler stuff and sought help from her girlhood friends in England. By the time Ulick packed his bags and left home, he was assured of a teaching post with the Earl and Countess of Ilchester.

Like the rest of their circle, the Cazenoves disapproved deeply of the way England's great public schools were developing. For more than a decade, there had been increasing emphasis on team games, sportsmanship and general physical prowess at the expense of intellectual development. All the men in the group had attended Eton, Winchester or Charterhouse, but in their

15

day, they said, it had been different and the schools had struck more of a balance between physical and intellectual attainment. Not that their criticism prevented them from sending their sons to their own old schools. They regarded it as an unpleasant necessity in preparing for adult life. All except the Cazenoves – or at least, Laura. As usual, Gregory was dragged in her wake, half convinced that he had thought of the whole scheme, half wishing he could insist they conformed with the rest.

Laura's passion for her boys was unfeigned. She adored them. When Tristram reached the right age, he was shipped off to Eton. At thirteen he had no love of team games and fell victim to severe bullying. Determined not to tell his parents, he went into a visible physical decline. When a distraught Laura questioned him closely, he confessed that he was regularly beaten and taunted by his classmates. Overnight, she persuaded Gregory that neither of them could bear their son to be treated thus, although Gregory started by saying that most boys went through something of the sort and got used to it. Tristram was spirited away from Eton and Laura spent the next four years telling all their friends it was a matter of civilised principles. He was educated at home by private tutors. There was no choice in their plans for Ivo's future. He, too, remained at Lyonesse for his education.

Tristram had soon begun to develop physically and now, at seventeen, was strong, self-confident and competitive. He was fortunate in his parents' friends: they all had boys of about his age, so when he went up to Cambridge next autumn he was unlikely to be isolated or rejected. He had always been intellectually promising, but Ulick Farrell had proved the making of him.

The aged cleric who taught Tristram was to be pensioned off when the boy was ready for university, and a new tutor engaged for Ivo, who was then just thirteen. Previously he had shared Charlotte's governess. The old man complicated matters by dying suddenly a year before Tristram's instruction was complete. Ulick, already recruited to teach Ivo, was asked to take over the final intellectual polishing of Tristram, too. He had performed his task with such skill that Tristram was now expected to be the star of his year, and hopes for Ivo were boundless.

Farrell was a natural teacher, and he knew it. Fired with enthusiasm for any and every subject, he was incapable of confining himself to his speciality, but so well-read that his digressions were almost complete educations in themselves. His good looks were in the class that made decent women blush when he glanced at them, convinced that he was speculating on the design of their undergarments. Laura Cazenove was as susceptible as the next woman to such charms, but her high-mindedness led her to dress up her interest as admiration for his intellect. Thus deluded, she found it fairly easy to take the next step, of consigning her precocious daughter to his intellectual care. A more philistine woman would have walled Charlotte up in the east wing and fed her through a hole in the brickwork rather than let her within touching distance of Ulick, but aesthetic refinement made Laura oblivious to such thoughts.

Anyway, Charty was becoming something of a problem.

Charlotte Cazenove was the one cloud in her mother's sunny life. Lady Ilchester had gained an unrivalled level of popularity by concealing her iron will and icy selfishness behind a screen of beauty, good taste and apparent

16

helplessness. Everyone in her circle was bewitched by it, except her daughter. From the earliest days, the two had disliked each other instinctively. Laura had the advantage, because she was an adult and knew how to hide her feelings. Charlotte was forced to learn by her own infant mistakes. Now, in her mid-teens, the loathing was even greater than it had been in her infancy, but she had learned to veil it in conventional politeness for at least some of the time in order to survive.

She was at a loss to explain her antipathy, except that what Laura wanted from life seemed to be the reverse of anything she herself desired. Charlotte had always been as straightforward as a healthy young animal, with a sharp sense of humour and natural impatience with artifice which doomed her to eternal discontent in her mother's essentially artificial world.

By her tenth year, she had achieved a compromise between ideal and reality which ensured that her mother was no happier than she herself. It involved strenuous use of the forbidden expressions she heard bandied about the stable yard; the acquisition of a range of working-class accents from cockney to Somerset peasant; and a knack for leading her brother Ivo off into the most hair-raising adventures, from which they returned dirty, bruised and supremely happy. Anything less like Laura's ideal of a pale, remote, poetic girl child was hard to imagine. Sometimes Lady Ilchester caught herself secretly speculating that a brisk dose of consumption might cause an improvement in her daughter's disposition.

Charlotte paddled about in the lake for fifteen minutes or so, unaware of Farrell's rapt attention. Finally, chilled by the water and bored by the lack of company, she waded ashore. She was sitting against a fallen tree trunk, pulling the black stockings up her still-damp legs, when a shadow fell across her.

She glanced up with a startled gasp, her expression swiftly relaxing into one of relief when she recognised Ulick. 'Oh, thank goodness for that! For a moment I thought it might be Nanny!'

'Now is that any way to greet your new schoolmaster?' he asked, mock-serious. 'You're supposed to show at least as much fear of my opinion as Nanny's, you know!'

She gave him a frankly lecherous smile which momentarily made him forget she was still a child. 'You and Nanny might have different ideas about whether I should show off my legs in public!'

'If you keep up that tone, young woman, your mother might change her mind about her educational plans for you.'

Charlotte wrinkled her nose contemptuously. 'Mama never thinks about me long enough for anything like that.'

'I'm sure she does. You're lucky to get the chance of being taught with your brothers. Most girls are never given an opportunity to read Ovid.'

'And d'you think it makes any difference to the way they're treated in the end? Mama's only doing this because she can't think of a more genteel way of controlling me.' She glanced around to make sure they were quite alone, then dropped her voice ostentatiously. 'I have other plans. I'll tell you, if you promise never to breathe a word.'

'I promise. What had you in mind?'

17

'Nothing to do with Latin and Greek, for a start – the French will come in jolly useful, though.'

'Don't tell me – you're going to run away to sea!'

'Stop making fun or I shan't say any more!'

'Very well. You have my undivided attention.'

'I'm going to be a world-famous actress. There – what d'you think of that?'

He looked at her face, glowing with the conviction that she could achieve anything, and swallowed his instinctive, mocking response. Careful, old man, he thought. She means every word of it. Aloud, he said: 'Charlotte, I'm sure a young lady of your background has no idea of what an actress has to go through, what a debased life it is . . . but surely you've noticed that they are never received in decent society?'

She waved her arm with such a regally dismissive air that he almost believed she might make it. 'Why d'you think I want to be an actress? It would be absolutely marvellous if Mama were to cut me – just think, she'd never be able to tell me what to do again.'

The flirtatious little encounter was getting out of control. Ulick had intended to tease her, he told himself, to strengthen the pupil–teacher relationship by showing her he was a man of the world, albeit a trusty one. Now, unaccountably, he found himself really believing it was important to dissuade the child from going on the stage. He took a deep breath and swallowed the rush of indignant fatherly advice which had bubbled up in response to her confidences. That would range him squarely on her mother's side. Come on, Ulick, give her the impression you think she's a grown woman . . .

'That's all well and good now, but you'd regret it later,' was all he could find to say.

Charlotte laughed scornfully. 'You obviously don't know Mama very well! No one in their right mind would regret being frozen out of her life.'

Now it was Farrell's turn to laugh. 'Really, Charlotte, you must be blind if you believe that! You know your mother is generally regarded as the great beauty of her generation. She's got admirers lining up from here to London just hoping for a smile from her.'

'Yes, and look at them! Talk about niminy piminy! I don't see any men like you joining the queue.'

'Charlotte, what can you mean?'

Once again, he was struck by the girl's unexpectedly adult attitude.

'You know precisely what I mean. I'll tell you why I despise Mama so much. It's because she's the sort of woman who only wants men to look, not to touch.' She moved so close to him that he could smell the delicate odour of her warm young skin and clean, silky hair. It was suddenly very hard for Ulick to keep his hands off her. She went on: 'You're not a man who'd be willing to be kept at arm's length like that – I can tell.'

He felt himself smiling foolishly. 'How can you tell that?' Momentarily, she was perplexed. 'I – I don't really know. I just have this feeling . . . If you took hold of a woman, you'd have to finish it before you let go.'

Ulick was staring at her now. 'And how would a child like you get to know about that?'

She blushed and looked away. 'I don't; not really.' Abruptly, she became angry. 'No one will tell me anything, not even Nanny, but I shall find out! I know there's something, something to do with the way the footman caught hold of that girl . . . it's all tied up together.'

Farrell was bewildered. 'Footman? Girl? What have they got to do with anything?'

'Something I saw, and when I told Nanny she was cross, because I said it was like what Mama wanted from those silly young men. But she wouldn't tell me what they were doing, and it was so . . . so –' she caught his eye, and realised he knew what the unidentified pair had been up to, and that she herself might be closer to finding out than she had expected ' – exciting,' she finished, breathlessly.

Later, he asked himself again and again why he had done it, but at the time there seemed only one possible response. He reached out, put his arms around her, drew her against him and kissed her. It started reasonably chastely, a mere brushing of lips, but then he got her scent again and his mouth opened over hers, his tongue seeking, demanding something whose nature she did not understand. Her body understood, though. She arched against him, moaning encouragement, and momentarily all his self-control vanished. Holding her with almost savage intensity, he pressed her back against the grassy bank and began caressing her neck, shoulders and breasts as he kissed her again.

Then the everyday world intruded and saved him, temporarily at least. A faint gust of laughter was carried to them on the breeze – probably from guests strolling on the lawn below the house. The very normality of the sound made Ulick realise what danger he was in. He sat up abruptly, holding the girl away from him and giving her a little shake as he did so. Charlotte's eyes were closed and her body was limp and malleable with the intense physical arousal that had swept through her. She blinked, and with an effort focused on him. 'What is it, Ulick? Please don't stop now . . .' She swayed towards him once more and only the rigidity of his grip kept her from him.

'Come on, now, quick – pull yourself together, child!' Panic made him brusque, but he still needed to reinforce his determination by calling her a child.

She winced as though he had slapped her, hurt flaring in her eyes. She said: 'I was wrong after all – you *are* the sort of man who lets go before he's finished. Perhaps Mama would suit you better.' Then she pulled away from him and scrambled to her feet.

He was sweating now, acutely conscious of the folly of what he had been about to do. As he stood up and moved to follow her away from the quiet lakeside glade, he realised his passion was not lessened for all his sudden caution. Even now, upset, very much a child, Charlotte Cazenove possessed some inner magnetism that made her irresistible. She walked away from him, stately and graceful in spite of the rumpled pinafore and damp petticoats. No one would ever need to teach Charlotte how to hold back her shoulders, to keep her chin up or to move smoothly from the hips. Her body knew the answers already, even if her mind was barely on the brink of womanhood. And she was still just fifteen! What would it be like when she was twenty . . . or thirty?

He called after her, his voice low so that she could barely hear him.

19

'Charlotte, you weren't wrong. I haven't finished yet. We need more privacy, more time, that's all.'

She turned to face him, the misery banished from her face. 'I wouldn't have let you escape that easily in any case,' she said. 'I'm going to find out about it all, and you're the one who's going to show me! Now I'd better go and change before Nanny sees what a state I'm in.' With that she ran off towards the house, the black stockings twinkling provocatively against her white petticoat frills.

CHAPTER THREE

Ulick Farrell was crippled by two character flaws: reckless courage and an insatiable appetite for women. During the summer of 1895 the two combined to destroy his future in polite society.

A more timorous man would have taken fright at the ease with which he had slid into Charlotte's arms. Ulick did so for four days, then decided it was scarcely worth the trouble. Anyway, by then Charlotte's mother had begun to draw him with a siren call which left no room for competition. Ulick cursed himself for a fool over Laura. He was an intelligent, sophisticated man, and he had met her sort before. He did not even like her, and yet her incomparable beauty, combined with the possibility that he might be the one to waken the sleeping sensuality others had never stirred, urged him onward to fulfilment and self-destruction.

Had anyone dared ask Laura why she ever encouraged the young man, she would have recoiled in horror. Laura believed there was nothing unseemly about a handsome, cultivated woman asking an equally handsome, cultivated man to read hot-blooded verse to her in the orangery or on the terrace. Had it been pointed out that she was a married woman, she would have laughed, and retorted that this alone made it obvious nothing indecorous was taking place. So sincere could Laura Cazenove be at such protestations that all but the most world-weary cynic would have been ashamed at having impugned her honour.

Ulick was never under any illusions about why Lady Ilchester wanted him to read to her. She could not keep away from him. He was not immodest about his physical magnetism,; he had seen it at work before, since he was a young boy. It seemed he had only to let his gaze linger on certain types of older woman to set their blood and their imaginations racing. He had no idea why it happened, but he was always ready to take advantage of it.

So now Charlotte found her new idol all too eager to be gone from the schoolroom when they had finished their morning lessons. She had started them convinced that after classes, Ulick would lure her back to the lake and complete the sensual education he had begun with her. Instead, he was the picture of businesslike detachment, somehow managing to give her his undivided attention without any personal involvement slipping in. Charlotte was furious. She grew even more angry when she realised he did not notice her tempestuous exits. He was obviously too bound up with what he planned to do next.

> 'Then murmured Arthur, "Place me in the barge."
> And to the barge they came. There those three Queens
> Put forth their hands, and took the King, and wept.

21

But she, who rose the tallest of them all
And fairest, laid his head upon her lap,
And loosed the shattered casque and chafed his hands,
And dropping bitter tears against his brow
Striped with dark blood . . .'

With a snort of impatience, Ulick set aside the leather-bound copy of *Le Morte D'Arthur*. 'Really, Lady Ilchester, if you're going to ask me to read to you, you have to choose better than this poor stuff. It's trash – romantic trash!'

Laura was startled from a softly tinted daydream in which she was the ministering Queen and the dying Arthur looked very like a somewhat etiolated Ulick Farrell. 'You're talking about the great poet of his generation, Mr Farrell. If you're so ready to criticise, perhaps you can do better?'

'I should think half the young poets of the kingdom could do better than that. If you want to read Arthur's story and get real pleasure from it, try the Malory version. It's a little harder to understand than this, but that's because it has guts instead of straw inside it.'

Laura blushed, scandalised at the man's indelicacy, but she need not have bothered. Ulick was only beginning to hit his stride.

'If you want a real bit of glowing, sensual verse, I know the poet to give it to you – Swinburne!'

She gave a little squeak of disapproval. 'I never said I wanted sensual verse, Mr Farrell. And if half of what I hear about Swinburne is true, his work is unfit for a gentleman's library!'

Ulick laughed at that. 'I never claimed to be a gentleman, ma'am, but I do claim to know good verse from bad. Wait – I have something of his with me . . .' He riffled through the soft-covered notebook he always carried, until he found the poem he had copied out. 'Listen to this:

'And Pan by noon and Bacchus by night,
Fleeter of foot than the fleet-foot kid,
Follows with dancing and fills with delight
The Maenad and the Bassarid;
And soft as lips that laugh and hide
The laughing leaves of the trees divide,
And screen from seeing and leave in sight
The god pursuing, the maiden hid . . .'

He had her undivided attention. She was leaning forward, listening to the insinuating flow of the verse, made doubly alluring by his beautiful voice. Ulick got up and began to move across to her, continuing to read:

'The ivy falls with the Bacchanal's hair
Over her eyebrows hiding her eyes;
The wild vine slipping down leaves bare
Her bright breast shortening into sighs;
The wild vine slips with the weight of its leaves,

22

But the berried ivy catches and cleaves
To the limbs that glitter, the feet that scare
The wolf that follows, the fawn that flies.'

Laura came out of her reverie with a visible shake. 'I – I must ask you to keep such indecent material to yourself, Mr Farrell. It's less what he says, than what he implies. Disturbing, most disturbing . . .'

'Why? Does it come too close to the way real grown-up people feel? Does it step outside the magic, safe walls of Lyonesse?' He was very close to her now, half bending over her chair, gazing intently into her eyes. Laura attempted a dismissive laugh. It petered out, and she remained, helplessly returning his stare. 'What's wrong, Laura? Afraid the world is going to touch you?'

She swayed forward, almost imperceptibly. The woman in her was aching to touch him but the lady still had some control. Her lips were slightly parted, and her small hands gripped the arms of her chair as though she feared they would embrace him if she let go. Ulick said nothing more. He reached out, slipped two fingers under the soft lace flounce which finished her dress sleeve halfway down the forearm. Finding the silk-smooth fold of flesh on the inner part of her elbow joint, he began a slow, repetitive caress, continuing to stare at her as he did so.

Laura moaned, on the edge of ecstasy, then collected herself as abruptly as she had begun to surrender. 'Wh-what are you doing? Stop it at once – this is unpardonable!'

His voice was soft, persuasive. 'What's unpardonable about a little pleasure? I guarantee that nothing will be the same again.'

'Th-that's what I'm afraid of. Now, please, move away from me. This is most improper. If you don't, I shall have to . . .'

'. . . to call for help? Tsk, tsk – don't you think your dear Gregory might think you'd been the teensiest bit to blame yourself, going off alone to a very private place with a hot-blooded young Irishman?' Ulick could have baited her like this almost indefinitely, but she was too easy prey. He liked them to struggle a little when they were backed into a corner. This one was so stupid under her veil of artificial culture that it was like soothing fish in a barrel. He stood back, and gave a little ironical bow. 'Forgive me, Milady. I can only plead that I was swept away by your beauty.'

Laura knew as well as he did that he was mocking her, but she was unable to think of a counter-strategy at present. God, he thought, what a pity the ravishing ones so seldom have any brains!

Now that he had given her sufficient space to regain her grande dame persona, Laura was recovering fast. She gave him a pretty fair approximation of a wintry smile. 'I think, perhaps, we should forget this entire incident, don't you, Mr Farrell? Sometimes, I fear the warmth of the afternoon air and the stimulus of passionate verse can distort one's proper sensibilities.'

Ulick lowered his head to prevent himself from laughing in her face. She chose to take the gesture as a sign of penitence, and added: 'Come, you are forgiven. Perhaps I was at least a little to blame. I think, though, that we should postpone any further readings until you have had time to change your opinion of dear Tennyson.'

With that she was up and on her way out of the orangery, gliding along as

23

serenely as a ship in full sail. 'Hmm,' he murmured, watching her go, 'there's more to you than meets the eye, Milady.'

He had made a rod for his own back with Charlotte. Never one to prescribe texts when there was an opportunity to make pupils use their own minds, he had set her loose on her father's library to find a different poem for each day of that week, which she must copy out, study and then be able to discuss with him each morning. She had made her debut that day with a long extract from Macaulay's *Horatius*. Apart from the fact that he would have expected a boy rather than a girl to choose it, it was much what he had anticipated from a fifteen-year-old educated by governesses until now. In his view, it was about as much like poetry as an advertising slogan.

The surprise came when he expressed that view to Charlotte and she gave him a withering look. 'I know that, silly,' she said. 'It's no more moving than a piece of wood, but Mama loathes Macaulay, so I really had to choose him, didn't I?'

Farrell sighed. 'That is not an objective criterion for judging the quality of poetry. Why should you choose something simply because your mother dislikes it?'

'Because the things she likes are so awful, of course! If I hear another line of Tennyson, I'll be the one they find floating down to Camelot, dead in a rowing boat!'

'Mmm, well, I don't blame you for that. But there are other poets, you know. Why not take a look at some of the Romantics? That should keep you happy for a while.' At the end of the lesson, when she scampered off armed with a list of Romantic poets to follow his advice, he wondered if it had been sensible.

He got his answer next morning.

Ulick was used to the sort of encounter he had been through with Lady Ilchester. Unmarried girls might be taboo, but it was surprisingly easy to get comely married women alone, both at home on his father's estate and at English country house parties when he was an undergraduate. Laura might be a variation from the norm, but their dalliance had been trivial to him and he had almost forgotten it. His morning lesson with Charlotte soon reminded him.

'I hope you found something a little more inspirational than *Horatius* for today,' he said.

Charlotte chose not to answer him. Instead, she moved over to the window, where she had room to be properly theatrical, and introduced her poem: *La Belle Dame Sans Merci*, by John Keats.

He had known and loved the poem since his not-too-distant boyhood, but he had never heard it delivered with such force and conviction, particularly when she got to the point where former followers of the Belle Dame came back to warn the narrator:

> 'I saw pale kings, and princes, too,
> Pale warriors – death-pale were they all,
> Who cried, "La Belle Dame Sans Merci
> Thee hath in thrall!" '

She was glaring at him intently by now, and Ulick began to feel vaguely embarrassed. It was almost as if she knew something . . .

Then the recital was over and she resumed her seat at the scarred school-room table. 'Now,' she said. 'I'll tell you what it was about.'

'You feel confident of your ability to do that without my guidance? No doubts about whether you understood it properly?' She shook her head, her expression truculent. 'I probably understand it a lot better than you do,' she said. Then she launched into what Farrell remembered for ever afterwards as her Awful Warning, a highly coloured break-down of the men who had pursued her mother – the original Belle Dame Sans Merci as far as she was concerned – and ended up alone and palely loitering, like the rejected knights in the poem.

'So you see, although it's tempting to run after empty beauty, you're doomed if you do,' she concluded. 'I hope you see that now.'

The last sentence tipped Ulick over the edge of indignation into helpless mirth. As he shook with laughter, Charlotte sat opposite him, watching coldly with a patronising expression which would have been offensive in an adult. Eventually she said: 'Perhaps you wouldn't think it so funny if you knew I'd seen it all.'

She was right. 'Seen all what? What are you talking about?'

'It's a very big orangery, Ulick.' Inconsequentially he thought, I should insist on her calling me Mr Farrell, but perhaps the time's not right . . . She went on: 'I came in to find you, because at the beginning I had about three poems I liked and I couldn't make up my mind. I heard you reading as I came in, but then you left Tennyson and started reading that other stuff. And I . . . I just stayed by those thick palms that screen the draughts from the inner door and – and listened. To all of it. After a bit I crept forward and peeped through the foliage. You were both far too busy to notice me.'

Charlotte had not known quite what to expect when she started her confession to Farrell. Guilt? Shame? Fear? Whatever it was, the effect was unlike anything she had imagined. He regarded her in silence for what seemed like centuries, his expression growing colder with each moment that passed.

Finally, when she was at breaking point, he said: 'If you have any bright little ideas about blackmail, dear child, I suggest you go through with them immediately. I'm the wrong sort to be kept twisting on the hook while I wait to be finished off.' His tone was deadly and he looked as if he would have killed her with little further provocation.

Almost in tears, Charlotte said: 'But I didn't mean anything like that – honestly I didn't. I . . . I just l-like you a lot, that's all, and I couldn't bear you going off in such a rush after lessons. I knew you'd be reading to Mama, and I thought, if I had an excuse with the poems, I'd be able to join in. When I got there, I knew I wouldn't be welcome, but somehow I just couldn't leave . . . and then, afterwards, I thought, I'll show him – show him I know what they're up to and warn him she'll throw him over . . . that's all I meant, Ulick, honestly it is!' And she began to cry, sitting at the table, hands clasped in her lap, making no attempt to conceal or stem the tears.

His anger vanished. In a moment, he was around the table, holding her, murmuring words of comfort, and almost before he realised it, they were kissing. Temporarily regaining his sanity, he stood back from the girl. The tears still glistened on her cheeks, but she was radiant now. She gave him a huge smile and said: 'Anyway, Ulick, she's far too old for you!'

CHAPTER FOUR

Laura Cazenove felt restless and irritable. How could she ever have enjoyed listening to Gilbert Aynsley reading Tennyson? She studied him covertly as he concentrated on the text. Had she once thought him handsome?

Aynsley was one of Laura's crowd of male courtiers, and typical of them all. Tall and lanky, he affected the languid manner which most of his group seemed to associate with artistic sensibility. His honey-gold hair was slightly crinkled and women often told him it gave him a boyish look. A silky golden moustache curled over his upper lip, accentuating a petulant mouth which the same ladies thought cherubic. Limpid, heavy-lashed brown eyes and a short, straight nose added the crowning distinction to his attractions. Today, though, Laura remembered one of Charty's more penetrating comments – that Aynsley looked remarkably like a Cavalier King Charles spaniel in a Norfolk jacket.

It's just that wretched child and her endless sniping, Laura told herself, although she had seen Aynsley several times since Charlotte said it and had continued to find him attractive. Now, for some unknown reason, her mind kept returning to Ulick Farrell. Ulick's hair was straight and black and fell forward across his forehead when he made one of his sudden, unpredictable movements. His eyes were bright blue – the most piercing shade Laura had ever seen – and his nose crooked, the legacy of a school boxing match. The mouth was straight and wide, wide enough for countless passionate kisses. Laura daydreamed, then stifled the fantasy.

Aynsley gestured with a white, long-fingered hand to illustrate the verse. Mr Farrell's hands are square and powerful, mused Laura, hard enough to subjugate the most spirited horse . . . or woman. She gave a little shudder and forced herself to concentrate on the reading.

Aynsley was declaiming the Guinevere idyll, always a favourite of Laura's until today, and now he was reaching the section she loved most of all:

> 'And then they rode to the divided way,
> There kissed, and parted weeping: for he past,
> Love-loyal to the least wish of the Queen . . .'

'Oh, do stop, Gilbert. I'm tired of that thing. It has no – no guts!'

He stared at her, aghast. 'Laura, what did you say?'

She was too excited to realise or care how she had shaken his ideal of her as ethereal lady, and rushed on: 'I've been realising lately that Tennyson is a mere scribbler compared with some more adventurous poets. Listen – what do you think of this?' And she strode a few paces across the orangery, to where a backdrop of foliage would highlight her beauty. Breathless, she flung herself into the verse:

'Where shall we find her, how shall we sing to her,
Fold our hands round her knees, and cling?
Oh that man's heart were as fire and could spring to her,
Fire, or the strength of the streams that spring!
For the stars and the winds are unto her
As raiment, as songs of the harp-player;
For the risen stars and the fallen cling to her,
And the southwest-wind and the west-wind sing . . .'

'I-I say, Laura! That's rather . . . well . . . intense, don't you think? I
mean –'

Before Aynsley's fluting tones could express his feelings about Swinburne,
another, deeper voice took up Laura's ode:

'For winter's rains and ruins are over,
And all the season of snows and sins;
The days dividing lover and lover,
The light that loses, the night that wins;'

To Laura, Gilbert Aynsley faded from sight. She gazed at Ulick, hypnotised
by his voice and his eyes, and moved towards him as though drawn by invisible
wires, as he went on:

'And time remembered is grief forgotten,
And frosts are slain and flowers begotten,
And in green underwood and cover
Blossom by blossom the spring begins.'

'So you went and found the rest of it. Well, well – maybe I was wrong
about you after all!'

Laura spoke almost automatically. 'Perhaps you were. Perhaps you need to
know me better before you judge me.'

Aynsley attempted a tactful cough. He might as well have remained silent
for all the attention he attracted. Farrell and Laura were now only inches
apart and Laura had started to reach out to him. Momentarily, some dim
memory of her status and attitudes made her hesitate. Gilbert decided he was
better off elsewhere and backed out, muttering an inane excuse which went as
unheard as his cough. Finally he felt the pressure of the doorknob at the small
of his back, turned, let himself out and fled.

Ulick was accustomed to clandestine affairs, but he tacitly acknowledged his
amateur status beside Laura Cazenove. Over the ensuing six weeks, she
found more secret, romantic meeting places than he would have dreamed
possible in such a modern house.

'One of the advantages of retaining the original landscaped park around
the new building,' she murmured, smiling, when he brought it up. 'And even
in such a new house, there should always be odd, private corners where one
can withdraw to . . . er . . . free one's spirit.'

28

'You certainly free mine, my dearest.' Ulick bent to caress the perfect curve of her long neck.

She sighed and disengaged herself. 'Your conversation is really too coarse at times, Ulick.'

He grinned, unabashed. 'Surely that's part of my charm? You can have an orangery full of smooth young niminy piminy types merely by snapping your fingers.' He advanced on her like a big, lithe cat. 'But – I am – different. I – am – a – glamorous – enigma!'

'You are also in danger of overstepping the mark.'

He was within reach of her again. 'Oh, I wouldn't say that, Laura. I'd say I'm pretty well indispensable to you.' As he spoke he bent again and embraced her, his mouth crushing hers deliciously and stirring her sense of danger as much as her passion.

For long seconds, she abandoned herself to the kiss, but then opened her eyes and said, with surprising detachment: 'No one is indispensable. People forget that clichés only become clichés because they are true.'

Normally such a remark would have made Ulick apprehensive. Until now, Lady Ilchester had shown all the symptoms of obsessive passion for him. Today there was a distinct coolness in her tone. But he was more deeply involved than he cared to admit, and his rational faculties were blunted by her devastating physical glamour. His hands moved from her shoulders down over the smooth bodice of her gown, sliding around her waist to unfasten the multitude of hooks.

'Not now – not in the daytime. Anyone might find us. This evening, before I dress for dinner. I'll meet you in the Chinese summerhouse.'

He liked this game of temptation, delay and reward almost as much as she did. Now he freed her for a moment before taking her hand and raising it to his lips. 'I shall be counting every moment.'

Again, that chill echo of detachment. 'If I didn't know better, I'd think you had taken to reading Ouida,' she said.

Parting from her, Ulick cursed himself for a fool. That bloody child mightn't have been so far wrong a couple of months ago when she flung *La Belle Dame Sans Merci* at him. Laura was beginning to take on a distinct resemblance to Keats's anti-heroine. But he was ensnared, and knew he would not be ready to free himself from her for a long time yet. Lady Ilchester had been the supreme challenge – a woman who seemed so bound by convention that she would never succumb to the attraction he held for her. But she *had* succumbed, and very abruptly at that. The suddenness of her surrender and the intensity of her passion had bewitched Ulick, and he still found it impossible to shake off the enchantment. Now he had to while away the afternoon and early evening until he could see her again and, this time, make love to her. It had been more than a week and he was half crazy for her. Strange, he mused, that such a sheltered, conventional woman had proved so inventive both in finding places for their rendezvous and in removing, then resuming, her complicated dress without any noticeable dishevelment. Just as well, though. He was prepared to swear no one was aware of their liaison.

He was almost right. Only one person at Lyonesse was fully aware of Farrell's relationship with Laura Cazenove: her daughter Charlotte.

Throughout the afternoon, Ulick attempted to conduct a French conversation class with Charlotte and Ivo. The girl's efforts were exemplary, but she was mutinous and unco-operative, making her contribution in flawless French, then slumping back in her chair to glare at him across the schoolroom table. He had been irritable enough before their lesson began. By the end of it, his temper was near breaking point and he would dearly have loved to slap the girl.

Finally he dismissed them twenty minutes earlier than they had expected. It was a soft, golden September afternoon and Ivo rushed off to look for early conkers in the woods. Charlotte made no attempt to depart.

Ulick made much of tidying away some books from morning lessons, acting as though the girl were not present. But after a while she had still not moved and he was forced to speak. 'Surely you have something more interesting to do out in this beautiful weather than to stay caged up in a dusty schoolroom?' he said.

'Stop humouring me.' The words sounded ominously adult but the accompanying scowl was straight out of the nursery.

'My dear child, I have no reason to humour you. I am here to teach you, not to keep you in a good mood.'

'Ulick, how can you treat me like this, after . . . after . . .'

Sensing danger, he attacked. 'After what? I repeat, I am here to teach you.'

'You didn't seem to think that's all there was in July,' she said. 'You didn't treat me like a boring little nuisance then.'

'Nothing happened in July. You've been indulging in some childish fancy, I should think.'

That really hurt her. 'Ulick, how can you say that when you know I love you?'

The tragic tone of her voice caught at his heart but he sensed that his survival hinged on detachment. 'I know no such thing. You are my pupil and I am your tutor. Any other relationship would be improper.'

'But you said . . .'

His control slipped momentarily. 'Charlotte, for God's sake! You can be very adult at times and a complete child five minutes later. You're a very attractive girl and I temporarily forgot myself. But that's all, do you understand? Anything else would ruin me for life.'

She was crying now. 'You know I wouldn't want to do that. I told you, I love you.'

'Perhaps you do. Perhaps you're not old enough to know how you feel yet. In any case, if you're so besotted, think of me for a change. If anyone had the slightest suspicion that for one second I'd regarded you as anything but a pupil, I'd never work again. What use would that be to either of us?'

'It wouldn't matter. Love always wins in the end!'

'If you believe that, I've been teaching you the wrong subjects! Only someone of your age, living in a rarefied atmosphere like Lyonesse, could show that degree of faith. The world isn't like that. Now please, if you really think you love me, stop endangering my future.'

Fighting back her tears, she nodded reluctant acquiescence. He sighed with relief and finally gave her a smile. 'That's better. From now on, we'll concentrate on making you the best French speaker north of Paris, and forget all the other nonsense, shall we?'

Charlotte still found it hard to speak without crying, but she nodded again, this time with a watery smile. Hoping he had weathered the storm, Farrell picked up his books and left the schoolroom.

Twice, on his way to the summerhouse, Ulick thought he heard someone following him. In the end he dismissed the sounds as those made by birds or small animals. The park was thickly wooded in this section; it was one reason why he and Laura often used the summerhouse for their assignations. When he reached the small ornamental wooden building, it was empty. Hardly surprising; he had taken pains to arrive early, knowing Laura hated to get there first. Now he strolled across the octagonal room, smiling at his own vivid memories of the use to which they had put the upholstered willow daybed along the far wall . . . the use to which they would put it again soon. Pleasantly distracted by the prospect, he sat down and half reclined, savouring in memory the silky touch of Laura's skin, the surprising lustiness of her responses. Ulick's daydreams made him incautious.

He failed to hear the slight creak as a foot pressed on the doorstep, and started with a low cry of alarm when Charlotte, not her mother, opened the door. 'What the devil are you doing here? No – no time for explanations – out, out, I tell you, this minute!' His mind was somersaulting at the possible consequences if mother and daughter should confront each other here.

But Charlotte showed no signs of going anywhere. She slid on to the daybed beside him and moved so close he could feel her warm breath against his cheek. He was on the edge of panic now. 'You must not stay, child, don't you understand? I'll come and see you later – anything – but not now. I beg you to go . . .' At that point his pleas were cut short, as she wrapped her arms around his neck, puppy-like in her enthusiasm, and kissed his mouth.

Laura would be here any second. There must be something he could do to prevent this demonic child from ruining him. If he could first disengage her . . . Farrell raised his hands and tugged at Charlotte's loving arms, but as he gripped her, she merely wound her fingers through his and entrapped him more deeply. Frantic, now, he jerked his arms down with a savagery born of desperation, breaking her hold with such force that he drove her arms back against the daybed, momentarily pinioning her there and evoking a sharp cry of pain.

After that events became somewhat blurred. He was seized from behind and in the ensuing struggle realised that Laura Cazenove was shrieking at him.

It took Laura the better part of a minute to bring herself under control, and a much longer time to reclothe her own behaviour until it emerged as sufficiently decent to spare her blushes when she thought of it. Panting, she stood away from the pair on the daybed. Ulick leaped to his feet, stammering and gesticulating, confused as she had never seen him before. Charlotte, calm as a madonna, remained in her place, tranquilly massaging one bruised wrist and watching them both.

'What is the explanation of this appalling scene?' Laura was regaining her dignity but she could still hear the hysterical wobble in her own voice.

'N-not what it seems, truly, nothing at all is as it seems, Lau – Lady Ilchester. If you'd just sit . . .'

'Sit down, here, after what I just witnessed? If your sanity were not thrown into doubt by your behaviour when I came in, it is highly questionable now! Charty, come here at once. Mr Farrell, you had better stay precisely where you are. I shall send someone to deal with you the moment I return to the house.'

She seized Charlotte's shoulder in a grip which would have done credit to a workhouse master, and almost frog-marched her out of the summerhouse. The girl went along without protest, bestowing a last soulful look on Ulick as they brushed past him.

After that, Ulick was prepared for destruction. The only cause for conjecture was the form his retribution would take. It might be anything from straightforward dismissal to a horsewhipping by Lord Ilchester. That thought made him wonder why he was still sitting here awaiting his fate, instead of slipping away. At least if he disappeared now he might escape a beating. Gregory Cazenove was as big as Ulick, and totally unlike the spineless young men who followed in Laura's wake.

But flight was not in Farrell's nature. He might have attempted to vanish if criminal prosecution had been a likely outcome, but he knew instinctively that the Cazenoves would never expose themselves to such public disgrace. What a little bitch that Charlotte was! As his mind dwelt on her sudden appearance and passionate descent on him, he realised that she had set it up deliberately. Of course, the noises in the woods behind him! She must have followed, waited outside until he had closed the door, and then . . . Ulick went over to the window and glanced along the tree-fringed path. Yes, she must have waited until she caught a glimpse of Laura approaching in the distance, then rushed in and flung herself on him.

It was so farcical it amused him even now. He might have been flattered at the intensity of the girl's passion for him, had it not been for the appalling consequences. All thoughts of Charlotte and her romantic obsession fell away. Yes, the consequences . . . His belly felt hollow. There'd be no indulgent mother to get him out of this scrape. From now on, he was alone. Alone, penniless and homeless. 'I suppose I could always run away to sea,' he murmured, recalling his old teasing remark to Charlotte.

He decided not to await judgement in the summerhouse. They could hardly make a worse fuss in the house. In fact, he might get off more lightly up there, with all the servants eavesdropping to find out what had really happened. Ulick strode away along the path, forcing himself to move with his customary swagger. 'Might as well die on your feet, old man,' he said.

Confronted in the library by his wife, Gregory Cazenove wished he were anywhere else but here, listening to the appalling tale of how the tutor had attempted to violate their only daughter. Worse, Laura took care to imply, Charty had probably co-operated enthusiastically.

'How on earth did you happen on them?' he asked. 'You always dress for dinner between half-past six and eight.'

She did not meet his eyes. 'I felt restless, and I thought a short walk might help. I'm sure now that it was a mother's intuition, warning me Charty needed me . . . I was just about to turn back to the house when I heard her cry out.'

'Cry out? You didn't tell me the brute had managed to hurt her! I thought you implied she had gone there of her own free will.'

'I'm sure she did. Surely you can see what happened? Once she was there, his base desires got the better of him and it frightened her. I still think she's almost as culpable as Farrell.'

'I will not have you say that of our daughter. She's no more than a child – it's our responsibility to see that she is protected from vicious influences, and if she comes under them, we are to blame.'

Laura bit her lip. She had never seen her husband's anger directed at her. For Gregory Cazenove, Laura could normally do no wrong. 'Perhaps I was somewhat hasty. It's simply that I was so concerned in case she had come to harm.'

Gregory was determined not to be placated. 'I knew there would be trouble when you suggested we engage Farrell to teach her as well as the boys. It's most unseemly, Laura. Why d'you think girls are taught by governesses? To protect them from precisely this sort of influence, of course. From now on, I shall make all such decisions. Kindly remember that.'

'But what shall we do in the meantime? I've sent Charty straight up to the nursery with Nanny. Mr Farrell was still in the summerhouse when we left, and I told him to stay there. You'll have to do something immediately.'

'I'm aware of that. I shall dismiss the man on the spot, of course. He'll get this quarter's salary, and count himself fortunate to receive even that, no doubt. But he'll have no references and I shall make it my business to see he never holds a similar job in an English household.'

Laura was almost gaping at him. 'That's all? You're not going to do anything further? He's dragged the Cazenove name in the mud!'

'What do you suggest? A horse-whipping in front of all the servants?'

'At least that would ensure he never forgot the incident.'

'I imagine the inability to earn a respectable living will be a far more lasting reminder.'

She should have read the warning signs, but did not. 'Really, Gregory, you must do something to impress the gravity of what he did . . .'

'As I am powerless to impress upon *you* the gravity of what you did – or, I hope, merely almost did – I think it unjust even for one as low as Farrell to suffer retribution alone.'

Laura met his eyes for a moment and began to demand an explanation, but the words died on her lips. 'I – I have done nothing to be ashamed of . . .' She fell silent.

'I am infinitely relieved to hear it.' But he did not sound convinced. 'My dearest, I love you sufficiently to forgive you almost anything, but I think it is time you stopped believing I am a fool. Love and foolishness may be close friends, but they are not the same thing, and love does not blind a man to the way his wife looks at someone else.' He turned away from her. 'We will not go any further into your role in this affair, but I must insist that you allow me to handle it as I think fit. Farrell was not the only one to come close to besmirching the family name. Now, we shall be late for dinner if you do not go and dress. Dismiss all this from your mind, if you can.'

He moved across to the windows and stared out into the garden. Realising he had nothing further to say to her, Laura withdrew.

She never learned what was said to Ulick Farrell who was called in to see Lord Ilchester within minutes of his arrival back at the house. He was dismissed, paid his salary in sovereigns, and told to be out of the house that evening. There was a train to London just before nine o'clock, and Ulick was left in no doubt that he should be on it. He had packed his belongings in less than an hour and when he came downstairs for the last time, the butler told him a carriage was waiting at the servants' entrance to take him to the station.

Noblesse oblige to the very end, eh?' Ulick said. 'Doubtless it would have demeaned the family name if I'd been seen trudging to the station.'

The butler's sphinx-like expression remained set. 'I wouldn't know anything about that, Mr Farrell. I'm merely passing on the master's orders.'

'All right, Slater, I understand.' He lowered his voice. 'Tell Master Ivo and Master Tristram I'll be wishing them luck when they go up to the University.'

'Very well, Mr Farrell. Goodbye, Mr Farrell.'

The Cazenoves were dining with only four guests that evening: the vicar and his wife, and George Devauden, an elderly baronet whose estate adjoined Lyonesse, who brought his sister. Gregory and Laura regarded it as a social obligation to offer hospitality to both couples, but invariably did so when they were not entertaining their fashionable friends. All four had arrived by the time Farrell made his departure, and were talking with their host and hostess in the drawing room.

Breaking off a tedious discussion of fishing with the baronet, Gregory told them all: 'I shall have to beg your indulgence for a few minutes while Laura and I deal with a tiresome matter that has come up today.' He turned back to Devauden. 'George, do tell the vicar and Mrs Waring about that remarkable pike while we're gone. Won't be five minutes.'

Outside, Laura said: 'What on earth has happened now? I thought you had dealt with everything before they arrived.'

'I did, with Farrell. But I thought it prudent to see Nanny this evening and give her instructions about Charty. I know I shall have to talk to the child eventually, but I prefer her to have a day or two to settle down. I still haven't decided what to do about her. I think perhaps she should spend a few months with Isabel in the Highlands – in any case, I shall send her away from Lyonesse for a while. But I don't want it to look like a punishment, so my decision will be more appropriate after Farrell is well clear of the place.'

'Are all your edicts to be issued like this from now on?'

'Really, Laura, I think you should consider how gently you have been treated today, and try to refrain from such remarks. After this incident is over, I hope we shall return to our old, happy ways.' He sighed. 'No one wishes more deeply than I that none of this had ever happened.'

She reached out and touched his hand, but he disengaged himself gently and walked away towards the library, where Nanny was waiting for them.

'There has been a small – er – irregularity with Mr Farrell, Nanny, and we

34

have been forced to dispense with his services. You know, I'm sure, that Miss Charlotte was unreasonably fond of him, and she might be upset. Lady Ilchester and I have decided, therefore, that she should stay in the nursery for the next few days. She can go for walks, of course, but only if you are with her. We have not decided about her future education yet, but the governess will resume her old timetable next Monday, and we can make permanent arrangements later. Until then, keep the child amused and don't let her feel like a prisoner, but please watch her at all times.'

Nanny glanced warily back and forth between Lord and Lady Ilchester seeking any hint of the tempest which must have resulted in these new orders, but she could discern no indication of disunity. Never did trust that Farrell, she thought, and never liked the way he looked at my Laura, neither. We'll all be better off without him. Rotten apple . . . Her thoughts moved to Miss Charty, who had drifted into the nursery in a very strange mood an hour or two ago, saying Mama was cross with her and there'd probably be trouble. Cocoa and bed had been Nanny's panacea, even if it was only half-past six. There were times when young ladies needed to be treated as children, and this was one. Within ten minutes, Miss Charlotte had been tucked up in her room, still looking a bit funny and distant, but not making a fuss. Nanny wondered if she would ever find out what had happened this evening.

The evening train drew in at Handford station and Ulick found himself an empty second-class compartment. Now that it was all over, he felt curiously light-headed. No, wait, that was wrong: light-*hearted* was more like it. He'd never been cut out for schoolrooms anyway. Maybe this had been just the jolt he needed to set him on the road to fame and fortune . . . his thoughts veered to Gregory Cazenove. Poor bastard! I'd rather be me than him, any day, he thought. Imagine loving – really loving, not merely desiring – Laura Cazenove. It must be like being eaten slowly by an insatiable monster.

The train was ready to depart. Ulick vaguely heard a whistle blow somewhere and felt a surge of anticipation. Tomorrow he'd start a new life. Who cared that he had a little over a hundred pounds in the world and no prospects at all? Nothing like having your mind made up for you when you needed a fresh start. What a woman that Charlotte would make one day. Talk about single-minded! She had seen what she wanted and gone for it, ignoring any rules and showing utter indifference to the probability that her efforts would ruin the object of her affections. Now it was all over, he almost admired her for it. And what a beauty she was going to be!

Smiling ruefully at the memory of her calm expression as she confronted her mother in the summerhouse, he stood up and moved to the carriage window, intending to take a last look at the village which had so briefly been his home. As he lowered the sliding glass panel on its leather strap, the guard blew his whistle again and the engine let out a few explosive bursts of steam, then the pistons slowly began to move.

A commotion erupted outside the ticket hall, and as the train edged forward, a female figure came flying through the wooden barrier, a bag in one hand, the other pressed to the top of her head to keep a broad-brimmed straw hat in place. Long, black-stockinged legs flashed against a flurry of white petticoats. Momentarily, Farrell was caught between outrage and incredulity. 'It isn't – it can't be . . .' he muttered.

The train was picking up speed now, but the running girl managed a final surge of energy and drew alongside his door. 'Open it, you beast,' she gasped, 'I can't keep this up forever!'

He never knew what made him obey her, but he did. Charlotte flung her bag on to the carriage floor, then reached up and grabbed Ulick's outstretched arm. He heaved her inside just as the train cleared the end of the platform.

Well nigh speechless, he turned back and stared at her after grappling to shut the door. Eventually, he said: 'When you're ready, perhaps you'd care to explain why you ruined me. Then, as an encore, I'd like to know what the merry hell you're doing here now.'

She gave him a dazzling smile. 'Simple, Ulick darling. I'm going to take care of you. You need looking after if you let yourself fall in with women like Mama!'

CHAPTER FIVE

The train journey to London had an air of unreality. Remembering Charlotte's mad dash along the platform at Handford, Ulick expected the train to be stopped at any minute. Once the station staff had thought over the incident and, inevitably, reported it to Lyonesse, they would be intercepted, the Cazenoves' rebel daughter forcibly returned to the fold, and, unless he was very fortunate, he himself would end up behind bars. For some reason the notion amused more than it daunted him. At this moment, he was smiling indulgently at the crazy child who had caused his downfall, savouring her unconscious grace as she sprawled across the seat opposite him.

'You realise, I take it, that you'll enjoy my company at best as far as Paddington, and probably no further than Reading?' he said.

Charlotte frowned. 'You're not going to shake me off that easily. Not even you would jump off the train at a country station and leave me alone.'

'That's the last thing I have in mind. How long do you think your parents will be ignorant of your whereabouts? Half the population of Handford must have seen your hundred-yard sprint. They'll pass on the news to Lyonesse in the time it takes a youngster to bicycle up there.'

'If that's all you're worrying about, stop it. Mr Perkins was on duty at the ticket barrier and the other station staff were off having their supper.'

'Then Perkins will obviously raise the alarm.'

'No, he won't, silly. Mama tried to have him dismissed a year or so ago because she said he was rude to some guests of hers when they arrived at the station. She'd got the wrong end of the stick as usual, but of course she wouldn't climb down. If Papa hadn't intervened, Mr Perkins would have been out of work and homeless. He hates Mama.'

'But probably feels he owes your father a lot, you goose.'

'No. Papa saved the man's job, but he said it would be an act of public disloyalty to Mama to let Mr Perkins know it. So Mr Perkins thinks the Railways people supported him and everyone at Lyonesse is his enemy now. Cook heard him say he wouldn't send a warning to Lyonesse if the Russian Army was arriving on the 3.45! Weren't we lucky he was the only one on duty?'

'Hmm, perhaps. I tend to the view that a runaway daughter will rank higher in his mind than invaders. If he didn't report it, he really would lose his job. Still, he might delay until morning, and after that you could be anywhere.'

Until now Ulick had been assuming that their time together could be estimated in minutes. Now the picture had changed. What on earth was he going to do with a fifteen-year-old girl who looked exactly what she was – a spoiled sprig of the aristocracy?

'You can't stay with me, Charlotte. It's out of the question.'

'I shall have to. I have nowhere else to go and I did it all for you.'

'I wish you hadn't bothered! Until you threw up everything for love, I had a comfortable billet and a reasonably interesting existence. Now I'm about to embark on a career as a gentleman of the road. As far as I can see, the only thing I did to deserve it was to attract your attention.'

'Don't be absurd! You encouraged me. I didn't know about kissing, or . . . or anything like that, until you came. And what about you and Mama? I couldn't let that continue, not with poor dear Papa to think of.'

'You're a shameful little liar, Charlotte. Dear Papa couldn't have been further from your mind. You acted out of good, old-fashioned, grown-up jealousy. You thought your mother was doing what you fancied and you were determined to stop her. I was just a casualty in the war.'

She had the grace to blush. 'Well, perhaps. What are you going to do with me now?'

'If we get to London without capture – and it's a big if, in spite of your Mr Perkins – I suppose I shall have to look after you.' He studied her critically. 'We shall have to get rid of those white clothes as soon as we can; too conspicuous by half. A lower class girl of your age would look quite different and no one would care that she was too young to be out with an older man. But that frock of yours will get us both arrested unless I'm very careful.'

'Oh, Ulick, thank you! I'll do anything you say, honestly! And I really am sorry about your job and everything, but you do see it was the only way, don't you?'

He gazed at her bemusedly. 'I confess that had escaped me. Still, I always did believe in making the best of what I had.' Charlotte launched herself on him from across the compartment, flinging her arms around him and showering him with kisses. Emerging briefly, he added: 'And the situation doesn't appear to be wholly without its advantages.'

The train arrived at Paddington station soon after eleven o'clock. Ulick leaned cautiously out of the window, half expecting a uniformed policeman to be waiting at the ticket barrier with the guard. But there was no sign that they were discovered. The first passengers off the train were streaming out through the gate and no one was being stopped for questioning.

He turned to Charlotte. 'Now listen carefully. It's far too late to find somewhere reasonable to stay tonight. We'll need to change your looks before we do that. Until further notice, you are my younger sister, understood? I'm taking you – let's see – to Wales, yes, that will do, to Wales to stay with our father's sister while Mama is recovering from an illness. Thank God you brought a bag with you. No one would have believed us with no luggage except mine.'

At the barrier he apologised profusely to the collector for having lost his sister's ticket, and bought one on the spot. The story was accepted without demur and they emerged from under the great glass station canopy into the mild autumn evening, both excited by the adventure ahead of them. As they walked up the exit road and round the corner to register at the Great Western Hotel, Charlotte gave him a conspiratorial grin. 'Go on, admit it,' she said, 'you're enjoying every minute of this!'

'I believe you're right. Let's hope I get the opportunity to go on doing so.'

An hour later, alone in his room with the mournful late-night sounds of the nearby railway terminus occasionally breaking the silence, Ulick marvelled at the unlikelihood of his circumstances. Here he was, chastely locked up next door to the precocious child who had ruined him, content to conspire with her against her parents and to take both of them off into a penniless future. And yet he still found it impossible to shake off the tingling anticipation which had gripped him ever since Charlotte had grabbed his hands and hauled herself aboard the nine o'clock train from Handford.

Next morning, she gazed at him accusingly across the breakfast table. 'I thought it was wicked to go to hotels with men like you, and that all sorts of exciting things happened,' she said. 'The most exciting thing that happened to me was almost falling out of bed when the noise of the early morning trains woke me.'

'If you're going to pretend to be a woman, you'll have to learn to act the part convincingly,' Farrell told her. 'This is a respectable hotel. I can just imagine what the staff would have done if brother and sister had promptly gone off to the same bedroom. I'd have been in Paddington Green police station before my feet could touch the ground. As long as you look as you do now, we preserve the illusion. When we've bought you some new clothes and settled up here, we shall see.'

She grinned. 'Is that when I become your femme fatale?'

'Don't be in such a hurry to grow up. I think we should talk about that later – much later.'

He refused to discuss it further, and Charlotte consoled herself by plunging into the sort of breakfast which had always been forbidden her at Lyonesse. Ulick watched, fascinated, as porridge, kippers, tea and slice after slice of thickly buttered toast vanished.

'I've never seen a female eat so much! Where do you put it?'

'That's because you've never seen Mama's idea of wholesome nursery food. When I have children, they'll never have to eat bread and milk, or coddled eggs.'

'If you go on like that, you may find yourself disappearing inside an overcoat of fat.'

She merely gave him a sceptical sniff as she buttered her fourth piece of toast.

An hour later they were in a department store in Oxford Street. 'My wife needs a couple of completely plain ready-made dresses and a skirt and some blouses,' Ulick told the assistant. 'She and her sister here are about the same size, so perhaps you can work something out.'

The saleswoman nodded. These two were definitely at the carriage trade end of her normal run of customers. You didn't get many of their sort buying ready-made stuff. Probably come down in the world.

They emerged with a modest but complete adult wardrobe which Ulick hoped would permit Charlotte to merge unnoticed with other young female Londoners. She was complaining steadily about the drabness of the clothes. 'I haven't spent my life in white muslin and brown Holland frocks to go on to things like these,' she moaned. 'I thought you'd get me something smart.'

'You are the most exasperating girl! For the next few months, my sole aim is to make you as inconspicuous as possible. With looks like yours, that would be difficult enough even if you were wrapped in sacking. In the latest styles it would be damn' well impossible. In any case, every penny we spend now is taking us closer to beggary. You can't have anything better until I make some money.'

They returned to the Great Western, where Ulick told Charlotte to dress in her new clothes while he settled their bill. Their luck was still holding. By the time Charlotte came down the broad staircase to join him in the hotel vestibule, it was the height of the mid-morning rush, with departing guests arranging luggage, cabs and appointments, and the staff in too much of a hurry to notice anything very much. As a result Charlotte, transformed from a dazzling child into a quietly respectable-looking young woman, received not so much as a second glance as Farrell escorted her out.

He did not relax until they were inside a cab, clattering away along Praed Street towards the West End. 'I was convinced they'd rumble us, you know!' he said. 'Now, I think we can assume we got away with it, and start working on what to do next.'

He had told the driver to head for the Strand, for no better reason than that it was safely remote from Paddington. Now, though, he had to come up with some sort of plan for living accommodation. Another hotel was out of the question: too risky to try that more than once. On the other hand, good lodgings close to the centre were quite hard to come by, and outfitting Charlotte had depleted his funds too much for a false start to be affordable.

The idea came to him as they crawled along the Strand in a mid-morning traffic jam. A new show had just opened at the Vaudeville Theatre, starring Nellie Tolliver, the musical name of the season.

'That's it, Nellie!' Ulick clapped his hands in pleasure at the prospect and called up to the cabbie: 'Pull in at Romano's for a few minutes, there's a good chap.'

Charlotte had seen the theatre billboard. 'Do you know this Nellie Tolliver?' she asked, impressed.

'Never met her. She just put me in mind of another Nellie, that's all; and one right out of her class. I just need to find out where she is . . .'

A few minutes later they drew up outside Romano's, the restaurant which served as a meeting place for everyone who mattered in music hall. 'You stay here – shan't be long,' Farrell told Charlotte. He hurried inside Romano's which was just opening for the day. Returning, he gave the cabman an address in Bloomsbury and they turned off up Drury Lane.

'Where are we going now?' Charlotte asked him.

'Home, I hope – or somewhere that will serve as home until we're set up. You are about to meet a music hall legend in the making.'

The Georgian house in Gower Street was neat as a pin, with window boxes of brilliant flowers and dashing striped awnings giving it a rakish air lacking in its more sober neighbours. When Ulick rang the bell, the front door was opened by a maid dressed in keeping with the house front, in a beautifully cut black worsted dress with the frilliest muslin apron and cap Charlotte had ever seen. Her mother would have dismissed such clothing as flashy and thoroughly inappropriate for a servant. Charlotte loved it.

'Will you please tell Miss Standish that Ulick Farrell wishes to see her?' The maid left them at the door and disappeared into the depths of the house.

Moments later, a full-throated yell erupted from inside. 'Where's me bloomin' Irish boy?' Nellie Standish arrived in a cloud of French scent and frilly lingerie.

'Come in, come in! Maud knows better than to leave friends outside, but I get some funny strangers turning up from time to time, so nobody she doesn't recognise gets into the hall to wait. I'm in the morning room, finishing breakfast. Let's go back in there and Maud can bring another pot of coffee, all right?'

Charlotte was entranced by the woman's accent, a potent mixture of cockney, theatrical and some other element she could not pin down. Nellie Standish was the most exciting female she had ever seen and at the moment Charlotte would have given anything to be her.

Inside the morning room, Nellie ushered them to a small circular table. As they waited for the coffee she gave Charlotte a long, inquisitive look, then turned to Ulick and said: 'Back where I come from they put men in jail for taking up with little girls. What's the game?'

'More convoluted than any I've played before. I was rather hoping we'd managed to make her look grown up.'

'Well, yes, you've not done too badly, but I'm a pro when it comes to disguises, remember. Tell you what: she looks too well bred to be the age she's dressed. She'd pass for nineteen in a crowd, but to anyone with a nose for it, she's probably well short of sixteen.'

'Absolutely spot on, Nellie. Perhaps I should introduce her before she explodes. This is Lady Charlotte Cazenove, known to her family as Charty. Charlotte, meet Nellie Standish, who will be the Marie Lloyd of the twentieth century.'

'Blimey, what an intro!' Nellie peered at Charlotte as though she were a zoological specimen. 'Lady, eh? How did you strike up an acquaintance with this Fenian hooligan then?'

'He was my tutor. I didn't want to stay at home when he left.'

'Something tells me you've missed out a big piece of the story, but we'll get to that later, no doubt. I need to talk to Ulick.' She turned back to Farrell. 'Right, my darling. I told you last time we met I owed you a favour. I take it this is payday.'

'If you can help me now, I'll be in your debt forever, Nellie.'

'I'll certainly try, love. That little song you wrote for me gave me just the boost I needed. It would have taken me a couple more years to get a break without it. How much trouble are you in?'

'That remains to be seen, but the favour I want from you is fairly straightforward. D'you still own those two houses over in Covent Garden?'

'Course I do. I told you, I bought them with the first big piece of jewellery I got given, and I'll keep them 'til I'm old and grey. They might be all I've got by then.'

'Any vacancies?'

She laughed. 'As simple as that! Bless you, of course there are. Always find room for you. There's two rooms and a kitchen on the first floor front at Number Three, or the big ground-floor apartment in Number Four. Take your pick. Can you afford to pay me rent, or is it charity for a while?'

'Oh, no – there are certain matters on which I believe it's a mistake to be a sponger. The roof over my head is one of them. I'll pay the going rate, and given the state of my funds, that means it'll have to be the two rooms at Number Three.'

'You just got yourself a landlady. Tell you what; I'll come round there and settle you in myself. I'm sure you won't mind sitting around here for an hour while I get myself dolled up.'

'I'm perfectly happy to do so, and I think our young friend here has plenty to occupy her.' Charlotte was wandering around the room, oblivious to their conversation in her fascination with the flashy but attractive baubles with which Nellie had covered every surface in the place.

'It's one of the hazards of this game, love,' Nellie told her. 'You don't arf pick up a lot of bric-a-brac from so-called admirers. I keep telling myself it's not worth having unless it's assessable in carats, but then I go all soft if they give me a Toby jug or a china dog. Daft, innit?'

'I don't think it's daft at all. I think it's wonderful . . . all those people loving you so much they just want to give you something. You must feel as though the whole world adores you!'

'Gawd strewth – *you'll* be going on the stage next! Believe me, there's a lot of malice in between the china dogs and paste earrings. Sometimes it's hard to remember anyone loves you, even your old mum. Anyway, you go on looking at the knick-knacks if it keeps you amused. I'm going to get dressed.' She raised her voice to a melodious bawl: 'Maud – more coffee for my visitors! I'll be upstairs forever!' Then she left them.

'What a wonderful woman!' said Charlotte as soon as Nellie had gone. 'Are we really going to live at her house?'

'Well, for a while, anyway. As you heard, it's her investment against an obscure old age – though that's hard to envisage, looking at her now. It's two adjoining houses divided into about eight apartments and she lets them out to theatricals. We'll be right at the heart of things and if I ever run short of the rent, she won't throw us out for a few weeks.'

'How did you manage to meet her? I never had any idea you'd led such an adventurous life.'

'Hardly the sort of background that would land me a job at Lyonesse, is it? I used to spend a lot of time in town when I was up at the University. Part of the fun was meeting the actors and music hall artistes and one lucky evening, someone introduced me to the delectable Nellie.' He paused and eyed her suspiciously.

'I must say, for one so love-struck, you don't seem to be at all jealous.'

'Don't be silly, Ulick! Even a child can see there's nothing more than friendship between you two. What man in his right mind would leave a woman like that to go and do a boring old job in the country?'

He sighed. 'Wouldn't it be splendid if the world were as clear-cut as you imagine! Young men of my background and young women of Nellie's have been loving and leaving each other as long as England has had a professional Stage. In this case, though, you're right. Friends we were, and friends we remain.

'She wasn't at all well-known then – just doing a rather threadbare serio-comic routine halfway down the bill around some of the East End halls. Her material was appalling. I'd been playing at writing poetry and my tutor had told me I was wasting my time. Said the closest I'd ever be to a poet would be a writer of popular songs. He was mocking me, but I took it seriously and tried my hand. The song I wrote for Nellie got her noticed by someone from the Royal Standard and she's been working her way steadily up to West End headline billing ever since. She would have got there anyway, but I managed to speed things up for her.'

That sent Charlotte off into further transports. 'So you write songs for the stage, too! Oh, Ulick, every few minutes I'm finding out something even better about you!'

The continual childish enthusiasm was beginning to irritate him. 'For God's sake, I only wrote three or four songs, and you can sell just about anything if it's literate and rhymes.' Then he caught her stricken look and reminded himself that after all, she was just a child. 'I've been wondering, actually, whether that might prove to be a good way of earning a living. Nobody in show business cares what skeletons you have in your cupboard.'

She brightened again. 'Then it will be all right?'

'Charlotte, unless you are prepared to be murdered within the next few days, you must at least begin to grow up. There's more to it than wearing your hair in a chignon and throwing away your muslin frocks.'

'What have I done now?'

'Nothing, nothing – except that you're so bloody determined all is for the best in the best of all possible worlds. Life isn't like that, certainly not theatrical life.'

'But you said . . .'

'I know what I said, dammit, but the moment the words are out of my mouth you pick them up and dash off with them like some mad colt. I'd have to be selling at least two good songs a week to keep us, and no one produces that many good music hall songs. I simply meant it might be a start.'

'How much do you get for each song?'

'Depends on the artiste, and how badly they want the material. Someone unknown like me will never get more than a fiver a time, and that's if a Marie Lloyd or an Albert Chevalier is interested. If it's a middle-of-the-road piece for a middle-of-the-road artiste, it's more likely to be a guinea.'

'Five pounds? I had ten in my moneybox in the nursery.'

'Then I sincerely hope you brought it with you. We're likely to need it before this month is out.'

He stopped talking and sat peering gloomily at the grounds in his coffee cup. Charlotte got up and came to stand behind his chair, twining her arms around his neck. 'I'm truly sorry to be such an ass, Ulick, but that's a lot of the reason I hated it so much at Lyonesse. You know I'm not stupid, and I knew the rest of the world didn't live like that. But I wasn't allowed to see how they *did* live, and Mama would never have relented over that.'

Ulick was unimpressed. 'That's not so unusual. Mothers from far more modest backgrounds than your own would move heaven and earth to see their ewe lambs remained ignorant of the ways of the great unwashed.'

'Don't you see, I didn't want to grow up bored? The trouble is, I don't know anything about anything. If I couldn't have what I wanted, it was never because we didn't have enough money; it was because Mama or Papa decided it wasn't good for me. If I wanted to do something useful, like grooming my own pony, Mama had forty fits and dragged me back to my stupid embroidery. I've wanted to get out for as long as I can remember, but now I've done it, I still don't know the smallest bit about how people earn their livings or even how much they need to stay alive. Please don't be cross with me.'

'I should apologise to you. Of course you don't know anything yet. It's just that I'm getting a bit frantic about what the big bad world is capable of doing to us both. Are you absolutely positive you won't consider returning to Lyonesse? It might be a lot better in the long run.'

She had been starting to sniffle, but instantly all signs of tears were banished. 'I'd rather starve! At least I'd learn first what it felt like to be really alive.'

'Hmm, brave words. As I recall, I used to declaim them after the second bottle of claret. With you, infatuation substitutes for wine. Either way, I fear the sentiment is equally unreliable. We'll give it a try, but never forget that I can be a terrible weakling when things get really bad.'

'I don't believe you! You're twice as much of a man as any of those snivelling suitors of Mama's.'

'Perhaps, but they never had to prove they could survive in the real world. I have to. I think I might need to be a lot more than twice the man they were.'

'Well you are, so there! And if it gets hard, I can always help.'

Her serene confidence that she could make a contribution, in spite of all he had said, moved Farrell to exasperated mirth. 'Come on, you wretch, sit down and have another cup of coffee before it gets quite cold. Nellie should be down soon.'

Eventually Nellie rejoined them, swishing dramatically in an extravagant worsted and silk outfit. Ulick went out to find a hansom and they set off to Covent Garden, Nellie chattering all the way about what fun it would be to have them as tenants.

Her two houses were part of a terrace of artisans' dwellings in Wilson Street, off Drury Lane. They were tall, neat buildings, their casement windows divided into regiments of square white-framed panes, their heavy front doors loaded with well-polished decorative brasswork. 'I get a cleaner round twice a week,' Nellie explained. 'Well, I want to keep me investment up to scratch, don't I?'

She led the way in through the bright red door of Number Three and moved ahead of them up the wide dog-leg staircase. The first-floor front apartment looked down into the pleasant street, and the house was far enough along Wilson Street for the noise of Drury Lane to be all but lost. It percolated here as little more than an interesting background buzz.

The rooms were spacious, with gleaming, polished wood floors, but the place gave Charlotte her first qualms. 'Oh – there's no furniture! I thought . . .'

Nellie laughed. 'Yes there is, the piano. All my apartments have them. Stands to reason, my tenants are always theatricals and they can't be lugging a joanna about everywhere. So I lay one on. They always treat it right, because a useable practice instrument's their bread and butter just as it is mine. But of course there's nothing else. I rent unfurnished.'

'But we can't . . . that is . . .' Ulick's outburst about poverty had gone to Charlotte's heart and now she was contemplating the impossibility of furnishing this place from scratch. Why, she remembered Mama telling Papa once that one could scarcely get a small sofa table for fifty pounds nowadays. Would they ever see such money?

'No need to worry your head about that. I've been thinking, Ulick: I never did pay you for that song.'

'Of course not. It was a present. You were poorer than I was then. You've paid me now with this place.'

'Yeah, but I haven't, not really. You're just the sort of tenant I can do with, and you'll be paying a fair rent, so I haven't done you much of a good turn. What I was thinking was, why don't I stake you to a few sticks of furniture? Nothing grand, mind – just a few simple chairs, a table and a nice big feather bed.' This last item was accompanied by a lewd wink in Charlotte's direction.

'No one will ever accuse you of excessive subtlety, you wonderful woman! I'll repay every penny some day, I promise.'

'No promises of that sort. With your prospects, I'll be glad enough ever to see the rent. Come on – there's a so-so place over beyond Great Queen Street. We'll get the basics there, then while they're delivering it I think we'll take your little country girl and introduce her to Romano's. With a bit of luck, by the time you get back your place will be furnished and waiting. All right?'

'All right? Nellie, you're my guardian angel.'

To Charlotte at that moment, the older woman seemed more goddess than guardian angel. In the cab, she hardly took her eyes off Nellie, and Nellie basked unashamedly in her worship. At Romano's, it was different. Romano's was a big pool stocked with an infinite variety of theatrical fish, and Nellie was still no more than a middle-weight here. In a hierarchical system every bit as strict as that of a duchess's drawing room, lesser lights were expected to fade when one of the top stars put in an appearance. On days when Marie Lloyd or Vesta Tilley was on hand, Nellie might as well have stayed at home. On a normal day, though, she was already sufficiently important to be escorted to a good table and thereafter to be courted by everyone. Today was not such an occasion.

Nellie glumly contemplated an overblown middle-aged star who was the centre of everyone's attention. 'What d'you think they see in her, Ulick? She's carrying at least two stone more than she should be, and the hair's getting right brassy, and yet the minute she comes in, abracadabra – I might as well be invisible.'

'You don't need me to tell you her secret. You have the same quality yourself, but you're not at the top yet. Have patience. Her voice will start going soon enough, and when that happens they'll notice the hair and the figure faster than you'd believe possible.' Ulick's tolerant tone took on a sadder note. 'Just remember, though, Nellie, you're no more immune than she is. The time will come when you're teetering there on the edge of the precipice, enjoying that last glow of worship before you fall off.'

She laughed at this. 'Not me, ducky! I'm not going to grow old.'

'We all say that, but we do.'

'No, you don't understand. I don't mean I'll be mutton dressed up as a

45

ballet girl when I'm fifty. I just mean I'll never *see* fifty – or forty, for that matter.'

Now it was Ulick's turn to laugh. 'Is this the vibrant Nellie Standish, threatening to be cut down in her prime by a gypsy premonition? Oh, Nellie, do spare me the melodrama!'

She glanced at Charlotte and did not reply until she was sure the girl was too absorbed by the scene across the restaurant to heed their talk.

'Don't be daft. You know me better than to think I'd trust fortune tellers. I may be dying.'

He choked on his drink. 'But you look fitter than me!'

'That's because I keep myself in good nick, innit? I've been getting awfully tired the past few weeks. And you should see how much paint I need to put on before the face looks like this any more.'

'You're probably working a damn' sight too hard and having too many late nights. You know it's an occupational hazard for artistes.'

'Yeah, and I know I lost a stone in two months. I'm not exactly skin and bone yet, but I wouldn't take bets on being the right shape for Christmas panto.'

He stared at her, aghast. 'Have you seen a doctor?'

She shrugged. 'Course I have. Best Harley Street could offer. They don't know much, do they? I'm going to see him again next week and then he swears he'll have some news for me – a second opinion from some colleague.' For a moment, the shell of her flippancy cracked. 'Christ, Ulick, I'm terrified! My mother died of cancer when she was twenty-seven. I'm twenty-six next week.'

He patted her arm. The gesture seemed a crass understatement. 'That doesn't mean you have it. Are you in pain?'

'Sometimes so bad I can hardly see straight. Deep in my gut, like a vulture clawing me.' She smiled. The fabricated merriment stretched across her lovely face and concealed only a little of the panic beneath. 'Doesn't half make me concentrate on doing all I've got in mind as quick as I can.'

'Have you told anyone else?'

'No – course not. You've been on the fringe; you know what they're like. It'd be everywhere in five minutes and then they'd stop giving me work in case the trouble started to show on stage.'

'But, Nellie, you told me . . . we aren't even close.'

'I know. Daft, innit? I think I had a weak moment, seeing you pop up out of nowhere like that. Truth of it is, there's nobody close I can tell. I was playing house with someone really special for the best part of last year. Just as I got the first hint of this trouble, I found out the bastard was stringing me along.' She paused, considering a painful memory. 'I even did a quick trip to America as an excuse to get away from him . . . afraid I'd weaken and take him back if I stayed too close.'

'Maybe I could contact him for you now. You need someone.'

Her eyes blazed. 'I don't need anybody, least of all that one, and don't you forget it! This is between you and me, all right?'

'What's the matter? Nellie, why are you so upset?' The sudden intensity of her tone had finally distracted Charlotte's attention from the show business carnival all around her, and now she was looking at the pair with perplexity.

Nellie, always a good improviser, quickly diverted her.

'Don't take any notice of me, love. Just trying to make sure Ulick here didn't get any big ideas about shelling out rent for a couple of weeks before you're properly settled in, and he was being a bit awkward.'

Charlotte gave a proprietorial swagger. 'You leave him to me. We'll soon see about that!' Catching sight of Nellie's pleading face, Ulick took advantage of the girl's arrogance to change the subject and began a bantering argument with her. A few minutes later, it was difficult to believe he and Nellie had been discussing life and death with such intensity.

When Nellie left them outside Romano's, it was after five o'clock. Ulick and Charlotte walked back to their new home, through the warren of Covent Garden back streets and across the vast piazza. Charlotte was so enchanted by Romano's, by the music hall performers she had seen there and above all by Nellie Standish, that she hardly noticed the bustling neighbourhood they were passing through. For the moment, Farrell was glad of her continual chatter. It enabled him to digest Nellie's appalling news and come to terms with it. The last thing he wanted was to alert Charlotte that something was wrong with their benefactress.

Nellie had given them keys to the apartment when they parted at the restaurant, telling them someone would have let in the carriers who delivered the furniture. When they got into the rented rooms, the place looked as if it had been lived in for months. Nellie had slipped in some extras neither of them had noticed at the saleroom – a solid, fatly upholstered goose-neck sofa, a hearth rug and a big armchair. Clearly her idea of a few sticks was rather different from theirs. No carrier arranged this lot, thought Ulick. Nellie must have nobbled her cleaner, or one of the neighbours who owed her a favour, about setting it up. Apart from the bare floorboards beyond the hearth rug, the apartment was now fully furnished, right down to bedlinen and blankets.

'Oh, isn't it wonderful?' gushed Charlotte. 'I'd never have believed everything could work out so well. Aren't we lucky?' She was bouncing on the big brass bed as she spoke, her face aglow with pleasure.

'Luckier than you'll ever know,' Farrell said. The shadow of Nellie's mortality leered at him. He went to the little kitchen to boil water for tea. At the moment, he would have given anything for an endless supply of whisky.

CHAPTER SIX

Charlotte explored the flat with minute care, mentally itemising all their new possessions. Just like a little girl with a new dolls' house, Farrell thought bitterly. The juxtaposition of this spoiled child with the generous-hearted woman who had made them so comfortable killed his nascent sexual desire. It's quite a joke, he thought. There's Milady down in Lyonesse, probably in a frenzy of jealousy at the idea of me tumbling her baby girl, and His Lordship aching to get at me with a horsewhip for the same reason, and all I can think of is a dying music hall singer!

He made an excuse to get away. There was a twist of tea and some sugar in the kitchen, but nothing else. He could get milk and bread. He waited for Charlotte's pleas to go with him, but she seemed too happy in her new home to leave it yet. Walking along the noisy streets as darkness gathered, Ulick tried to set his thoughts in order. What a mess. What a bloody awful mess. Nellie Standish had been no more than a likeable acquaintance until today. Now she was a bosom friend on the strength of having confided her darkest secret to him. Somehow that one act had knocked Farrell's world askew.

Before he became her confidant, nothing had been very serious. He was scarcely more than a boy himself – still in his mid-twenties. In spite of his turbulent past, life had been easy. To his quick intelligence, academic studies had been childishly simple. At home, his mother had indulged him until he reached an age when his father took control, and when the inevitable clash took place between them she still managed to intervene to ease his passage. He had never really been short of money, never come closer to having to fend for himself than when he took the job at Lyonesse; and even then he had been shielded by the self-confidence his own aristocratic background bestowed, the self-assurance which whispered that money and comfort would always be easily come by.

Now he felt as if he were seeing the world for the first time, and he was appalled by his own position. Instinct told him Nellie was right to fear she was dying. He was almost the same age as she. What if it had been him? What was it she had said – doesn't half make me concentrate on doing all I had in mind as quick as I can? She would probably manage it, too. Whereas if he were struck down . . . memory offered him no more than a few cheap tokens: boyish claims to patriotism as he swore to die for a free Ireland; women seduced and told he loved them, rejected when they clung too closely or became too expensive. His mother, always hoping the best of him, always stifling her pain and humiliation when he delivered the worst. And finally, this latest shabby adventure, the seduction of a shallow, bored woman whose husband he rather admired, followed by the virtual abduction of the same man's daughter. It no longer struck Ulick as a dashing piratical escapade, but as a sordid act of theft.

No question of it, Charlotte Cazenove was a child and, however hard she

49

tried to inveigle him into making her a woman, he must send her home intact. If he knew his aristocracy, they'd have doctor and midwife checking her condition before the nursery door had been locked behind her. Once they realised she was still a virgin, they would never pursue him – better let it die, they would say, than face the scandal. Charlotte would spend a year or two at school abroad, then she would be restored to the life which had been pre-ordained for her before he arrived at Lyonesse. By the time she reached her twenties, she would have forgotten him, even if her father and mother had not. Now the solution was in his mind, he wondered why any alternative possibility had occurred to him.

Bright yellow light suddenly enveloped him and a welcoming smell of beer and tobacco seeped out beneath florid doors of engraved glass. He had stopped under the flaring gas lamps of a large street-corner pub. Remembering his earlier craving for whisky, he went inside and ordered one. It seemed incapable of working its usual magic. Nellie's tragedy and his own profligacy lay heavy on his mind and he ached to demonstrate his redemption as before he had ached for alcohol.

Might as well leave now, get a few groceries as he had promised, then send a telegram to Lyonesse and pack Charlotte off on the last train. She would be back in Wiltshire very late indeed, but better that than an extra night away with a dissolute young man . . . Farrell left the pub and found a small shop tucked away off Drury Lane where he bought bread, bacon, sugar, tea and a few eggs. The shopkeeper directed him to a dairy on the way back to Wilson Street and he got the milk there. As he headed north up Drury Lane, his heart was already lighter.

He remembered that the nearest post office open at this hour was some distance beyond the apartment. Might as well drop off the groceries on his way, then go on to send the telegram. He could collect Charlotte afterwards and whisk her off to Paddington station before she realised what was happening.

As he turned into Wilson Street, the vulgar, spell-binding sound of a barrel organ wafted from the alley. Ahead of him, under the street lamp, was a commonplace sight which never failed to stir him. The organ grinder had set up his little show and a group of children had come out of the houses to dance in the puddle of lamplight as happily as if they were on stage at Drury Lane. Tonight, though, it was different. The children had formed a ragged audience around two dancers who wheeled together with perfect timing and a grace uncommon in such an impromptu setting.

The boy was undersized and shabby, with ragged trousers that flapped free of his worn-out left sock, and clumsy boots which should have made his movements clownish. But his natural talent and his joy in his partner gave him wings. The tall, white-clad child who circled him so gracefully could have made a donkey dance. It was Charlotte Cazenove.

As the notes of the barrel organ died away, Farrell moved into the charmed circle. The children turned to gaze up at him and he felt like an intruding giant. Boy and girl finished their dance, then she curtsied and he bowed. One of the watching urchins said: 'Ain't they lovely, mister? Wouldn't see nuffink better dahn the Royal Standard.'

Ulick ignored him. He was gazing at the white-clad girl. 'Charlotte, what

50

the hell are you up to? I thought you'd got rid of that frock.'

She looked at him strangely, as though returning reluctantly from a great distance. 'Get rid of it? Why, no . . . it was still in the luggage.' She glanced up at their window. 'I was standing up there and I saw them, and – and I just had to come and dance.'

'But the clothes, Charlotte – why are you dressed like that?' It was difficult to keep the anger from his voice, and already he could sense the hostility of the little crowd.

Charlotte shrugged. 'I don't know . . . I don't think I could have danced in my new grey skirt, that's all.'

'Hey, mister, you leave her alone, all right? It was my fault. You fight me if you like!'

It was the small scruffy boy who had danced with Charlotte. 'Wasn't her as started it,' he reiterated. 'I was doing a bit o' step dancing, see, and she come an' joined in. You seen how well we was doing it. Wasn't nuffink woulda stopped us.' He was taller than Farrell had first thought, and older, the Irishman estimated sixteen at least. But he lounged instead of standing straight and was so painfully thin he appeared more like a child of twelve.

Ulick made an irritable gesture. 'I'm not doing anything to her, you young fool – but I'm not having her dancing out on the streets in the dark, either. Come along, Charlotte, back inside.' He was so put out at this obstacle to his plans that he failed to notice he sounded like an outraged parent.

Charlotte bristled at him. 'I'm not going anywhere until Tommy and I have had a last dance together. You go if you want to.'

Belatedly he accepted that he must humour her for the present. Time was slipping away and the last thing he could afford now was an ugly scene. 'Very well. I'll watch with the rest and you have one last dance.' He caught the organ grinder's eye and realised he was the only cash-carrying patron of the show. He threw a few coins into the man's battered collecting bag and the music started again.

Ulick's anger melted as soon as the pair within the circle began working their magic again. Whatever the street children had felt, he was picking it up now, too. The tune ended and another began, and then, after only moments, it seemed, the organ grinder was saying: 'Off for me supper now, guv, sorry. Show's over for tonight.' And he realised the urchins were drifting away as the evening chill deepened.

All thoughts of a telegram and an inglorious dash for the last train to Handford were gone. Another, far bigger plan was stirring somewhere in his mind, its details still unclear. All he knew at the moment was that he had to keep track of this boy, and to get someone else, an expert, to see them.

'Tommy, is it?' he asked. 'Sorry I was so sharp just then. Charlotte's only just come to London and I worry about her.' The wizened, street-wise young face returned a flat cynical look of patent disbelief. Ulick pushed on, trying not to make heavy weather of it: 'You must be a bit chilly in those thin clothes. How would you like to join us for a bite of supper? Nothing much. I'll just go down to the fried-fish shop.'

'And I could come and 'ave it wiv you an' Lottie?'

'Lottie?' For a moment indignation boiled again in Ulick's breast, but then he thought, why not? No one would ever associate that name with a

51

lady . . . 'Yes, you and me and Lottie, how about that?'

'You got yourself a bargain. I'd even offer to get the fish, only you wouldn't trust me wiv the money.'

'Oh, I think I would.'

'Then you're a bloody mug, mate, that's all I can say.' His grin disarmed the words of malice. Laughing, Ulick handed over the price of three fish suppers and shooed Charlotte upstairs to the apartment. 'I'll leave the door on the latch, Tommy. I'm going round the corner to get us some beer,' he told the boy.

'Porter for me. Sticks to the ribs better,' Tommy called back as he headed towards Drury Lane.

He was a street boy, he told them, who slept rough under railway arches or in the cellars of ruined houses when he could not earn enough to buy a cheap bed for the night. At first he was reticent about where he got any money at all, then admitted he sold ballad broadsheets, having first picked enough pockets to buy his stocks from the printer.

'I'm surprised a lad who dances as well as you isn't making a living round the pubs or halls,' said Ulick.

Tommy's snort of merriment spattered half-chewed fish and chips everywhere. 'You blind, mate? They won't let me in nowhere wearing rags and needing a wash. Any case, whoever heard of a clog dancer in worn-out boots?'

'Wouldn't it be worth saving a bit of what you get for the broadsheets?'

'A comedian like you should be on the stage hisself. Most I ever got from that lot bought me a pie an' a bed. Sometimes it's just a penny sit-up.'

'What's a penny sit-up?' Charlotte was spell-bound.

'Just hope you never have to find out the 'ard way, Lottie. You sit on a wood bench and lean forward on this rope, see, on your arms, and get a bit o' rest if you can. Come the morning, they cut the rope and all fall down. Saves 'em having to go round an' wake everybody up.'

'But that's terrible!'

'You're tellin' me. Unless it's too cold, gimme the railway arches any time.' Tommy fell silent as he wolfed down the rest of his supper, finally pushing his plate away and saying: 'Best bit o' grub I've 'ad this year. You can 'ave me to supper any night. Hey, mister, don't say you've finished with them chips! I'll take 'em, shall I?' Without waiting for Ulick to reply, he scooped them into his filthy palm and finished them off.

'For God's sake call me Ulick. "Mister" makes me sound like some businessman with a waxed moustache!'

'What's your other name, then? Mine's Fanshaw.'

'Fanshaw? Where on earth did you pick that up?'

Tommy threw back his skinny shoulders and stuck out his jaw. 'That was all they knew about me, wasn't it? My ma died before I was old enough to know 'er and all I had was the name. Thomas Fanshaw, that's me.'

'How have you lived until now – before you started on the ballads, that is?'

'Li' any other workhouse kid. They pushed me around for a few years, 'til I was old enough for a bit o' work, then everybody else took their turn having a go at me. I'd be hired out to all sorts of odds and sods. They called it learning a trade. I called it being a slave. In the end I buggered off and kept goin'. I think that was three or four years ago.'

'But the . . . the dancing! Workhouse boys don't dance like that.'

Tommy shrugged. 'Not the only one under the arches, am I? I bunked up for a bit with an 'armless old type who'd been on the halls. He was drunk half the time, but the rest, Christ, you shoulda seen him! He did turns to keep us amused, singing or whistling a bit o' music while he was dancing. The only thing he had left was his last good pair a' clogs. Taught me how to dance, how the shoes helped, all the fancy steps and so on. I used to go an' find him summat to eat and drink when he got too sick to fend for 'imself.'

'What happened to him?' Farrell almost could not ask. The answer was inevitable.

'Died, didn't he? Everybody I like goes an' dies.' Tommy shot a fist across his nose, sniffed and blinked, then said fiercely, 'Gave me his clogs when he was dyin', an' all. Said they fitted an' I'd get a chance with them as my luck. Trouble was, I didn't want to leave him down there, dead, on his own in the night, so I slept down there. When I woke up, some bastard had gone off with Harry's old black coat and the clogs. I never even woke up while they was doing it, neither. Some luck, eh?'

Ulick swallowed hard. 'How long ago was this?'

'Ooh, 'bout a year or more. End of the summer. I didn' arf miss old Harry at first, then I thought, if I make myself the best step dancer there is, even without any clogs, he'll never really be dead, not as long as I'm around, anyway. So I practised an' practised an' practised. Every time I saw a barrel organ I'd tag along behind until he stopped and played the thing, then I'd dance. Didn't arf make 'em mad at first, then I got better and they started realising it was good for trade, because people was stopping to look at me and dropping money in the bag. After a while, one or two of them was givin' me a bit o' their take to dance on their patch.'

'But you weren't step dancing tonight with Lot – Charlotte. That looked more like a very graceful waltz.'

Tommy's bright grin sparked again. 'That was 'er Ladyship, wasn't it? I was doing me stuff down under the lamp – just for fun, no cash in that little mob – when this sort of fairy princess comes down and stands there staring. I couldn't take me eyes off her, and after a bit, she said –'

' – if I teach you my dance, will you teach me to dance like that?' Charlotte finished the sentence for him. 'And, Ulick, he bowed to me, right there in the street, and said, "My pleasure, Miss." And I said, "Not Miss, Charlotte." And we joined hands and started dancing.'

Tommy broke in again, as excited as Charlotte now. 'And I said, "I don't call nobody a stuck-up name like Charlotte-rhymes-wiv-harlot. You're Lottie to me, now and forever!" Then she taught me that dance you saw us doing later on.'

A small mean resentment clawed at Ulick and he said: 'Forever? That sounds like a very long season.'

'Aah, you know what we jolly cockneys is like! Hearts o' gold but can't trust us. We always promise the earth an' can't pay the rent.' But the eyes which threw back Farrell's tacit challenge did not echo Tommy's self-mocking tone. I want this girl, his eyes were saying, more than I ever wanted anything in my miserable life, and I'm having her, so watch out.

Then the tension subsided. Tommy's smile was friendly again. 'Well,' he said, 'you've 'eard my life story. Now let's 'ave yours, or at least the reason you spent all that money on me beer an' food.'

'I don't think our story would interest you,' Ulick lied glibly, 'but I have a proposition which might.' He turned to Charlotte. 'Were you just day-dreaming a couple of months ago when you said you wanted to be an actress, or did you mean you'd be prepared to work at it?'

'Of course I meant it! You know how I feel about hypocrites! I'd do anything to be a great actress.'

'I don't think it need quite come to that – and I don't think you're looking in the right direction. How about the variety stage?'

'Music hall? But would I have the talent for that?'

Farrell laughed in spite of himself. 'You were prepared to take on the acting profession and you don't think you'll manage the halls?'

'P'raps she's right, an' all,' Tommy broke in. 'A music hall audience is a lot tougher to work than them toffs in the legit theatre.' He pronounced it thee-ay-ter. 'She's going to need more than just talent for music hall.'

'Well, I shall probably regret saying this for the rest of my life, but I think perhaps she and you, both together, might just have that something more. I asked you up here to see if we could work up an act between us.'

'Christ! Are you serious? You'd set it up?'

'Yes. I know you couldn't afford to get clean and buy the clothes and clogs – from what I hear about the clogs, I'm not at all sure I could afford the good ones for you – but I'll back us all to get going, and I'll work out a routine. If you like it, and both you and Charlotte are able to do it, are you game, Tommy?'

'Game? Who d'you want me to kill first? One condition, though. You got to get rid of Charlotte-the-harlot. From now on, she's Lottie, all right?'

Ulick needed only to glance at the girl's radiant face. 'Very well,' he said, 'Lottie it is – but only for the stage, as far as I'm concerned. Now, let's drink to it.' He opened three bottles of stout and they drank to their shared, unknown future.

A week after moving into Wilson Street, Ulick Farrell called to see Nellie Standish at her house in Bloomsbury. He was acutely conscious that she had told no one else of her illness and that she would have received the doctor's full diagnosis by now. Ulick was unfamiliar with sickness, but he knew plenty about trouble. It was his way to take problems head on and deal with them like human enemies. This was no exception. Nellie needed a friend in her lonely fight.

She took him to her morning room and spent a few minutes chattering brightly about nothing. Finally Ulick broke in. 'It's bad news, I take it.'

Her set smile crumbled. 'The worst. Knew it would be, really, but it still came as a shock. You're never ready for that, I don't suppose.'

'How long?'

'Don't be bloody stupid! It's all so vague he wouldn't even tell me straight out I was going to die until I forced him. He hasn't got a clue.'

'Then maybe . . .'

'Uh-huh, he's not wrong. I could have told him before – said it to you, didn't I? Nothing that hurts this much is going to just disappear an' leave me alone.'

'What about work? How well placed are you financially?'

'You do me a power of good, Ulick. Always cut away the dead wood and

54

consider the important bits. I can work for a while and there's money put by
. . . quite a bit. You're a survivor, like me, aren't you? What a pity we never
got together.'

'You'd have loathed me in ten minutes. I've always been a better friend
than I was a lover.'

'Now where does that leave our little Charlotte?'

'Still in her bloody virginal state as far as I'm concerned.'

That succeeded in distracting Nellie from her own tragedy. 'After a week
in that love nest of yours, following God knows what fun and games in the
country as a warm-up? Do me a favour!'

'As God is my judge, Nellie, I could be her older brother for all the
satisfaction I've had there.'

'Well, I am surprised. She's the last one I'd have put down as a cold fish.'

'No question of that, believe me. Her intense curiosity about matters
carnal was what got us into this mess. What with one thing and another, it's
mainly my fault.'

'First I heard of you having trouble getting it up.'

'Don't be crude, dear girl. Nothing of the sort. I find it difficult to know
how to put this, but – well, we seem to have acquired a lodger, and as long as
he's there, Charlotte has made it clear I can forget about cosy amorous
twosomes with her.'

'How the devil did that happen? You must be stark raving, after I set you
up like that.'

'I told you, I know it's my own fault. I still think it could be the making of
us, though, and I was hoping to ask for your expert advice.'

'Lovey, if there's one thing I'm not expert about, it's lodgers. That's why I
live over here and keep all my tenants at a long arm's length over Wilson
Street.'

'No, this is about a possible music hall act. I'm too close to know whether
I've got real quality or just a flash in the pan. I need a pro like you to judge.'

'Any time. By the seem of things, I won't be good for much else for very
long.'

'Have you had the chance to make any plans at all?'

She laughed. 'Been upstairs, crying, haven't I? You don't make any plans
in that state. One thing I'm sure of, though, I'm going out with a bang. I'm
doing two shows a night at the moment – the Middlesex and the Royal
Standard. They're going all right, everybody loves me, and if it wasn't for this
sodding growth I could choose any gig in London after this run's over.'

'But you won't.'

She shook her head. 'I finish at the Standard in two weeks – three in the
Old Mo'. I planned the bookings months back to leave me clear for rehearsals
in panto. I thought I'd be in one of the top productions this year. But it looks
as if the time has come for me to announce I'm going into temporary retire-
ment to work on something really big, a long way ahead . . . maybe even hint
I'm going legit and taking on a musical comedy. You know enough about this
business to realise they'll forget about me after ten minutes' guessing what it
will be. Then I can crawl away and die in peace.'

'Do that and you'll kill yourself off in six months. You live for the stage.'

'Think I don't know that? But I can't come up with anything else that won't involve me fading away *on* stage. I couldn't do that to myself, even if it meant lasting a few months longer. I'd rather keep my rotten pride.'

Impulsively, he put his arms around her and held her close. She relaxed against him with a tired sigh, then stiffened and said: 'Come on, now, don't get me feeling sorry for meself. It'd be far better if you could come up with something to keep me occupied. All suggestions gratefully received.'

'I think I've already offered the best one you're likely to get. Help me with my two theatrical lame ducks.'

She began to dismiss the idea. 'I'm no nanny, Ulick, it's centre stage or nothing for me.'

'Well, you've just admitted you're vacating the limelight in a couple of weeks, so that's no longer true. Isn't the next best thing to create future star performers?'

'Destroy 'em, more like!' When did you ever know a feature artiste who was willing to give rivals a leg up?'

'Often, and you're well aware of it. How many times have you slipped money to a promising kid, or seen to it that a little dazzler gets pulled out of the chorus for something a bit better?'

'Yeah, but that's small beer compared with what you're suggesting.'

'Quite. Until now it's been a minor hobby. This could turn into your life's work.'

'The way things look, that could be a bloody short career, but all right, you're on. God knows what you've pulled together, though. It sounds like a right dog's breakfast. Do I need a bottle of fizz before I can nerve myself to watch, or will I be able to take it cold?'

'That's more like it. Come on over to Wilson Street and you can see them at their appalling worst. Oh, and by the way, Charlotte is now Lottie.'

Ulick's impromptu vision of theatrical genius had faded abruptly when he got Tommy Fanshaw stripped, bathed and dressed in fresh clothes. He turned the piano sideways on to the room so that he could play for Tommy and Charlotte while watching them dance, then started off with a medley of the tunes the organ grinder had played in the street. But Tommy's spontaneity had vanished with the dirt. He approached Charlotte self-consciously, held her stiffly and bungled elementary steps which he had grasped naturally before. Farrell was beginning to feel very silly.

If he had hoped Nellie's presence might galvanise the pair into some semblance of their original talent, he was sadly mistaken. As he opened the apartment door and ushered Nellie in, Tommy froze in mid-step and squawked: 'Gorblimey, it's Nellie Standish!' then seemed incapable of further speech or motion. Charlotte, dressed in her white muslin for the rehearsal, merely stood and simpered at her favourite female. Ulick did not know whether he wanted to roar with fury or slap them both like naughty children.

He had explained the dilemma to Nellie in the cab on the way over to Covent Garden. 'One day they were the best natural dancers I'd ever seen, the next they could have been a pair of automata! I simply don't know what went wrong.'

'I think I might,' she said, but after that remained enigmatic. 'Time enough when I've seen them,' she snapped when he pressed her for an opinion.

Now she sat through a repetition of the lacklustre routine he had watched with mounting despair for the past few days. At the end of the second tune, she clapped her hands to stop the music. 'Enough! Nothing here we can't change with a bit o' work, but we'll need to do it different.' She still refused to be more forthcoming, merely sending Tommy out for a couple of bottles of champagne. 'Drop of bubbly will loosen everybody up, me in particular,' she announced. When he came back from the wine shop, she told him to change into his ragged old clothes.

'Can't,' he said, 'Ulick burned 'em, except me old shirt.'

'That'll do. Put it on – and rough yourself up a bit – here, like this.' She rumpled his hair, then took a handkerchief and drew it across the sooty fireback, smearing the resultant grime down his cheek and on to his shirt-sleeve. 'That should be enough for now,' was all she would say.

The wine kept her going for a couple of hours, which she filled with music hall reminiscences that captivated Ulick as much as the younger ones, but got nowhere towards solving his problems. It was already dusk and he was about to start steering Nellie back to a second audition, when she tapped the table for silence and said: 'Listen! They're playing your song.'

Into the silence filtered the distant notes of a barrel organ. 'Coupla streets away, but it'll have to do,' she said. 'Come on, kids, pick up your traps and let's find 'im.' With that she was up and out of the apartment.

They did not catch up with the organ grinder until he set up in Bow Street, just up the road from the opera house. Nellie sniffed. 'As good a place to start your theatrical career as any, I'll be bound,' she said. 'All right then, young Tom, you got the right music, a decent pair o' clogs, and the prettiest partner I ever saw. Do your stuff.'

And he did. Hesitantly at first, then with a rising lyrical self-confidence, he swung Charlotte into first the waltz she had taught him, then the step dance he had passed on as her price for the first evening's instruction. After ten minutes, they had a sizeable audience and the organ grinder was gesturing madly at his black collecting bag in an effort to capitalise on them.

Eventually, Nellie signalled to the dancers to stop, and they withdrew reluctantly from the charmed circle of onlookers. 'No dawdling,' she ordered. 'Back to Wilson Street. We got a lot of talking to do.' As she stalked ahead of them, splendid in her off-duty showgirl rig, Ulick wondered briefly if the doctor had made a mistaken diagnosis.

Back at the flat she poured herself another drink, then turned on them.

'God save me from amateurs! Ulick, I'd have credited you with more sense, at least, but none of you saw it. What happened just now?'

For a while they all stared at her owlishly, bereft of an answer. 'Come on, come on – I haven't got all night, if you 'ave! What happened, from the beginning? Lottie: you tell me.'

'W-well, we tried again, up here, with the piano . . . you saw. We knew it was awful, didn't we, Tommy? Somehow it's not the same indoors, with the piano. And then, as soon as you took us out . . . well, it was all right again. I could have gone on forever.'

'Right – and that's your trouble, Ulick. You took away the contrast and you took away the audience. I dunno why, but these two brats are naturals and they can't do it right without an audience. You must have seen how they improved when the crowd started gathering.'

57

He nodded. 'It was more than that, though, Nellie, much more. You saw it was different right from the beginning. There was no audience then.'

'Course not, but that was the other thing you missed. I didn't just make Tommy change so's he wouldn't dirty his new trousers. They're not such brilliant dancers as you made out – not yet, at any rate. Reason they looked so marvellous was the contrast. You got to keep 'em just like that for the turn, you dunce. When you tarted up Tommy and took away the barrel organ, you ruined it, eh, Tommy?'

Realisation had dawned on the boy's face as Nellie began talking. 'Yeah, that's right: the first time, I felt all poor an' dirty and she was like a princess. When I got clean, we still weren't the same, but we were too close for the differences to show. An' anuvver fing – that piano sounds too stuck-up by arf!'

'Bravo, Tommy! Now, what are we going to do about it?'

'Well, you've started it already, haven't you? Get me ragged and dirty again. I'll keep the new clogs, though – make 'em a bit shabby, like, to match the rest, but you need good clogs for good dancing.'

'That's it. And for Lottie?'

'Ah, she've got to stay like she is, p'raps more so. You know, ribbon in 'er hair . . . she could even 'ave one o' them hoops like the toffs' kids have. We could make it a little story, couldn't we?'

Comprehension was dawning on Ulick now, too. Of course, it had been the setting and contrast that charmed him – that would charm a music hall given half a chance. Mentally, he began writing the sketch, choreographing the movements. 'Dammit all,' he said, 'where will we get an organ grinder?'

Nellie roared with laughter. 'Haven't you spent any time on the streets of London lately, mate? The place is crawling with 'em, all available to you for an evening's takings and a tip on top – a fraction of what you'll be paid for the act.'

Bedlam broke loose as Tommy and Charlotte started throwing in suggestions and demanding one of them should go now to engage an organ grinder. Nellie yelled above the din: 'Quiet, the lot of you! Nobody's doing anything else tonight. In case you'd all forgotten, I'm on stage at the Old Mo' in just over an hour. For the rest of the evening, all I'm interested in is Nellie Standish.'

She decided to go directly to the theatre. She was due to perform there at eight-thirty, after which she would rush over to Pimlico by cab to appear in the Royal Standard at ten o'clock. Ulick went downstairs to call a hansom for her while she gathered together gloves, boa and umbrella. Then she turned her attention to Charlotte. 'As for you, my girl, you're coming to stay with me for a while. We'll never make a star of you with this ragamuffin way of living.'

Charlotte bridled, torn between her heroine and her adored Ulick. 'But I can't move from here.'

'You certainly can't stay here with a street urchin sleeping on the hearth rug and a great brawny Irishman on the sofa, so get your things packed. I'll sort Ulick out; I'm sure he'll see it my way.'

'I bet 'e will,' said Tommy, grinning at the expression on Nellie's face.

'I'm not sure I do, yet,' Charlotte grumbled.

'Well you soon will. You're going to learn to be a music hall star, and you don't do that living like this – not unless you were born in the slums in the first place, that is. You get ready. I'll arrange for Ulick to take you to Bloomsbury while the show's on. Tommy – you watch yourself. I got plans for you, too.'

Then, in a flurry of skirts and feathers, she was gone.

Charlotte turned to Tommy, round-eyed. 'I think we may be on our way,' she said.

The boy shook his head. 'But you don't know where to, do yer?'

CHAPTER SEVEN

The jumble of new impressions and people which now thronged Charlotte's life had deflected her, temporarily at least, from her ambition to become Ulick Farrell's mistress. Apart from anything else, she was not entirely sure what the term meant. It was one she had seen in various books in her father's library, books normally kept out of reach of the children. Although the precise function of such women was never described in detail, it was clear from the stories that mistresses had a far more exciting time than wives: riding alone and glamorously habited in Rotten Row; visiting theatres and establishments evasively referred to as night-houses; enjoying the forbidden delights of something called a fizz dinner, which seemed to entail all the women sitting on the gentlemen's laps to eat and drink.

It all looked very exciting but Charlotte's natural intelligence warned her there must be a price for such pleasures, and something told her it had everything to do with what the footman and the village girl, and later Ulick and her mother, had done together. There was something disturbingly grown-up about it. Perhaps it would be better to postpone further exploration in that direction until she knew what to expect . . .

Anyway, other impressions crowded out thoughts of tying herself to one man. Ulick was no longer the only male in her life. Now there was Tommy Fanshaw, too. She never saw Tommy without wanting to hug him – not as she embraced Ulick, but the way she had once cuddled Nanny. And when he began to dance with her, she felt something she had never experienced with anyone. With Tommy and a little music, Charlotte knew she was an enchantress, and when people gathered to watch, she saw that enchantment reflected in their eyes. They never wanted to look away; when the music stopped and the barrel organ man trundled on his way, the onlookers trailed off reluctantly, glancing back as if hoping the boy and girl would give them one more glimpse of fairyland. Charlotte loved that feeling. If she could experience it all the time, she often thought, she would never ask for anything else, not even Ulick Farrell.

Now Nellie Standish added to it all by taking Charlotte into her own house. Charlotte started off with visions of long mornings in bed, luncheons at Romano's and evenings watching Nellie from the stalls at the Royal Standard. She was rapidly disillusioned.

When Nellie took her away from the Wilson Street flat, she was sent back to Bloomsbury where the maid installed her in a bedroom, produced a light supper and saw she got to bed early. Hearing Nellie arrive home very late, Charlotte emerged on to the third floor landing, intending to rush down and greet her heroine. Instead, she confronted a determined Maud, who chivvied her back to her bedroom and ordered her to stay there.

'Never assume a lady will be coming home alone at this hour,' Maud said severely. 'It's one of the most important lessons you learn in this line, my girl.'

In fact, she was treated more like a child than she had been for years. Nellie saw to it that she went out only with Maud, Ulick or herself. She was expected to go to bed and get up early, to spend the morning at Wilson Street practising; to read and rest in the afternoon and to see as much music hall as possible in the evening. She was always sent – with Ulick and Tommy – to halls that had early houses. They sat in the gallery and she was home in time for bed by eleven.

'It's like being in a convent', she glowered at Nellie one afternoon.

'Some bloody convent – since when do nuns wear frilly lace drawers and drink fizz?' said Nellie. 'You're here to learn, and you can't do that if you're gallivanting about with stars in your eyes. Right, then – let's see how well you memorised those songs I gave you on Monday.'

Her sessions with Nellie were limited as long as the singer was still appearing on stage. She had barely enough energy to take her through two shows a night, without further strain. 'Get her used to that routine you've worked out, Ulick,' Nellie told him. 'The minute I'm off the boards, I'll want her a lot more of the time.'

The act Ulick had concocted had a unique delicacy designed to play perfectly on the mixed sentimentality and snobbery of the urban poor. It was an idealised version of Charlotte and Tommy's first meeting. The curtain rose on a street scene, yellow-lit by a gas lamp. Beneath the lamp, an organ grinder set up his instrument and began to play, wearily at first, as if at the end of a profitless day. Then a ragged street urchin erupted on to the stage, holding a pie he had supposedly stolen from his unseen pursuers. Seeking to throw them off, he discarded the food, joined the street musician and began a clog dance in time to the man's tune. The shouts of pursuit died away, and the boy became absorbed in the dance. Watching him, the organ grinder appeared to shake off his weariness, enlivened by the vitality of the performance.

At that moment, a lovely young girl – Charlotte in a theatrical version of her white muslin – entered, bowling a hoop. She clattered to a halt in front of the dancer and musician, delighted at the novelty of the scene. Then she threw aside her hoop and big straw hat and, hesitantly at first but with growing confidence, began to mimic the boy's steps. The dance ended and the boy bowed awkwardly to her, as if in homage to her beauty. She gestured, indicating that now she would show him a dance. After that, they went into a more developed version of the waltz Ulick had seen them perform that first evening. When they finished it, they concluded the whole act with a lively polka to leave everyone with feet tapping.

Nellie loved the idea but was more reserved about its performance. 'It's brilliant, Ulick, but I warn you, it's ambitious enough to faze even a couple of old pros. These two are as green as grass and if they flunk it, there's plenty of pros out there ready to lift it and do it full justice. Are you willing to lose one of the best sketches you're ever going to write to give these two a chance? You could sell it now for a pretty penny.'

Farrell shrugged. 'I don't have much choice. I pulled Tommy Fanshaw off the street with something like this in mind, and Charlotte is stuck to me like glue. I can hardly let them down now.'

'So be it, but we're not going public with it until I've had that little girl of yours under my thumb for at least a month. She needs educating in more ways than you'd believe.'

Nellie's final performance served Charlotte as a life-long standard, an ideal she always aimed for but never felt she attained. At first, Nellie refused to let them come, but Ulick insisted. 'You may not feel like getting carted off to Romano's afterwards by your fellow artistes,' he told her. 'I've noticed how done in you look when you finish on normal nights now. Think about what that performance will take out of you. Be sensible. Use us as your shield.'

Reluctantly she agreed. 'Since you're coming, though, you can go in the gallery and let Tommy and Lottie soak up the atmosphere,' she said.

'I've been meaning to ask: why do you always insist they sit there? I could run to the dress circle now and again.'

'Tommy's all right, he's got the touch anyway; born to it. Lottie's different. I want her so used to them up there that she forgets there's anyone else in the hall when she gets on that stage. They're always going to be the ones she's got to please and I don't want her forgetting it.'

'I'm not at all sure you can teach that to anyone, Nellie. Either you're born with it, or you've missed it.'

'You'd better be wrong, or you've got a beautiful flop on your hands, Mr Farrell. I'm happy to say I think you *are* wrong, so why don't you leave it to Nellie?'

The Middlesex in Drury Lane was still universally known to regulars as the Old Mo', after its original name, the Great Mogul Tavern. It had a murderous reputation as one of the toughest top line houses. Getting the bird at the Old Mo' was the dread of most rising artistes; but it was also the great place for farewell performances. This was where the audience grew tearful as an old favourite, now creaking at the joints and short of wind, croaked out the hit song of his career for the last time. Nellie, still in the full glory of her talent, could think of nowhere better for her swan song.

Ulick persuaded the leather-faced old stage doorman to let him go backstage before she went on. He found her alone, gazing down at a piece of jewellery she was about to pin to her gown.

He glanced at it casually, then looked again, struck by its obvious value. 'That looks a little rich for prancing about behind the footlights,' he said.

Nellie gave him a wistful smile. 'Just this once, I'm allowing myself a bit of sentimentality,' she said. 'This was the last present I got from the fellow I mentioned to you.'

'Hmm, all those sapphires – he must have been very keen.'

'Not quite keen enough. I'd a swapped all the sapphires in Tasmania for him, only he was too daft to see it until too late. He never even knew I kept this. I didn't see him again – just sent a snotty note back with the doorman and sailed out past him on the arm of a South African millionaire. It cost me every ounce of acting talent I had to do it, an' all.'

The brooch was an exquisitely designed tangle of diamond hearts and sapphire forget-me-nots. 'I was singing a song called "Hearts and Flowers" in that show – maybe you remember it – it was all the rage just before last Christmas. They even gave away the words and music in the *News of the World* one Sunday, so everyone would have their very own Nellie Standish in the parlour, belting it out with Dad on the piano. I've never sung it again – and I've never worn the brooch, either. But tonight I'll do both.' She took a deep breath and blinked rapidly several times. 'Mustn't bloody cry, not with the paint already in place. Off you go now, love. Time for me final touches.'

Farrell headed for the door. As he reached it, she said: 'Thanks, Ulick. I don't think I could get through this without you and those two kids.' He stopped and began to say something, but she had turned back to her mirror and was smoothing her already immaculate hair.

He had seen Nellie perform countless times, but never so well. The Mo's stage and auditorium were still lit by gas and limelight, and Nellie was enough of a past master at makeup for such conditions to ensure there was no trace of strain or illness in her face. She looked reed-slim, but she had always been a tall, big-boned woman and now she carried the slenderness as well as she had her more voluptuous curves. She wore a gown of midnight blue velvet and a vast cartwheel of a hat in the same colour, trimmed with black cock feathers. She carried a tall silver-headed cane like those sported by major-domos, and paraded around the stage using it as an accessory to various statuesque poses while she sang. Only Farrell knew that half the time it was all that held her up.

She started them off with 'Brown-eyed Girl with Long Black Curls', the song Ulick had written to launch her into big-time music hall. After that, her act was a reprise of half the great songs of the 1890s. Maybe it was a poaching job, but the likes of Marie Lloyd and Maidie Scott were hardly likely to confront her with it if she had no plans to appear again.

She made no attempt to pass off the material as her own, but linked the songs with a stream of amusing patter which was almost a history of her rise to stardom, with pithy references to rival artistes. When she mentioned them, their names became pegs for her to sing their songs in her own inimitable way. The audience loved it.

Ulick was expecting her to save 'Hearts and Flowers' as the big finishing number, but she sang it midway through the routine. He never knew whether the professional in her decreed that this was the right artistic position for the song, or whether she distrusted her own ability to sing it unmoved as the last item in her act. As it was, she almost brought the house down with it.

Appropriately, it was the sentimental tale of a young girl who fell hopelessly in love with the handsome man who brought her flowers and sent her Valentine cards, but then left her alone and went off with another woman. Her stage presence was such that with no change of costume or makeup, she managed to convince them she was a young, dewy-eyed maiden, then a woman blooming at her best while their love lasted, and finally a fading flower after she was jilted. She started the song far upstage, with the limelight just off her, conjuring an atmosphere of spring sunlight in the country, then moved forward into the full white blaze of summer when she sang the verse that told of leaving everything for him. She crowned the performance by doing what none but the very best could get away with – she half turned her back on the audience and moved slowly upstage again, the words of the last verse drifting back:

> 'They say that hearts and flowers
> Are the sign of love that's true;
> But oh! They just remind me
> Of the heart I lost to you.'

In the gallery, Ulick blinked away hot tears and told himself impatiently that he was over-emotional because he knew the story behind the song. But he had only to look around him to know it was untrue. Nellie had just turned a few verses of music hall bathos into true emotion with supreme artistry. She can't be dying, she can't! he thought. It's so damned unfair. But the silent protest was swept away on a storm of applause as Nellie took her bow before moving on to the second set of songs in her act. After 'Hearts and Flowers', she could have recited Shakespeare and they would have cheered her to the echo.

What she gave them now was a series of rollicking comic songs, so that tears were forgotten and everyone was tapping their feet and roaring with laughter as she perpetrated the most appalling *doubles entendres* in songs like 'Have You Seen My Little Tiddler?'.

When the merriment had started to die down after this salacious epic, she strolled downstage, still apparently as fresh as when the act started, although God knew how she was still conscious by now, thought Ulick. Nellie raised her hand and gestured to quell the last of the laughter, then said: 'It's time to say goodbye, at least for now . . . There's only one possible song for this moment. It's not mine: I only wish it was; but some of the biggest names on the halls have sung it, and now I'm going to add my two penn'orth. This is for you lot up there –' she raised her arm higher '– the ones who made us all. God bless you, and thanks for everything.'

Then she sang 'The Boy I Love Is Up In The Gallery'. Farrell knew no performer could distinguish individuals in the stalls, let alone the gallery, thanks to the intensity of the footlights, but by some freakish chance, Nellie directed the full blast of her performance at Tommy Fanshaw.

It was the best thing she had ever done. All over the hall, people were leaning forward, entranced, tears streaming down their faces. Tommy sat as though turned to stone, and Ulick knew this moment would be burned on the boy's memory for the rest of his life. 'Not a bad thing, either,' he muttered to himself.

Afterwards, they tried to make her stay, to sing more songs, preferably to sing 'The Boy I Love' once more. But Nellie knew when to quit. The storm of applause subsided momentarily and she said: 'What more can I give you? You've had it all – with my love.' Then she made an abrupt sideways slice with her gloved hand and the stagehand killed the lights. When they went up again, she was gone, and she did not return for a curtain call.

The stage doorman had instructions to admit Ulick and Tommy and no one else. They left Charlotte outside in the cab. In her dressing room Nellie, face ghastly, eyes burning like spots of black volcanic rock, was raising a glass of gin to her lips.

Tommy let out a horrified gasp. 'Jesus, Nellie – what's the matter?'

'Nothing this gin won't cure, love. Hang on.' She closed her eyes, tossed it down and shuddered slightly. 'There, that's better.' Leaning forward to the mirror, she pinched her cheeks until the pressure and the liquor brought back some colour. 'See? Never know I was knackered, would you?'

Her dresser was fussing like a mother hen. 'Course they would – anybody wiv any sense, anyhow. Think we're daft or something? Do these two know?'

Nellie nodded, resigned. 'Mr Farrell does. Not Tommy, though. I had to tell Kitty, Ulick. She's close enough for me to trust her, aren't you, Kit? And it was getting obvious to her, anyway. Tommy, you mustn't tell anyone about this. It's our secret, right? I'm a bit done up and that's why I'm stopping for a while. D'you mind keeping the secret, just between us?'

'Nah, I'd do anything for you, Nellie, you know that. Is it really bad?'

For a moment it looked as if Nellie would try to fool him, but then she decided to make a small joke of the truth. 'Bad enough. Let's say I'm not planning to visit the Italian Riviera next summer.'

If Ulick had expected melodrama from the boy, he was disappointed. Tommy's face remained impassive. He merely said: 'I'll never forget the way you sang tonight. That last bit, I felt as if you were singing it just for me.'

'I was, Tommy, I was . . . Right, then, we've 'ad a good cry. Kit, where's me wrap? I'll take root if I stay in this damned dressing room much longer!'

She stood up as smoothly as if she had never been ill, permitted Kitty to robe her like some Roman empress, embraced and kissed the dresser, then strode out with Farrell and Tommy in her wake.

Ulick permitted himself a sidelong glance at Tommy and saw that now the boy was crying freely, tears trickling down his cheeks and dripping off his jaw-bone on to his collar. Silently, he handed over a handkerchief, pressing Tommy's shoulder as he did so. Then he said, very quietly: 'Try not to grieve. Let's hope she has a good long time yet.' Drying his eyes, Tommy merely shook his head, then handed back the handkerchief and moved on out to the cab where Charlotte waited.

True to her word, Nellie banished Ulick and Tommy for the week following her farewell appearance at the Middlesex. The newspapers did her proud, with fulsome expressions of regret that she would not appear in pantomime at Christmas, and endless speculation about the nature of the new show she planned the following year. Charlotte was told Nellie needed a rest from the stage, but not the nature of her illness.

The day after her farewell appearance, Nellie lay late in bed, but left instructions that Charlotte should walk in the park with Maud, then return for lunch at the house. Charlotte made a face when she heard the news. 'I thought at least I'd get lunch at Romano's the day after Nellie's grand finale,' she grumbled.

'Gawd, you haven't arf got a lot to learn,' Maud said. 'Don't you have the faintest notion what it would be like for Miss Nellie to have to go in there, won-dering if it was her last big entrance? Better do it on the stage, with the limelight blinding you to the audience. Once you can see 'em, that's when you start to cry. Any case, if I know my Nellie Standish, you'll have plenty of excitement later to make up for it.'

If Charlotte had expected Nellie to announce her plans over lunch, she was mistaken. Instead, the spotlight was turned on her. 'I'm going to be a right nosey parker now, and ask you all about yourself,' Nellie said.

Charlotte became defensive. 'Why do you want to know? I'm not very interesting.'

'Don't be silly, we both know that's not true,' snapped Nellie. 'I bet you've got a story fit for a novelette, and it's time for you to tell your Auntie Nellie.'

'You'll just try and send me back.'

'Oh, Christ, I haven't got time for this sort of nonsense! Why would I want to do that?'

'B-because I'm still a child and . . . and respectable . . . and you'll think I can't look after myself, and—'

'Enough! I've seldom seen a kid more capable of looking after herself than you. If you fell in Barking Creek you'd climb out bone dry with a plate of meat pudding in your hand.'

But Charlotte was nervous. She had seen the Cazenove name snap the lower orders into subservient attention for long enough to know it brought out the worst in people. She mumbled something unintelligible and stared down at the tablecloth.

Nellie tried again. 'If it makes you feel any better, I've been a grown woman to all intents and purposes since I was eleven. In them days I was scrubbing staircases in the morning and going onstage in Drury Lane as a fairy in the chorus at night. Sixpence for the staircases; shilling for the fairy – and that's just the bit I can tell you about. If you think I'm going to send you home because you've been up to some underage hanky-panky, think again. I've seen it all.'

Shamefaced, Charlotte unbent and told of the domineering mother and the restricted life, the beautiful house which offered her nothing to look forward to; she confessed to her entrapment of Ulick, at which Nellie hooted with merriment. 'That's the best laugh I've had since before I saw the Quack! No wonder he's still following you like a dog after a bit o' tripe. You're probably the first woman who ever got him into serious trouble.'

'Well, it got me into trouble too.'

'Do me a favour! Only trouble you got into was exactly what you wanted – a one-way ticket out of that country mausoleum, and a man to protect you while you got started. I'm not going to need to teach you as much as I thought.'

After that, she listened attentively, asking occasional questions, while Charlotte went through details of her daily life at Lyonesse. When the girl finally ran out of steam, Nellie shook her head. 'I take it back. I'll have to teach you a hell of a lot, but a bit different than I expected. The songs and dances are just the beginning.'

'But why? You've seen I know how to behave. Surely, if you take me to places like Romano's, I'll just get into the swim naturally.'

'I wish it was that simple. What do you know about music hall?'

'Not much, I admit. After all, I'd never been to one until a couple of weeks ago. But I shall learn, Nellie, really I shall!'

'Not the things you need to know, not unless I show you. You're coming from the wrong direction. Your sort goes to the theatre for entertainment, not

67

music hall. Theatre and concerts is Mayfair. The halls is the streets, and unless you know the streets, you'll never learn to handle an audience. However good Ulick got you, you'd go on stage somewhere like the Old Mo' and they'd have you on toast.'

'I don't understand.'

'Course you don't, but you will. You got to know them right through, know what it's like not to have money to buy supper, or a bed for the night; what they eat when they're flush; what they do on Saturdays. Ever been shopping?'

It had always been a bone of contention between Charlotte and her mother. 'Hardly ever,' she said. 'Mama said it was unnecessary until I was older. When we were in London I had to stay in the nursery or go out with Nanny when Mama went shopping.' From force of habit, she dropped her voice. 'My brother Ivo always said it was because Mama didn't want anyone to realise she had a daughter as old as me, but I think it was just to make me miserable.'

'Fine, that means we won't have any wrong ideas to put right. This evening we're going shopping, but not down Regent Street. It's time you got to know how the Other Half lives. I hope your little stomach is strong enough – but it looks to me as if you've got cast-iron guts, so I'm not too bothered about that!'

It was Saturday. Nellie had been playing Saturday-to-Friday at the Middlesex. This evening, she was free to show Charlotte how ordinary Londoners spent their Saturday nights.

They found what Nellie was looking for down a side turning off the Borough High Street. To get there the hansom had travelled through drab grey streets, which even had a different smell from the wide West End thoroughfares that were all Charlotte knew of London. Nellie dismissed the cab driver, then gestured broadly at the hive of activity all around them.

'This is what you need to have come from to understand the people you and Tommy will be entertaining,' she said. 'Bit like putting a bird of paradise in with a cage of fighting cocks to expect you to get on with them first off. That's why we're going on a grand tour. And when we've done it, I advise you to go off somewhere like this every time you've got a free afternoon. By the time I'm finished with you, you'll wake up with the sound of their talk in your ears and the smell of their sweat in your nostrils. You'll be more partial to pie and mash than pheasant, and you'll be prepared to swear you sucked porter from your mother's tit. All right, here we go.' With that, she plunged off into the street market which was coming into its own with the onset of darkness.

'What a funny time of day to go shopping,' said Charlotte. 'I thought they'd all be at home having supper by now.'

'This isn't just shopping, girl. It's social, too. Look how they're dressed up. That's their Sunday best. Besides, they don't get any money for shopping until after work Saturday, so the market doesn't get going much before seven. Where d'you fancy going first?'

'I want to see that funny restaurant over there. They have the oddest things written on the window.' Before she had finished speaking, Charlotte was off across the street to where a modest coffee shop front announced 'Good Food

For Working Men'. Underneath, written in white cleaning fluid on the window, were the star dishes from the menu. It read:

HARRY CHAMPION TODAY

and underneath, side by side:

BABY'S HEAD, 3d BAKED SIDE VIEW, 4d

ending with:

TWO-EYED STEAK OUR SPECIALITY

'I don't understand a word, Nellie. What on earth does it mean?'

Nellie laughed. 'See what I mean? A whole new world! Well, start with Harry Champion. You saw him at Collins's with Ulick last week. What was he singing – about food, I mean? Come on, that should be easy enough!'

'Oh, of course – "Boiled Beef and Carrots"! But I still don't understand the rest.'

'Told you none o' this was any good for them with weak stomachs. They cook steak pudding in a cloth. It comes out all wrinkly, just like a baby's head. Simple when you know. Side View speaks for itself, dunnit? Half a sheep's head, baked in the oven. That really takes a bit of beating.'

'I think I'd settle for Harry Champion,' murmured Charlotte. 'What about two-eyed steak?'

'Oh, that's positively genteel after the baby's head. It's a bloater – meatiest tasting fish you could hope to try. D'you fancy any of it?'

'Later, perhaps,' said Charlotte faintly, turning away.

'All right, but just you keep it in mind that this is the sort of food your customers will be eating when things are going well for them. Other times it'll be just bread and scrape, but they'll always find a few coppers to go to the show.'

Nellie eased Charlotte into the crowds that thronged the street market: respectable working families in their best clothes; stallholders dressed in more workaday gear; and, slipping among them seeking the odd honest or dishonest penny, the tramps and down-and-outs, crusted in dirt and wearing rags the poorest working men had discarded long ago.

Gradually the girl began to distinguish individual voices in the babble or noise around her. 'Luvly chrysamphs, tuppence a bunch', mingled with 'Fine almond celery and fresh-boiled beetroots!' The produce to match the cries was spread about her: pale creamy-green celery stalks next to great bunches of cress, both essentials for a working-class Sunday high tea when there was a guest to impress; close by, the brilliant purple-red of the boiled beetroot, its rich coloured juices staining the sides of the white enamelled bowl it was in. Next was the flower woman's basket with pungent-scented chrysanthemums, the cheapest blooms on sale and nothing resembling the rich man's nosegays commonly offered by Covent Garden and Piccadilly flower sellers.

Beyond the flower baskets was the first of the fish stalls. 'Now these you gotta try,' said Nellie, regarding with relish the neatly aligned saucers of winkles, shrimps and cockles, Brown bread-and-butter was provided, along with glass sprinkler bottles of vinegar, and pins to extract the winkles from their shells. 'Food of the gods!' Nellie swallowed a mouthful of bread-and-butter and winkles. 'Go on, don't be put off by their looks or you'll never eat anything down here!'

Minutes later, Charlotte was savouring a saucer of tiny brown shrimps and wondering why everyone didn't eat like this instead of sitting around an overloaded table with servants at their elbows. 'Don't kid yourself, love, half this lot would give their eye teeth to swap! A bit o' what you're not used to always does you the most good.' As she finished her shellfish, she was craning around, looking for something. 'Ah, there they are – thought I remembered seeing 'em down here. Come on, Lottie, I'm going to show you a bit o' first class street theatre!'

A few yards along the road a small riot was taking place. Two brightly lit shops faced each other across the street, their windows stacked high with assorted cuts of meat. Outside each stood a couple of men wearing butchers' aprons, but on their heads, instead of the traditional straw boaters, battered top hats. They also sported false noses and theatrical whiskers. Each time a potential customer passed, one or the other would start bawling: 'Don't buy nuffink from 'im, missis, he's a right swindler! Ain't got a decent bitta meat in his shop. Now come over 'ere an' let me show you our special . . .'

'Watch 'em,' said Nellie. 'What d'yer see?'

After a few moments, Charlotte said: 'Why, they aren't rivals at all! They're sharing out the customers, turn and turn about. But why are they making so much fuss about it?'

'Because they're all swindlers, that's why. Look at the shop on the left – more like a music hall than a butcher's, innit?' It certainly looked that way from outside. The windows of the upper floor had been removed, and coloured fairy lights had been attached around the openings. Just inside sat a small German band, reeling off an endless succession of popular tunes. Whenever a selection ended, the men outside the shop opposite let out a stream of insults and blew noisy raspberries until the musicians started up again.

'They're not butchers,' said Nellie. 'They're doing the same as I do and you will as soon as you know how – entertaining people. Only difference is that at least we don't con money out of our customers – they do. Their meat's lousy. Those blokes outside are drawers – some of them will be working outside fairground tents touting the dwarf and the bearded lady next week. In the meantime they draw people in there with that banter. That sort of shop's called a cutting house. The meat's inferior but you pay as much as you would at the good butcher's up the road. The drawers do their stint for a coupla bob and all the beer they can drink from the barrel at the back of the shop. Both o' them places are owned by the same firm. All the rivalry is just to make the show better and kid people they're getting a bargain.'

Charlotte went on watching, her interest tinged with growing distaste as she realised it was invariably the poorer people with least to spend who were drawn into the web of the spurious rivals. 'I don't like it,' she said. 'They're fleecing people who haven't enough to afford it.'

70

'That's why I wanted to show it to you. Don't you ever forget it. In this world you have to look after yourself. Nobody plays fair when you expect 'em to, and nobody believes you deserve kindness if you're poor an' stupid. They just take away the little bit you *have* got. That's the world you'll be entertaining – and surviving in, unless you reach the top straight away. Think you can take it?'

'But you're not like that – you've been wonderful. And Tommy . . .'

'I'm different, Lottie. I always was a mug for a sad story, and believe me, that means I've been taken for a ride myself a few times too often. The only way I've survived is by making enough money to protect me from my own stupidity. Don't expect other people to treat you the way I do. And Tommy? Bless us all, Tommy's a victim, same as those women with their ratty hair and their coupla coppers for a bit o' scrag end. Ignore Tommy and me. Take a good, long look at this lot, an' remember it. From now on, they're your world, even if you're living in more comfort than them.'

'Thank heaven for you and Ulick!'

Nellie gave her a strange look. 'Don't put too much faith in our Mr Farrell. I'd hate to see you let down.'

'But I wouldn't be doing anything like this if it weren't for him! I know how badly I behaved at home, and he's been splendid in spite of that. I'd trust him with my life.'

'Then you'd die in the gutter. Ulick Farrell is a different sort than you'd imagine.' She studied Charlotte's perplexed face for a moment, then said: 'Come on, you might as well go the whole hog and discover the London pub. I think we've got a bit o' straight talking to do.'

She led the girl a few paces further, to the corner of Southwark Bridge Road. There Charlotte confronted her first gin palace.

'Quite a sight, innit?' said Nellie, with almost proprietorial pride. 'It's not really a pub in the old-fashioned sense, but my God, it's a place to drown your sorrows!'

The location of the place was marked by two vast gas lamps which bathed the frontage in a blaze of light. The engraved glass double doors led to a long mosaic-tiled passage with an endless run of wood-panelled doors along one side. 'We'll be goin' into one o' them,' said Nellie, 'but come and see the rest before we settle down.'

At the end of the corridor was the saloon bar, all mahogany fittings and marble-topped tables. A potboy, wearing a long white apron like those sported by French waiters, darted from table to crowded table, vainly trying to mop up the spilled ale and clear empty glasses before a fresh crop arrived. As usual, Nellie looked sensationally attractive; but this was not a place where men sought out female company. They did not give her a glance. Everywhere, market traders, still in their work clothes, were taking a break to gulp down a couple of quarts before returning to their six-hour evening shift. Although they were drinking draught and bottled beers, a glance at the shelves above the bar made it clear why the place was called a gin palace. The upper shelves boasted cask after cask of gin, each labelled for a different manufacturer or type: Mountain Dew, White Satin, Old Tom, London Special and Hollands.

'I had the pleasure of starting my singing career in dives like this,' said Nellie. 'Once you've worked a coupla these, a music hall is a piece o' cake.'

71

Charlotte glanced around in dismay. 'I can't imagine ever even making myself heard in a place like this.'

'Take my word, it's difficult. But it does teach you voice projection, sharpish. Let's hope you get straight on the halls without having to be the belle of the taproom.'

Glancing at the counter, Charlotte said: 'What an enormous man there behind the bar!'

'Not as big as he looks,' Nellie told her. 'Just doesn't trust the staff, that's all. He's standing on a platform so he can get a bird's eye view of what they're up to. He also makes sure no one goes on sitting in here once they're skint. Finish your drink and sit over your glass for too long, and you're out before you can say Bob's your uncle.'

She turned away. 'No place for us in here. Come on back down the passage.' She walked along the row of closed doors, pushing them open until she found an unoccupied compartment. She grinned at Charlotte's bewilderment.

'Get a lot of secret drinking in these parts, and you can hardly call the saloon private.' Inside the cubicle was a long, narrow mahogany table with high-backed settles on either side of it. The far end touched the panelled wall, in which there was a small stained glass window. Nellie sat down at the table and opened the window. 'Barman – give us a quartern of gin an' two out, please . . . oh, and we'd better 'ave a jug o' water, an' all.' She turned back to Charlotte: 'It's heady stuff when you're not used to it, and I shouldn't think you got a lot of it down in the country.'

A quartern measure arrived, brimful of gin, with two small glasses. A pitcher of water was slapped down beside it. Nellie paid the barman five-pence and the window was closed again. She laced a half-glass of gin with water for Charlotte, but took her own neat. 'Now,' she said, 'about our Ulick – and about your future. I think it's time you did a lot o' thinking.'

Feeling nervous, Charlotte took a generous swallow of her drink, which rendered her speechless. Nellie took her choking silence for polite enquiry and carried on: 'He's a talented writer, Lottie, but he'll end up in the gutter. He's got all the gifts except persistence and that's the one that matters most in the end.'

Somewhat recovered, Charlotte jumped to his defence. 'Maybe he simply didn't have a proper incentive before. He'll stick to it now, you'll see!'

'Stick to what?' The singer's face softened and she squeezed Charlotte's hand in an effort to soften the blow. 'Oh, love, try not to build up this thing with him into a great love affair. It'll only end in tears – yours, not his, mind.'

'How can you say that? You said yourself you were never that close to him.'

'All that means is that we weren't lovers, you silly little girl! You don't get a bloke like Ulick knocking off a damned good music hall song and throwing it away on some woman he hardly knows. Of course I know him well, and if he hadn't had something going with one of my best friends, it might have turned into more. I know him all right.'

Charlotte started to speak again, but Nellie cut her off. 'Now just you listen to me: first, I'm sure he led you on, but you went after him from the start. Lesson one: a man like him thinks that gives him carte blanche to treat you rough in future.'

72

'But you know he doesn't.'

'Chance'd be a fine bloody thing! Correct me if I'm wrong, but he hasn't had you yet, has he?'

Charlotte blushed. 'No – but he must realise it's only a matter of time. I'm willing; more than willing.'

'Yes, dear, I'm sure; and I'm sure he's straining at the leash at the very thought of it. But the interesting thing about virgins is their virginity. He won't be paying you too much attention once he's got what he wants.'

'Why not? Am I that repellent?'

'I'm not even going to bother to answer that one! Nothing to do with you, apart from the fact that you're too available. No, Ulick's faults are all in the direction that'll give you trouble with him. Worst of all, he drinks.'

'So do you. So does everybody we've met since I ran away.'

'Not like Ulick Farrell. Now and then he gets his Irish up and starts feeling sorry for himself, then he goes off on a bender you'd never believe unless you saw it. He'll be like that for anything up to a week – not earning a penny and spending like Rothschild at the same time.

'By the time he's over the drinking bout, his hangover's so filthy he needs another week to recover. Sometimes he's so bad that the minute he's through the first binge, he'll go on to another. That's what finished him with my friend. He was on the whisky for nearly a month and she had enough.'

Charlotte was determined it would make no difference. 'He'll change with me – just you see.'

Nellie shook her head, her face sorrowful. 'Drunks never change, Lottie. But they don't arf change the people who love 'em. Much better if you stay clear of him from the start . . . but it's not just that; it's you, too.'

'That's plain silly! I'd never do anything to harm Ulick – I love him.'

'Lottie: you think you're another kid wanting to go on the stage, don't you? You think most other fairly musical girls could do more or less what you do if they really wanted to. Well, you're wrong. You're a one off. Some day you'll be so big, no one will notice Ulick. He couldn't stand that for five minutes.'

'But he's written that beautiful sketch for Tommy and me!'

'Yes, exactly – for Tommy and you. And what, pray, is your stage name to be?'

'You know. You already use it. Lottie.'

'Not that one, silly – the surname.'

'Oh, that.' Her spirited retaliation weakened. 'Carr. Lottie Carr. Ulick likes the sound of Fanshaw and Carr.'

'I bloody bet he does! Sounds just like a provincial performing dog act, aiming at the bottom of the bill and stuck there forever.'

'Now you're insulting Tommy, too! I thought you said he was talented.'

'He is – believe me, he is. That's the amazing thing about you two. Usually, when an act gets together, one partner is mediocre and the other carries the whole thing. Either of you could make it on your own, in a big way. He's as good as you are, Lottie.'

'Then why are you decrying Ulick's idea?'

'For a reason Ulick can't even see in himself. As long as you and Tommy Fanshaw are doing pretty little acts like that, you'll never get big and unmanageable, and Ulick will stay in charge. That sketch he's done for you

73

is brilliant, but have you ever considered how you'll follow it?'

'Don't be silly! You know better than I do that some acts have been succeeding around the halls without any changes for ten or fifteen years. If he doesn't write us something else, we'll stick to the street scene dance.'

'I've no reason to think either you or Tommy has stopped growing yet. You're both going to look bloody silly dressed up as a pair of children when you're twenty, aren't you?'

'Oh! I hadn't thought of that.'

'No, but I'd take money Ulick has.'

Charlotte stared at her in perplexity. 'Why are you doing this to him? I thought you were fond of him.'

'I am, but I'm getting fond of you and Tommy too, and whatever Ulick's good points are, his bad ones will destroy all of you if I don't say something. I'm thinking of him as well, though he'd never see it. Lottie, love, please say you believe me. I'd hate you to think I'm just being a crabby old bitch.'

'You, crabby? What an absurd idea! I'm only answering you back because I have this horrid feeling you may be right.'

'I am. Look, at least think about that name again.'

'I don't see any way of changing, unless I spoil everything from the start. I don't think Ulick would tolerate it.'

'No need for any quarrels – at least, not yet.' Nellie refilled the gin tots, this time not adding water to Charlotte's. 'The name will do for the moment, just as long as you do the street scene routine. But when you're on your feet, you and Tommy, I want you to promise you'll start talking to him about the pair of you doing separate things later on. When you – you and Tommy, not you and Ulick – decide the street dance has had its day, you'll be used to the business and you can start setting up independent routines. That's the time to change your name.'

'Do you really think it might work?'

'The amount o' consideration I've given the matter, it'd better. I've even got something lined up for you. Interested?'

'Of course I am. Do tell!'

'You must have noticed I've got a bit of an accent under the cockney, something you can't place. It's Italian. I was born and raised in Clerkenwell. My dad was a baker, name of Pirelli, and Ma was a pretty little thing from old Napoli who ended up working her guts out scrubbing people's stairs. I was doing me ballet girl routine in Drury Lane panto choruses and helping with the scrubbing before I'd finished learning to read properly. Never did get all the Eyetie out of my speech, and it was an advantage later – sounded exotic. You could do worse than follow the same route.'

'I don't quite see why.'

'Well, for a start, you *look* Italian, with those eyes like great juicy black olives and all that gorgeous dark hair. On top o'that, I've heard you imitating cockney in the songs I've given you. It's pretty good – the high falutin' accent underneath hardly notices at all. But you're not quite so good when you're talking it.

'There's two reasons we don't want anyone knowing you're a lady. For all we know, your parents are looking for you everywhere. There's precious few girls on the halls who sound and look like you. Second, even if your family

74

have cut you off, there's the audiences. They're funny. You've mixed with 'em now, you've heard them at it. They treat toffs as Aunt Sallies in there – it's their home ground, after all. They don't take kindly to that lot invading, and that's how they'd see it if they knew about you. So why don't we make sure none of 'em ever finds out you came out of the top drawer?'

'Nellie, you're a genius! But I still don't see what this has to do with my name.'

'I'm coming to that. It's the whole point of the Italian background. Give you three guesses what me mother's maiden name was.'

Charlotte shook her head.

'Casanova!' Nellie announced triumphantly. 'How's that for a coincidence? I don't s'pose it really is the Italian version of Cazenove, but it could be, couldn't it?'

Charlotte clapped her hands in delight. 'Oh, Nellie, it's gorgeous! I can just see it now, up in lights!'

'So can I, love.' Nellie raised her hand and wrote out invisible letters in the air between them: 'Starring Lottie Casanova – I think that'll do nicely, don't you?'

Charlotte's smile froze. 'Who's going to tell Ulick?'

'Silly girl – we're not going to do anything as rash as that!'

CHAPTER EIGHT

By early November the street dance sketch was as close to perfection as Ulick and Nellie could bring it. Ulick was beginning to think all their efforts were in vain, for as yet there was no sign of an opening for the act.

'You'll just have to lower your sights a bit and go somewhere like Hoxton to start,' said Nellie. 'I put up with it on me own. I can't see why two of 'em plus an organ grinder can't survive in front of an East End audience.'

'Don't be deliberately obtuse,' said Farrell. 'You know that by the time you played the Hoxton Empire, you could have out-cursed any meat porter or fishwife who dared to give you the bird. Charlotte's too green and Tommy's too bashful – and we're not paying the organ grinder enough for him to risk his neck. Therefore, my dear, I'm not letting them perform anywhere but a top line hall.'

'Then you'll be waiting this time next year,' said Nellie. 'They don't have the experience, Ulick. No manager is going to risk a fifteen-minute spot on two unknowns and a street-musician. If it was a five-minute filler, maybe, but not a full-blown act.'

The argument trailed back and forth between them while Tommy and Charlotte stood by, growing listless as they saw their chance of a music hall career receding into the uncertain future. Then, one raw afternoon when they had practised until they were too bored to go on, Ulick arrived back from what he called his tour of the contacts – an exercise which frequently produced symptoms of intoxication. He breezed into the flat, singing a slightly out-of-date comic song and bringing with him the usual faint whisky fumes. Slamming the living-room door behind him, he performed a flourish worthy of a circus ringmaster and said: 'Perhaps one day I shall be given credit for knowing what I'm doing. What would you two say to panto at Drury Lane this Christmas?'

'You're joking – they'd never 'ave us in that!' Tommy's expression said he would freeze on the spot if they did.

'But they will, bonny laddie, they will, as long as you perform as well at an audition as you do here. We are about to benefit from an ill-timed dance interlude.'

'Do you really mean it, Ulick? I thought they arranged all the pantomime acts three months ago.'

'They did, but someone slipped in a chorus of street urchins without realising it was too close to the next big set piece. Result: they have a fifteen-minute gap with a street scene already painted and the urchins gone to pixies, every one. They need something cheap but brilliant to slip in. Who else but you, my dears?'

'How long have we got?' asked Charlotte.

'Two hours, including rounding up the organ grinder. They want you on stage at six o'clock for a rehearsal-cum-audition.'

'Gawd almighty, I'll dry . . . I feel sick. Can't go . . .' Tommy was gibbering and looked every bit as bad as he felt.

'Nonsense!' Ulick told him. 'If you can't manage this, forget about the stage for good – and prepare to be back sleeping under the arches tonight.' He took out his watch. 'You've just time for a rehearsal to piano accompaniment before we go to the theatre. Come on, places!'

'But Nellie . . . I want her with us', Charlotte said.

'Out of the question. She's supposed to be out of circulation, preparing for her big musical comedy debut. If anyone sees her now, the cat will be out of the bag.'

'I don't understand.' Charlotte was standing very still and staring at him. He realised she still thought the star merely needed a lot of rest, and knew nothing of Nellie wanting to avoid public scrutiny. The whisky and impatience at her unenthusiastic response to his great coup loosened his tongue.

'Oh, do grow up! Surely you can see how ill she really is. If you can't, take my word for it that any journalist who saw her would know she's sick, not preparing for a big show. It would be all over town in moments, and that's exactly what Nellie doesn't want.'

Charlotte turned away and confronted Tommy. Her voice was savage. 'Did you know about this too? Was I the only one left out?'

Tommy shuffled his feet and looked vaguely towards Ulick. 'I . . . er . . . that is, nobody told me nuffink, honest. I just sorta guessed. She looks so tired all the time . . .'

'You beast! Something wrong with Nellie and you didn't tell me. I'll never forgive you, either of you!'

For a moment Ulick thought she would rush out of the apartment, but instead she strode to the window and stood glaring down into the street. Eventually, she snapped: 'Ulick, is she going to die?'

'We're all going to die, dear child.'

She turned on him, blazing, the first time he had seen her really lose her temper. 'Don't get bloody clever with me! You know what I mean. Is she?'

It might have been Nellie herself speaking, he thought, so like her idol had Charlotte become in recent weeks. He shrugged. 'She's certainly very ill, Charlotte. But let's not be pessimistic, eh? And above all, let's not talk about it now, before such an important evening.'

The girl digested that for a moment, then muttered: 'Very well, I'll do it – but for her, not you.'

They practised in their ordinary clothes, so that Charlotte's white dress would remain unmarked. They were terrible.

'For God's sake, you were better than this the first time I put you through the routine,' Farrell told them. 'What on earth is wrong?'

Charlotte dropped Tommy's hands and turned to face Ulick. 'Everything. Don't you care about anything at all except how clever you are?'

He chose to be flippant. 'Not about anything I can name offhand – and as I'm financing us all and funds are running pretty low, I suggest you concentrate on more important matters than my feelings. Now, there's no time for another try-out, so we shall have to leave it to chance. I'm going to find Jack

Andrews. He normally does Earlham Street at this time on Tuesdays, doesn't he?' Neither of them answered. Ulick shrugged and left them to their shared misery while he went looking for the third member of his cast.

An hour later he was in the vast, empty auditorium of the Theatre Royal, Drury Lane, a few seats away from Augustus Harris, the manager. Harris was the biggest fish in the theatrical pool; his nickname, Druriolanus, recognised his almost physical bond with the Theatre Royal. He was not to be approached uninvited by semi-professionals like Farrell. The Irishman, feeling cold and isolated, caught himself wishing Nellie had been with him after all. That would have made Harris welcome him within the charmed circle. Then he forgot everything as the manager signalled and the curtain rose, to the faint sound of barrel organ music.

It had been evocative in a living room in Wilson Street. On the best stage in London, with professional lighting and scenery, it was magical. The stage lighting contrived to look more like gaslight than the real thing. The organ grinder, huddled over his instrument, shabby, bored and down-at-heel, jerked believably to attention as the thieving street boy dashed on stage, clutching his half-eaten pie. Tommy's frantic glance around the stage conveyed real desperation.

Then he departed brilliantly from the script and stuffed the remains of the pie into his mouth, gulping it down as he stopped short in front of the street organist. Ulick did not know at the time that his agitation was real because the stage was bigger than he had expected and he was afraid of missing his cue; and that the pie improvisation occurred because Tommy did not dare throw down the pastry on the well-swept stage. Whatever the cause, the effect was exactly right, and panic about doing the wrong thing made Tommy throw off the paralysing stage fright which had crippled him earlier. Within seconds, he was dancing beside the organ grinder with just the right degree of mixed anxiety and pleasure. The organ grinder gloried in his first share of real limelight and was a properly hammy impressed bystander to the urchin's dance.

Charlotte's entrance sealed the success of the sketch. Watching her skip on stage, Ulick found himself half believing she was a well-brought-up child who had inadvertently stayed out late and strayed down the wrong street. By the time the pair had done the faltering follow-my-leader step dance and moved on to the waltz, the manager was leaning forward in his seat, spellbound. As they galloped off the stage in the final full-blooded polka, Harris stood up. Ulick got the impression that he did so to prevent himself from bursting into spontaneous applause.

Harris finally joined him. 'Congratulations. Quite a good little act,' he said. Ulick fought down jubilation. Here it comes, our break . . . 'I think I can offer them an engagement for the length of the run. Come round to my office in the morning, Farrell, and we'll settle terms.' They shook hands on the booking and Ulick went backstage, still half afraid Harris would change his mind, to tell his protégés they were now a working act.

But only Tommy and Jack Andrews awaited him in the poky dressing room. 'Where's Lottie?' he asked, instinctively using the nickname he still despised.

Tommy was sullen. 'Where d'you think? The minute we come off she was on 'er way to Nellie's. I'd a gone an' all if it hadn't been for these stage clothes. She couldn'ta got an hansom with me looking like this.'

'Come to that, where did *you* get the money?'

'Half-inched it, didn't I? Plenty of people would never miss that little bit, and she needed it.'

On the edge of striking him, Farrell suddenly lost his impetus. What was it about this little devil? He always knew how to stir things up. Ulick had come to tell them wonderful news and had ended up halfway to a quarrel over Charlotte. He gritted his teeth and barely managed a half-smile as he extended his hand to Tommy.

'All right, I admit defeat. I should have told Charlotte about Nellie's illness; should have told you, too, come to that. I'd like to make amends now and I've got good news which would give Nellie a lift as well as us. We're booked for the run of the pantomime. Now, Jack, let me pay you for your time tonight and we'll get together soon in time for a few last rehearsals, all right?'

Andrews smiled and nodded. 'Call it half the price tonight, Mr Farrell. Couldn't take the whole lot off you with all that work in the pipeline, could I?'

Ulick, conscious of his fast-disappearing savings, was on the point of accepting the offer when he caught sight of Tommy's contemptuous eyes on him and was forced into a noble gesture. 'Nonsense, you earned every penny! Here we are. Come along, Tommy, get into your street clothes, otherwise we shan't get a hansom, either.'

In Gower Street, Charlotte found Nellie in her first-floor drawing room, stretched out on a velvet-upholstered chaise longue and wearing an exquisite loose robe. In spite of the flattering lamplight and the softly draped gown, she looked thin and drawn. Charlotte wondered how she could have ignored such obvious signs that something was amiss.

In her agitation, she cut through Nellie's usual lighthearted greeting. 'Why didn't you tell me you were so ill? I feel frightfully guilty about being so selfish. I didn't even notice.'

Nellie's smile froze. 'Has that swine Ulick been telling tales out of school? I'll kill the bugger!'

'No, no – he accidentally let something slip. Th-then Tommy admitted he'd already guessed and I –' She faltered, on the edge of tears, shamed by her own lack of consideration.

'Come here and give us a kiss, you silly girl,' said Nellie. Charlotte rushed across the room and knelt beside the chaise longue, embracing Nellie fiercely and uttering a fresh outburst of apologies.

'Before we get over-emotional, may I ask what brought on this storm of revelation from Messrs Farrell and Fanshaw?' She interrupted herself: 'Christ, I never thought of it before, but that'd make a better bottom-of-the-bill dog act than Fanshaw and Carr . . . Hark at me. I ask a question, then start babbling. What was going on?'

'It should have been so exciting, and all this spoiled it! Ulick fixed us an audition at Drury Lane – a late fill-in for this year's pantomime. I said I wanted you there and he tried to put me off, then he got cross and said you couldn't let any journalists get a close look at you or they'd know how ill you were.'

Nellie was sitting very still, her arms loosely around Charlotte's shoulders.

80

In a dead voice, she said: 'And Tommy? What did he have to say?'

'Only that he'd guessed there was a lot wrong. Oh, Nellie, it was dreadful, because he looked so terribly sad. He must have been worrying and worrying and I was too selfish even to notice. I feel so ashamed!'

Nellie held her away. 'Well, at least you've got the guts not to blub all over me. I'm pleased about that, even if I'm furious with bloody Farrell for letting it slip . . . then again, the way I look now, I'd have had to tell you some time soon, wouldn't I?'

Charlotte nodded dumbly, fighting the tears Nellie had praised her for not shedding. The older woman's mood changed abruptly. 'You got an audition with old Druriolanus and you're sitting here all miserable? I'd have sold my whole family for that at your age. Let's hear about it, then.'

Woodenly at first, then with rising enthusiasm as the memory gripped her, Charlotte told her about the audition.

'Did he take you?'

'I don't know. The minute we danced off stage, I dodged out and came back to see you. That's why I'm still wearing this horrid dress.'

'You don't arf sound snooty when you're in a state!' Nellie teased her. 'You mean just because you wanted to pay me a sick visit, you didn't hang on for your big news? Silly little bitch!'

Charlotte's smile was conspiratorial. 'I didn't need to stay, Nellie.' She said it almost in a whisper, as though afraid she might be appallingly wrong. 'You see, I knew. The minute Tommy and I started dancing, I knew. We were the best we'd ever been. If that man hadn't loved us, it wouldn't have been worth going on, because we'll never shine as bright again.'

Nellie let out a huge sigh. 'I always thought you had it. Now I'm certain. You've got enough of an eye and an ear to know if it's not right. I think we can open a bottle of fizz and drink to your debut, my girl!'

When Ulick and Tommy arrived, expecting tears and recriminations, they found the two women halfway through a bottle of champagne.

'How the devil did you know there'd be anything to celebrate?' demanded Ulick, outraged at the realisation that he had been upstaged.

Nellie gave him a superior look. 'A pro always knows instinctively when something's right, and this one's a pro,' she said.

'Don't worry, there's another bottle. You can fetch it from the cellar. We'll celebrate and then you can let the invalid and her companion have an early night.'

Ulick directed a yearning glance at Charlotte and said: 'I thought Charlotte might come back with us this evening . . . give us an early start for rehearsals tomorrow.'

'Mmm-hmm, no chance, mate. She's staying here until she opens. After that, we'll see. She needs an awful lot of off-stage polishing yet.'

And with that, Ulick had to be content.

CHAPTER NINE

'And mind you always remember, keep in with the little people around the halls. Nothing to do with 'em being lovable – there's as many right bastards in music hall as there are in the city or the Law. You'll meet good, bad and indifferent, but my God, they've all got one thing in common: they can do you some damage if you get on their wrong side!'

Charlotte was listening intently but Nellie could see she was out of her depth. 'Look,' she explained, 'what would you do if you were the lighting man and I was topping the bill and cut you dead Monday night after the show when you complimented me on my performance? Nothing? Don't give me that – you'd be after revenge. So here's the great star on stage Tuesday night, and you adjust the lime that weeniest little bit on the harsh side.

'Even if you don't manage to make me look like an old boiler, you'll have my eyes smarting so much I'll be put off for the whole show. A good lighting man is hard to come by, so unless you muck up Marie Lloyd or Dan Leno, you're not going to get sacked for it. Meantime, the hall manager decides I'm slipping a bit and thinks twice about re-booking me. You multiply that around every dresser, callboy and doorman and you've got a lot of potential enemies. All it takes is the odd kind word and flashy smile, and they're your slaves. Just you remember.'

That lesson had been delivered immediately before Christmas and when Lottie walked through the stage door of the Theatre Royal at noon on Boxing Day for her debut, Nellie's words were still ringing in her ears. She produced a special smile for the stage door keeper, who scarcely seemed to notice her.

Hardly to be wondered at, she mused, looking around at the bustle which preceded the opening matinee. Behind her came a troop of young girls, drab as cygnets, in patched thin skirts and skimpy shawls, tightly folded across their thin chests as inadequate shields against the winter air. The first time she had seen them, at the Christmas Eve full dress rehearsal, she had assumed they were servants of some kind. Any more glamorous role was inconceivable. Then she found herself sharing a dressing room with six of them and she watched in awe as the ragged street clothes were exchanged for gauzy fairy robes complete with wings, wands and ballet shoes. These were the children of the chorus, learning their trade as Nellie Standish had fifteen years before, cleaning staircases and offices in the morning and then scurrying over to the theatre twice a day, from Clerkenwell, Hatton Garden and Holborn, to portray an illusory world of ease and beauty for spoiled rich children.

In spite of her tendency to chronic naivety tinged with romanticism, Charlotte was developing a healthy streak of realism. Her first reaction had been to admire and envy these children. What a start! What a story to tell the newspapers when you finally became rich and famous. Look at Nellie Standish.

Who could fail to admire what she had reached from such an unpromising start?

But there Charlotte's common sense intervened. There were swarms of these slender, pale girl children about. For every one who became a Standish, there were countless failures, girls who lacked quite the requisite talent, good luck or toughness to rise. They stayed where they were until their youthful appeal faded, and after that their lives were dedicated to more cleaning, poverty and too many children. For the first time, Charlotte began to accept that her privileged background had given her a better start than any of them.

She roused their interest too, and was careful to follow Nellie's advice about friendliness, along with a little of her own intuition. The girls had obviously heard that a new, untried act had been booked to fill the interlude left by the cancelled chorus routine. They were all curious about the new-comers and, when they learned that one of them was a girl not much older than they, slightly resentful. Nellie's counsel ensured she countered their curiosity with an open-hearted friendliness. She herself realised they would take her to pieces if they heard her speaking naturally.

She had been listening to Nellie for a couple of months now, as well as soaking up the robust cockney street talk she heard all around her. A year ago, she would have said she could produce a perfect costermonger accent. Now she knew better. It had sounded convincing only because there were no costers in Lyonesse. It had not mattered to Ulick and Nellie, or to Tommy. They all knew she was an outsider. With these little predators, it was vital she did not give herself away.

The answer proved childishly simple to one with her gift for mimicry. She merely imitated Nellie. The imposition of slightly Italianate pronunciation over the other accent fooled even the girls who came from the Clerkenwell Italian community. With so many other foreign influences crowding in on their speech, no two second-generation immigrants sounded the same. As long as she was not outrageously different, they accepted her apparent origins without suspicion.

That was when Charlotte changed her name, irrevocably, and without reference to Nellie, let alone Ulick or Tommy. Christina Minoli, one of the more hostile girls, whose own physical resemblance to Charlotte made her doubly envious of the girl's good fortune in the pantomime, was determined to provoke her. 'Lottie Carr? Funniest name I ever 'eard a Clerkenwell wop come up with, don't you think, girls?'

Biting back a scorching retort, Charlotte smiled with a humility that was almost convincing and said: 'I was quite happy with my own name, but Mr Farrell – that's our manager – he said it should be something English to go with my partner's. Course it's not me real name. I'm a Casanova – Lottie Casanova. D'you think maybe I should keep that as a stage name? I'd rather it than Carr, any day.'

That silenced the opposition for a while, as Tina, her would-be persecutor, withdrew to sulk about how an immigrant girl as lucky and pretty as Lottie should get the even better break of having been born with a good billboard name. Life just wasn't fair . . .

During and after the rehearsal, Lottie felt the ballet girls' resentment crank up a few more notches as they watched Ulick's delicate bit of choreography

84

weave its magic with everyone backstage. Even the great Dan Leno, playing the Dame at that year's production, paused and said a few complimentary words to Ulick as he passed him on his way to the star dressing room. By the time Lottie got back to her narrow space backstage, she knew she could look for no allies in the chorus.

Now she was about to see if she could survive a live audience. She went cold at the thought, but strangely, the enmity of the little ballet girls diminished her nerves and reinforced her determination to shine. 'If I could do it at dress rehearsal in front of a bunch of pros who've seen it all, I can do it anywhere!' she muttered into the long dressing room mirror.

'Talking to yourself already? That's really a bad sign. Don't tell me the star of Little Italy's frightened!'

For the first time in the theatre, Lottie allowed her own feelings free rein. Tina Minoli had to be put in her place now or never. With a smile that expressed infinite contempt, Lottie said: 'Nothing of the sort. It's the only way I get a chance of intelligent conversation with you for company.' Then she stood up, made a last adjustment to her white dress, and sailed out of the dressing room in a fair approximation of Nellie Standish's Big Star walk.

The first matinee was something of an anticlimax. By now, they knew the street dance routine so well that they could have performed it in their sleep, and after the first great gulp of nervousness had subsided, Lottie found herself lapsing into a state of automatic response. She felt a surge of disappointment. Was this all she had set her sights on, all she was working for? What had happened to the huge flood of love and veneration which an audience bestowed on its favourites? Their vigorous polka ended the sketch and earned them a round of enthusiastic applause, but now there was general stirring in stalls and circle as the children and parents prepared to see their idol, Dan Leno, who followed the street scene with a bustling bit of Dame's stage business. Lottie stood in the wings beside Tommy, clutching his hand and wanting to cry.

Her wretchedness seeped into him. 'Don't worry, girl,' he said with a reassuring smile. 'It can't *all* come at once, can it, an' we've 'ad more'n our fair share so far.'

He was right, of course. She choked down her disappointment and went back to the dressing room. Fortunately for her dented pride, the fairies had just gone on stage for the next big chorus. She was able to change, put away her things and leave before they returned and seized the opportunity to jeer at her disappointment.

It was much better at the evening performance, where there were far more adults. The sketch was rapturously received and at last Lottie tasted a faint flavour of what she was seeking. Still, though, she felt there was something wrong. As usual, Nellie Standish came up with the answer.

Nellie had decided she could disguise herself sufficiently to attend the pantomime without being recognised. 'Anyway, I'm so bloody skinny now that if I wear a veiled hat so they can't see me face, nobody'll recognise the rest,' she informed a dubious Ulick. 'If you think I'm not going to see these kids performing the act on stage, you've got another one coming. Now, are you going to sit out front with me?'

'Very well; I suppose you're right. In any case, it's your feelings I'm trying to save in keeping you from the press, Nellie.' Ulick's tone was deeply self-righteous.

'Well, now, and there was selfish Miss Standish thinking it might have something to do with 'em twigging I'd had a hand in coaching Lottie, and me stealing some o' your thunder.'

'What nonsense you do talk sometimes, Nellie.'

'Yeah, don't I?' She gave him a cheeky grin and went to inspect her hats for a suitable disguise.

The pantomime performance did not teach Nellie anything new about her recently acquired family. Perhaps she had hoped it would show her a confrontation was unnecessary. If so, she was not reassured. She was an intelligent as well as a talented woman, and believed in using both qualities to get what she wanted. As her illness advanced, her goals had shrunk, but they still existed. Now, she wanted to enjoy Charlotte's rebirth as Lottie, and to ensure that the creation to which she had contributed so much of herself had a chance of survival after she was gone.

She also wanted to savour at least some of the drama of the situation.

At the end of the first act of *Dick Whittington*, she slapped Ulick on the thigh and said: 'Right; I've seen Dan Leno's Dame act enough times to write his script, and fond though I am of him, I've other fish to fry tonight. Go backstage and get the kids.'

'I don't even know if they'll have changed yet. And what about the finale?'

'Bugger the finale! If you're that het up about what it'll do to their futures, I'll have a quick word with Druriolanus myself while you're fetching them. He's got a soft spot for me; says I'm a good advertisement when he's recruiting ballet girls. Promises 'em all they're the Nellies of the future. Notice, he doesn't say the Nellie *Standishes*!'

'But what will you tell him?'

She gave him a weary smile. 'The truth, Ulick. Once I pull up me veil and show Harris my face, he'll know I'm not conning him. I'll just tell him tonight's his last chance to make a dying woman very happy.'

Moved in spite of himself, Ulick clasped her hand. 'Did I ever tell you how brave you are, and how much I admire you?'

'Not once, you bastard – but we'll take it as read. Now, you get Tommy and Charlotte, I'll see Augustus Harris.'

She had booked a private room at the Café Royal – and she had been right about her influence with Harris. He had seen her and instantly given his youthful team dispensation to be absent from the finale for this one evening. 'Sorry you have to miss all the fun of the main restaurant,' Nellie said, 'but even I know it's best that the hyenas out there don't take a close look. Never mind, at least we'll get a good celebration.'

And celebrate they did, their jubilation at this first stage success bolstered by the Café Royal's wonderfully excessive combination of red plush, gold cherubs and pink champagne. Nellie had taken considerable care with her makeup, and although her appearance had shocked Augustus Harris after he had not seen her for a long time, to Ulick, Charlotte and Tommy she looked wonderful. Her exuberance and gaiety carried them through the evening on such a wave of exhilaration that Ulick even forgot for once to make longing remarks about taking Charlotte back to Wilson Street. Shortly before midnight, they parted on the pavement outside the Café Royal, Ulick and Tommy for Covent Garden, Nellie and Charlotte for Bloomsbury.

Back at the house, Nellie ushered Charlotte into the drawing room, yelled for Maud and then gave a long, luxurious sigh of contentment. 'One thing about losing all this flesh,' she said, 'it isn't arf comfortable without the stays!'

They sat together beside the well-banked fire, and Maud brought them a bottle of the inevitable pink champagne. Charlotte, tired herself after the rigours of two stage performances that day, was more anxious about Nellie. 'Should we be staying up so late? Wouldn't it be better if you went to bed?'

Nellie's laugh carried a rasping undertone. 'You die in bed, girl – that makes it less tempting to one in my condition than one in yours. No, I feel grand tonight, and you and I have a lot of talking to do.'

'Do we? Was I terrible? I was quite pleased with it.'

'Bless you, child, stop being so defensive. You were better than I've seen you in that part. But there's the rub – *in that part.*'

'I thought you loved the sketch.'

'Mmm, wonderful – if you're promoting the writing talents of Ulick Farrell, that is. It's a masterly bit of stagecraft and they'll still be performing it thirty years from now – but that'll be Ulick's immortality, not yours.'

'We have a booking until the end of February. Surely by then we'll have something else planned?' Charlotte's expression pleaded for Nellie to agree with her.

'I wish I shared your optimism, love. Trouble is, that sort of act doesn't give you many places to go. It's a springboard more than anything else.'

'I thought there would be opportunities to take the sketch on the halls.'

'There will be. But remember what I said to you down the Borough Market that night. It's not an act you can do forever. You're going to grow up; and after seeing you tonight, I'd say you've all but outgrown it already.'

'But I can't have! We're only just beginning.'

'That's no reason to go on with it if it isn't right. How does it feel up there?'

Charlotte began to speak and then hesitated. Finally she said: 'N-not what I expected . . . actually, I was a little disappointed.'

'Yeah. Thought you were. Truth is, Lottie, it's the sort of little sweetener that does you the world of good for cutting your teeth. But take it from me, you were born for grand gestures and big audiences. You're never going to get that done up as a little girl dancing by a street organ.'

'You said you liked it at the beginning . . . liked me and Tommy in it, I mean.'

'Yes, I did. But it's done its work, Lottie, and you're ready to move on when the run ends.'

'What about Tommy – and Ulick?'

'Don't fret too much about Tommy. God knows how you found each other, but he's cut from the same piece of cloth and he needs to break free as much as you do.'

'And Ulick?'

'We had to get back to him in the end, didn't we? Tell me something, Lottie. What d'you really want from life? Do you even know yourself yet?'

'It's much easier to say what I *don't* want.'

'Tell me.'

87

'Lyonesse. Getting like my mother. Marrying a suitable young man. Reading suitable books and being the power that stands behind a suitably successful English gentleman.'

'That's all well and good, but it doesn't explain why you want to go on the halls, and you haven't said where Ulick comes into all this.'

'That's because I'm not at all sure I know myself yet. Music hall certainly wasn't my idea, as you know. But until today I thought it was exactly what I wanted. At first I just wanted to go on the stage – and to me that meant being another Sarah Bernhardt.'

'Stop there a minute. Even that's a pretty odd ambition for a girl from your walk of life, I should think.'

Charlotte smiled, remembering something. 'It was inevitable, I suppose. You see, that was how I learned I could escape from Mama. She and all her frightful friends thought it would be diverting to have all the children put on a play during one house party when I wasn't much more than a baby – about nine or ten, I suppose. Someone cast me as the little girl from the manor house who runs off with the gypsies.

'At first I hated the very thought of dressing up with all these silly children and showing off for the grown-ups. But then, I went on to the stage they'd erected in the ballroom and started the little song . . .' She clasped her hands, childlike, in front of her, swayed back and forth and chanted:

'My mother said I never should
Play with the gypsies in the wood . . .

'And as I sang, and then acted the part, I realised that if I was someone else, Mama couldn't bully me any more – there'd be no one there to bully. So I decided to be an actress.'

Nellie sighed. 'Christ almighty, and I thought you'd been moved by some great earth-shaking insight into your own talent!'

'But don't you see? In a way, that's just what happened. I discovered I had a talent to do the one thing I really wanted – be someone else – and I've never stopped wanting it since.'

With some difficulty, Nellie resisted the temptation to pursue the illogic of that argument. At times it was hard to remember how young and inexperienced Charlotte still was. Perhaps her mother had been the original spur to rebellion, but Nellie was willing to gamble that since then pure talent had taken over. Otherwise, the girl would not have been working like a dray horse for the past three months. She would have been wrapped lovingly around Ulick Farrell, content to be having an adventure far from home and family and with no more than a passing interest in either legitimate theatre or music hall.

She turned her mind back to the thought that had started this latest hare. 'That still doesn't tell me how you feel about Ulick. I may as well be frank with you. At your age, if some big bully of a music hall singer called Nellie Standish had come along and dragged me away from a tasty bit of male flesh I'd just run off with, I'd have sent her packing. Instead of that you came like a lamb to the slaughter, and I haven't exactly had to twist your arm to make you stay ever since. How come?'

To her surprise, Charlotte blushed furiously and turned from her to stare into the fire. At last she said: 'It seemed to be such a good idea at Lyonesse . . . he'd kissed me, and touched me, and every time he did, I was terribly excited—' she cast about for an appropriate expression '– as if I was being turned upside down and held up by the ankles! I thought it would be fun to find out more, maybe try the thing I'd seen one of our footmen doing with a girl in the woods . . . but then it all changed.'

'And a bit of hot breath somewhere more intimate than your neck suddenly seemed all too grown-up, did it?'

Charlotte nodded silently, ashamed of her own gaucherie.

Nellie grinned at her. 'Nothing to worry about. At fifteen, I'd probably have done just the same, given the chance. Didn't have any alternative then, though, and I got to like it later. That's all past now, but you and Ulick aren't. You may have cooled off, but he seems to have started panting a bit harder lately.'

'Oh, Nellie, what *can* I do? I really ruined him, didn't I, and now he's bound to expect something in return. I can't just keep holding him off!'

'I'd forgot that bosh about ruining him. Ulick Farrell's quite capable of ruining himself in ten seconds from a standing start. And he's hardly suffered by your talent so far, has he?'

Charlotte was bewildered. 'I can't see that he's gained anything. The poor man has been slaving away at that wretched sketch almost since we got to London. I'd hardly call that profiting from my presence.'

'Lottie, me love, it would take too long for me to explain. You'll just have to take my word for it. Ulick isn't suffering as a result of you getting him into trouble, and he hasn't sacrificed his precious time teaching you a stage routine. Now that's out of the way, tell me straight out. Do you still fancy him?'

Eyes downcast, Charlotte muttered: 'Yes, he's terribly attractive, isn't he? But I'm not ready to be his m-mistress yet.'

'God Almighty, but you use some quaint expressions at times! Half the types round the halls wouldn't know what that was anyway. They'd call you anything from a donah to a brass, but they think mistresses are women in velvet gowns who order you about and pay your wages!' Abruptly she stopped laughing. 'I'm sorry. You were trying to answer a difficult question and here I am making fun. Right, I've got the picture. Have another drink and listen to my plans.'

She had thought out her strategy with the greatest care. The really big names on the halls were not partnerships, they were soloists. And although many of them were excellent dancers, that was a secondary skill. To reach the top as a female artiste, you sang. And you sang alone.

'I can teach you that, Lottie. Not Ulick, me. What's really tearing out my guts isn't this growth – it's knowing I'm finished almost before I got started. I'd only barely reached the top, and it was bye bye, Nellie. I've still got all the tricks locked into me, and I can pass them on to you. You're a natural, I can tell that from the way you've been handling those songs I gave you to learn. You know already you're quite a dancer. When I've run you through handling stage business, and sharpened up your timing, you'll be fit to take on Marie Lloyd.'

'And Ulick?'

'Told you, no need to be bothered about that one. With any luck, he'll accept things and settle down to write songs for you . . . manage you, too, p'raps,

89

when he gets a bit more experience of his own. He's one of the best song-writers I've ever run into, if he'd only keep his mind on it. But he's short on staying power and he's no long-term planner. You mustn't let him shape you, Lottie – ever, understand? It'll always be Farrell first with that one, and some day what's good for Farrell won't be good for Casanova.'

Charlotte giggled guiltily. 'I haven't said a word about that name. I think he's going to be frightfully cross.'

'Yeah. I get the same feeling. Maybe it should wait a bit.'

'Too late. I tried it on one of the ballet girls at Drury Lane. They think it's my real name and that Carr is the false one.'

Nellie burst out laughing. 'He'll bite your bloody head off when he knows – and mine, I'll be bound. Never mind. There's more important things than that for you to worry about. From now on you'll be practising here with me in the mornings and again between the early doors and the evening show at Drury Lane. After that it'll be straight to bed and no late night fun an' games. By the end of the run you'll be ready to go solo – in a small way, at least.'

Studying her reaction, Nellie realised there was still something wrong. 'Come on, you can't still be worrying about Ulick. He'll survive all right.'

'No . . . Tommy. I thought you were fond of him. What will he do? You can't simply say he has talent too and then cut him loose.'

'Of course not, you idiot. Tommy is going to spend his mornings with an old boy who taught some of the best dancer-comics of the eighties. By the time your name's up in lights, his will be next to it – but for a different act, that's all.'

'Oh, Nellie, I do love you. How d'you manage always to think of other people when you're so ill? Anybody else would be brooding over it all the time.'

Nellie's smile melted. 'Hasn't it ever struck you that's just why I interfere with other people's lives? It doesn't arf stop you having to remember your own . . .'

CHAPTER TEN

The day of the last pantomime performance at Drury Lane, Ulick had lunch alone with Nellie at her house. She was eating like a bird these days, although she still drank plenty of stout and champagne. After they had talked in superficialities for twenty minutes or so, he said: 'All right, tell me. I'd be a fool not to know you have plans for our infant prodigies.'

She took the plunge. 'Then you must also have a pretty good idea that you've got to break up the act.'

He glowered at her. 'No such thing. All I said was that I'd guessed *you* had plans for them. It doesn't follow that I agree.'

'Come on, you must. Tommy's shot up nearly two inches and put on a stone since he's been eating properly. And Lottie – well, every day she goes on stage in that frothy frock she looks more like a French parlour maid and less like an English schoolgirl.'

'That simply means a new sketch. I thought they could do the street dance in a couple of suburban halls while I'm dreaming up something else, then move on to the new routine.'

'Ulick, you saw their individual talent before I did. You don't need me to tell you they'll go a lot further apart than together.'

'And what happens to me, dammit?'

'Don't be so half-baked! You'll manage one or both of 'em, of course . . . I suggest just Lottie. Handle the two and you'll really lay up troubles for yourself.'

'What are you getting at now?'

'Nothing, nothing . . . reminds me, though; you seem to have cooled your ardour over little Lottie.'

He uttered a mirthless laugh. 'What alternative have I had with you standing guard over her morning, noon and night? Honestly, Nellie, if you were older I'd be thinking you were her mother!'

'Come off it – if you'd been that keen you'd have got me out of the way in five minutes. There's another reason, isn't there?'

He told her about the evening he was returning to the flat and planning to pack Charlotte off back to Wiltshire. 'It was only the heart-stopping sight of them dancing in the street that prevented me, Nellie. But it didn't delude me altogether. That evening, for the first time, I truly realised how much trouble I could be in, merely for permitting her to run away with me. For a start, they'd have called it enticement or abduction.'

'You can't still be taking that seriously! Why, it's – let's see – five months since you left the Cazenoves. Lord Muck would have been up long before now with his horsewhip if he was coming at all.'

'Hmm . . . I wish I shared your optimism. You don't know their sort as I do. Charlotte's disappearance would have put them in a virtually impossible position. Everyone in Handford would have known within five minutes that she ran to get on the train with me. Laura Cazenove had enough enemies in the village to make sure someone would have said so publicly if the family had claimed I took the child by force.

'The mother hates Charlotte so much she'd be the first to say, "Never mention her name again; she's dead." The father, I think, would want her back at all costs, but he'd be looking for a way of doing it without causing too much scandal. After all, one day they'd want to marry her off.'

'All this seems to be a hell of a long-winded way to explain why you've kept your mitts off her for such an age.'

'Because, my dear, if they did track her down, she would still be intact and a medical examination would prove it. Perhaps they'd have second thoughts about getting me locked up then.'

'Well I'll be damned! That's the first time I've ever heard you being cautious.'

'It's the first time you've ever known me to be in quite such a pickle. D'you realise what the aristocracy do with bounders like me who run off with their girl children?'

Her eyes twinkled. 'No, but it'd be damned interesting to find out. When they catch you, can I watch?'

'Unfeeling bitch! Anyway, there you have my reasons. I still find her unbearably attractive, but every time you hold me off, a little warning voice inside my own head helps you.'

'Right then. At least I know where I am over that one. Has it occurred to you than once she reaches the legal age of consent, you'll be safe on the abduction? After that, even if they did track you down, all they could do was drag her off back home.'

'There are times, Nellie, when you're a great comfort to me. I shall mark her birthday in my diary and come along with a very special present for her.'

'Dirty old man! And you old enough to be her kind uncle.'

She decided he was sufficiently softened up to listen to her plans, and outlined what she had in mind for Charlotte. 'She's going to need you every step of the way, Ulick. I've polished her like a jewel these last two months, but she needs new songs if her original talent if ever to shine through. "Up In The Gallery" is a great song, but sing it as your big number and everyone in the hall has memories of Nellie Power or Marie Lloyd. Lottie'll make your fortune, but you'll have to make hers, too.'

She reached out to a side table and picked up a notebook. 'I've put down a couple of agents in here that you might like to contact. Lottie's weakest point is that she doesn't know the streets, and so she doesn't know how to climb out of the gutter by her own efforts. You'll need to tout her round the agents and see she gets to the right auditions. Without that she could still be playing Aldgate ten years from now. Promise you'll tackle it and not slope off on the booze till she's fixed up?'

'I promise. This can be the making of us both, I see that. And what about Tommy?'

'No, Ulick.' Her eyes said, I tried to warn you off before; don't make me spell it out . . . but he was irritated by her flat rejection.

'Why on earth not? I spotted him, for heaven's sake!'

'Yeah, you spotted him, and you've given him a start. But your talents don't lie where he needs help now; and . . . well, you and he just rub each other up the wrong way, that's all.'

For a moment she thought he was going to pursue it, but he made an exasperated sound and merely said: 'With your soft spot for him, I'm sure you've recommended him to somebody, too.'

'Of course. He'll have an agent by this time tomorrow, and for him, I don't think a manager will be necessary.'

Then a new thought occurred to Ulick. 'Just a moment; I don't hear you saying anything about your own involvement in all this.'

'Sometimes, I wonder how a big strong boy like you has survived for twenty-odd years without a brain. I won't be here, will I?'

He had the good grace to blush, but then said: 'We're talking about next week and next month, not next year. Of course you will.'

She smiled tiredly. 'No, Ulick. I'm not thinking of dropping dead tomorrow.' Her tone became deliberate: 'I – shall – not – be – here. In London; in England, for that matter.'

'Why the devil not?'

'Because I can't hold on much longer. It's happening faster than I thought . . . hurts almost all the time now, and when it doesn't hurt, I'm so tired I could drop.' She forced optimism into her voice: 'So, I've booked Maud and me a little trip off to the Riviera. Always did fancy Nice in the spring. I shall blow a big chunk of what money I've got left on a suite at the best hotel on the sea front, and spend my last days enjoying the wages of my sinful life. Just let's hope I don't last *too* long, eh? It'd be so embarrassing to run out of money and have to leave before they carried me out in a wooden overcoat.'

She refused to listen to reason and turned the talk determinedly back to the careers of Charlotte and Tommy. When she had covered all the possibilities, she said: 'One last thing. If I have to say goodbye to those kids, I shall crack. Tomorrow, I intend to send Lottie over to you early on. Take her and Tommy to Romano's for lunch – and don't be stingy with the fizz. My treat, I'll give you money before you leave this afternoon. When you get back to Wilson Street, give 'em these.'

Again she reached over to the side table, this time for three envelopes. She handed them over: 'Yours is the money for Romano's tomorrow, and a little something to get by on while you're getting Lottie organised. The others are a bit of working capital for each of them. Oh – and you've got three months rent free in Wilson Street, too. My lawyer will be looking after things like that from now on.'

Ulick was looking dazed. 'We can't just part like this, Nellie. I know it's only really been the past few months that we've been so close, but . . .' He hesitated, shamefaced, for a long moment, then said in a rush: 'It wasn't simply cold feet that put me off Charlotte. Somehow, when I caught up with you again, she was just a pretty child. In other circumstances, you would have been all I could ever want.'

Her eyes misted over. 'I think that's the nicest thing anyone ever said to me. It makes it even more important that I just waft off tomorrow. Something tells me you'd take on shocking when you saw what this sort of illness does to a girl in the end. Go on now – we've both said enough. Just don't ever forget me, all right? I've an awful feeling everyone else will, except you and Lottie and Tommy.'

As they were speaking, she had managed unobtrusively to ease him across the dining room and into the entrance hall. Now she led him forward to the front door. She looked so frail that he did not dare to argue with her. At the open door, he turned and embraced her, then kissed her, deeply and passionately, on the mouth. 'I shall never forget you if I live to be a hundred – and if I ever pray for anyone, it will be for you,' he said.

As he went down the flight of steps on to the pavement, she said with forced gaiety: 'Thanks, darling – where I'm going, I'll need all the help I can get!' They were the last words she ever said to him.

He had hoped that Tommy and Charlotte would take the news of Nellie's departure stoically. After all, he told himself, they both knew she was desperately ill; had both commented to him in private on how far she had slipped since Christmas. They must have been expecting something like this.

It seemed they had not. When he took them off to Romano's, they demanded to know why Nellie was not going with them, on the grounds that they could use another restaurant if she was still reluctant to be recognised. He told them she felt too weak, but that depressed them instead of reassuring them. The lunch was a sombre affair and without Nellie's effervescent company the champagne made them morose. Back in Wilson Street, when he delivered the envelopes, there was an outcry.

Charlotte's fluttered unnoticed to the floor as she wailed over the letter it contained. Ulick glimpsed the edges of a number of white five pound notes as he retrieved it for her. She could not have cared less. 'But she mustn't do this – she can't – I won't let her die by herself!' she cried.

Ulick attempted cool reason. 'She won't be alone, Charlotte. Maud is with her, and she and Maud have been together since long before any of us knew her. Please try to understand that for Nellie, part of the dignity is in bowing out on her own terms. She doesn't want any of us to sit round her deathbed. We must respect that wish.'

'But what will we do without her?'

Before he could stop them, the words were out: 'Anyone would think she was your mother.'

'Don't dare to mention Nellie in the same breath as my mother. I'd give up Mama ten thousand times for Nellie to live another year!' She was sobbing, now, and when he went to comfort her she shook off his arm and ran out of the apartment. As he started to follow her, Tommy said hoarsely, 'Leave it! She'll need to be by 'erself.'

'I suppose you're an expert in the behavior of Charlotte Cazenove?'

'No, but I don't arf know me Lottie Casanova, and I'm telling you she needs to be by 'erself. All right?'

For the tenth time that week, Ulick wanted to thrash the boy. But then he noticed the tears flowing unchecked down Tommy's cheeks and softened towards him. 'Oh, dammit, you're as badly affected as Charlotte, aren't you?'

Tommy nodded, wiped his eyes and said: 'Now if you'd said she might be *my* mother, that'd be another matter . . . not the real one, you understand, but a lovely dream, the sort of picture you see in your wakin' dreams under

94

Waterloo arches when you're lying cold of a night and can't get to sleep. Warm, and beautiful, and generous, and always young. She was everything to me, mate.' His mouth twisted into a grotesque parody of a laugh. 'Course, we all know mothers is really a bunch of drabs who drink gin and sling you out to fend for yourself, but Nellie always did say she was the best "let's pretend" player who ever lived.'

It was the longest speech Farrell had ever heard him make. He scrubbed at his eyes again, then turned and followed Charlotte out of the flat. Ulick stood staring disconsolately after them for almost five minutes, then he picked up their envelopes, put them on the table and gazed at Nellie's round, childish handwriting on the two letters. Finally he muttered: 'Dammit all, I'm not staying here alone. I need another drink,' and stalked out.

When Tommy returned to Wilson Street three hours later, the flat was in darkness. Assuming everyone was still out, he went through the living room to the kitchen to boil a kettle and make tea. While he waited for it to heat, he wandered back into the outer room to light the lamp. Charlotte was sitting in the armchair, her profile silhouetted against the gaslight which spilled in from the street.

'Gawd, Lottie, you give me a fright!' he said. 'You shouldn't be sitting here all by yourself in the dark. It won't make anything better.'

'You know as well as I do that *nothing* will make anything better. Oh, Tommy, why her? Why does she have to go and die when there are so many horrid people in the world?'

His laugh was bitter. 'Sooner you stop asking that question, love, the better you'll be. Didn't they never tell you down Wiltshire? Only the good die young. The right bastards 'ang on forever and get fat on our misery.'

'I don't think I can go on without her . . . I've been dreading this moment ever since I realised she was so ill.'

He squatted in front of the chair and took her cold hands between his own. 'If you can't manage without her, she'll 'ave failed, don't you see? The one thing that's kept her going these last few months is training us up. We both got to get on – it's the least we can do for her, innit?'

Charlotte sniffed and nodded. 'Yes, you're right.' She managed a shaky laugh. 'Think of what she'd say to me if she could hear me now: "I mighta known a gutless little rich piece like you couldn't stand the pace. Wotta waste a' my valuable time!" '

'You know, you even sound just like her? P'raps you never saw it, but she did. You an' she were so alike you could have been her little sister.'

'I wish I had been!'

'Oh, no you don't, Lottie. No rosy specs about Nellie's world. I grew up there an' all, remember? Who wants to live wiv wolves?'

'Was it really as bad as that?'

'Worse. She knew you and Ulick come from another world than ours, and the last thing she ever wanted to do was whine, so she just talked to me about it.' He smiled, remembering. 'We useta top each other's rotten stories for hours, but both of us knew we weren't laying nuffink on. It really was bad. You don't need none o' that . . . Now, I bet that kettle's boiled. What if I make you a nice cuppa tea, and then light this lamp?'

95

'All right.' As he rose, she grasped his hands tighter and said: 'I'm so grateful to you – you let me grieve about her.'

Tommy thought of Ulick and knew what she meant. If Ulick cared at all about Nellie, he would hide his sorrow beneath swagger and tough talk, and that was not what Lottie needed now. 'Don't you worry about nuffink. You do all the grievin' you like, only do it wiv me, all right?'

Minutes later, he was back with the tea. 'Put some of 'is Nibs's whisky in it to warm us up. Be blood on the moon if he ever thought it had gone in tea, but cheers – we need it!'

The hot sweet brew bit into Lottie's throat and comforted her. For the first time in hours, she relaxed, and leaned back in the big chair while Tommy lit the lamp. He sat at her feet, propped against the chair, and for a while they talked quietly and easily about Nellie and all she had given them. Eventually they had talked themselves out and sat on in companionable silence. Then, uncertainly at first but strengthening as the player hit his stride, music began to filter into the room; barrel organ music.

Tommy listened for a moment, then stood up in one fluid movement, turned and bowed to Lottie with the perfect formality of the ballroom. 'Miss Casanova,' he said, 'shall we have the pleasure of this last dance for Nellie Standish?'

It was a gentle, haunting waltz, and as they swung together into the rhythm that was now instinctive to them, both were weeping and smiling at once. The waltz music melted into a polka, and Tommy said: 'Come on, this one's more like our Nellie!' and they flung themselves into an abandoned gallop, skilfully avoiding furniture as they raced around the restricted space.

Still crying, but as much in exhilaration as sorrow, Lottie said: 'You're right – if we win through, she'll never be dead!'

The music stopped and silence invaded the room again. They separated and stood, still facing each other, panting from their exertions. Then, tentatively, Tommy reached out and touched Lottie's cheek, easing away the last tear stain. 'Beautiful,' he murmured. 'Oh, you're so beautiful, Lottie.'

Their embrace was so natural that afterwards she wondered why it had not happened sooner. His arms encircled her and his mouth was on hers, gentle, loving, comforting. Why had she thought they were like brother and sister?

'I love you. Always been afraid to say it before, but I do.'

He did not press her to declare any love for him, but a wave of tenderness overwhelmed her and she stammered out: 'I – I love you too, Tommy . . . only I never realised until now that it was this sort of love.'

He blew out the lamp and led her to the bedroom. Nellie Standish, Ulick Farrell and the whole world had temporarily ceased to exist. They were together in a world where they were the first beings.

There was a gas lamp in the bedroom, and now Tommy lit it. 'I want to see you, Lottie,' he said. 'Never want to take me eyes off you again.' He sat on the edge of the vast brass bed and started unlacing his boots. He chuckled ruefully. 'Wish I knew how them toffs managed to do this bit an' still look good, but I don't suppose I ever will. Anyhow, this is the first time I ever did it in company.'

'Me, too,' said Lottie, undoing her skirt fastening. 'D'you think we'll make a frightful mess of it?'

His grin was wicked. 'Well, whatever we do together, we don't arf improve with practice, so we'll just have to go on trying until we get it right, won't we?'

'Oh, you horrid, common boy! I'll teach you to have more respect for a lady!' Giggling, she leaped on him and they wrestled like a pair of puppies on the bed. But then, in the horseplay, her blouse worked loose from her unfastened skirt and in seconds the scuffle had turned to passionate exploration of each other's bodies.

There was a wonderful intensity about that first love-making which Lottie remembered for the rest of her life. They both lacked finesse, but it scarcely mattered. Their awkward fumbling caresses were so buttressed by their friendship and common experience that they seemed to learn together. Throughout the night, as they slept and woke and slept again, reaching for each other each time with fresh pleasure, Lottie lost all consciousness of herself and felt she and Tommy were melding into one. She wanted it to last forever.

Ulick drank throughout the night and well into the next day, snatching a few hours' sleep in a nighthouse down a back street behind Leicester Square. He had never felt so isolated. On other occasions, whisky had brought with it welcome oblivion, but this time he seemed to be immune. Even in the depths of his drunkenness, his memory tortured him with pictures of Nellie saying her last goodbye, followed in rapid succession by Charlotte dashing out of the Wilson Street apartment and of Tommy going after her. No one wanted to be with him . . . nothing lasted . . . a man was always alone at the end . . .

As the arid afternoon declined into evening the following day, he began to think with maudlin sentimentality of Charlotte. Little Charlotte – now there was a girl who wouldn't leave him alone for long. Of course, why hadn't he thought of it before? It was Nellie's presence which had separated them until now. With Nellie gone, Charlotte would be back at Wilson Street, anxiously awaiting his return, waiting to comfort him in his time of sorrow . . . and he would comfort her, too; soothe the pain of her loss. He knew just what she needed to make her forget . . .

Convinced, now, that he had straightened out his trouble, and so drunk he thought he was quite sober, Ulick walked stiffly out of a pub at the bottom of St Martin's Lane and reeled off through Covent Garden.

CHAPTER ELEVEN

Charlotte was still in a world of her own, bounded by the walls of the Wilson Street flat and having only two inhabitants, herself and Tommy Fanshaw. They had stayed in bed throughout the night and most of the day, and by early evening both of them were very hungry.

'Never let it be said I'm no gentleman,' said Tommy at last. 'You keep the bed warm. I'll go round the corner for something. Fish and chips and porter, how about that? Same supper as the night we met.'

'Don't be too long. I'll miss you.' She rolled over and stretched luxuriously in the soft depths of the bed.

Tommy threw on shirt, trousers and shoes and went off without bothering to put on any more clothes. Ten minutes later he was back, bringing the papers full of steaming hot food straight into the bedroom and leaving again only to get glasses for the beer.

'Come on, then, slowcoach – get your things off and come back to bed for supper,' said Charlotte.

'Nah – we may want more beer or something an' I'd have to dress again. Shift over 'til we've finished and I'll just sit on the top.'

Lottie attacked her meal with vigour. 'I can't remember ever being more hungry,' she said.

'Certainly gets you more peckish than a day's rehearsal, I'll say that for it.'

'You must be the most unromantic talker I've ever heard. Shut up and eat this.' She took a piece of fish in her hand and reached over to put it in his mouth.

He swallowed the food but then caught her wrist and pressed her hand against his cheek. 'You know I *feel* romantic, though, don't you?' he whispered. She nodded and he bent over her to kiss her.

That was when Ulick arrived back at the flat.

They were so engrossed in each other that they did not hear him come into the outer room. Farrell had heard sounds from the bedroom but inebriation left him confused about identifying the low voices. He was at the open bedroom door before it dawned on him that Lottie and Tommy were in bed together.

At that moment his drunkenness cleared like a morning mist. 'You bloody slut – I'll kill you for this!' he yelled, and launched himself at the bed.

Lottie, taken by surprise, reacted instinctively and plunged sideways on to the floor to avoid him. His flying tackle caught Tommy and knocked him, breathless, across the bed in a welter of spilled food and drink.

Immediately, Farrell's target changed. 'No, it's you, isn't it – you've been itching to get at her . . . Nellie warned me but I didn't see it.' As he spoke he pinioned Tommy across the chest with one powerful arm, and took the boy's jawbone in his other hand, squeezing inward until the pressure was unbearable. Choking and spluttering, Tommy eventually managed to disengage the hand, but by now Ulick had straddled him and appeared ready to beat him senseless.

Meanwhile, Lottie had jumped to her feet and rushed round the bed to defend Tommy. She grabbed Ulick from behind in a futile attempt to break his grasp, and succeeded only in enraging the big man still further. He half turned and delivered a ringing slap across her face and skull which sent her reeling back across the room, then heaved himself off Tommy and dragged the boy upright on to the floor.

The first murderous drive of Farrell's rage had diminished now, but had been replaced by something far worse. Still holding Tommy in a vicious grip, he wheeled the boy towards the door and said: 'All right, you've asked for this and now you're getting it. I'll show you just how unfair life can be!'

Before Lottie could clear her head from his blow, Ulick had dragged Tommy out of the bedroom and across the living room, pausing as he went to pick something up from the table. She staggered to her feet and started after them, forgetting until she reached the outer door that she was still naked. Sobbing, she turned back to the bedroom to find her clothes.

Moments later she was dressed and down in the street, but there was no sign of Ulick or Tommy. Lottie turned right, away from Drury Lane and towards the warren of back streets leading down to the fruit and vegetable market in Covent Garden. Wilson Street was something of an island of respectability among these rookeries. The narrower streets were scattered with rubbish and foul smells emanated from the disreputable lodging houses, shops and tenements beyond. On the corner of Wilson Street and Endell Street, an old woman sat at her regular pitch with a basket of fruit and vegetables for sale. Lottie stopped beside her, hesitating until she could trust her voice to sound relatively normal.

'Nancy, have you seen Tommy Fanshaw or Mr Farrell in the last few minutes? I don't know where they've gone.'

The old woman sniffed. 'Tellin' me I saw 'em, and 'eard them, along with arf the people in the Garden! That Tommy was yelling 'is head off about summat an' Mr Farrell was carrying on even worse, sayin' they'd lock up Tommy an' throw away the key. Best show I seen all week!'

'Yes, but where were they going?' Lottie was on the edge of panic now.

'Shoulda thought that was obvious. Mr Farrell stopped a Peeler just along there and they've all gone off down Bow Street nick.'

'But why? I really don't understand.'

Nancy regarded the girl as if she were mentally retarded, and said very slowly: 'Because your Tommy 'as stole some money off that Mr Farrell, that's why. The way the gentleman was carrying on, it must have been a tidy sum, too.' She paused and examined Lottie again. 'Well, go on then, off you go after them. You won't 'elp neither of 'em stuck up here gawping at me.'

'No . . . no, you're right . . . but perhaps it would be better if I just went home and waited.' Lottie turned away and headed back down Wilson Street. If the fruit seller's eyes had not still been fixed on her, she would have broken into a run.

100

The police station! How could she go there? Come to that, how could Ulick have the nerve to be seen there? Since her flight from Lyonesse, Lottie had regarded any brush with the police force as highly dangerous. Early on, in an attempt to teach her caution, Farrell had told her that her parents might have notified the police of her disappearance and that they might be searching for her. Ever since, she had been convinced that any contact with a policeman, let alone appearance at a police station, would result in her immediate forced return to Lyonesse.

The prospect was unthinkable. Now, it seemed to her, the only way of finding out what was happening to Tommy was to venture into the lions' den. She would have done it gladly, had she not been sure she would never have seen him again after that, because they would have sent her home. It never occurred to her that the authorities had most likely never heard of her.

It was a couple of hours before Ulick returned, alone. After pacing around the small apartment like a caged tiger, Lottie had decided activity would make the time pass more quickly. She turned to and stripped the beer-stained sheets from the bed, putting on clean linen and removing the debris of spilled food and glass from the floor. By then, although she was still deathly afraid of the police, she had calmed down and begun to think about the future.

Whatever happened at Bow Street, it was unthinkable that she and Tommy would remain here with Farrell after what had just occurred. She had inbred good timing, and the idea of having to pack her few belongings under Farrell's mocking eye before making her big exit would have been laughable had circumstances been less painful. So she collected her things, found the travel bag she had brought with her from Lyonesse, and stowed everything inside. When they got the booking at Drury Lane, Nellie had insisted they should have four of the frilly white dresses made up. They hung together in the bedroom closet, protected by a big linen bag. Lottie eyed them with disfavour, and almost left them where they were, but for once prudence told her she might soon need every asset she had. She packed them, with some other bits and pieces, in the canvas hold-all Ulick had given her to take things to and from the theatre.

When everything was ready, she moved her luggage over to the door and hid it behind the screen they used to exclude draughts. Then she went to the table to get the money Nellie had left for her. She and Tommy would need every penny until they were set up, and if she was going it alone . . . No! Her mind rejected that thought as too terrible. She pocketed her envelope.

Something was missing from the table. As she realised what it was, she went cold. 'Oh, Tommy, no!' she moaned. 'He's got you, hasn't he?' For she has remembered Ulick, vibrating with vengeful rage, pausing to pick up something from the table as he frog-marched Tommy out. The other envelope . . . the envelope with Tommy's fivers in it. Without that envelope, who would believe that a street boy had honestly come by fifty pounds in notes?

Lottie's first impulse was to flee now. It was not fear which drove her, but distrust of her own reaction to Ulick when she saw him again. What if she did something to him and he treated her as he had Tommy? But she could not leave matters so completely unresolved. She must simply try to control herself. She slumped in the armchair to await his return.

He arrived soon after that, quivering with bitter triumph. No hint of his earlier drunkenness remained. He was every inch the Anglo-Irish gentleman, and Lottie found it all too easy to imagine the figure he had cut at the police station.

He shut the door firmly behind him and turned to her with a crooked smile. 'Well,' he said, 'that seems to have solved that problem . . . now I must decide how I teach you a lesson.'

She stood up. If dignity was to be her only weapon, might as well use it to the full. 'Since when have you the right to teach me lessons?'

'I thought that was why we met in the first place.'

'From where I stand, it looks as if everything has changed since then.'

His smile vanished and his mouth was cruelly twisted by some half-suppressed emotion. He padded towards her like a big, dangerous animal. Stopping inches in front of her, he said: 'Ever since we met, you've been a curse to me, but I thought it was all worth while, because I wanted you. I wanted you so much I was prepared to put up with that nonsense about running away, all Nellie's bloody nannying, everything, just so that I could have you in the end. And guess what part of it was? The thought that you didn't know much about any of it, that you were aching to find out . . . your mother all over again, but without the inhibitions. What a challenge . . . what a prize!'

'Don't you *dare* compare me with my mother! I'm not at all like her!'

He had turned aside momentarily. Now his eyes snapped back at her face: 'But you are – you're her damned double! Look at you, playing me along, talking me out of a job, fluttering your petticoats and promising me everything – and then the minute my back is turned, opening your legs to some vagrant from under Waterloo Arches! Substitute a degenerate nobleman for the vagrant, and you could be your dear mama all over again!'

If Lottie could have killed him at that moment, she would have. She had forgotten Tommy; forgotten Farrell's perfidy in betraying the boy. All she could see in a red haze was a vision of herself as a copy of Laura Cazenove. Lacking other weapons, she lashed out wildly at him with both hands, breaking the skin of his cheeks as her nails raked the flesh.

She had been right about Ulick at the beginning: he was no namby-pamby chevalier worshipping at the feet of womankind. When he was hurt, he struck back. Now he let out a great roar of pain as her nails tore into him, and started striking her methodically back and forth across the face. Lottie was determined not to admit defeat, and she was a big, strong girl. But Farrell was over six feet tall and heavily muscled. He drove her steadily back across the room, raining open-handed blows across her face and head at such a rate that the best she could hope for was to shield herself. Almost before she realised she had moved, she felt the edge of the brass bedstead biting into the backs of her legs. He had harried her across the length of the apartment. She tried to dodge sideways, but he caught her off-balance and knocked her flat on to the bed.

'Now we'll see how inexperienced you really are, you cheating bitch!' he snarled, and threw himself on to her much as he had pinned down Tommy hours before.

The memory of that scene knocked all the fight from her. Lottie's body went limp and she lay, spent and listless, her head turned aside from Farrell's triumphant leer. He pulled her face back towards his own – again the gesture reminded her of what he had done to Tommy – and kissed her violently. She neither fought nor responded. He began running his hands over her body, as he had with such exciting effect when she was a curious child and he a less sinister figure than he had become today. She remained still, limp as a waxwork mannikin.

Ulick took her by the shoulders and shook her. 'What's the matter? Not used to a real man, I suppose? Only a boy will do, and a dirty one at that. Come on, you owe me, remember.'

But still he failed to rouse her from her torpor. He began to raise her skirt, sliding his hands up over the silky thighs he had so long wanted to touch. They were cold and motionless under his fingers. At last he gave up, standing up with a gesture of disgusted dismissal. 'It'll wait. Don't think you'll get away with it for good. In the end you'll be begging me for it.'

He left her and wandered out into the kitchen in search of his whisky. After a minute or two, Lottie followed him. She was still light-headed from the attack and from the rain of blows that preceded it, but she had to find out about Tommy.

'Ulick, you can't simply act as if there are just two of us when there was three a few hours ago. What did you do to Tommy?'

He had found the whisky and one swallow seemed to have brought back the effects of his two-day spree. He giggled mischievously. 'That's for me to know and you to find out, as Nanny would say!'

Fighting her resurgent rage, she said: 'I've guessed most of it. I know you pretended he stole from you – that money Nellie left for him.'

Farrell looked up sharply at that, a shaft of sobriety cutting through the whisky haze. 'What if I did? Serve him right . . . ingratiating himself with the two of you when he had me to thank for dragging him out of the gutter. Well, he's got what he deserves, now. You can forget any notions of seeing him again.'

'D'you mean they'll send him to prison?'

'I should say so! He can thank his lucky stars they've stopped transporting people! As it is, he'll be too old to think about a music hall career when he gets out – or to interest a little whore like you, I'll be bound.'

He sat back on the kitchen chair, grinning lazily and awaiting Lottie's next outburst. He was disappointed. She gave him a look of freezing contempt, and said: 'In that case, I'm on my own.' She turned and began to leave the room.

Farrell straightened and called after her: 'Don't be damned stupid! I know you have Nellie's money, but you won't survive five minutes out there on your own.'

'Nellie did.' Her voice drifted back faintly from the other room.

'But Nellie grew up on the streets – God knows she told you that herself often enough! You're different . . . coddled . . . Charlotte! Listen to me, you silly girl. We'll sort all this out. I was angry, that's all; jealous that little swine

103

had beaten me to it. We'll settle down together, you'll see. Six months from now, you'll have forgotten this ever happened. Charlotte, come on, stop sulking . . . Charlotte?'

Growing impatient at her prolonged silence, he got up and went to the living room. It was empty, and the front door swung open. Wherever Lottie Casanova's future lay, it seemed she did not intend to spend it which Ulick Farrell.

CHAPTER TWELVE

The privy was the worst thing about every place she looked at. In the beginning, Lottie thought she was merely unlucky. As she backed away, gagging, from the pestilential shed in the back yard of the Clerkenwell lodging, she assured herself the next place would be better. In fact it was worse. Nothing in her pampered life had prepared her for the everyday sanitary conditions endured by the poor. When she remarked on the stench and the filthy condition of the hut, the landlady regarded her with surprise and said: 'Well, some o' me fussier tenants keeps chamber pots upstairs and just slops out in there a coupla times a day. P'raps that would suit you better.' Inwardly cringing, Lottie said she thought not and moved on to the next place with rooms to let.

Her search for accommodation began the morning after she fled from Ulick Farrell. She had spent the night at the Temperance Hotel for Single Ladies which she had noticed down a Bloomsbury side street while she was staying with Nellie. The following day she caught a horse bus to Clerkenwell and walked the streets for half an hour, inspecting any houses which had signs in the windows advertising rooms to let. Lottie chose Clerkenwell because, in her new rootlessness, it gave her some sense of belonging, however remote, for Nellie Standish had started out from here. Besides, she told herself, trying to be rational, if I'm to claim I come from Clerkenwell, I'd better know the area.

After looking at single rooms and small flats in four houses, all of which would have been suitable had it not been for the noisome lavatories, she realised she must set her sights lower or remain homeless. By now she had moved south into the heart of Clerkenwell and was looking at the streets just off the Green.

She glanced listlessly at the shoddy modern houses along Newcastle Place. Nothing here as attractive as dear Wilson Street, and she shuddered to think about the plumbing . . . but the morning was almost gone, her feet were aching and she knew she must find something soon. There were two houses with signs offering lodgings. One said 'Clean rooms to let for single professional people'. The paintwork looked stale and cracked and Lottie was nervous about describing herself as a professional person. To one of her background, that meant lawyer or doctor, not aspiring music hall artiste.

The second house was altogether brighter, with fresh green and white paintwork on the mean window frames and flimsy front door. Its sign said: 'Small two-roomed apartment suit single or couple. Furnished'. Striving to thrust earth closets and wet middens from her mind, Lottie rang the doorbell.

The wallpaper in the narrow hall was bright and brash. Like its owner, it exuded an air of cheerfulness. The woman was wearing a skirt and shirtwaist with a pinafore. Her hair was piled into a ridiculously elaborate Pompadour and there was hint of paint on cheeks and eyelids. Instantly, Lottie felt at ease.

'The apartment . . . I'd like to look at it, if I may.'

As they reached the half-landing on the first floor, the landlady, Mrs Benson, gestured at a door, elaborately half-glazed with coloured, patterned panes. 'Bathroom there. I'll show you on the way back. This way.'

'No wait. I'd like to see.'

Lottie turned the doorknob and confronted a large, cast iron bath with scrolled lion feet and, joy of joys, a white porcelain lavatory pan with a mahogany seat, an overhead water tank and pull-chain. 'Oh, how wonderful,' she breathed, sounding as if she had found the Holy Grail.

Mrs Benson beamed. 'Nice, innit? Course, this house is nothing special. The whole street have got them. This block was built when they put up the Peabody Buildings around the corner, see, an' once they had the drains down for them, it was just as easy to connect us, an' all. You know what the builder said when he advertised Newcastle Place? "Indulge yourself with the amenities enjoyed by the Gentry for a fraction of the price, and buy a good investment, at the same time." It wasn't nuffink to do wiv the investment, luv,' here she nudged Lottie in the ribs, 'it was the sheer bloody luxury of being able to sit there for ten minutes without getting gassed.'

Her raucous laugh was inoffensive to Lottie. That morning she had come to understand the full value of running water and mains drainage. After that, the apartment could have been a cramped hutch and still have met with her approval. It happened to be light and attractive, although it looked as cheap as the house-front, the hallway and Mrs Benson herself.

The rent was considerably higher than at the older houses Lottie had seen around Exmouth Street, but she would have paid twice as much to avoid the stench and indignity of the cheaper apartments. Lottie was buttressed by the crisp feel of Nellie's ten five-pound notes, and the confidence that she would find lucrative work as soon as she knew her way about. She paid Mrs Benson a month's rent in advance, then set about unpacking her meagre luggage.

Now she was not mixed up with Ulick and his possessions, there was precious little: her clothes, in three scanty categories – child's garb from Lyonesse; the theatrical copies in their linen shroud; and the skeleton ward-robe of what she called governess clothes that Ulick had brought for her that first morning in London, so many dreams ago. Apart from that there was a fully-equipped theatrical makeup box, which Nellie had bought for her; a couple of pieces of showy paste jewellery, for stage use, from the same source, and a little stock of books. A couple of these were old schoolroom textbooks which she had stuffed into her bag before the headlong flight from Lyonesse. The rest were second-hand classics Ulick had picked up for pennies and brought home to Wilson Street for her to read. She surveyed it all with a sinking heart, then resolutely turned her back on it. Only one way to change all that – she needed money, and money meant work. Lottie Casanova made herself a cup of tea and then set out to seek a venue for her music hall debut.

As a pub, it had been called the Rose of Normandy. Officially, at least, it was now the Marylebone music hall, but it still bore traces of its old identity and regulars used the old name just as patrons of the Middlesex still referred to it as the Old Mo'. There was no proscenium arch or curtain. The turns walked on stage up steps and performed to a noisy mob who were more interested in their mutton chop and baked potatoes than in the songs and gags which were belted out by the artistes.

Cut off from the orthodox routes to audition and booking by her estrangement from Farrell, Lottie had hung around the pubs and halls of Marylebone, Holborn and Clerkenwell for a couple of days before deciding how to approach her problem. In that time she had seen enough of the Rose's clientele and performers to get its measure. It was a third-rate house, although considerably better if regarded as pub rather than music hall. She was never going to walk in off the street and win a booking at the Oxford or the Tivoli, so this was her choice of beginning. She was not at all sure what she intended to do if they booked her, beyond a vague determination to sing.

A waiter pointed out the landlord, a Mr Nelson. It was three in the afternoon and he was sitting at a table near the stage, sipping a pint of porter after finishing his lunch of chops and vegetables. Lottie stood in front of him, hands clenched together on the frame of her small bag, and said: 'Good afternoon, Mr Nelson. I want you to book me for your music hall.'

His eyes swept over her and failed to be very impressed. 'What did you have in mind,' he asked, 'teaching them the six times table?'

Lottie jerked her head at the stage, where a quartet of over-sized chorus girls were wobbling uncertainly through a rehearsal, and said: 'If I did, it would probably get a bigger hand than that lot.'

Nelson eyed the girls with disfavour and sighed. 'Yeah, maybe you're right. Still, they're cheap.'

'So am I, Mr Nelson – and better value than they are, I assure you.'

His scrutiny became sharper. 'Well, you seem to be put together the right way. Without that drab get-up you could be a good eyeful, even if your voice was no good.'

'I am and it is. Just try me.'

'Mmm . . . got your costume?'

'Not with me,' she improvised. 'Hardly worth trailing around with it when I'm only calling to see if there's work available. You don't think I audition for halls like this in full costume, do you?' Dear God, she thought, can I buy something suitable in time to start here?

'Where have you worked before?'

She took a deep breath and plunged. 'I've just finished a season in pantomime at Drury Lane.'

His guffaw turned the heads of the lumpen chorus girls. 'That would be Drury Lane, Huddersfield, I take it? Nobody does a season for Druriolanus and then comes running around to the Rose for their encore. If you were in *Dick Whittington* you must have been back o' the chorus!'

She did a creditable impression of an affronted prima donna and said: 'As it happens, I was part of a double act, a fifteen-minute speciality spot. But the act has broken up and I'm starting alone.'

She had his full interest now. 'Stage name? Act?' he said.

'The act was the Street Urchins' Dance. Our stage names were Fanshaw and Carr, but I've gone back to my own name now – it's more distinctive than Carr. I'm Lottie Casanova.'

'Lottie Casanova . . . hmm, yes, like that; got a bitta class but not too much. But I dunno about a solo dance act. Very specialised, that. Not the sort o' turn for a house like this.'

'No, I told you, I'm a singer. Really, Mr Nelson, wouldn't it be better just to hear me? You don't need character references for a ten-minute spot at the Rose, surely?'

He shrugged. 'S'pose you're right.' The chorus lumbered into a tuneless song-and-dance routine. 'Come to that, if they go on much longer, *you'll* be asking *me* for character references! Get 'em off, Joe. I gotta girl here wants to audition . . . Go on, then, tell Joe what you want him to play. One song's enough.'

Her palms were wet as she went up the six steps to the stage. The chorus girls stumped down at the other side and stood sullenly watching her as she approached Joe Smith. He was a big man with a bull-like neck and a choleric complexion. A curly-brimmed billycock hat gave him the look of a comic villain, but his friendly smile disarmed Lottie and made her feel a little more at ease.

'Hallo, darlin', you'll make a change from them dray 'orses down there. What can I play for you?'

Nellie, help me, she prayed silently, then said with an assurance she did not feel: 'D'you know "Hearts and Flowers"?'

'Not only know it – I heard Nellie Standish bring the house down with it at the Old Mo' a coupla months back. Aren't you aiming a bit high?'

'Come on, cut the cackle!' yelled Nelson from his table. 'I want these silly cows rehearsing for at least another hour when this is finished.'

Smith gave Lottie an enquiring look. 'You sure it's "Hearts and Flowers"?'

'Yes – I'm no Nellie Standish yet, but I will be one day.'

Smith went into the elaborate introduction and Lottie took up her position to the rear of the stage. Then she sang, with a technique as close to Nellie's as she could get it. She loved the song, and already could see places where she would perform it differently, but now was no time to experiment. To sing it in tune would be enough at the moment.

She managed to get through it without making a fool of herself, but she was too keyed-up to remember much of her performance. She eyed Nelson nervously and he stared back in silence for a while.

Finally, when she was becoming convinced he would reject her, he said, 'Fine. As long as your costume's all right, you're in. Only don't expect much appreciation. My customers scarcely hear half o' what goes on up there, and it's up to you to grab their attention.'

Lottie subdued her impulse to rush down and fling herself at his feet in gratitude. Instead, she managed a cool smile and said: 'How much will you be paying me, Mr Nelson?'

He glanced sideways at the chorus girls. 'Better come round to my office an' discuss that,' he said, getting up.

She started to leave the stage. As she passed Joe Smith, he said, very quietly: 'You were a lot better than Nelson's average turn. Don't let him beat you down too far.' Lottie gave him a brilliant smile and hurried off in Nelson's wake.

108

Lottie had no idea what constituted a good wage. Ulick had never told her what they were paid for the Drury Lane act, and she had never handled money at all until now. In the end she decided that Nelson would deliberately pitch his offer lower than he was prepared to pay, so she refused his first two proposals and accepted the third sum he offered – thirty shillings a week and a cooked supper every evening after the show.

'Start tonight if you like,' he said.

Alarm flared in her again. Where would she get a gown?

'I . . . ah . . . think not, Mr Nelson. I'm moving house and I need a few hours to sort myself out. Tomorrow, perhaps.'

'Tomorrow perhaps? Tomorrow or nothing, you mean! I'll have forgotten what you sound like if you put it off longer than that. I'll book you for the rest o' this week and all of next. After that we'll see, all right?'

Back out on the street, Lottie was close to desperation about acquiring a suitable costume for her solo debut. She knew what Nellie had spent on a single gown and the thought took her breath away. It would take an unconscionable number of thirty-shilling weekly pay packets to finance such splendour. Lottie knew that the Rose would not require so much, but she must put on a reasonably glamorous show if they were to remember her. How could she manage it?

Then it dawned on her. Why did she have to go to a couturier? Theatrical costumiers worked in tens of dozens of costumes, running them up to look sumptuous at minimal cost, taking them back to refurbish them or make them over into new designs. Now if she could get hold of one of those . . .

Half an hour later she was in Stinchcombe's Drury Lane showroom, trying to charm the fitter who was checking racks of brocade robes as she came in. He was not so much unco-operative as unable to comprehend what she needed. She was making her third attempt to explain when Stinchcombe himself came in. His initial air of cool detachment melted when he realised what she wanted.

'You go back to your brocades, Mr Hartley. I'll attend to this young lady personally. Now, did I hear you say you required something for an . . . er . . . musical interlude?'

Sensing what was required of her, Lottie fell effortlessly into the appropriate role. 'Well, it's my first real solo spot an' I know I can't afford couturier's prices. Then I thought, Stinchcombe's! They dress their actresses better than any music hall star I ever saw. So I came straight round to see if you could fix me up.'

He ran an expert eye over her figure. 'It would be a great pleasure, Miss . . . er . . .'

'Casanova. Lottie Casanova.'

'Charming. I look forward to seeing it outside the Tivoli or the Oxford! Now, to business. What is the . . . er . . . ambience of your act?'

She twinkled at him: 'Romantic going on naughty, I think would best describe it. Do you think you could fix me up with the right costume, without breaking the bank?'

'Without the slightest trouble. I'll fetch a lady fitter at once. Please come this way.'

She was shown into a fitting room which strongly resembled a lady's boudoir. Soon afterwards, Stinchcombe returned, followed by a small bird-like woman who was pushing a metal rack containing about a dozen gowns. He had selected all dark, rich jewel shades. 'Partly with your own colouring in mind, partly because dark colours look richer than pale ones in harsh light,' he explained. 'Now, Miss Fletcher, let's see what we have.'

Lottie eventually selected two gowns, both recommended by Stinchcombe as suiting her better than the rest. She knew they were only theatrical imitations of couture – and second-hand models at that – but they were so skilfully cut to minimise the effect of cheap fabric and hard wear that they looked as good as the real thing.

One was a garnet-coloured velvet, with a deep square neck cut back almost to the armpits, and big puff sleeves. 'If it's one of the more – ah – informal halls, I think this would work best without gloves; nevertheless I recommend you take some. We can supply silk stockinette fabric dyed to match the gown for a fraction of the price of leather.'

'Oh, you are so kind to me!' Lottie was the perfect Italian-cockney sparrow and relishing every minute. 'Nobody's made so much fuss o' me before!'

He simpered at her. 'I'm sure I shall merely be the first of many, Miss Casanova. And now, if I may, I recommend the black satin, too. It's a little mature for you at present, perhaps, but it will look magnificent and should you wish to appear rather more grande dame, this is the gown in which to do it.'

He was right. The black had a deep vee-neck which left the shoulders bare and swooped between her breasts. It hugged her body closely to the waist and then belled into a short train at the back. A frou-frou of tiny silk net frills burst through the back skirt as though a frothy underdress had been accidentally exposed. 'It's gorgeous!' said Lottie, momentarily forgetting her smoky street accent as she appreciated the gown. 'But it will be far too expensive for me!'

'I think not. It's been re-made and it had a long run on the back of one of our premier leading ladies. That means it can't be seen again in the West End. I think we could offer you both gowns, and two pairs of the garnet jersey gloves, for ten guineas. Would that suit?'

It sounded like a give-away price for what they were offering, and probably was. It still made Lottie gulp at the thought of the inroads it would make in to her small capital. Thirty bob a week wouldn't finance too many rig-outs like this once Nellie's money was gone. 'Done,' she said, 'but if they need alteration, I'm not sure I can run to the extra.'

'Any alterations will be included in that price; and of course, if you wish to acquire different costumes later, we will allow you a certain amount on return of these.'

'Oh, you are a darling! How can I thank you?'

Miss Fletcher looked as if she could tell her, given half a chance, but she merely smiled behind Stinchcombe's back and went on re-hanging the unwanted dresses.

Stinchcombe reddened and said: 'It's my pleasure, Miss Casanova. I'm sure Miss Fletcher will keep my secret if I confess I have a great weakness for music hall. I shall expect free seats when you reach the top.'

'And you shall have them, sir! Now, hadn't I better try this lot on?'

The gowns looked sensational. The black made her appear to be at least twenty-five and dramatised her smouldering beauty. The garnet gave her a softer, more pliant look, which she knew would be good for her debut. This one fitted her as if it had been made for her. The black needed alteration and she arranged to collect it two days later. Then, heart singing, she said good-bye and went off to Clerkenwell to experiment with makeup and hair styles. For the first time in her short life, Lottie was her own mistress and she was enjoying every minute of the experience.

Onstage at the Rose of Normandy the following night, she realised she was going to need all the help her gown and makeup could provide. It was ten o'clock. The cumbersome chorus had clumped off, having lost the attention of the audience within moments of starting their routine. By the time Lottie mounted the steps to the platform, they were concentrating on their chops, their porter and their chatter.

But not for long, you bastards, she told herself. I'm here to entertain you, and entertained you will be!

She started with 'A Little Bit Of What You Fancy'. By the end of the first verse, they were still swilling beer and guzzling their supper. Remembering a comprehensive lesson from Nellie on voice projection, she put enough volume into the first chorus to cut through rush hour traffic. Some of them were paying attention now. But in spite of the gown, in spite of her sparkling good looks, there were still too many indifferent faces looking the wrong way. She ended the first song to a patter of applause. Well, at least *some* of them had begun to listen. By the end of the act, they'd begging for more if she had any say . . .

Lottie rapidly rethought her repertoire for the evening. She had five songs, and had planned to alternate sentimentality with humour. 'Hearts and Flowers' was to have been next on her list. Now she signalled hastily to Joe Smith – the Rose only ran to an orchestra on special nights – to play an unscheduled number. Moments later she was launched on 'My Old Man Said Follow The Van', a song she had learned in one of Nellie's education sessions but had never performed before, even in the privacy of Nellie's drawing room. Now, singing the first verse, she sauntered over to the stage-side steps and walked down them. As she ripped into the chorus, she was in among the tables, tweaking an ear lobe here, blowing a kiss there, even, in a breath between lines, snatching a morsel of potato off a man's fork as he raised it to his lips. By the time she was halfway through the song, they were with her to a man, hanging on every word. She finished:

'But you can't trust a Special like an old time copper
Now I can't find my way 'ome!'

'I'll take yer, love!' 'No, me!' 'How about me, darlin'? I'm smoother than them buggers!' Smiling, blowing more kisses, she regained the safety of the stage. She had them! Now to hold them for another three songs and leave them wanting more . . .

Somehow, she managed it. Never would she more fully appreciate the welcoming gloom of the wings in a conventional proscenium arch theatre. Here, descending the steps before she could slip through the door which led back to the primitive dressing rooms, she felt naked.

Harry Nelson was sufficiently pleased with Lottie at the end of her initial booking to extend it another month and raise her pay to two pounds a week.

111

When she thanked him, he looked faintly embarrassed and she realised he had been prepared to give her more. 'I don't get many acts in here good enough to make a noticeable difference to the bar profits,' he told her, 'but you're one, so it's only fair you should 'ave a share of the take, innit?'

When the first month ended, Nelson offered her a regular spot, and promised to raise her wages again after three months if the takings went on improving. She accepted, but also started looking around for bookings in what she still regarded as 'proper' music halls – theatres with proscenium arch and curtain, a full orchestra every evening and a large enough audience to spread her name further afield than the immediate vicinity. She still had no knowledge of the business end of variety, of the agents who held court in offices along York Road, just south of the river. She was trying to pluck up courage to go along to one of the catch-all auditions which some music hall managers held in the afternoons on a fortnightly or monthly basis, so for the time being she was stuck at the Rose. Then Joe Smith came to her aid.

He had joined her for supper one night backstage after her act. 'You'll wear yourself out for small beer in this hole and never make the big time,' he told her. 'Isn't it about time you got yourself an agent?'

She laughed derisively. 'Look at me, Joe – sixteen years old last week with two stage dresses, a season in panto and two months at a converted beer house to offer as professional experience. They aren't going to be standing in line for my business, are they?'

'I know a couple that might, if they ever got to see you. Trouble with the Rose is it ain't a fashionable house for new talent any more. Leave it to me; I'll see if a friend of mine is interested in a pint and a plate o' grub here one night this week.'

The friend was Larry Nash, a successful young agent who had recently set up on his own after a few years learning his trade in one of the big York Road partnerships. By the time he came to the Rose a few nights later, Lottie had worked harder than ever to polish her routine, which was already unrecognisably improved since her first uncertain evening on stage.

Now the regulars greeted her appearance with yells of approval and ribald appreciation. She treated them with easy familiarity, and once she had kicked off with a good rousing song, she was able to revert to her original plan of alternating rough and sentimental numbers throughout her spot. After her performance, Harry led her over to Nash's table and introduced her.

He was genial-looking man with a rosy country boy complexion, a dusting of freckles across the bridge of his nose, a mass of curly brown hair and bright hazel eyes which missed nothing. The air of innocent jollity was deceptive, though. He was a tough man who put business before everything; and Lottie Casanova meant business to him.

'I think you could have a first-rate career ahead of you, Miss Casanova,' he said, 'but your material needs a lot of improvement.'

She bridled. 'Some people would say songs that are good enough for Marie Lloyd and Nellie Standish are good enough for me.'

'That's just why they're *not* good enough for you, if you're ever going to make a reputation as anything but a copyist. Without some really good original songs of your own, the best you can hope for is bottom-of-the-bill bookings in dives like the Hoxton Varieties – all right when you're eighteen, but lousy at twenty-eight.'

112

Lottie remembered Nellie saying much the same thing to her, centuries ago, it seemed. 'But where am I to get original songs?' she wailed. 'I don't know anyone, and I can't write the damned things myself!'

'One of the things a good agent is for,' he said, soothing her with his boyish smile. 'Before we talk percentages or anything else, I'll put out some feelers and then come back in a few days' time with a good songwriter. I know one or two who are on their way up. One of them is bound to be interested in joining forces with a talented girl like you.'

It was not an entirely satisfactory meeting, but at least Lottie felt she was getting somewhere now. Outside her life at the Rose, things were not running altogether smoothly. Her landlady was a cheerful, friendly soul who did not interfere unduly. She never saw the tenant of the other apartment in the Newcastle Place house. Instead of welcoming the peace, she felt lonely and cut off. Grief for the loss of Tommy, ruthlessly suppressed in her waking moments, began to dominate her dreams.

At first she woke weeping two or three times a week. By the time the agent came to see her act at the Rose, she was reliving the separation from her lover every night. It was made worse by a nightmare vision of Ulick Farrell, lurking as a giant, menacing shadow just outside her line of vision. In the dream, the shadow gradually engulfed Tommy as he tried to run to her, and when it swallowed him up he gave a gurgling cry, as if he were drowning. Before the evil shape had time to resolve itself into Farrell's physical likeness, she invariably awoke, sobbing and shivering.

The constant disturbance began to make her physical health suffer, to such an extent that the day after her first encounter with Larry Nash, she had visited a doctor with a practice beside Clerkenwell Green. When she described her symptoms, the doctor looked at her perplexed for a while, then said: 'How old are you, Miss Casanova?'

'Sixteen, but I can't imagine that has anything to do with it.'

'Surely, by now, someone has explained to you the consequences of certain acts of physical intimacy between men and women?'

She blushed furiously, wondering how he could have guessed about her and Tommy, and shook her head. 'The only consequences I've noticed are dreadful dreams I've been getting lately.'

'Ah, then you do admit to such intimacy?'

She tossed her head indignantly. As she had told Ulick, she loathed hypocrisy. 'Yes. I've done nothing I'm ashamed of.'

The doctor sighed. 'I think, however, you have done it without being aware of the inevitable consequences. You appear to be expecting a baby.'

For a moment, she thought she would faint. 'But I can't be! How could I be . . . ?' Then she faltered into silence, finally, too late, realising the nature of the missing piece in the puzzle of the coupling of the footman and the village girl . . . so that was why it was secret and shameful . . . that was what they all feared. Briefly, her horror was swamped by shame at her own gross naivety. Even inside the raffish society she had entered last autumn, everyone had assumed she knew so it had never come up . . . Within seconds, the terrifying reality came pounding back to displace all other thought.

'What am I going to do?' It came out as a whisper.

The doctor was sympathetic, but powerless to offer a material solution. 'Is

113

it possible for you to go to your parents . . . or to the father? You'll need support from somewhere.'

She squared her shoulders and tried not to cry. 'I'm on my own. I have no one else to rely on. I shall manage.'

For a few seconds, despair had made her forget the cockney accent which was not quite instinctive. The doctor studied her intently for a long moment and said: 'My dear, are you quite what you say you are? Are you sure there is no one I can contact on your behalf?'

'No, nobody. Don't worry, I'll manage. Should I come back and see you again?'

'Most certainly. If you have been unable to make any suitable arrangements when your confinement is due, perhaps I might fix something. In any case, you will need a midwife to help you. And you are rather young to become a mother, so try to pay me a visit every few weeks.'

She shrugged and contrived to sound blasé. 'Won't be the first, nor the last, I dare say. When will it be?'

'From what you say, the relationship has ended. Can you put a time on it?'

She blushed at this, remembering the blissful night and day that ended in such misery. 'Th-the last week in February. I'm sure.'

'Then you will come to full term early in December. Not an easy time to stay warm and healthy if you have only a little money.'

'I should have enough if I'm careful.' Already, her mind was shifting to Larry Nash and the prospects of work he might offer. Her knowledge of pregnancy began and ended with recognition of the pear shape which women developed as the process advanced. That would make work difficult. 'Will it be long before it shows?'

'Well, you're a tall, big-boned girl and you carry yourself properly . . . with a good corset and regular exercise . . . sensible diet . . . you might manage to conceal it right up until the seventh or eighth month, although people would certainly be aware you'd put on weight by then. And of course, it might be a big baby . . . All in all, I don't think you need worry too much until August or September, as long as you take care.'

Four months and a bit at least to get some well-paid work, she thought. She had the remains of Nellie's nest-egg behind her, and her two pounds a week from the Rose. Somehow, she'd get through. This song writer of Nash's had better be good . . .

Two nights later she was talking to a couple of regulars at the Rose when Joe came over. 'Nash has arrived with his pet song-writer,' he said. 'They know they're too late to catch the act tonight, but they'll come back tomorrow, and in the meantime they'd like a chat. All right?'

'Yeah, where are they?' Joe turned and led her through the crush to the long mahogany bar which occupied the entire back wall of the room. As they drew near, Nash, who was facing them, glanced up with a smile and started forward. The other man had his back to them.

The outline of head and shoulders gave Lottie a jolt of recognition, and at that moment he turned. 'Hello, Lottie,' said Ulick Farrell, 'where have you been hiding? I've looked everywhere for you.'

She turned and ran.

CHAPTER THIRTEEN

There was no question of staying at the Newcastle Place flat. It was too expensive, and too exposed. Harry Nelson knew her home address and would have no reason to withhold it from Nash. Nash would lead Ulick to her and that would be the end of everything. By now Lottie's attitude to Ulick was so irrational that she did not stop to ask herself just what he could do to her. The mere fear of another confrontation was enough to make her flee.

There was another good reason for moving. Now that she had no prospect of working the halls, and needed every penny she could earn, the little apartment was too expensive for her. Any better-paid work in proper halls was beyond reach. Ulick would see music hall bills and inevitably would find her again. He had told her himself that he had looked everywhere for her since she left Wilson Street. Only the lucky accident of a job in an unfashionable pub had kept her hidden from him so long. That meant her only chance of earning a living in the foreseeable future was singing in another pub. But how would she get a job?

Then she remembered Joe Smith. Joe had been very kind to her when there was nothing in it for him. Perhaps he would help her.

When Smith stepped out into Marylebone Road the following afternoon for a breather after the busy lunchtime session, Lottie hissed at him from her hiding place in a doorway: 'Joe – over here, I want to talk to you!'

He hurried across. 'Lottie! What the hell is going on? I dunno what there was between you an' that geezer Farrell, but Larry wasn't 'arf mad at having come all the way to the Rose twice for nothing.'

'Please believe me, Joe, I'm ever so grateful to you for all that, but I can't go ahead with it . . . that man – he really is my worst enemy and I have to disappear.'

Smith was gazing at her incredulously. 'You can't just up stakes an' run! How will you earn a living?'

Lottie glanced about frantically. 'Look, there's so much to explain . . . isn't there a coffee shop or something we could go to?'

'Yeah, o' course. Come on, just down 'ere.' He led her down Harcourt Street, past Queen Charlotte's Lying In Hospital, and she winced as she saw the nameplate on the door. Beyond it was a little working men's restaurant where Joe got them a mug of tea and a sandwich, then led her to a table away from the scattering of afternoon customers. 'Come on, then,' he said. 'Out with it – what's the big trouble you're in?'

She told him a lot of it, carefully avoiding her family background and Nellie Standish's involvement. When she told him about the baby he looked at her in real alarm. 'How the devil are you goin' to manage with that? I can see now why you want to avoid Farrell, but you're going to have to get an agent an' go on the halls, girl, otherwise you'll starve.'

She refused to budge on the matter of an agent. 'No, Joe. I know I must work, but I cannot face knowing Ulick might find me.'

'What if he does? He can't eat you, for Gawd's sake!'

'I can't tell you just what he is capable of, but believe me it's enough to make me hide from him. If he ever found out about this baby . . .'

Joe thought he was beginning to understand and nodded sagely. 'All right, then. What d'you want to do and how can I help?'

'Well, for a start, you can tell Mr Nelson I'm ill and I won't be back. Will you?'

'Course I will. He won't be best pleased; you're the best draw he's had this last two years or more. But I'll tell him – get you the half-week's wages, too. You'll be needing them.'

'Oh, thank you, Joe . . . there's more, though.'

'I can always say no. Out wiv it.'

'Are there any pubs like the Rose where I could find work – far enough from here to be away from Ulick, but somewhere where I could get cheap rooms nearby? Could you find somewhere and have a word with them?'

He scratched his stubbly jaw for a while as he thought about that one. Finally he said: 'Yeah, there's a coupla places would do up around where I live, Camden way. Plenty of cheap lodgings there, an' all. They're much the same as the Rose and they'd pay about that much, 'long as I told 'em how good you are.'

'Would you, Joe? I'd never forget it, I'd be in your debt forever.'

'Don't be bloody daft. I'm your friend, ain't I? Don't expect no favours for being a friend, you know. But Lottie, you got to promise me somefink. If this goes bad, come to me and my missis. We've only got a small place or I'd take you back there now. But if you get in real trouble, you remember us.' He took out a pencil stub and tore a corner off the newspaper he had been carrying, then laboriously wrote down his address. 'There you are. Mind you keep that safe. You're gonna need all your friends before long . . . I'll see about the pubs tonight on me way home. You live over Clerkenwell, don't you? Can't see how I'll manage to get over there an' back tomorrow afternoon.'

'Oh, don't worry about that! Let's meet here again.' She managed to summon up a grin: 'After all, they do such a good cuppa tea!'

The pub was called the Prince of Denmark and it was near the Caledonian Road cattle market, a busy, boisterous location with plenty of cheap housing within walking distance. Another pub, in the heart of Camden, had also been interested in booking her, but the Prince of Denmark wanted two performances an evening and the landlord was prepared to pay double the wages she had received from Harry Nelson for the privilege.

'Joe, you're a jewel!' she said. 'One day I'll find a way to repay you.'

'You know what I already told you about that,' he growled, 'and anuvver fing: Frank Giles wants to 'ear you do your stuff before he confirms. I know that won't give you no trouble, but do the audition before you count your chickens, just the same.'

'What are the rooms like up that way?'

He made a face and waggled his down-turned hand. 'Very mixed. Some old tenements they should have pulled down when Adam was a boy. You don't wanna touch them, however cheap they're going. Some of the newer places was built within the last twenty years, so you should find somewhere the bugs haven't taken over yet.'

She shuddered, and broached her own pet requirement. 'Any chance of running water in any of them?'

'Yeah, in the better sort. But you'll have to look 'ard and when you find something it'll be a lot dearer than the places where the night soil cart still calls.'

She wondered if she would be able to afford the rent, but decided she must. The doctor had warned her she could expect to go on being queasy for some time, and the idea of locking herself in an outside privy when she felt like that was monstrous.

As a result, it took her the best part of four days to find suitable accommodation she could afford. Even then, it was nothing special; a seedy lodging house on five floors with rudimentary bathrooms on two of them. She rented a small furnished room on the second floor for a quarter of what she had been paying for the apartment, and the new place was less than half a mile from the Prince of Denmark.

On her first night in her new quarters, she stowed away her belongings and sat down disconsolately to count her money. Harry Nelson had proved more generous than she had expected, and had paid her in full to the end of the week. With that, the remains of Nellie's nest egg and what she had managed to save since she started working, she had thirty-five pounds. She began to feel better. That should see her through, as long as she could go on working and saving more until shortly before her confinement.

She planned to admit herself to a lying-in hospital rather than risk giving birth in this shabby place. Once the baby was born, Joe had promised his wife would find someone trustworthy to look after it so that she could go back to work. She would not hear of giving it up, although Joe told her it would be for the best.

'What would become of it? I can't just hand it over to strangers. It's my fault I'm having it, even if I didn't know what I was doing.'

At first it looked as if she would be lucky. Frank Giles, the landlord at the Prince of Denmark, was very taken with her, and so were his customers. She had learned a lot about self-presentation at the Rose of Normandy, and although she had gone back to using unoriginal songs popularised by the stars of the day, the Caledonian Road audience did not care. They enjoyed looking at her, and liked the earthy relish with which she delivered the old favourites. Once she had settled down and got used to the rougher neighbourhood, the customers she entertained were much the same as those in the Rose.

After a couple of weeks, she started giving thought to her costumes. The dark red velvet was not going to fit her for long; it had originally appealed to her because it accentuated every curve of her slender girlish body. She did not want to spend her tiny savings on another expensive theatrical costume, only to outgrow that, too, within a few weeks. Then she found a solution. She was singing cockney songs to an audience one step removed from the East End, who saw East End life through slightly rosy spectacles. What better than a Pearly Queen get-up? The loose bead-encrusted blouse and voluminous skirt would hide all manner of bulges until she was ready to quit the stage.

117

This time she went to another theatrical costumier. She could not quite face Mr Stinchcombe with his appreciative eye for a trim young female, and flaunt her very un-maidenly condition before him. The costume cost her only a fraction of what she had paid for the elaborate gowns, and did everything she had hoped of it. The audience at the Prince of Denmark loved it.

Her good fortune seemed set to continue when the summer proved to be cool and breezy, making it easier for her to give her twice-nightly performances in the hot, crowded saloon bar. When she left the Prince of Denmark each evening, she was more isolated than she had believed possible. She held herself aloof from the other tenants in the lodging house and limited her acquaintance with the pub customers to easy familiar chatter between and after her act. She spent a great deal of time alone, reading her few books, trying to make plans for after the baby was born, and missing Tommy Fanshaw and Nellie Standish.

Sometimes Lottie wondered whether the Tommy her memory conjured up was more than a dream. Had he really been that affectionate, that undemanding, that tolerant? Had he really been the one who held back and played the diplomat while Ulick, almost a decade his senior, had been provocative and vicious? When doubt assailed her, she always quelled it with the same answer. Nellie Standish had thought the world of Tommy, and Nellie was no fool when it came to judging men.

Lottie ate sensibly and took a long walk in Regent's Park each day. Together with her energetic stage routine and a murderous corset, this regime ensured that she kept the secret of her pregnancy. By September she was beginning to tire easily, but at least she felt she might stay the course. These days she looked back with growing disbelief on the girl she had been. The face she saw in her mirror looked as fresh as it always had, but it seemed to be the only relic of her old life which remained. The Italian-cockney pastiche accent had become second nature to her and slipped only in moments of extreme stress. One night she awoke from a dream in which she had spoken with the new accent, and giggled to herself. It was the infallible sign you had mastered a foreign language when you started to dream in it.

With the accent, her outlook had begun changing too. She would never lose the streak of arrogant self-assurance that came only from being brought up at the very top of society. But now she also understood what it was to be at the bottom of the heap. She had experienced the sad invisibility imposed by nondescript clothing; the terror of waking at midnight with no idea of where she would be next year – or even next week; the strange mixture of panic and elation which came from knowing she would survive only by her own efforts. Now she understood what Nellie Standish had been trying to put over to her: that each experience shared with the poor and downtrodden brought her closer to excellence on the stage. As her secret pregnancy progressed, she could feel her act improving with each performance she gave, and wondered whether, once her child was born, she would master her terror of Ulick sufficiently to have another try at showing herself off in music hall.

The problem of keeping her stock of money safe was a constant worry. Her room had a lock, but she had no way of knowing how many keys there were, and on two occasions she had arrived home early in the afternoon to find the landlady moving furtively along her landing. The first time it happened, the

118

woman had greeted Lottie without meeting her eyes, and had made some remark about sweeping the floor – an odd excuse as she was not carrying a broom at the time. The second, she merely gave a shifty grin and slid past towards the top of the stairs.

Back in her room, Lottie had hurried to her little pile of books and opened two of them. The money was still safe, laid flat in single five-pound notes between the pages. She always carried five guineas and a few shillings in small change with her. The rest was entrusted to the books. She knew she should put it somewhere safer – preferably out of this wretched building – but could think of nowhere. She would gladly have entrusted it to Joe Smith, but was reluctant to burden him with the responsibility. There were now eight fivers, and she guessed Joe had never seen that much at one time, unless he was around when Harry Nelson was paying the artistes and bar staff at his pub.

When autumn came, she began to realise the lodging house had more disadvantages than she had foreseen. It was impossible to get her room really warm. The fireplace was too narrow and mean to get a good blaze going, the window frame so ill-fitting and the curtains so thin that a vicious draught constantly circulated. When she was not working, buying her small supplies of food or out walking, Lottie began spending most of her time in bed. She bought a couple of heavy woollen blankets in an effort to keep warm.

By early November, she was forced to call a halt to her act. She wanted to go on; she was as popular as ever with the audience and Giles was sufficiently happy to have raised her wages in September. But she was no longer sufficiently agile to carry off her lightning sorties into the audience – and the routine had to be fast or she was likely to be grabbed and fumbled by the enthusiastic on-lookers. Finally she admitted defeat and confessed her condition to Giles.

As she had expected, he was surprised but showed no moral outrage. The Prince had seen far worse than an expectant mother singing and dancing on its cramped stage. 'You'll be giving your notice then, will you, Lottie?' he said.

'That's why I wanted to see you. I shall have to stop performing, but I can still work and I need the money. As your girl Alice left last week, how about keeping me on as a barmaid?'

He gave her a long look. 'You know what the money is? Small change compared with what I pay for your act.'

'Yes, but I've seen the tips the girls get; and I know you let them take out the drinks they get bought for them as cash instead of stock.'

He chuckled. 'Don't miss much, do you, dearie? How am I to know you'd be any good as a barmaid? It may not need the talent you show up on that stage, but it's a skilled job for all that.'

'I know, Mr Giles, but I got Kate to show me how to pull a pint last week, and I'll work for nothing if you like for the first night, just so you can see I know the ropes. I promise you won't regret it.'

'You're a game, 'un, I'll give you that. Forget the trial night. I'll take a chance on you being all right. You learned your trade fast enough on that stage.'

'I don't understand you.' Momentarily her accent was pure Lyonesse.

'I'm not daft, child. You're a very talented singer – have to be, to survive here for so long. But I know you could count your time on stage in weeks when you first came here.' She could not meet his eyes and stood, head down, trying to think up an explanation. 'Don't get in a twist,' he said kindly. 'If you hadn't made good, you'd have been out in a week. Come to that, I know Joe wouldn't have recommended you in the first place. I don't mind; I just wanted you to realise I knew, that's all. I like a trier! Go on – off home now and turn up ready to run the bar tomorrow at noon. You can do four hours on, two hours off, two hours on and see how we go. That suit you?'

'Very much, Mr Giles. Thanks a lot.' On her way back to her lodgings, she wondered how on earth she would stay on her feet for six hours a day, six days a week, with just a two-hour afternoon break. Finally she sighed and said aloud: 'Stop worrying about how – you've got to and that's that.'

Because of her altered working hours, she did not know for a couple of days that a new woman tenant had moved into the back room across the landing from her own. The woman and the landlady seemed very close, and that made Lottie doubly nervous about the landlady's intention to break into her room. As far as Lottie could judge, the newcomer was in her late twenties. She was also in an advanced state of pregnancy.

The hard work and longer hours began to take their toll, and Lottie soon stopped noticing the comings and goings of the landlady, her new tenant and everyone else. Life rapidly became a drawn-out torment of trying to look wide awake and work efficiently while wanting only to rest indefinitely. She went to see the doctor in mid-November and he was clearly displeased at her condition.

'You've lost some weight since your visit last month,' he said. 'You certainly should not be doing that at this stage of your pregnancy. You also look very tired. I hope you're not still working.'

'I've eased up', she said, willing brightness into her voice. 'I'm not too interested in food at present, so I expect that's why I lost weight.'

'Hmm, I don't like it at all. Drink as much milk as you can, particularly if you eat less than usual. And you really should have given up work altogether by now. What arrangements have you made for the confinement?'

'I – I haven't made any, yet. Perhaps I should do it now.'

'Should have done it weeks ago. Do you still intend to go into a lying-in hospital? If so, I shall arrange it immediately. You will probably stay there for two weeks after the birth, and considering your youth and – er – isolation, I strongly recommend it.'

'How much will it cost?'

'Between five and ten guineas, depending on what treatment you require. That would be Queen Charlotte's.'

It would take a terrifying bite out of her savings, but she knew he was right. She bit her lip. 'Very well. How do I go about being admitted?'

'If anything happens between now and the date you come to full term, have someone put you in a cab immediately and get around there without wasting any time. Otherwise, report there for admission on the date I give you. They will keep you until the baby is delivered and for a couple of weeks afterwards. Come and see me again before you are due to go in.'

Lottie began feeling ill the following day. It was nothing concrete, just a

general malaise with aches and pains in her legs and shoulders. She determinedly thought of something else and went on with her work, rested every
minute she could and tripled her consumption of fresh milk. Three days later
she was feeling even worse, and when she tried to get up to go to work,
discovered she was unable to stand without stumbling. She went to the
window and waited until a scruffy child passed, heading towards the
Caledonian Road Market.

'Hey, you, little boy! Would you like to earn sixpence?'

'Yeah – what d'ya want me to do?'

'Just go up to the Prince of Denmark and tell the landlord, Mr Giles, that
Lottie is ill and can't come today. I'll give you the money the minute you
come back.'

'Righto – don't go away, missis!' and he was off. Lottie staggered back to
bed and dozed until he returned. He came up to her room for his money, and
she sent him to get her bread and milk, knowing she would be unable to go
out and preferring to trust him than any of her fellow lodgers.

For the rest of the day she slept and woke unevenly, vaguely aware from
time to time that her temperature was climbing alarmingly. She wondered if
there was some epidemic going around. These were certainly not the
symptoms of labour which the doctor had told her to expect.

When she woke again it was dark. Every muscle in her body was aching
and her head pounded. She managed to sit up, find matches and light the
lamp, then her confused mind fixed on the thought that a warm bath would
soothe the muscular aches. When she had made her unsteady way to the
bathroom, she was so relieved to find the water was still hot that she sat crying
weakly on the rickety chair while the tub filled. Then she slid into the
comforting depths and tried to relax. Inevitably, she slept again and woke to
find the water barely tepid.

She clambered out, shivering, towelled herself vigorously to restore the
warmth, pulled her flimsy robe around her now-bulky body, and started for
her room. Halfway down the landing, she hesitated. If only her head would
clear, she would know what was wrong . . . the door . . . something about the
door to her room . . . open. She never left it open. Always locked it . . . she
had the key here, now, in her pocket. Still confused, instead of hurrying back,
Lottie stood swaying on the gloomy landing, fumbling for the key. Yes, here
it was . . . I remember locking it . . . keep the thieves out . . . can't afford to
lose my savings . . .

But her door was open, just a crack. The light of the oil lamp spilled dimly
out. Was someone inside? She hesitated again. What if she caught an
intruder? She was in no state to send them packing . . . but even on the edge
of delirium, Lottie was not prepared to lose everything she had. With a huge
effort, she forced herself to move steadily down the landing and fling the door
wide.

The room was empty. She heaved a sigh of relief and turned back towards
the bed. But wait . . . surely she hadn't gone to the books since becoming ill?
So why were they stacked in the middle of the table? She always kept them on
the shelf in the fireplace alcove. Heart lurching, she sat down at the table and
pulled the top volume towards her. Virgil's *Aeneid* – hardly a piece of
popular fiction that a casual visitor might pick up. This morning it had

121

concealed four five-pound notes. Tonight it was empty. Her second hiding place, a collection of Molière plays, had also been rifled. She had been robbed, and unless the culprit had missed the guineas in her bag, she was completely penniless.

After this first tragedy, Lottie lacked the strength to investigate further. She put her head down on the table and began to cry.

She lost track of time and remained slumped at the table until cold and returning stiffness sent her stumbling back towards the bed. Her one clear memory of that night and the following day was of tugging down the two new blankets from their place in the clothes cupboard. At least she still had warmth . . .

Lottie awoke with a start, perfectly lucid, after dark the next day. She still felt abominably weak but at least her mind was clear. As she remembered the rifled books and glanced across at the table to confirm she had not been dreaming, she almost wished she was delirious again. Then she was distracted from her own crisis by a repetition of the noise that had roused her – scream after agonised scream coming from the room across the landing.

She managed to get out of bed, stumbling to the door and peering round it. Phyllis Noakes, the shifty landlady, was at the new woman tenant's door. Forgetting this was her sole suspect for the theft of her money, Lottie said: 'Mrs Noakes – what's wrong? It sounds as if someone is dying.'

The woman's small bright eyes moved knowingly to her bulging abdomen and she said: 'No such thing – just a little taste of what I dare say you'll soon be going through. I'm off for the midwife . . . nothing to worry about.'

Lottie drew back into her room, horrified at the realisation that she could expect such suffering within a week or two, and cowed by the woman's contemptuous treatment. Now she was certain Mrs Noakes had taken her money. Before, she had preserved at least an element of respect. Now it was clear that she knew Lottie was destitute. Only the thief would be aware of that.

Lottie rekindled the dead fire, heated some milk and sat in the armchair as close as she could get to the warmth. The night wind whistled viciously at the window and she knew she would be better off back in bed, but the spasmodic cries which still came from the other room made her want to stay as far as possible from the wall adjoining the landing, against which the bed stood. Eventually, though, she ceased to have much choice. The muscle pains, chills and sweats of the previous day began to build up again, and she knew she would be helpless soon. Bed was the safest place she could be, and if she got as bad as she had been yesterday, she would scarcely notice the cries from outside.

But this time the attack was more spasmodic. In one interlude of clarity she heard Mrs Noakes walking down the landing with someone else, talking as she went. They entered the room and the door closed. Still the cries continued, endlessly, it seemed. The silence was what woke her next. After the mayhem of the last few hours, the quiet was sufficiently shocking to jolt her from her comatose state. Then she heard a less strident noise – a baby's cries. Thank God, it was over at last! The poor woman had come through it and given birth to a healthy child.

Momentarily, she relaxed, then became fretful. Perhaps she hadn't come through . . . her silence might not be the satisfactory end of labour, but something far worse . . . Already more than half identifying with the other woman, Lottie pushed herself out of bed again. She must go and see . . . make sure everything was well . . . they'd understand, even that awful landlady . . .

This time she did not even wait to put on her robe, but went out in her nightgown. The door opposite was closed. Lottie thought she knocked hard enough, but there seemed to be some sort of minor commotion going on inside and they must have failed to hear. The baby had stopped crying now. Lottie pushed open the door. Three pairs of eyes confronted her with unrelieved hostility. The mother was lying on the bed, hair awry, face still slicked with sweat from her recent ordeal. Mrs Noakes was sitting beside her, leaning close as if in the act of reassuring her. The third occupant of the room, wearing midwife's cap and apron, was putting something swathed in newspaper on a small table against the wall.

'What do *you* want?' snapped Mrs Noakes.

'I – I just wondered . . . did everything go well?' she asked limply.

Their hostility hit her again, like a wave. 'Hardly. It was a stillbirth, wasn't it?' Mrs Noakes's tone was venomous.

'But it can't have been – I heard it crying just a few minutes ago.'

She heard the hissing intake of the midwife's breath as the woman put down her burden and turned back towards the bed, with a questioning glance at Mrs Noakes. The landlady shook her head almost imperceptibly and said: 'From what I've seen of you yesterday an' today, you've been out of your head. Of course you didn't hear it crying. It was born dead – got that?'

As though to illustrate her point, she stood up, strode past Lottie to the table and pulled aside the newspaper. Lottie was confronted by the screwed-up, empty face of the lifeless child. She uttered a terrified sob, turned and stumbled back to her own room, slamming and locking the door behind her.

Now she was submerged in a nightmare. The shock of the robbery, followed by exposure to the apocalyptic scene she had witnessed next door and the resurgence of her illness combined in an all-pervading fever dream from which she was powerless to escape. Now it was *her* baby who lay dead on a cheap table, surrounded by her enemies. She no longer had the strength or the incentive to keep hold of reality, and she drifted temporarily into the refuge of unconsciousness.

CHAPTER FOURTEEN

Ulick spent months trying to forget his attack on Tommy and Lottie. First he got drunk, surfacing to semi-sobriety only for brief interludes over two weeks. When he was sufficiently cogent to remember what had happened, he blamed Lottie, Tommy, and even Nellie Standish, but never himself. That came later.

He was jolted from the first self-destructive binge by the need to do something about Tommy.

Lottie's horrified guess about what Farrell told the police had been true. He had discarded the envelope in which Tommy had received his fifty pounds, and crammed the cash into the boy's pocket. Tommy was still so dazed by the attack and his subsequent forcible removal from the flat that by the time Ulick accosted the policeman in Endell Street, he had still not fully grasped what his persecutor planned to do. By then it was too late. The policeman was shown the cash stuffed in his pocket as though in frantic haste, and assumed Tommy had stolen it, just as Ulick intended. At Bow Street police station he was cautioned and charged, then Ulick made a statement that it was his money, and Tommy was locked up.

If the law had said Tommy must stay incarcerated until Ulick took the matter further, the boy would have remained in the cells for ever. But once the initial complaint had been processed, it was necessary for Ulick to appear as the sole prosecution witness in the case. By then, Lottie had left him and he was some days into his drinking spell. Now that the first vicious surge of jealousy had subsided, he felt deeply ashamed of what he had done.

He knew he could not live with himself if he permitted Fanshaw to be jailed. In the end he stayed sober long enough to report to the police station and say he was dropping the complaint. When the desk sergeant pressed him to proceed, he told a makeshift story about his sister telling him she had borrowed the money, adding that a mutual friend had also said she gave Tommy the fifty pounds found in his possession.

The sergeant looked sceptical but there was nothing he could do to change Ulick's story. The charges were dropped and Ulick left the police station hurriedly before they released Tommy. He had no wish to face the boy, given what now lay between them.

But he was not to shake off his conscience that easily. Tommy Fanshaw loved Lottie and had no intention of giving her up. As far as he knew, she was still at Wilson Street with Ulick. The following morning, Ulick was dragged from drunken slumber by his knock at the apartment door. He wanted to see Lottie and would brook no evasion.

Farrell still had no wish to see Tommy prosper, but there was more to his response than just that: his vanity would never let him confess the girl had left

125

him. Now he glared at Tommy blearily and said: 'No use you coming here for her. I'd had enough after what I saw between the two of you. I sent her packing back to the country. Her uncle came to get her three days after they arrested you.'

'Well where did he take her?'

'Home, where else?' Tommy's hopeful expression moved him to a mirthless chuckle. 'And you might as well forget about any hare-brained scheme to go and set her free. If you think *I* was hard on you, you have no idea what that type of family can do. You'd be jailed for vagrancy before you got past the lodge gates.' In case Tommy still harboured ambitions to see Lottie again, he added: 'In any case, her uncle said they planned to send her off to a French convent school for two years the minute she'd been back to Lyonesse and seen her parents, so you'd better just forget about her. She'll be safely abroad by now.'

He watched with grim satisfaction as the hope died in Tommy's face, then said: 'Now, if you've no further questions, perhaps you would care to go off and leave me in peace. You've done me more than enough damage already.'

Aware that in comparison to the damage he had inflicted on Tommy, his own injuries were minimal, Ulick waited for a spirited counter-attack. But the boy merely gazed at him, almost absently, and said: 'I just hope you can live wiv what you've done, mate. I couldn't, not for five minutes.' Then he turned and went out, like Lottie, leaving the living room door gaping open behind him.

After that days and weeks became a blur to Farrell, usually seen through the bottom of a glass, if at all. He was saved by a bout of sickness of such savagery that he eventually regained consciousness to find himself lying in a pool of dried vomit, in clothes he had not changed for days, and sufficiently sober to be revolted by all of it.

After several attempts he managed to get up, go to the kitchen and clean himself enough to be seen out of doors. Then he went to the Jermyn Street Turkish baths and sweated himself back to relative cleanliness and well-being. Once he had put on fresh clothes and forced down a large cooked breakfast, he felt that some day he might rejoin the human race. In the meantime he resolved to find something less destructive than whisky to take his mind off his recent troubles.

A solution arrived in the shape of work. Ulick realised that even with the money Nellie had left him to get started on the new act, he was now close to penury. He took a couple of sovereigns from his almost-vanished savings, and went off to Romano's to see if any crumbs were available for the picking. It seemed his luck was due to change that day. He ran into an old drinking crony who now worked as a writer on the *Sporting Times*.

The reporter, Sam Walton, seemed uncommonly glad to see him. 'Ulick, my friend, how goes it? Come and let an old acquaintance buy you a drink – you're just the chap I needed to see!'

Over several glasses of hock, he explained that his paper had recently been developing its music hall coverage, on the principle that these days the sporting fraternity patronised the halls with as much enthusiasm as they visited the racecourse.

'We had an ace reporter lined up to work up our coverage, but he dashed off somewhere or other to write bloody songs!' Walton regarded such action as evidence of insanity. 'That got me thinking about you, because I recalled you used to pen the odd ditty, and I thought, wonder if Farrell would be interested in a couple of guineas a week for a few columns of reviews and snippets. Well, would you?'

Ulick hoped the wild elation he felt did not show in his face. Impassively, he said: 'Precisely how many guineas, for how many columns, Sam?'

'Mmm – they said up to five – guineas, that is. No "up to" about the columns, they want three a week, Monday, Wednesday and Friday or Saturday. Mind you, to get the full five guineas you'd have to make the snippets really top notch. No tired old gossip. Free admission to every hall in town, of course, and reasonable expenses for the odd noggin or business supper . . . How about it?'

Ulick gave him a helpful, anything-for-an-old-friend smile and said: 'I confess it would be useful to me to keep abreast of what's going on, if I could get round the halls regularly like that . . . Yes, all right. If they'll throw in the expenses on top of the five guineas, tell your editor he's got a winner.'

'Glad to hear it, old chap . . . don't suppose it would interest you, but there's more and more scope for that sort of thing; Press is crying out for informed music hall writing, y'know. You could pick up all sorts of commissions from other publications, as long as it didn't queer the *Sporting Times*'s pitch.'

By God, he was right, thought Ulick. Why had he been wasting effort scribbling at songs for a guinea a time when he could be paid more for repeating juicy gossip?

After that, he was on the road to recovery. Walton's editor was impressed by Ulick's credentials – academic and show business – and confirmed Walton's offer as soon as he had talked with Farrell. Once the first two articles had appeared under Ulick's by-line, he started receiving commissions from the weekly illustrated press and from national newspapers. If only I had the application, I'd be in danger of making my fortune, he told himself.

Whatever the job lacked, it prevented him thinking about his perfidious treatment of Lottie and Tommy for days at a time. After a while, he was even able to take out his guilt, dust it off and tell himself he had done nothing any reasonable man would not have done. After all, between them they had broken his heart, hadn't they?

He also tried to convince himself that Lottie must have become Charlotte again and gone home to Wiltshire. How else could a gently born girl survive in the city without someone like him to protect her? With something close to desperation, he stifled the voice which said the girl would starve rather than go home, and which then insinuated itself into his nightmares with visions of just how Charlotte Cazenove might be driven to keep body and soul together.

Within a month of starting work as a columnist, he scarcely thought of Charlotte at all – but at night he dreamed about her too often. When he scanned variety bills he found himself not merely seeking interesting prospects for his column, but wondering if her name – or that of Tommy Fanshaw – would crop up anywhere. He never saw either name, and concluded that Tommy must have changed his. He forced himself to refrain from any such assumption about Charlotte, preferring to believe she was back in Lyonesse.

His acquaintance in the music hall world, already wide, grew day by day, and

127

after an interview with the rising agent, Larry Nash, he found himself growing increasingly friendly with the man. Nash was a little older than Ulick, but still of the same generation. He lacked Ulick's polish, but possessed qualities the Irishman would never aspire to. He was tougher, sharper and more single-minded than Farrell, but admired the other's talent with words and music and enjoyed his company. He gave Ulick leads for several good stories which he sold as colour pieces to periodicals, making hefty sums in addition to his regular payment from the *Sporting Times*.

It was with such a piece in mind that Nash invited him to the old Rose of Normandy one Tuesday evening. 'Shouldn't think there's much else to distract you this early in the week,' he said, 'and there could be a good line in it for you, as journalist and as song-writer. Ever considered how all these kids with ambition but no contacts manage to get on the halls?'

Ulick did not want to tell him he had personal experience of helping just such a one before destroying her. He looked intrigued and shook his head.

'The pub-halls are one way,' Nash went on. 'The Rose likes to think of itself as a music hall these days, but you can't compare it with a place like the Oxford – or even a dive like the Hoxton Varieties, come to that. It's still a pub with a stage rather than a theatre without plays, if you see what I mean. There are scores of hopefuls appearing in places like that, just on the brink of making the profession proper.

'An old friend asked me to take a look at one of them last night. I did; I was impressed but I told him she needed a good original song-writer. I said I'd be back with one. There are a couple of men I know would be interested, but I think you can get some good journalism out of it, too.

'I can't get there this evening until after she's been on, but I said I'd at least go back and introduce you tonight, then possibly you could go back tomorrow for her act if you agree she's talented. Could at least make a piece for you if she's any good. If you're as keen as I am, you'll do well to start writing for her as well as about her.'

He was right, thought Ulick. Even forgetting the song-writing opportunity, the general idea was a good one for an article. And if the first piece proved interesting, he could put aside one evening a week to look in on such places and tip the more likely talent in subsequent articles. Some of them would inevitably make their names and he might build a reputation as a talent spotter. 'What's this girl's name?' he asked.

Larry shook his head. 'No, no preconceptions. I'm leaving her as much a blank page to you on first exposure as she was to me. I think she's special, but it may just be that I'd like to get her between the sheets, so I don't want to prejudice you. If you think she's impossible, I shan't ask you to go back there with me tomorrow, never fear.'

'Oh, I think I might enjoy it. I haven't been in that sort of place since my undergraduate days.'

Nash grinned at him. 'In your undergraduate days, I was *working* in that sort of place!'

He was aware of her before she saw him, which at least gave him an opportunity to armour himself against the encounter. Nash greeted Joe Smith, who joined them at the long bar. 'Just missed her by five minutes, Larry,' he said. 'Pity, she was 'specially good tonight.'

128

'Never mind. She was pretty good last night, in my eyes. I've kept my song-writer here in the dark about her. As he won't see her on stage tonight, go ahead and tell him a little about her.'

Joe turned to Ulick with the pride of a father. 'She needs a lot o'polish yet, but she's got what it takes to get right to the top. Good timing; big strong voice; marvellous shape and face . . . and then there's this funny accent . . .' Ulick was beginning to sweat as Smith went on, 'You'd never pin it down in a 'undred years if you didn't know – she's Clerkenwell Italian. Name's Lottie Casanova, of all things!'

Nash looked up. 'Ulick, are you all right? You look as if someone spat in your porter.'

'Er . . . yes, of course. Just wool-gathering, that's all. Nothing important.' Covertly he began casting about for some means of escape. He might come back here alone some time, but he could not handle a confrontation now, with these two on hand to witness God knew what recriminations.

But before he could work anything out, Smith said: 'Ah, here she is now, large as life as twice as lovely . . . I'll get her.'

Still hoping for a miracle, Ulick remained facing stolidly away from the direction Joe indicated. At that point he realised he had no alternative to brazening it out. As if in slow motion, he saw Larry Nash's growing smile of appreciation as Lottie approached from behind him. He knew, as clearly as if he too were facing that direction, just what his friend was seeing. The thought raised a semi-hysterical, mimicking smile on his own face, which was still pasted there when he turned, so, so slowly, in an effort not to make a fool of himself.

There she was, heavily painted for the stage but looking even more glorious than when he had last seen her. Her maturing beauty hit him so hard that instinct took over from there and the bland lie tripped easily off his tongue: 'Hello, Lottie, where have you been hiding? I've been looking every-where for you.'

One terrified sob escaped her before her hand flew to her lips as though to suppress all further sound. She stood rooted to the spot for a long moment, then turned and ran from him, pushing aside surprised customers who turned to gaze curiously at the three men beside the bar.

Joe stared at both of them in turn, then said: 'What was that about? No – don't tell me. I'll go an' find 'er first.' Then he slipped unobtrusively after Lottie towards the back corridor.

Larry Nash had seen more of the incident than Joe, and had realised Farrell knew a great deal more than either of them about this new performer. His formerly friendly expression had melted into neutrality and now he stared at Ulick, not speaking. Ulick could not think of an explanation which would even begin to cover the situation, so he sat staring back, trying unsuccessfully to remove a sheepish smile from his face.

The two men were still silent when Smith returned about five minutes later, deeply embarrassed. 'Terribly sorry, Larry, but she's scarpered. Didn't even change, just pulled 'er coat on over her costume, grabbed her street clothes an' went. What can I say?'

For form's sake, Nash assumed the scowl of a thwarted impresario, but Ulick could see the agent was more intrigued than angry. 'Not your fault, Joe, but don't expect me to risk coming back here a third time. If your young protégée decides to show, let me know and I'll try to see Mr Farrell makes it later in the week. Judging by the speed she took off just now, she doesn't plan to come back.'

Still apologising profusely, Joe withdrew, promising to let Nash know when Miss Casanova was appearing again. As soon as he was gone, Larry turned to Ulick and said: 'Now, how about you and me going somewhere out of all this spit and sawdust and you telling me all about that little scene. I have a feeling you're the one I should be choking off, not Joe Smith.'

They went to Romano's for a late supper. Ulick drank a lot and ate almost nothing while he told Nash a savagely edited version of his life with Charlotte Cazenove. It included her roots but barely touched on Tommy Fanshaw and certainly failed to mention that Ulick had wrongly accused him of theft. In his version, he had caught them in bed together, had driven Fanshaw out of the flat and then beaten up Lottie, who had fled.

'I felt so ashamed about it all – I'd never hit a woman before – that I couldn't face trying to find her . . . that remark about looking for her was purest bluff . . . Oh, Christ, no wonder that poor girl was so frightened. She probably thought I'd start on her again . . .' By now he was drunk enough to believe his own fantasy.

Nash was gazing at him as steadily and as neutrally as he had in the Rose. 'So what are your intentions now?'

'I don't think I have any say in the matter. She made her feelings clear.'

'Ulick, she's barely sixteen – although I'd never have believed that if you hadn't told me; she's alone in London and she shows all the signs of possessing great talent. Don't you think you should suppress your gentlemanly delicacy about having beaten her senseless, go and apologise and try to make some sort of restitution? She needs protection both as a woman and as an artiste. You hardly need me to tell you what a savage world music hall is.' Farrell failed to respond. 'Dammit, man, you *owe* it to her!'

Farrell looked up, haggard now. 'I can't, Larry! I only wish I could . . . she has to come back to me. If she does, I know I'm forgiven and I can start again.'

'Balderdash! If she does, your male pride will remain intact – and before too long you'll knock her about again. I don't think we have any more to say to each other. I still think you should try to repair the situation, but if you won't, I shall go back to the Rose myself in a couple of weeks. If Miss Casanova has returned – which I doubt – I shall offer my professional services.

'And now, I shall settle the bill and leave you over your wine. Somehow I find your company less enjoyable than usual.'

After that, he saw little of Nash. The agent did not avoid him, but Ulick found it impossible to be comfortable in his company, always feeling he was being judged and found wanting.

He was moderately relieved to find he did not turn immediately to the bottle to forget the painful encounter with Lottie. The day after she ran from him, he received two major commissions, from a national newspaper and a monthly magazine, and the magazine job was his first venture into general journalism, unrelated to the stage. The work absorbed him sufficiently to get him over the first days of self-loathing, and after that it was easy enough to push Lottie back into the mental lumber-room she shared with so many of his past sins.

Weeks turned to months, and in mid-November he was putting the finishing touches to a long feature article for the *Illustrated London News* about the development of pantomime. He was still living in the Wilson Street flat, but beginning to consider moving somewhere more fashionable now that his earnings were rising so fast. In the meantime, he discouraged professional and social contacts from visiting him at home, preferring to keep up appearances by entertaining them in restaurants. He was surprised and irritated, therefore, when someone knocked on his door just as he was checking the final version of the pantomime article.

When he greeted the visitor, irritation instantly turned to astonishment. It was Hillary Fane. He and Fane had lived in rooms on the same stair at their Oxford college. They shared an interest in the more raffish side of London night life and had taken endless pleasure trips to the city together, admiring the same Gaiety Girls, topping each other's discovery of outlandish music hall characters and even collaborating on a few shaky songs.

In other circumstances, they would have remained close friends for life. As it was, Ulick's dispossession by his father meant he could no longer enjoy a sybaritic existence in London. To complicate matters further, Fane was Laura Cazenove's first cousin. Ulick had visited the family mansion in Warwickshire several times, and Lady Fane's enthusiastic testimony to his good character had clinched the teaching post at Lyonesse for him.

Now Ulick fought an impulse to gape at Fane. He could scarcely fail to be aware of what had happened at Lyonesse. Even the Cazenoves would find it impossible to explain away the disappearance of their only daughter on the very day they had dismissed her tutor. Whatever their past friendship, this man must now regard him as an enemy.

When Fane spoke, he certainly did not sound like a friend. 'Farrell, forgive me for disturbing you at home –' his tone said he was indifferent about whether Ulick did so '– but the family has asked me to perform a most delicate task, and I think you might be the one to help.'

'B-by all means, if I can. But do they know you're coming to see me?'

Fane glanced with distaste along the open landing. 'Must we discuss such a private matter in public? I assure you I shan't become violent if you let me in.'

Silently damning himself for being so crass, Ulick stood aside and ushered the other man into the living room. 'I have a feeling a drink would help us both through the next ten minutes,' he said, and hurried out to the kitchen.

When he returned with whisky, water and tumblers, Fane had mellowed somewhat. He said: 'Let's not mince matters: I don't blame you for being taken with young Charty – sometimes found it difficult to keep my own hands off her – but it put Mama into the most appalling position with the family, having vouched for you and all. Things will never be the same at Lyonesse, y'know.'

'I'll bet! How is the fair Laura taking it?'

Hillary took a long swallow of his whisky and said: 'Odd, that. She behaves almost as if she were pleased. Pays lip service to the great tragedy when there's a family conference about it, of course, but underneath I think she's glad the competition has gone away. Poor old Gregory is another matter. That's really why I'm here.'

Ulick nodded. 'I really regretted doing such a thing to him. He always treated me well. But look, old chap, I don't know what they told you . . . I didn't take Charlotte – she ran after me.'

Fane chuckled grimly. 'If Gregory didn't know that, you would have heard from the family before this, I assure you. It's the sole reason for his restraint until now. But he's become quite desperate recently; sufficiently so to snap Laura's head off when she told him for the umpteenth time he should regard Charty as dead. That finally pushed him over the edge and he said he was bringing her home whatever the cost to Laura's pride.

'Laura had a real tantrum then, and in the end they compromised with Gregory saying Charty could go to stay with his sister in the Highlands for an indefinite time. I think that calmed Laura down because she sees Scotland and Isabel as a punishment worse than Dante's Inferno and could think of no one she'd rather inflict it on than poor Charty. So, having settled that, and knowing I was the only trustworthy soul they knew who was familiar with your pre-Lyonesse stamping grounds, they blackmailed me by saying it was all my fault that you'd ever met Charty, and sent me to track you down.'

'Are the police involved?'

'Really, Farrell, don't be absurd! Can you see my crowd doing anything so indiscreet? I am their Sherlock Holmes; there is no Inspector Lestrade.'

Ulick brightened perceptibly. 'What must I do?'

'Help me to track her down, of course. I found you from our old information post, Romano's. And before you start seething about that, let me assure you they only passed on your address because they remembered all the time and money we used to spend there together, and believed me when I said we had accidentally lost touch. Now, to business. I take it that as you've failed to produce her from behind the arras, you and she are no longer living *à deux*.'

'Not for a long time. I won't bore you with sordid details, but please try to believe me when I tell you I was never Charlotte's lover.' Fane raised a sceptical eyebrow. 'Strictly between you and me, only because someone else beat me to it,' Farrell added hastily. 'I'm telling you that now merely to explain why we are not together any more. I'd never have been enough of a bounder to throw her out if there had been anything important between us.'

'So you did throw her out?'

'No – really, it wasn't like that. We had a row and she left. Disappeared.'

Fane sighed. 'Then this visit is a wild goose chase?'

'I didn't say so. I've run into her since, to my considerable embarrassment. She may not be where I saw her any longer, but we could start there.'

'Will I be shocked beyond words if you tell me the exact location of "there"?'

'Couldn't say, old chap; she's not my cousin. When were you last in the Rose of Normandy?'

'Good God – I may have been there once or twice, when we were up at Balliol, but not since then.'

'Don't worry – she wasn't selling her fair body for a plate of meat pie. She was trying to break into music hall as a singer.'

132

Hillary's jaw dropped, then he began to laugh. 'You hardly need me to tell you that's almost as bad!' he said.

'Oo's asking? This ain't an information bureau, ya know!' Harry Nelson was at his most obstreperous.

'We're old friends of Lottie's, Mr Nelson. I called to see her act the last night she appeared here, but I haven't seen her since.'

'Nor me, neither, more's the pity. That girl really had somefink. Look, sorry I went off the deep end, but you're the second one to come asking questions. I've had a music hall agent round here twice now – last time only about a fortnight ago. I get sick of having to say I dunno where she went.'

'Would that have been Larry Nash?'

'Yeah, that's right; said he wanted to talk to her about some bookings. I said join the queue, so do I.'

'So you couldn't direct him anywhere.'

'Only to Joe Smith. Joe saw Lottie after she walked out of 'ere. Picked up her last wage packet an' delivered it. Maybe he'll know. He's out the back, by the dressing rooms. Go on through if you like . . . I got work to do.'

In the back corridor, Joe gave Ulick a hostile look and stood up a little straighter, as though preparing himself for violent action. Ulick hoped it was no more than bravado. He was in no mood for dealing with a man who looked as if he had been surviving street fights when Ulick was still in petticoats.

Joe listened to him courteously enough, then said: 'No idea where she went. You'll 'ave to try someone else.'

'But you took her last wages . . . you must have known where she was!'

'Yeah, then I did. She 'ad a place over Clerkenwell, didn't she? But as soon as she had her money she was off. And she didn't leave no forwarding address.'

'Does she know where *you* live?'

'May do. What of it?'

'In that case, at least take my card, and if you hear from her, send to let me know at once.'

'What if she don't want me to?'

'I promise I shan't do anything to harm her, Smith. I – we – just want to talk to her. Her family are worried half to death about her.'

'Yeah. It 'appens. Tragic. If that's all, I'll be getting along.'

'The card, Smith. Please don't forget. It's as important to Lottie as it is to us.'

Joe took the card between thumb and forefinger, with an expression which suggested it might contaminate him. 'As I said, I'll be getting along.' He turned his back with a finality that prevented Ulick from speaking again.

Outside, Fane said: 'That seems to be that. How can we hope to track her down when she could be anywhere?'

'Don't give up hope yet. Smith would have been a fool if he'd missed the effect I had on Charlotte. She bolted as if she thought I was about to attack her . . .' He stopped talking, abruptly remembering he had not told Fane about beating her up.

'Why would she do that?'

He improvised wildly. 'Probably thought I was there on much the same errand as I was running today. Face it, Hillary. She wants no part of Lyonesse.'

'Nevertheless, Lyonesse wants a part of her. You were saying, there might be another way. What is it?'

'Well, first, it's going to be a slow job. No use your hanging about, hoping I'll come up with an answer overnight, but I think I might prise something out of that agent.'

'If she didn't want to see you, she'd hardly see him, either.'

'Don't be too sure. She wants to be a music hall star, remember? The temptation to get a good agent might be too strong to resist. After all, if she really wanted to go on the halls and avoid me, she need only change her name again. Then I'd have no idea who she was unless I happened to go to one of her performances. Not that likely when you consider the number of halls in London, is it?'

'So what do you propose to do?'

'You go back to the Cazenoves and tell them you've set enquiries in motion. I'll sound out this agent chap, explain the family concern and so on, and then we'll see.'

'Doesn't sound too hopeful to me.'

'Perhaps not, but it's all you've got.'

Phyllis Noakes decided it was time she did something about her second-floor front lodger. The rent had been due two days ago and she did not believe in encouraging arrears. The fact that all the lodger's money was tucked into a strongbox in her back kitchen did not deter her from putting on the pressure. After what the nosey little bitch had seen, the sooner they were shot of her, the better.

She puffed up to the second floor and called into the back room first to see her temporary tenant. 'How you doin', then, Mary? Feeling a bit better today?'

The woman smiled shakily. 'Very much, ta. Once that doctor produced 'is death certificate, it worked wonders for me condition. Pity about that damned kid blundering in, though.'

'Nah – no need to worry about that one. She's so ill she's arf daft anyhow . . . oh, now don't take on, girl. You know it wouldn't 'ave worked.' As she dismissed Lottie's significance,the other woman's bravado had crumbled and she started crying weakly. Now Mrs Noakes sat down beside her and put an arm awkwardly around her shoulders. 'Don't take on, love. You'll soon get over it.'

'B-but he was so little and – and helpless . . . oh, Phyl, I didn't want that midwife to do it! I'll never forgive meself.'

'Now look 'ere, if you hadn't gone through wiv it, and the brewery had found out you'd had a brat, Bert woulda lost that pub in five minutes. And then you, he and the baby woulda been out on the street in half a minute. You can 'ave other kids when you got a pub o' your own. You just stop fretting and get some rest . . . Bert'll be around to take you 'ome tomorrow and you'll be better in no time. Oh, an' when he comes, he will 'ave the money, won't he? That woman'll need paying tomorrow, then there's the cash for this room and the doctor and so on.'

134

Mary turned her head away, an expression of disgust on her ravaged face. 'Yeah, don't worry. You'll get your pound a flesh.'

Mrs Noakes turned on her like a viper. 'If I was you, my lady, I'd watch me tongue. You owe me a lot, you do, and don't you forget it!'

'I wish I *could* forget, but I never will.'

The landlady glared at her for a moment longer, then turned and stalked out to go and see Lottie.

When she walked into the front bedroom she wondered if for once she had gone too far. There was an appalling smell, and the room was icy cold – by the look of the grate, the fire had gone out at least twenty-four hours ago. The oil lamp, too, had gone out. Mrs Noakes muttered an oath and groped in her pocket for some matches. Some tenants just wouldn't look after themselves . . . why use the oil lamp when there were perfectly good gas mantles? She turned on the tap and put a match to the small wall-mounted gas jet near the door. Once the mantle warmed properly and the first flaring light had spread to a more even glow, she glanced round and gave a sharp gasp at what she saw.

The source of the stench became obvious. Lottie had gone through a labour of sorts, and lay in the appalling, decomposed fragments of what she had produced. Mrs Noakes had seen enough genuine stillbirths to know this was one where the baby had been dead a long time before the mother went into labour. At first she considered simply leaving the room and pretending she knew nothing of what had happened. Then, almost automatically, she moved across to the still, twisted form on the stinking bed and bent to feel for a pulse.

She was still alive. There was a vague fluttering there if she pressed very firmly . . . Again the hesitation. Was it worth all the fuss of nosey parkers coming around, just to stop one little forsaken drab dying? She remembered the money in her strongbox. One way and another, it had been a pretty profitable tenancy. She went to find the girl's bag. Perhaps there would be some hint of who could be contacted to take her away and get help for her.

Mrs Noakes had come across the loose change and guinea coins when she ransacked the room a couple of evenings earlier. She ignored them now for the same reason as before – a victim who still had some money was less readily believed than one who was quite destitute.

She pushed aside the little purse of money and looked in the pocket of the bag. There she found a crumpled corner of newspaper. On it was scrawled: *Joe & Hilda Smith, 48 Wrotham Road, Camden Town.* It was the only identification of any kind she found in Lottie's possession, apart from a book plate pasted inside the front cover of the Molière which she had raided earlier that week. The plate showed a Pierrot offering a slim volume to a Columbine, and on its cover was the legend *Charlotte Cazenove: Lyonesse, Wiltshire.* Talk about upper crust! Just because she found some second-hand book that had been owned by a toff with a name like hers, this un had spent good money on it. Serve her right if she got robbed! She didn't have any idea of what the world was like.

The stink in the room was becoming oppressive, even to one with sensibilities as blunted as Phyllis Noakes's. She left everything else and took the dog-eared piece of newspaper, then set off back downstairs to find someone who would go to Camden Town.

Just as well my Hilda's seen it all, thought Joe Smith, as he reeled out of Lottie's lodging house room a couple of hours later. How could women nerve themselves to clear up after something like that, when they knew it might be their turn next month or next year? He shuddered, and turned his thoughts back to Lottie.

Once Mrs Noakes had summoned them, all Joe and his wife could do was arrange for the girl to be taken to Queen Charlotte's. He had bluffed that by saying he was contacting her family and they would be along to square the account. He knew all too well that Lottie's few guineas and the tiny savings he and Hilda owned would never cover the bill. Now he had to find someone who could bail Lottie out. He thought again of her yellow-ashen face against the pillow. Maybe she wouldn't need no one to bail her out . . . looking like that, she might never come out of it at all.

He still had two business cards. He knew he must alert one of the men, but which one? That first chap, the agent – he'd swear there was no trouble for Lottie from that quarter. He'd known Nash a long time, and heard nothing bad of him in that direction. If only she'd stayed all right a couple of days longer, he could have asked her himself.

On the other hand, the second one, the one Lottie had been really scared of . . . he'd been far more concerned about her than the agent. Joe had no wish to involve Larry Nash if the man had only a business relationship in mind. He had never taken Lottie's fear of Ulick too seriously. Joe came from a society where men beat women for no good reason save that they were there. Lottie seemed to have suffered no permanent ill effects from whatever Farrell had done to her.

He stood outside the bedroom, puzzling about the whole business, and then finally decided he must rely on Lottie's sincerity about her fear of Farrell. Once Lottie was safely dispatched to Queen Charlotte's, still just clinging to life, he set out for Larry Nash's rooms off Theobalds Road.

When Joe arrived, Nash was locking his front door before leaving for an evening out. He wore full evening dress and carried a fancy silver-headed cane. As Joe softly called his name, he looked up with some impatience, anxious to be gone.

'Yes, what is it, man? Good God, you look dreadful! Half a tick and I'll let us back in. I think you need a brandy.'

Embarrassed, Joe grinned. 'Reckon you may be right, an' all. Funny, I thought I was tough.'

In the warm drawing room full of overstuffed furniture and gleaming polished wood, Joe took his brandy at one gulp and told his story. Nash stared at him, aghast. 'You mean you and I are the closest she has? No family, nothing?'

'Well, I reckon that geezer you brought the night she cut an' run knew her better than either of us ever will, but I didn't like to get him, in case it set Lottie off again. Thought you was safer, Larry. You've always got a calm head on your shoulders.'

'I don't feel calm now. Farrell, Farrell – how much of this was your doing?' He gazed into the fire for a while and said: 'I suppose we shall never know the answer to that one. Nevertheless, I think we'll have to get him, Joe. If the girl survives at all, she'll need more than one friend and one casual acquaintance to pull her through. Don't worry about the hospital bill. Farrell and I can sort something out between us. Go back to the hospital, give them my name and address for that, and I'll find Ulick. And he'd better be sober!'

CHAPTER FIFTEEN

It was a long time before the hospital was able to tell Ulick Lottie would recover. For a week, her mere survival was in question, and the physician thought she might be a permanent invalid even if she lived. But she was stronger than she had looked when they admitted her, and halfway through the second week she began drifting up towards consciousness.

Ulick had sat at her bedside every moment they allowed him to stay. During the lonely vigil, he had thought over his mistreatment of Lottie and had finally confronted his responsibility for what had happened to her that year. If she did not panic and shrink from him when she regained her sensibilities, he would make a home for her and nurse her back to full health. After that, he would make her into a music hall star who would put all others in the shade. The strategy was as stimulating as fine wine. Once he had thought it through, he decided it might suit him as well as it did Lottie.

Dim dreams, pain and weakness had comprised Lottie's awareness for the time since her collapse. The terrors of her last days at the Camden lodging house had temporarily wiped out earlier troubles. Now, emerging from the dark mists of illness to find Farrell there as her protector, she welcomed him with open arms. So much had happened to her since they parted that the quarrel seemed a minor matter in comparison. Now she needed someone strong to look after her, and Ulick fitted the bill.

Once she was on her feet again, being helped shakily around the ward by a nurse, Farrell did some serious thinking about what he would take her home to. Hillary Fane had contacted him again the previous week to ask if he had made any progress in tracing her, and he had evaded a straight answer, saying he still had leads to follow. At first he had thought he was co-operating with Fane in trying to reunite Lottie with her family, but now he recognised he had acted solely out of self-interest. He had thought Lottie was lost to him forever, and the knowledge that she was at least materially secure would have salved his conscience.

Having seen her helpless and mortally ill, he was more in love with her than he had ever been, and she seemed miraculously to have been restored to him. It would have amounted to betrayal if he had sent her back to the Cazenoves now. But if he did not send her back, he must get away from Fane. That meant giving up Wilson Street and not blabbing to anyone at Romano's about his new address. The move would be no great hardship; it was the logical consequence of his desire for more elegant surroundings. But where should he go?

He decided he need not move far. Covent Garden suited him too well for the suburbs to exert any attraction, and the other central areas of London were either too rough or too expensive. If he moved westward, beyond the fruit market, there were far more graceful apartments available than the Wilson

Street flat, and it might as well be on the moon as far as any connection with the old address was concerned. As long as he concocted a story which would satisfy Fane and stop him prowling around after Lottie in future, everything should go smoothly.

He found an attractive flat in Henrietta Street. Like Wilson Street, it was on the first floor, but after that all resemblance ended. The new place had spacious rooms with high ceilings and elegant plasterwork. It had a small kitchen – perfectly acceptable, as neither he nor Lottie was any sort of cook – and its own bathroom. There was a large bedroom at the back, a drawing room looking down into the street, and a well-appointed third room which would serve admirably as rehearsal space and study. Farrell signed a three-year lease on the place, then set about furnishing it, starting with a good quality upright piano.

By the time he had finished, he had exhausted the funds he had built up over the past six months and run up a certain amount of debt. But these days he came by money easily enough, and he told himself he owed it to Lottie.

After setting up their new home, he sat down to compose a letter that would throw Fane off the scent.

Dear Hillary

I had hoped to have good news in our search for Charlotte, but all to no avail. Yesterday I tracked down someone who had been in touch with her until a few weeks ago, who satisfied me we would never succeed in finding her. It seems she went to sing at another pub-music hall and while she was there, she took up with some sort of commercial traveller from the North of England. The theatrical life must have started to pall, and after a week or so she cancelled her pub booking and went off with him. She told the girl whose dressing room she shared that they were going to Darlington and planned to marry. I fear you and her parents will find this news most painful, but that you will agree with me that she has now passed beyond the reach of all of us. I wish there were more I could do, but there is nothing.

Ulick Farrell

He chuckled grimly as he sealed the envelope. The Cazenoves might have accepted a slightly soiled daughter, rescued after a disastrous romantic elopement with one of their own kind, but a commercial traveller from Darlington? Never! Pity about Gregory Cazenove, but then, Lottie would never willingly have returned to the bosom of her family, so better to sever the connection quickly and cleanly now. He posted the letter, then went to find the lawyer who managed Nellie's Wilson Street properties to give notice of his departure.

At first he thought she was no longer the Lottie Casanova he had seen developing during the months in Wilson Street. She seemed subdued, too serene. It went ill with her flamboyant looks, and furthermore it augured badly for her talent. Shrinking violets seldom came across well on a music hall stage. He need not have worried. After a week or two at the new apartment, during which she sat at the window most of the time and looked out like a spectator rather than a participant in the life of London, she announced abruptly that she was ready to go for a walk on her own. Farrell's first impulse was to say he must accompany her, but something held him back. Perhaps it was wishful thinking, but there seemed at last to be a spark of independence regenerating itself.

That first solo expedition tired her, but she persevered and by the end of January she was making longer and longer trips on her own. She seldom talked about where she had been, merely reappearing in the early evening, looking better than when she had left. He grew so accustomed to her absence during the afternoon that one day, coming in early after delivering an article, the sound of the piano took him by surprise. Now who the devil could have come to see her? The only people who knew her whereabouts were Joe and Hilda Smith and Larry Nash. Both Joe and Nash played the piano – which of them was it?'

The thought provoked a stab of jealousy and Ulick hurried up the last few stairs to the first floor landing. He opened the front door and that was when he heard her voice:

> 'They say that hearts and flowers
> Are the sign of love that's true;
> But oh! They just remind me
> Of the heart I lost to you.'

Ulick rushed into the rehearsal room. Lottie was alone, sitting at the piano, accompanying her own song. She heard the door open and turned to smile at him. 'It's coming back, Ulick – I can feel it. Will you write me a song as good as the one you wrote for Nellie?'

He pulled her to her feet and smothered her in a great hug that combined relief, love and re-emerging desire. 'I'll write you a hundred songs, and you'll take them around the world, my love!'

That night he made love to her for the first time, gently, persuasively, more the experienced husband with his virgin bride than the playboy with his runaway houri. She had lost the fire he had sensed in her an age ago in Lyonesse, but had acquired a tenderness that transported him to heights he had not known with any other woman.

In the small hours of the next morning, lying on his back with a sleeping Lottie cradled against his shoulder, he wondered if the wild girl would ever return to displace this pliant mistress, just as the talented performer was advancing to reclaim her territory from the frightened child he had brought back from hospital. He decided that on balance he would prefer her to stay as she had been tonight . . .

Ulick woke just after dawn, and she was missing. He slid out of bed and went out into the drawing room. Lottie was sitting at the window on the upholstered seat, gazing down into the street. She wore his dressing gown.

'What are you doing out here? You'll freeze to death!' he said.

'I was thinking Ulick . . . thinking about Nellie. I went to her house yesterday.'

'Why? You know it was let to a new tenant months ago.'

She nodded. 'Yes, but I needed to bring her back, and somehow, with all that's happened lately, she was getting blurred in my mind. So I stood in the square, and looked up Gower Street – the window boxes and awnings are still there – and squinched my eyes up, and it almost seemed as if she'd just gone in.

'I walked back here, and all the way I made myself remember her, what she said to me, what she taught me. She was right, you know. You can't *get* at an audience until you really know what they've been through. Knowing that was part of what made her so good. Well, now I know, too, and it will help me . . .' the little gush of words dried up and she began to cry. '. . . It must help me, mustn't it? All that misery couldn't have been for nothing?'

He swept her into his arms and held her close until the sobs subsided. 'Nothing's ever for nothing, my love,' he murmured against her hair. 'Everything matters in the end, although sometimes we don't realise it at the time.'

Something of the old, fiery Lottie began to re-awaken. He felt it stir in her as he kissed her, his compassion giving place to desire so abruptly he could not remember the moment when it changed. He eased the harsh woollen dressing gown down off her perfect shoulders and gazed at her. Lottie stared back at him – the Lottie he had known, when was it, a century ago? Surely more than a few months? Ulick was swept by a vision of Botticelli's Birth of Venus. Here was Venus re-born, emerging from a prosaic blanket of concealment, passionate, desirable, forever unattainable. But he could attain her . . . he had, hadn't he? She was here, now, all his . . . a memory of Tommy Fanshaw intruded and he forced it out of his mind.

Lottie had slipped the dressing gown further down her snowy arms and had edged close to him. She took his hand, raised it and pressed it against her left breast. 'Show me, Ulick. Please show me how to love you properly,' she murmured. She leaned back against the tall shutter at the far end of the window seat. Ulick's hand, apparently with a will of its own, caressed her breast in a hypnotic, circular motion. His other hand gently displaced the lower edge of the robe, exposing the long legs. A sigh escaped her as she watched his fingers slide up the satiny inner surface of her thigh, and her legs parted, magically, to receive his exploring caress. She gave a small shudder of delight as he touched her, and murmured, 'Don't stop, please don't stop . . .'

Momentarily, he stopped stroking her breast and untied the silk cord which held the dressing gown at the waist. He pushed it back off her and her body arched against the exploring fingers now deep inside her. She snatched at his free hand and clamped it back against her body. Ulick cupped her breast and bent forward, engulfing the nipple with his lips. As his tongue played against it, he felt it swell and harden in his mouth and she moaned with excitement. Her hair had tumbled loose over her shoulders and it intensified his own arousal as he felt the heavy, silky mass brushing the side of his face. Now she was pressing his head hard against her breasts, breathing harshly, her whole body thrusting rhythmically towards him.

Briefly he broke free of her, and she opened her eyes to look at his nakedness. He took both her hands and pressed them around his hugely erect penis and murmured to her, 'I want that in you, I want you on me, quick, now!'

'Show me how!'

'Like this,' he said, lifting her bodily and shifting her into a sitting position above him on the wide window seat. He pinned her on to his body from behind, pressing her down against him by her shoulders, thrusting into her repeatedly while she cried out in mounting passion.

When she reached the high pitch of excitement it was as though a dam burst and he was deluged with her explosive pleasure, triggering his own fulfilment.

Ulick collapsed, shuddering, against her perfect back, moaning small endearments. Lottie slumped over his restraining arms, and leaned back on him. They remained thus, exhausted, for long minutes, then he eased her off him, turning her so that she was sitting across his lap.

He brushed aside the moist tendril of hair that had fallen across her forehead, and kissed the corner of her mouth. 'There,' he whispered, 'how does that feel?'

'Better than anything I ever felt before, Ulick . . . is that the way it should always be?'

Chance would be a fine thing! he told himself, but to Lottie he only said, 'Yes, my darling, always.'

'Oh, Ulick – why did I ever leave you?'

Farrell fought to keep the Cheshire-cat smile off his face. 'Hush, now . . . we all make mistakes, don't we?'

He led her back to bed, and soon she was asleep in his arms again. But he lay wide awake until it was time to get up, wondering whether there was any truth in what he had just told her with such conviction.

The bookings began in April. Farrell had not considered Lottie ready for public performances until mid-March. Then he went to Larry Nash and asked the agent around to Henrietta Street to see what he thought of Lottie. Nash had called to see her a couple of times when she was convalescing, but had not been there since she started rehearsing in early February.

He sat through her routine and bowed gravely to her when she had finished. 'I've been waiting to hear you sing material like that since last spring,' he told her. 'If you want one, you now have an agent.' He glanced at Ulick. 'I take it you already have a manager.'

Ulick smiled smoothly at him. 'She has, and about time, too. From now on, Lottie's going to have her work cut out becoming a first-rate artiste, without having to worry about all the off-stage business. That's where you and I come in.'

'Then I suggest all three of us meet for supper tonight and discuss some details.'

Before Lottie could speak, Ulick waved his hand dismissively. 'Lottie will have supper with us some other time – Friday, perhaps, if you're free. If there's business to discuss, just talk to me at present. I don't want her worried about non-essentials yet.'

Nash gave him a long, cool look. 'I'd hardly call planning her own professional career a non-essential. Surely she should be involved in that?'

'Of course, of course – but she's been ill, and she's starting from scratch, remember? I think it will be better all round if I take on that part of the burden for the moment. Shall we say eight o'clock this evening, at the Café Royal?'

Nash glanced at Lottie but she was flicking through a pile of sheet music, an expression of acute embarrassment on her face. He shrugged, dismissing the problem. 'As you wish. We'll need to go over just what sort of money, and what sort of spots, you're looking for, before we get her started. I'll see you at eight.'

He got up to leave, pausing for a couple of minutes at the door to discuss some business afterthought that had occurred to him.

143

Lottie hovered inside the rehearsal room, wondering why she felt so left out when it was her future and her wellbeing they were discussing. She had agreed that it was best for her to keep out of that side of things. Ulick had the experience, she didn't. Still . . . it would be nice to know where she was going. She tried to dismiss the feeling of unease, and went back to run through a tune on the piano for the twentieth time that day.

Between them, Ulick Farrell and Larry Nash planned out for Lottie the hardest year's work of her life. Neither man intended it to be so strenuous; it was simply that once the bookings started, it was hard to stop the flow.

Three months into Lottie's new career, Nash said to Ulick: 'A year like this and she'll be well on her way to the top. I may have my doubts about your autocratic methods, but by God, you get a good performance out of the girl.'

In a business which was fragmented among hundreds of halls in and around London alone, not to mention the huge provincial networks, all but the biggest talent took years to become a household name. The system had advantages in that one song or comedy routine could be used and re-used almost forever. The drawback was that even for the brightest talents, the climb to the top was slow and often painful. No one made a name overnight in music hall.

Lottie started out with a series of one-week bookings in a scattering of different halls, largely in the East End and south of the Thames. It was rough, but Ulick was always ready to escort her home after her performance, and no artiste could hope to start even with lowly billing at Collins's or the Royal Standard.

She went over well. When Ulick started rehearsing her again after her illness, he had discovered a confidence and maturity that had been entirely lacking before. Watching her in the rehearsal room at Henrietta Street, he wondered how he had ever thought of casting her as a dancing, innocent child. No one could mistake her for anything but a knowing, delectable woman now. He rapidly set about exploiting her new personality with a whole run of specially written songs.

The East End audiences took to the new Lottie Casanova, glamorous, brash and beautiful, and so did the managers. One-week bookings were rapidly extended in Whitechapel, Hoxton and several other halls which had seen less assertive talents sink without trace. Within a couple of months, managers of better, more central halls were seeking out Larry Nash and asking him about his new girl. The week Lottie got her first multiple booking, she really felt she had arrived.

She also discovered, to her delight, that she could handle it effortlessly. The mad dash by hired brougham through London from one hall to another, to repeat on a second stage the performance she seemed barely to have finished on the first, suited her temperament. Sometimes she felt as if the sound of applause never died from her ears.

Within six months she was opening the second half at the Surrey Gardens in Kennington. Although not the West End, the Surrey was a better class of hall than she had played so far, and the second half opening was a good spot for one so new to the business. This was where an astute music hall manager put the brighter unknown comic turns, or the more comely female serio-comics. The second half opener had to be a good act because it was there to gain the audience's undivided attention for the big bill-topping name which always came on immediately afterwards. The artiste who played the spot well was invariably remembered, and proximity to the top-of-the-bill act always enhanced the newcomer's future value.

Sometimes the act was so good it caused the headliner to throw a tantrum, and for that reason skilful managers took care not to follow like with like. Thus a female balladeer might precede a slapstick comic, or a male dramatic monologist would warm up the audience for one of the great women stars. Even so, it was invariably a good spring-board for the aspiring newcomer and a tightrope for the hall manager.

For her first week, Lottie was doubly blessed. Top of the bill was the great juggler, Cinquevalli, a name so big he did not need to worry about a tyro girl singer, and an act so different from hers that there were no possible points of conflict. Larry Nash saw to it that two or three of the more prominent figures in West End management took in Lottie's act that week, and after that the way was clear for some minor billing at the Royal Standard and the Grecian.

For once, he was able to get Lottie when she was not tied to Ulick. Farrell was off on a journalistic assignment that night, and had grudgingly agreed that Nash should escort Lottie home. The agent had laughed at him. 'What are you afraid of, Ulick? She's not a Gaiety Girl! Music hall artistes don't get abducted by sinister Hungarian barons or anything, you know. She must be the only girl on the halls who doesn't have to find her own way home every night.'

'And that's the way it stays. I've almost lost her once already, remember!'

Privately, Nash did not believe Farrell's watchdog stance had anything to do with the past. He was convinced Ulick thought someone else would supplant him professionally, not romantically, with Lottie, and that above all the Irishman wanted to control her professional life. Seeing her work an audience, Nash began to understand why. He had no idea what Miss Casanova was like in bed, but she treated that crowd as if it were her lover. Perhaps it was the audience Ulick feared?

On the way home to Henrietta Street, he said to Lottie: 'Fancy a quick trip to Romano's? I hear it was meat and drink to you when you first came to London.'

She sparkled. 'Oh, could we? Yes, Larry, please. I feel as if I haven't been out for years.'

Over supper she unbent in a manner Nash had thought never to see. So she did have ideas about her professional image, and somewhere close to the surface they didn't bear too strong a relationship to the Farrell version. 'I can feel a good song,' she was saying, 'and I know Ulick is a brilliant songwriter, so I'm lucky. Perhaps that means I shouldn't complain, but . . . oh, never mind!' She held out her glass for more champagne.

'No, go on, Lottie. It's your act. Tell me what you feel for once.' He poured the wine, hoping it would loosen her tongue a little more.

'Well, he seems to think in – in little plays. You never saw our panto sketch, so that probably doesn't make much sense to you. It's as if he can only write for me if he has a certain picture of me in his head. The trouble is, although he writes a marvellous song for the girl in that picture, she has to stay the same girl all the time.'

'And you don't want to stay the same?'

'No, there's that; but the other thing is that the girl he's thinking of isn't me.'

'She looked pretty good from where I was sitting in the stalls tonight.'

She made a throw-away gesture. 'Oh, yes, of course. But Ulick was the only one who didn't understand it was no use doing a dance sketch about children for two young people who would be a man and a woman within a year. It's the same with the Lottie he's writing for the stage. I'm going to change, Larry, and the woman I change into won't fit with the picture of the girl he's drawing on stage.'

'What would you do if he gave you your head?'

'Don't mistake me – I'd keep that girl, she's gorgeous. But I'd be other women too. I did a pretty good coster girl in my pub act, and if it passed muster in Camden, it'd go across anywhere. I'd love a chance to do the knowing middle-aged woman routine – you know, all little winks and nods – oh, God, I'd like to try a bit o'them all! Perhaps I'm being too greedy.'

'I don't think so. I believe you've just made a very telling point, and the sooner you pluck up the courage to broach it with Ulick, the better. The act you have now is good, but you're right; it won't last forever. Ulick presumably thinks as long as he changes the songs from time to time, he can keep the stage personality in the same mould.'

She nodded, then said gloomily: 'He's been so good to me over the past few months that I don't like to bring it up. It seems so ungrateful.'

'I'd offer to do it for you, but you know how he'd react. He'd decide on the spot I was trying to steal his star and cast me into outer darkness.'

She giggled. 'Oh, dear, Larry, you know him as well as I do!'

'Better, Lottie dear. Much better.'

Shortly after that he took her home, but as the hansom carried him on to Theobalds Road he thought again about what she had said. She was right. Farrell had created a very pleasing character whom he now called Lottie Casanova, but it was not the girl he had just taken back to Henrietta Street, any more than Ellen Terry was really Lady Macbeth.

All very well for Ellen Terry; she was an actress, and being someone else for the evening was the essence of the job. But it was not the essence of being a music hall singer. All the great ones, at least, stood up there and threw out projections of their own personalities. Tonight Lottie had talked of many different roles, but as she outlined them, he saw each as another aspect of the real girl. The smooth, knowing ingénue in the tailored clothes and the neat button boots who sang smooth, knowing little button-booted songs about leading on young men in omnibuses was not all there was to Lottie Casanova and never would be.

She was getting away with it now, because she was fresh and had not grown over-used to the routine. But when she did, it would look every bit as hollow as it was. Nash wondered whether Lottie would find the courage to challenge Ulick and demand a change, or let it go and end up being just another variety also-ran. He suspected she would finally risk the confrontation. She was too addicted to that audience to let it go without a struggle.

146

CHAPTER SIXTEEN

Lottie had the physical strength of a robust young animal. The fragility that Ulick had ascribed to delicate health was nothing of the sort. Her body had recovered rapidly from the punishment she had inflicted on it during her pregnancy. Her spirit had proved more vulnerable. In the months when he was coaxing her back to full wellbeing, the slowest injuries to heal were those that did not show.

Now her first modest stage success was banishing the terrors of her Camden existence, and her boisterous personality was beginning to reassert itself. Ulick had his first brush with it the evening when she arrived home after supper with Larry Nash.

It was later than Lottie had realised by the time she got back to Henrietta Street, and when she walked into the drawing room Ulick was pacing in front of the fireplace, more like an enraged paterfamilias than a lover.

'And where, may I ask, have you been until this hour? You must have come offstage by ten o'clock at the latest. It's after one-thirty now.'

She answered him mildly enough at first. 'Larry collected me as you asked him to, and he took me on to supper at Romano's. Nothing wrong with that, surely?'

'Nothing wrong, the girl says! Do I count for nothing?'

'Don't be silly, Ulick. It was supper, not a trip to Le Touquet! He's my agent, remember. Surely I'm allowed to speak to him.'

'You know I prefer to be there. It's best that I make the decisions about your business interests, haven't I told you that often enough?'

Before their first parting, he would never have dreamed of talking to Lottie like this, for she would not have endured it. Since the move to Henrietta Street, though, she had been so pliant that he had all but forgotten the old, fiery girl. Now he was forcibly reminded.

'Yes, you have,' she snapped, 'until long after I got sick of hearing about it. What makes you think you're such a genius at managing my career?'

He was so surprised that he did not counterattack, saying lamely: 'You're getting plenty of bookings, aren't you?'

'That's Larry's job, not yours. Your job is to write songs for me and to help me develop my act. I said *help me*, Ulick, not dictate the whole bloody caboodle!'

'You've taken it all without kicking before now . . . wait a minute – Nash has put you up to this, hasn't he? I knew I should never have let you out of my sight.'

She was so angry she turned, fists clenched, and stamped her foot. '*Listen* to me, damn you, it's nothing to do with Larry! You're making me into a different sort of act to the one I want to be, and I want to change it, now!'

'Oh, so suddenly you have the ideas about what will take you to the top. Perhaps you'd care to share them with us mere mortals.'

The contempt in her face made him flinch. 'I don't pretend to be a songwriter,' she said. 'It's not something the singer usually does for herself, remember? But most singers tell their writers what they want. You never give me the chance!'

'If you're so damned clever, tell me what's wrong with Mimi!' Mimi was the nickname they had given the knowing girl who had become Lottie's stage image.

'With pleasure, since I've already tried to explain it to Larry – and before you get going again, I was telling him, not the other way round ... Yes, Mimi. Ulick, I am not a knowing little seamstress on her day off up in town. I think I'm turning into a good actress, and that means I can "play" Mimi. But don't you see, she's not me?'

'Then who the hell is she? I created Mimi as a reflection of the way I see you ...' He tailed off as he sensed he had laid himself wide open to attack.

Lottie nodded slowly, an exasperated smile spreading across her face. 'You said it. And isn't she easy to handle? Doesn't she have all the right things a sparky girl should – pretty ankles, a knowing way with her, quick on the back-chat ... but she's *yours*, lock stock and barrel. That little girl you've made would never go off by herself and have adventures. She'd never expect to go to and from the music hall on her own ... she'd never dream of going out to supper with Larry Nash. She'd much prefer to curl up at home and wait for her Prince Charming to come back. And guess who he'd be? Why, Ulick Farrell, of course!'

She had shamed him to silence, for as she spoke he realised every word she said was true. He had been blissfully unaware of it as he wrote the songs for his bouncy heroine, but now he saw he had re-created Lottie with her claws drawn. Drained of his righteous indignation, he slumped back against the chimneypiece. 'Very well, let's say I agree you have a point. What do you want to do, throw her away and start again?'

'Of course not – she's a good character!' She shushed him as he began to protest at her inconsistency. 'But don't you understand, she's only one of a regiment of girls I could play? They're all bits of me, just as she is, but I don't want to be any one of them for good. That may come when I'm really established.'

She went through the variety of females she had described to Nash in the cab. 'You're a first-class songwriter, Ulick. You know you can make me any one of those parts if you set your mind to it. It's just that Mimi's really the only one you want me to be. Well, it's got to change, or I shall never get anywhere.'

Having finally nerved herself to voice her discontent, she tried to lighten the atmosphere. 'Phew! Finally got it off my chest. Now, can we be friends again and make plans over a bottle of something?'

Long after she had gone to bed, Ulick sat in front of the dying fire, drinking too much and brooding about what she had said. He could see it all right ... and if he tried hard, he could even stand back and view Lottie with the objectivity he had exercised at Lyonesse. In those days, he had understood her better. Somehow, in taking responsibility for her, part of him had come to fear her.

Ulick enjoyed being clever. He could not live with the idea that his was an inferior talent. But every time Lottie Casanova stood up on a stage, he saw a little more expertise creep into her routine. One day she would be the biggest of stars. What would he be? At best, Ulick Farrell, the hack songwriter, Mr Lottie Casanova . . . He did not fear losing Lottie. He knew she had a deep underlying dependence on him. He feared being eclipsed by her, an infinitely worse fate for an ego as monstrous as Ulick's.

Lottie sailed into Romano's one October day to meet Larry Nash for lunch, looking luscious in a garnet velvet coat with a fur stand-up collar, and a matching fur hat and muff. Nash stood up and bowed formally as she reached their table. 'Good afternoon, Lottie, ravishing as ever, I see. You really are a pleasure to look at.'

She beamed at him. 'Glad someone appreciates it! I never thought the day would come when I'd land the part of Dandini in Drury Lane pantomime, and bloody Farrell would take it as though I'd got the bird in the Hoxton Varieties. It's nice to go somewhere where you're loved and cherished for a change!'

'That bad, eh?' said Nash. 'Same old complaint, or a different one this time?'

'More a variation on a theme than a complete change. This time we started off with the "Why won't you be guided by me" routine, but then came a new twist: "Trying to put me out of business by singing someone else's songs." Fat chance I'd have of singing my own in a feature part in the panto.'

'I take it he'd prefer you to be staying on the halls over Christmas, not having the Drury Lane season.'

'No doubt about it, chum. He started off by kicking up a fuss because we hadn't let him in on the discussions, so I asked him straight out if he'd have agreed. And he said no. There was a bit of a row after that, and by the time I'd calmed down he was well into this moan. Sometimes I wonder how much longer I can put up with it.'

Nash ordered some wine then turned to her, his face full of concern. 'Why *do* you go on putting up with it, Lottie? You're earning more than enough now to survive on your own, and although he's a good songwriter on his day, there are plenty of others.'

'I wish I could explain . . . even to myself. Sometimes I kid myself that it's just gratitude to him for pulling me out of that misery last year. But if I'm honest, it's not that. I still love the silly ass.'

Larry smiled wearily. 'I cannot imagine why. I don't remember when I last saw him sober. His newspaper writing has gone down the drain, apart from the column in *Sporting Times*, and he tries to belittle everything you do. You must be sick and tired of it.'

'Yeah, I am. The trouble is that I understand why he gets like that.'

'Then I wish you'd explain it to me. It can't be jealousy of you with other men. You work far too hard for any nonsense like that.'

'He could cope with other men better than this. He'd go on a one-day boozing spree, slap me around a bit and then make up with me. My bruises

149

would go away overnight, his pride would be satisfied, and he'd carry on all right for three months or so before it happened again. I could handle that without trouble –' Nash's face made it clear he did not understand why '– but I can't cope with a man who's jealous of me and the stage. I can't give that up, and anyway, if I did he'd tire of me in a minute. But I'm even less capable of turning into the dancing doll he'd like me to be.

'So there we are. He sits around drunk and snarling all day, and I take on twice as many engagements as I'd like so we can pay all the bills.'

'Ah! That's why you've been grabbing every booking in sight these last three months. Is he so short of cash?'

'Larry, if you knew the half of it . . . He spent so much on setting up that apartment in Henrietta Street, half of it on tick, that he needed to go on earning top whack with his writing to pay it off. Instead of that, he eased up to write material for me, and then to rehearse me exactly as he wanted me, although I was begging him to go back to his own work and let me do mine. And then the rows started and he slackened off even more and started spending more than you'd believe possible on drink.'

'Oh, no one knows better than me how expensive Ulick's thirst can be.'

'To tell the truth, Larry, I was in two minds about auditioning for Dandini. I wanted it so much, but I knew I couldn't fit in any halls for the whole run, and although the money is so good, it doesn't come near what I get for four spots a night. I'll have to pray he does some work at least while it's on.'

'You know what I told you. After Dandini, you'll be able to ask a lot more for your appearances on the halls.'

'Believe me, darling, if I didn't know that, I'd have had to turn it down, much as I want to do it.'

Lottie was beginning to find the conversation profoundly embarrassing. She liked and respected Larry Nash, and had she not been involved with Ulick her feelings for him would have run a lot deeper than friendship. But Larry had come up the hard way and he found it incomprehensible that someone as talented as Lottie would insist on staying with a self-destructive egomaniac like Farrell. Now, in an effort to regain his approval for Ulick, she said: 'You must admit he's written me some wonderful songs this past few months, Larry.'

'Oh, he's done that all right. But he's used them as his excuse for having produced practically nothing else – which is as good as blaming you for his own idleness – and he's interfered repeatedly with your ideas about how the material should be presented.'

'Some of his ideas work out very well.'

'No better than your own. Don't you see, you have an instinct for the way your act should go, but you'll never get an opportunity to develop it while you're tied to the apron strings of his notions.'

'He paces an act better than I'll ever do. I make some real bloomers in that quarter.'

Nash was really exasperated now. 'For precisely the same reason you haven't developed your own talents in the other direction. He always jumps in before you can try it. I remember you at the Rose, even if that's an interlude you prefer to forget. There was nothing wrong with the

150

way you paced that act, and I know that was all your own work.'

She shrugged it off. 'That was small beer, though.'

'Not so small. Who d'you think makes up the music hall audience? You know as well as I do – the same artisans and labourers and small tradesmen who patronise the Rose. If you did it well for them, you can do it well for anyone.'

Really, this argument was getting too serious . . . Larry's powers of persuasion were beginning to break her down . . . Lottie summoned up a flippant smile and said: 'Y'know, Larry, if I didn't know better, I'd say you didn't altogether like my Ulick.'

He glowered at her for a moment, then threw back his head and laughed. 'Oh, God, if you're prepared to put up with him so uncomplainingly, I don't see that it should matter so much to me. Let's have another drink.'

'And *one* and skip, and *two* and skip, and skip-skip-skip-skip-skip-skip-skip!'

The ballet-master, an unlikely aesthete in his heavy woollen suit and curly brimmed bowler hat, was bending forward and moving across the vast Drury Lane stage in a crouching position, to bring himself down to the level of his pupils. He carried a wooden clapper, with which he was marking time for the children who followed him. They were a motley collection of little girls, some straight out of a fairy story illustration in their gauzy dresses and wings, others, later arrivals, still wearing their drab street clothes. He led them in a Pied Piper procession along a lightly chalked line, while behind them scene shifters lugged rocky grottos and magic fountains into position. To the side a blasé group of grown-up chorus girls looked on idly as they waited for their cue. The Theatre Royal was about to rehearse its famous transformation scene.

Arthur Collins had taken over as manager when the legendary Augustus Harris died the previous year, but the spectacular melodramas and pantomimes pioneered by Harris lived on as gloriously as ever. Now Lottie stood, revelling in the sound and the smell; feeling, for the first time in her life, that she was truly part of a family, and one to which she wanted to belong.

She was dressed and made up for a scene in which she, a woman masquerading as a man, took the confusion even further by appearing as the man masquerading as his master. For this scene, Dandini the valet was pretending to be Prince Charming. Not that there was any danger of confusing Lottie with a real man. She was wearing the pantomime version of the uniform of colonel of the regiment – a heavily frogged and braided military-cut jacket which fitted like a second skin and ended abruptly at the hips. Her legs were exposed to advantage in theatrical tights and tall kid Hessian boots with silken tassels at the tops. She carried a sword and wore a brilliant blue military sash which trailed to saucy effect from her left hip. On her head she wore a soldier's shako with a nodding plume on the crown.

'Rummest looking colonel I ever saw!' she had told the costumier when he made the first fitting.

The man stood back and glared at her, his professional vanity affronted. 'And, of course, Clerkenwell was full of colonels when you were a girl! Look, dear, you just concentrate on being Dandini and let me see to the frills and furbelows, all right?' After that, she guarded her tongue, remembering

151

Nellie's advice so long ago: always make friends with the people backstage.

The rehearsal went badly enough for everyone to say it would be all right on the night. Old stagers left, muttering that Druriolanus would never have let them get away with such a slipshod run-through. But it was all bombast: they knew Collins was as professional as his illustrious predecessor and that *Cinderella* would enjoy its usual run to rapturous applause from children and appreciative ogling from their fathers.

Lottie was passing the star dressing room on her way to the stage door, when the dresser, a small chirpy middle-aged woman, peeped out. 'Miss Casanova, if you've got time, would you care to step inside for a minute?'

Would she care to, when the greatest woman music hall star of all time was behind that door? There were only two short scenes that they played together, and so far there had been no non-professional conversations between them, because Lottie had stood and gaped in awe at her idol. Now she tried to prevent herself from elbowing the dresser aside in her eagerness.

'Here she is, Miss Lloyd. Told her I'd get 'er for you before she went.'

Marie Lloyd, that year's Cinderella, turned from her mirror and gave Lottie her own private version of the smile that lit up the theatre audience every night. Imperceptibly it slid from an all-embracing beam to a cheeky grin and she said: 'Cor, I had to tell you, with legs like yours I'd never 'ave played girls, either. You look sensational in that Dandini get-up.'

Lottie stammered something unintelligible and felt like a simpering schoolgirl. Marie, still smiling, went back to removing her makeup. 'Gawd almighty,' she said, 'if I get any more lines showing I'll be playing one of the ugly sisters next season!'

Lottie's awe collapsed. This greatest of stars was another woman, after all, and a generous one. 'Thank you for saying that to me,' she said. 'Tomorrow afternoon, just before the matinée, I'll need it.'

'Nothing to worry about. With Collins doing such a good job down here and ol' Druriolanus Up Above, willing us to be a success, we can't go wrong.' She paused. 'Course, it helps having Dan Leno as Sister Anne an' all . . . Off you go, and remember tomorrow – you look gorgeous.'

Lottie left, fighting tears of gratitude, and walked home through the wintry Covent Garden streets, feeling as if she had been blessed by a kind enchantress.

As usual, that year's Drury Lane pantomime was hailed as the best ever, with the appropriate number of effusive compliments to scenery and star performances, and enough screams of moral outrage at the brevity of the chorus girls' costumes to ensure full houses to the end of the run. By the time *Cinderella* came off in February, Lottie had so many offers of work that she felt like weeping at the amount she would have to turn down.

Her relationship with Ulick had not improved. He was still co-operating, reluctantly, with her plea to be allowed more say in her own act, but his bouts of drinking lengthened in direct proportion to her growing success. He attended only one performance of *Cinderella*, and drank so much during the interval that Larry Nash practically had to hold him up when they came backstage.

Even his work for the *Sporting Times* was falling off now. The editor dropped first his Monday column, then the Wednesday piece, saying he wished to ring the changes between a stable of writers. But Ulick knew the truth: the quality of his work was deteriorating and if he produced one good column a week nowadays, it was about as much as he managed. The rest of his material was straight puffery for artistes who sought him out and bought him a drink, or tired old articles dusted down and given a new introduction to cover the fact that yet another week had passed without him producing anything worthwhile.

He was not a messy drunk, and always looked immaculate in public. Only on particularly bad days, like his evening at *Cinderella*, was he seen to sway or to speak indistinctly. Watching his steady deterioration, Larry Nash decided to try and reason with him. With a bit of effort, the agent reasoned, it was not too late for Farrell to regain both sobriety and livelihood.

The pantomime season had just ended and Lottie had taken a flood of simultaneous engagements to pay the bills. The pick of the bunch was the Tivoli, the hall to which all artistes aspired. Her spot there was midway through the bill, giving her time to perform at the Middlesex beforehand and the Royal Standard afterwards. Ulick reflected privately that it was bitterly ironic she should be playing the same two halls at the beginning of her career as a headliner as Nellie Standish had at the end of hers.

That was for the first fortnight. The following week she was really over-doing it and adding a fourth engagement to an already crowded evening, with a mad dash from the Royal Standard in Pimlico across the Thames to the Canterbury. This punishing programme was what made Nash decide he must talk to Ulick.

After an hour or so of trivial pleasantries, Nash said: 'You know Lottie can't go on indefinitely, pushing herself as she is, don't you?'

Farrell was, as usual, not quite sober. He waved his hands about irritably. 'Then talk to her about it. She never listens to me any more, and you seem to have been the one to encourage her in that.'

'Don't be puerile. You know damned well that she's made some wise decisions. Even overextending herself like this, she's aware of what she's doing. It's only because she needs the money to keep you both.'

'Oh, listen to him, the man of affairs! What makes you think I need a woman's earnings to keep me?'

'I know just how little work you've done since last summer, and how much you must be spending on whisky, Ulick. Two and two usually make four.'

'You wouldn't understand any of it, so stop trying to interfere.'

'Sorry, but it's not that easy. Lottie is well on the way to the top. In normal circumstances I don't intervene in my clients' private lives, but you're about to wreck her professional career for no better reason than that you can't control yourself.'

'I should beat you to a pulp for that!'

'But you're not going to because you couldn't stand still for long enough, so shut up and listen to some sensible advice for a change. Lottie is as bad for you as you are for her. It's about time you went your separate ways, then you'd both have a chance.'

Ulick managed an uneasy laugh. 'W-wait a minute . . . just exactly what are you saying?'

153

'That if you said goodbye to her now, then put the cork back in the bottle for a few weeks, you'd be back at your writing in next to no time, with your self-respect intact and making a reasonable living. Over the past few months you've gradually become a drunken parasite. It's a criminal waste of talent and it's quite pointless. However much you drink and spout self-pitying opinions about Lottie, she'll go on rising and you'll eventually dissolve into a pool of whisky.'

'Quite the little parish priest, aren't we? I don't suppose this has anything to do with my noble friend the agent wanting to get his leg over?'

Nash smiled at him bleakly. 'Just as well I don't claim to be a gentleman,' he said, 'or I'd now be the one who felt obliged to beat you to a pulp. As it is . . . no, I don't want to supplant you with Lottie. She's a beautiful girl, but I'd be as disastrous with her as you are. Perhaps that should be a consolation to you.'

'Can't see why.'

'Oh, come now, I'm sure you can. Drunk or sober, you're a perceptive fellow. Lottie's lover is the audience; has been since the day she went onstage at the Rose, will be until the day she collapses and dies onstage. No man will ever compete with that. Why try? All you have to do is pack your bag and leave the Henrietta Street flat to her. Remember, it's not the journey, but the first step that counts.'

'As I recall, that was said of a saint who walked sixty miles with his severed head in his hands.'

'Perhaps that's not as inappropriate as you choose to think.'

Farrell managed a croaking laugh, but he was close to breaking point. 'Look, Larry, I know there's a lot of sense in what you say. But I can't break away from her . . . I've lost the will. God, sometimes I hate her, and that alone is bloody unfair to the girl. I know she's half killing herself to keep us both, and when I see her at it I hate myself. She's like a drug, though. You have no idea you're addicted until you try to stop. The only way I'll ever be cured is if she leaves me . . . and I'm not at all sure it isn't too late for that.'

'All right, Ulick; I tried. I don't believe in wasting words when it's obvious I'm not getting anywhere. But if that girls burns herself out within a couple of years, it will all be down to you.'

'And what if I burn myself out in a couple of years. Will that be *her* fault?'

'No. She can't help having talent, any more than a flame can help attracting moths. You just seem to be a moth, you poor bastard.'

Nash got up and left him to his drink. There was no more to be said.

154

CHAPTER SEVENTEEN

Jake Kadar arrived in Lottie's life at the wrong time. A natural cynic, she would have seen through him in five minutes in other circumstances, and sent him packing. But in the foggy, rain-soaked autumn of 1898, with Ulick going through yet another bad drinking spell, she was defenceless. She needed a bright dream and Kadar provided it.

He was a New York booker, one of a breed that was appearing in increasing numbers in England as American vaudeville expanded at a rate which insatiably devoured home-grown acts and called out for more. Lottie had six weeks opening the second half at Collins's. Kadar arrived in a slack week, when she had no engagements in other halls to keep her dashing around London repeating her act. When he knocked on her dressing room door, instead of finding a hive of activity, he found her pouring herself a glass of stout.

'What, no champagne? I thought all you English stars drank it non-stop!'

She glared at him over the rim of her glass. 'I dunno who you are, mate, but if I was you, I'd tone it down. I'm in no mood for soft soap or jokey strangers tonight.'

She might not have spoken. Kadar closed the door behind him, gave her a half-bow, reversed a chair and sat astride it, facing her over its back as though that put them on a relaxed, friendly basis.

Lottie's expression had not changed. She took a big gulp of her drink, looked him over closely, then said: 'Well, what d'you want? You don't look rich enough for a masher, but you're certainly not one of the backstage regulars.'

'Permit me to introduce myself.' Kadar dipped into his jacket pocket and produced a card case, from which he presented her with a floridly printed piece of pasteboard announcing his status as an American booking agent.

Lottie drew a fingernail over the card. 'Hmm – not a very successful one, either, unless things are a lot different in New York. You don't even run to engraved cards.'

If he was confused, it did not show. 'Not at all, Miss Casanova. Too successful, if anything. I had to get some new ones done here, that's all – so busy I'd run out – and engraving would have taken too long. Never judge a book by its cover!'

'I've always found it a very sound principle to do just that, Mr . . . ah . . . Kaydah?'

'That's Kahdahr, ma'am – Hungarian ancestry, you know . . . anyway, enough about me. I came backstage to find out if you were interested in visiting the Land of Opportunity.'

'I can only assume that's your quaint, colonial way of referring to

155

America.' Irritation made Lottie drop her studied cockney and for a moment she went cold as she realised that with that last remark she'd sounded just like her mother. Fortunately, her visitor appeared to have noticed nothing.

'Ha-ha, very droll!' he said. 'I'm sure you'd be more friendly if you realised what scope there is in the USA for rising young stars like yourself.'

'What do you take me for? Opening the second half can't be any more star billing in New York or Boston than it is in London. I'm an artiste on the way up, no more, no less. If you're larding it like that, you must be trying to sell me something.'

'Only to the advantage of us both, Miss Casanova. It's not all headliners that we're looking for. A season in North America could make you. Look at Vesta Victoria . . . just another fetching serio-comic before she dipped her toe into the Atlantic. Now she's topping bills on both sides of the ocean. Given the right promotion, you'd come home a star, too, even if you left as something, shall we say, a little less. I can give you half a year touring right across the States.'

That got through to her, he thought. Give her time to think, and you've got her . . .

Lottie had switched abruptly from hostile indifference to sharp interest. 'Six months? On the strength of one short turn here? Do me a favour!' But he could see she was struggling to maintain her cynical façade.

'You do me an injustice, Miss Casanova. I've been in the audience four times this week. I know your act inside out – and two others who interest me.' Better not lay it on too thick, he thought.

'What others? Who else are you interested in?'

'Ah, I can't divulge that. One of them will never know I was interested unless I fail with you . . . you're my first choice in that line.'

'Say no more! I know what you mean.'

Then you know more than me, little girl, he thought. Tonight, Lottie was his sole target, and he had made only one previous visit to the hall.

'So where would these six months be played?' she asked.

'Well, for a start, where else but Koster and Bial's?' That always got their mouths watering.

'You could start me there?'

'Certainly could, young lady!' And it was true; Koster and Bial's specialised in European acts and they could always find room for an up-and-coming girl as pretty as this one. He made a lordly gesture and added: 'Then we'd finish up on the West Coast. A month with one of the Orpheum Circuit halls is available now – nearer the date, they'll probably extend to two if you still have the time to spare – then of course it's up to me to fix up dates across the country to give you the easiest schedule.'

'Where else will you put me?'

'That's the complicated bit, Miss Casanova. Why, if it were that simple, you English artistes wouldn't need our American expertise, would you? I don't work on spec like that. Once I've contracted you for the beginning and end of the season, I go back to New York and fit in all the intermediate dates on the spot. That way you have a smooth journey with the least possible hassle.'

156

A slight frown marred her perfect face. 'Sounds a bit risky, agreeing to go all that way for just two sure dates, doesn't it?'

'Far riskier to commit yourself at this stage and then get to New York to find the dates I've fixed are in towns so far apart you spend all your time on trains, or even worse, miss some of the best theatres. Yvette Guilbert had one hell of a time because of problems like that. Some clown of a booker fixed her up in Philadelphia, closing Saturday, and New Orleans, opening Monday. She made it in time for the first house Tuesday, by spending sixty hours on trains and hanging around railroad depots, but she was half dead, and New Orleans is still wondering why everyone thinks La Guilbert is such a smash.'

There was much more like this. Kadar was a good talker, and by the end of the evening Lottie almost believed him. A couple of hours at Romano's, with the American lavishly dispensing champagne, won her over completely. She even introduced him to several other up-and-coming performers who liked the idea of an American season. The next day, she met him at a solicitor's office and signed a contract for the East and West Coast bookings which would begin and end her season.

Once he had her signature, Kadar smiled winningly and said: 'Look at it this way, Miss Casanova. If you find you're not satisfied with the other dates I offer you, you can always cancel the contract and not lose anything by it. That can't be so bad, can it?'

Fired with enthusiasm for the new audiences who would unquestionably make her a star, she shook her head and gave him a radiant smile. 'Lottie – call me Lottie,' she said. 'I can't have the man who gave me my big start addressing me like a stranger!'

'All right, Lottie, here's to a great partnership.' And Kadar kissed her resoundingly on both cheeks before departing from her life forever.

'Christ, Lottie, you're not fit to be let out on your own! For the hundredth time, why don't you leave all the planning and booking to me?' Six months later Ulick, relatively sober again, was beside himself with fury at Lottie's naivety. 'You should have seen the bastard coming! You can usually suss a home-grown villain faster than I can. Why do you lose your reason at the sound of an American accent?'

With just a month to go before her first American engagement, the agent had written to inform her that he had not managed to secure any further bookings, and that unless she felt able to pay almost as much for a return ticket across the Atlantic as she would earn in New York, she was free to cancel her trip. She would, however, still be liable for his commission on the contract.

'I-it wasn't like that . . . he was so plausible,' said Lottie. 'The two bookings were genuine, and he didn't seem to have anything to gain by falling down on the rest.'

'Well, now you know he did have something to gain, you silly little bitch! He does nothing; you have to fork out his commission on the two dates you cancel. *He* certainly saw *you* coming, didn't he? And I bet he's cleaned up on all those other hopefuls you introduced him to in Romano's. He got quite a return for a couple of bottles of house bubbly!'

157

She was beginning to get angry. 'Come on, Ulick! I can just let him whistle for the commission. He's hardly likely to come over here and sue me for his money, is he, and if he did, what English court would give it him?'

'You get worse every time you open your mouth. Presumably you have no further ambition to play in America.'

'Course I do! He was right about one thing: a good season over there would bring me back here as a star.'

'Then forget about withholding his commission. If one of his kind has got a hold like that on you over there, you'll never work as long as you're in hock to him. Nobody will trust you. Don't make an even bigger fool of yourself, Lottie. His commission isn't all that big, even if we'll go hungry for a couple of weeks to pay it. It'll cost you a hell of a lot more if you refuse to pay up and lock yourself out of America as a result.'

'It's not the bloody money, it's the principle! Why should that bastard earn his bread by conning me? I'll not pay – and I'll not turn myself into an untouchable in America, either.'

He was almost sneering now. 'In that case, my dear, you'll have to find ten times his fee for that passage to New York – and unless you can rustle up some work sharpish when you arrive, you'll starve to death in the four months between the two dates he's fixed for you.'

'I'd rather do that than pay him for nothing! And I'll find work all right, just wait and see.'

'It will be a very long wait, I fear. Six months, to be precise. I certainly can't spare the money or the time to come with you. I have a career too, remember.'

'Oh, yeah, we've all seen where it's leading you, too – straight to the bottom of a whisky bottle. You've never earned a farthing yet you haven't blued on booze. What's so great about staying here to do that?'

Ulick was staring at her, something like fear in his eyes. 'You mean, you'd go without me?'

'Why not? You've made it clear I shan't be going with you!'

'But we've never been apart, ever . . . ever since I came to get you from Camden.'

'P'raps it's overdue, then. About time I found out if I can stand on my own two feet.'

'You know what happened last time you tried that.'

She blazed at him: 'And we all know why I was in that bloody position in the first place, don't we? In case you failed to notice, this time, I'm not.'

'But Lottie, you're barely nineteen. You know nothing of the world.'

'Oh, that's a bloody laugh an' all. Who d'you think has been protecting me from reality since I left Lyonesse, you? The shoe has been on the other foot most of the time. The way I remember it, every time I've needed help since you so famously rescued me from Camden, you've been lying under a table, drunk. Do me a favour, Ulick – apart from having more room in bed, I'll hardly know you're gone!'

The moment the words were out, she regretted them. She loved him, in spite of the whisky and the lost dreams. But he had provoked her with his insinuation that he was a better businessman than she, when it was her money that had kept them solvent for the last year.

He did not give her an opportunity to recall her words. He stood up, glared at

158

her and merely said: 'Well, go then, you ungrateful bitch!' and slammed out of the apartment.

Lottie stood staring after him for a while, then turned away. 'Oh, sod you, too!' she muttered. 'I'm not letting this bastard cheat me just for the sake of staying with a drunken Irish scribbler!'

She was no saver, but she had enough to buy a passage to New York. She gave no thought to what sort of passage it would be until she arrived at the booking offices of the Cunard Shipping Line. There she discovered that a return second-class fare aboard the *Campania* was almost the same price as a one-way first-class ticket. There was no contest. In the cab on her way back to Henrietta Street, Lottie reasoned: 'Might as well start as you mean to go on, my girl. Like Nanny always said – cheaper is never better.'

After the first shock of finding her willing to go abroad without him, Ulick made a strenuous attempt to please her and to make her relent. He stayed sober; he was loving and attentive; he even tried to be helpful with her preparations for the trip. Underneath, though, Lottie was certain he believed she would have second thoughts before the departure date, if only he kept her sweet.

Perhaps if he had made less of an effort, she would have changed her plans. In her calmer moments, she was the first to admit that she had no idea whether she could survive alone. The thought excited and frightened her in almost equal measure. But to her young, unforgiving eyes, his sudden good behaviour seemed little short of emotional blackmail. If he can do it when he's losing me, why can't he be bothered when I'm his for the asking? she thought, watching him coldly one evening as he mixed Black Velvet with a bottle of champagne he could ill afford.

Ulick, painfully aware that he had left the romantic gestures until a little too late, grew daily more desperate and thereby further reduced his chances of holding on to Lottie. Eventually, the night before she left for Liverpool, and thence New York, he tried total surrender. 'All right, Lottie, I give in. You won't stay with me, so I'll come with you – though God knows how we shall survive!'

She had been bending over her theatrical trunk, carefully packing her more delicate clothing on the top layer. His remark stopped her in her tracks and she remained immobile for a long moment before she straightened and stared at him. Her expression was enough. Now it was Ulick's turn to wish he could recall his words.

But it was too late. Inevitably, she responded. 'Twelve months ago I'd have run across the room and squeezed the breath out of you if you'd said that.'

'And now?'

'You already know, don't you? If you came with me, it'd be just the same as if I stayed here with you. We'd both end up in a puddle of spilled booze with our dreams spoiled. No, Ulick, I'm going alone. I might as well spell it out. If I didn't want to kill that swine Kadar so much, I'd be grateful to him. At least he pushed me into changing things.'

'You can't walk out on me like that . . . don't you think you owe me anything?'

159

She gave him an incredulous look, teetering on the edge of outrage, but then humour won and burst out laughing. 'Me? Owe you anything? I'd like to hear the reasoning behind that one!'

Her laughter stung him more than anger could have done. 'All right, then, you shall.' For a terrible moment she thought he was going to refer to the incident of Tommy and her brush with death after she left Ulick, but even now he was not quite that reckless. Instead, he blustered: 'When you set your cap at me, I was a valued member of one of the best households in England. If I hadn't got tangled up with you, when your brothers went off to university I'd have been welcomed in the best educational institutions. I had it all in front of me . . . and I gave it up for you.'

Lottie did not even stop laughing. Almost before he had finished speaking, she broke in: 'And of course, fifteen-year-old girls from my sort of background are depraved women of the world, we all know that! As I recall, the first time I led you astray I was up to my knees in the lake, looking for newts, and I didn't even know what you wanted to do, though I must say it felt interesting! And then there was that bit of unfinished business between you and Mama – if anything was ever going to end in tears, that was.'

Farrell was almost too angry to speak coherently. Since he had brought her back to the Henrietta Street flat, he had privately persuaded himself that she was the sole instigator of their relationship and that therefore she, not he himself, was responsible for his social ruin. Because he had never confided this view to her before, he had never heard it laughed to scorn. It was an unbearable experience. Now he managed to splutter: 'And I suppose I kidnapped you and dragged you off on the London train against your virginal wishes, too?'

The merriment was gone from her face now. 'Oh, don't try that one, my lad! You were already ruined, remember? It was what you were up to before we ran away that did for you, not our elopement. If you're tempted to blame me for that, think about how you'd have coped alone. P'raps it's just as well I scrambled on that train with you. If I hadn't, you might be dead in a gutter by now!'

He slapped her face so hard that the cracking sound as his palm struck her cheek echoed around the room. Lottie staggered, almost losing her balance as the open trunk hit the backs of her legs. Ulick experienced an appalling sense that they had lived through this before . . . the bedroom in Wilson Street, the night he caught her with Tommy.

Horrified, he reached forward and clutched her forearm, steadying her. In a flash, she said: 'What are you doing, holding on to me to get a better shot next time?'

It was more than he could take. He flung her aside, turned and stormed out of the flat. She heard his footsteps hurrying down the stairs, then the street door slammed. She shrugged. At least there wouldn't be any reproachful goodbyes now . . . every time he'd left like that in the past, it had been days before he showed up again; and then the rows had always been over far smaller matters.

Lottie was catching an early train to Liverpool the following morning, and, as she expected, she set off alone. The cab driver wrestled her luggage

160

down from the first-floor landing, she slammed the street door – for the last time, perhaps – got into the hackney and they clip-clopped off to Euston. 'Hardly the best curtain call you've ever taken, my girl,' she murmured, then set her thoughts firmly on the future.

CHAPTER EIGHTEEN

Arriving in New York, Lottie offered silent thanks to Tolly Dwyer, a much-travelled illusionist who had supplied a list of addresses where she might find lodgings. Otherwise, she felt the great city would have swallowed her whole.

It was a shining May morning. Lottie's striking looks and familiar manner had speeded her through Customs in near-record time and secured her a horse cab from the line drawn up at the pier entrance. The easy availability of the cab was a relief. Lottie had never been daunted before by crowds, but the dockside hubbub between the Customs sheds and West Street was in a class of its own. She peered at the two addresses which Dwyer had scrawled on the back of an old playbill, then said doubtfully to the cabby: 'Which would you say is the better neighbourhood, East 14th Street or Great Jones Street?'

From his perch high above her, he pondered momentarily and then said: 'Can't say there's a lot to choose between 'em, lady. Ask me, an' I'd say you could be well fleeced in either one.' He paused, regarding her impressively bulky luggage and flashy-stylish dress, then added, 'Theatrical, are you?'

She laughed. 'Does it show? I thought I was on my best behaviour, too!'

He unbent a fraction. 'Vaudeville's the only business that could be taking a pretty girl like you to East 14th – 'specially if you've just got off an ocean liner. Most fares I pick up at the pier want Fifth Avenue, or maybe Greenwich Village if they're arty.'

'Can you ever forgive me for not going there?'

'Yeah, lady, easy. Cost ya more to get to Great Jones Street than Fifth Avenue or the Village. Which o' these addresses is it gonna be?'

'I-I can't make up my mind. It's so difficult, in a new city . . .'

'Look, we ain't got all day. Where're you booked to appear?'

'Koster and Bial's . . . of course! Why didn't I think of that? Which of these places is closest to the theatre?'

'Hmm, take ya forever to get to West 34th from the Bowery. I'd try the 14th Street joint.'

'Right – you've got yourself a fare. But be prepared to take me on to the other place if I don't like the look of this one when we get there.'

He sniffed and whipped up his horse. 'Surprised anybody likes the look a' New York these days.'

Ada Scully was a boarding house keeper by profession and a theatrical boarding house keeper by inclination. She loved anything to do with show business, but vaudeville was her idea of heaven. Her establishment at 311 East 14th Street had long ago spilled over to occupy the adjoining five-storey brownstone too. Now it had the capacity of a small hotel, providing an apartment for Mrs Scully on the ground-floor back, residents' dining and sitting rooms to the front of the ground floor, and on the upper floors, sixteen bedrooms of various sizes to house the boarders. Although she took anyone who performed on a stage, like all good vaudeville troupers she despised straight actors and referred to them as Harolds and Arthurs. They got rooms only if she could not fill up with variety artistes.

When she saw Lottie she was bewitched. English performers only ever came to America for big money – it was not worth their while to make the trip otherwise. Invariably, they were established acts with an entourage of helpers, and their accommodation was booked in advance at suitably grand hotels. Apart from the occasional gypsy of the likes of Tolly Dwyer, Mrs Scully had never given house room to a genuine English music hall artiste, and she was bursting to do so.

'Hope you don't mind things a bit rough and ready,' she said. 'Probably a lot plainer than you're used to. Mind you, I got more bathrooms here than many hotels, and you get clean linen every week – two changes of towels.' She paused, assessing the cut and quality of Lottie's outfit, and added: 'Second-floor front is free right now. I don't think anything less'd do for you. It's nine dollars a week, though.'

Lottie bit the bullet. 'Does that include meals?'

'Hell, yes – I ain't no thief! Good cooked breakfast and an evening dinner. If that's inconvenient, I sometimes do a mid-day dinner for performers with a lot of evening commitments.'

'No, that will suit me perfectly, Mrs Scully. May I see the room?'

Ada practically bowed her into the big double directly over the boarders' dining room in what had once been the house next door. It was a pleasant, bright room, the south-facing bay window eliminating any gloom. The furnishings were sufficiently comfortable to make it a sitting room as well as a bedroom and Lottie was well pleased. She tried to put out of her mind the fact that the weekly rental was all but double what it would have been in London. The sooner she got some more engagements lined up, the better.

'You'll have had yer breakfast aboard the ship, I expect,' said Ada Scully.

Lottie laughed sheepishly. 'No, as a matter of fact I was so keyed up I couldn't eat a thing. Look, I know it must be well past your breakfast hour now. Just give me the address of a good place for coffee and rolls and I'll do a little exploring while I get a snack.'

'Right you are, then. There's one place, a few blocks away – best coffee and bread in Manhattan – Fleischmann's.'

Fleischmann's Vienna Model Bakery was at the north-east corner of Broadway and Tenth Street. The original Fleischmann, a retired Austrian army officer, had started his bakery in 1875 and had been on the edge of failure when he realised the potential of advertising and took a stand at the Philadelphia Centennial Exposition. Visitors flocked to see the bread-making process in the working bakery he had set up on his stand, and when they tasted his goods at the adjoining restaurant he became established overnight. By 1899 the firm was a New York institution, much sought out by Austro-German visitors and fashionable city dwellers alike. Lottie loved it on sight. She sat out on the restaurant's leafy terrace to eat crisp warm rolls, sweet butter and black cherry jam, accompanied by better coffee than she had ever drunk in England. The day's newspapers and a lively buzz of conversation all around her were bonuses.

After her third roll, a feeling of supreme wellbeing crept over her. She said aloud: 'Well, Lottie, things are never so bad after a good breakfast.' Then she turned to the newspapers to see what prospects of work they might offer.

It looked impressive. There seemed to be almost as many halls in New York as there were in London. And where there were halls, there was an endless need for new talent. Why was she hanging around getting fat on bread and jam when she could be out taking the city by storm? Lottie paid her bill and walked out through the baker's shop on to Broadway. She took a deep breath of the sweet spring air and gazed north towards the theatre district. I wonder if Columbus felt this way when he arrived? she thought.

John Koster and Adam Bial wanted no part of the clean-up campaign which the likes of Pastor, Keith and Albee were imposing on vaudeville in an effort to attract family audiences. They had started off as brewers in Chatham Square, moving into show business with a hall on 23rd Street just west of Sixth Avenue. Bial managed the music hall and Koster looked after the liquor – and liquor always came first. But by the 1890s, the entertainment centre of New York was moving inexorably uptown and the partners noticed the migration through a sharp drop in liquor sales.

They compromised on location, but their antipathy to the clean-up brigade remained. Soon after they opened their new music hall on the block near Herald Square that ran from West 34th to 35th Street, half their feature players wound up brawling in police court when Bial mounted 'An Affair of Honour', a fencing duel between female protagonists naked to the waist. At the behest of the law, they put the girls into costumes after that, but it was always a hall that specialised in highly visible cotton tights and frilly petticoats displayed at every opportunity.

Free of any obligation to satisfy a home-grown family audience, the partners went a little further and booked as many good European acts as they could get. These played as exotic counter-point to the more outrageous American acts, and Koster and Bial's always retained a reputation as the place where New York blades, bohemians and expatriate Europeans combined to make a rich soup of cosmopolitan cultural low-life. This was where Lottie Casanova was to begin her American vaudeville career.

When she arrived at the theatre, the staff were getting it ready for the afternoon performance and the main doors on 34th Street were wide open to let a little air circulate. Lottie was in an odd position because of the irregular nature of her booking. English acts were almost never cast up alone in New York. Either they came as part of a company, or an agent awaited them, with arrangements and contacts complete to cover their whole tour. Lottie had no tour schedule apart from the two dates with the four-month gap between them, the used stub of a one-way steamship ticket, and the letters of confirmation of six weeks from Koster and Bial's, New York, and of four weeks from the Orpheum, San Francisco. Beyond an awareness that she must be there to open for the Monday matinée, she had no idea where to start. Hence her presence in the music hall now.

In search of someone who could direct her to the house manager, she went into the foyer, which was empty. The auditorium doors were as wide open as the street entrance, so after a moment's hesitation she went in. What she saw bore a tantalising resemblance to an English music hall, and yet it could never have existed in England.

The West 34th Street house followed the traditional music hall pattern of an open floor without fixed seating, furnished with groups of tables and chairs, with a stage at the far end. Around the walls were ranged closed-off tables and chairs behind a sort of ornamental garden fence, more expensive and offering greater privacy than the main floor. The upper storey comprised a promenade gallery with smaller tables and chairs ranged along the balcony where drinkers could sit down and take in the acts on stage before replenishing their glasses at the bar. The main hall was decorated with cast iron columns disguised as palm trees, with a scattering of fairy lights which gave the whole theatre an appearance reminiscent of the town square in some picturesque French Polynesian colony, but did little to improve the view for the blades who frequented the upstairs promenade. The stage was large, and instead of a curtain, sported an ornate screen in the shape of a fan, which appeared to serve the same purpose.

Curious about the acoustics, Lottie inhaled deeply, then let out a few good strong notes. They filled the auditorium satisfactorily. 'Mmm,' she said. 'Nothing wrong with that, anyway.'

'What's going on here? Hey, miss, does your mother know you're out?'

The voice issued from the gloom of the unlit upper promenade, and Lottie started in fright before swiftly recovering her composure. 'Who wants to know?' she retorted.

'Wait – I'll be with you right away.' She heard the man's footsteps receding in the silent hall, then returning at ground level moments later. He was a short, thickset individual, with a wiry black beard streaked with silver. He was expensively dressed, but had discarded his suit jacket somewhere. He wore a well-cut silk shirt, the sleeves rolled up above the elbows, and a fancy waistcoat, wildly out of keeping with the plain worsted trousers. He stopped a few feet from Lottie and looked up at her, his face wary. 'This ain't no beginners' house, kid,' he said, 'and I don't invite amateurs in off the sidewalk to practise their pitch.'

'You're no judge of talent, either, if you think an amateur could have found her pitch like that, straight away,' Lottie responded. 'Now, I don't want to waste your time or mine. Is Mr Bial here at the moment?'

'Maybe, maybe not. Who's asking? I can tell you now that if you want an audition, ya wasting your time.'

'I haven't come a couple of thousand miles to audition. If he's in, please tell him Miss Lottie Casanova wants to see him.' She ended her request with a poisonously patronising smile, and wheeled away from him to sit at one of the little tables close by. Exercising every atom of control she possessed, she refrained from glancing around to see whether he had gone to find Bial.

Moments later, she was carefully studying the floorboards in front of her when his short, sturdy legs intruded into her line of vision. She looked up, irritated now by his reluctance to co-operate. 'Look, if you can't – oh!' As she began to speak, she realised that his cautious expression had been replaced by a smile and he was extending his right hand in greeting.

'I'll be a sonofabitch if I ever got no act step right in off the sidewalk all the way from England before!' he said. 'Adam Bial in person, Miss Casanova, and pleeztameetcha! If ya'd care to come up to the promenade, we'll toast your arrival.'

'That's the best idea I've heard all day. Lead on, Mr Bial.'

He perched her on a high stool by the promenade bar and went behind the counter to open the champagne. 'Now, maybe you'd like to tell me how come you landed up here with no announcement or manager or nothing. It's so long since I heard from Kadar, I wasn't really expecting ya at all. It wouldn't be the first time.'

'Nor the last, if he makes a habit of treating artistes the way he did me,' said Lottie. 'I'm only here from sheer bloody-mindedness . . . Look, before I bore you with my life history, can we get something straight? Am I booked for the next six weeks, and will you pay me $250 a week?'

He laughed. 'Yes and yes. I dunno what music hall's like in London, but over here we always bet on a coupla acts. The programme stretches to cover it if they don't come, but if they do, well and good.'

Something else was troubling Lottie, though. 'How on earth can you book an act blind, through a villain like Kadar, and have any faith in the standard? He could have scraped me off the pavement, or, worse, out of some suburban parlour.'

'You don't look as if you've ever been near no suburban parlour, Miss Casanova. But even if you had, there's a simple answer to that one. I book likely-sounding English acts unseen 'cos I can't spare the time to go to England and audition my own artistes. But I operate about the only hall in New York that runs a Monday matinée, and guess why? My new acts open Monday afternoon to a quiet house, and if they bomb they get a second chance Monday night, another quiet session. If I still don't like 'em, they're out on Tuesday, with one third of a week's pay. Easy.'

Lottie felt cold. 'So I've come all the way to New York on the promise of just $80 and change?'

'Not if you've any sense. Ya just brush up yer act and move on early to settle in for your next booking.'

'What if I don't have one?'

'Then you'd better have a rich old uncle out in the Hamptons to stake you, honey.' He seemed to decide she had been teased enough, leaned across the bar and patted her hand. 'Don't worry – looking the way you do, you'll have to sound like a frog not to make it here. If we like you, you may even get offered an extended engagement, but I can't promise anything 'til I've see ya go through yer paces.'

Lottie gazed morosely into her champagne for a moment, then tossed her head and glared back at him. 'Why the hell am I getting stage fright? I've played the Mo' in Drury Lane second half on a Saturday night. Hell couldn't be worse than that.'

'Ever hear of the Bronx-cheer?'

'Enlighten me, Mr Bial.'

'I think you Londoners call it getting the bird. I've no idea what the Mo' is, but believe me, getting Bronx-cheered in Koster and Bial's is something fearsome.'

But Lottie had her courage back now. She laughed at him. 'I'll live with it. With any luck, I'll never know what it sounds like.'

167

'Good girl. Looks like you're a real trouper, Miss Casanova.'

'I think you can call me Lottie now.'

Bial shook his head. 'Not quite yet. Save that for after I see yer act. I hate to fire a friend.'

By the time they had finished their drinks, the hall was beginning to liven up. Bial emptied the last few drops into Lottie's glass and said: 'Better get going. Never know what they'll get up to if I don't watch 'em. Might be a good idea if ya stay and see the first house. Give you a taste of the place, ya know?'

'Thanks, Mr Bial, but I prefer to come back tonight. Somehow I never get much feel out of an afternoon show.'

'Looking the way you do, you'll get plenty a' feel if ya come back alone tonight. Be lucky to catch half an act in peace. I dunno what London audiences are like, but I can tell ya, it's not long since Koster and Bial's was a stag establishment. Things haven't changed much. Course, I could always keep ya company . . .'

'But surely, you'll have your hands full looking after the show?'

'Nah – long as I'm where they can see me, they'll do all right. How about it? Only way ya'll get to see the show in peace.'

'You're on. I hope it won't be too boring for you, that's all . . . Oh, before I go, just tell me one thing. Why have you got that big fan up front instead of a curtain?'

Bial chuckled. 'Never let it be said that Koster and Bial's was lawbreakers. Music halls ain't allowed to instal drop curtains. Against New York municipal laws. Only, if ya ain't got drop curtains, yer not a theatre. An' if yer not a theatre, ya can't open Sundays. There's no way K and B's is going to miss out on a day's takings for some chickenshit law, so we put the fan in. Fulfils all the legal requirements of drop curtains without legally bein' them, if ya know what I mean.'

'And to think I imagined it was something to do with the decorative theme!'

Bial glared around him. 'Ya mean you can see a theme in this joint? I think ya better have another drink.'

Mrs Scully's was as quiet as the grave when Lottie got back. The landlady peered around the door that led to her private quarters. 'Everything all right, Miss Casanova? Gettin' yer bearings okay, are ya?'

Lottie smiled. 'It's all so much faster than I expected, I feel quite exhausted already. Doesn't anyone go anywhere slowly in this city?'

'Seems not. They're all too busy trying to get some place else – top of the heap, usually! Now, what're you gonna do about dinner? Six o'clock too early for ya?'

'I think I'd better give it a miss tonight, Mrs Scully. I'm taking in the show at Koster and Bial's and I expect my escort intends that we should dine there.'

'You planning to eat in that dump? No offence, Miss Casanova, but if I wuz you, I'd fill up here before ya go, and leave them to eat as has to. It's tasty enough, but every so often a few customers ends up in the hospital. Safer to stick to the liquor.' She reflected on what she had said, then added, sorrowfully, 'S'pose it's a come-down from what yer used ta?'

Laughing, Lottie shook her head. 'Nothing of the sort, Mrs S. It sounds like Old Home week. The only difference is that in England I don't have good home cooking to fall back on.'

Mrs Scully's face lit up. 'Well ya do now, my dear. Six o'clock it is – and I jest hope yer hungry.'

Fortified against the world by Mrs Scully's beef pot roast, apple pie and endless cups of coffee, Lottie left East 14th Street just after seven, resplendent in one of her most flamboyant evening gowns. The landlady saw her off, regarding her with something approaching awe. 'Ain't nobody going to miss you in that rig-out, dear! I hope yer escort is big and strong!'

'What he lacks in stature he makes up for in clout, I think, Mrs Scully. Don't expect me too late. I'm aiming for an early night.'

Ada Scully hooted in derision. 'Then yer doomed ta disappointment! The blades up there'll never let ya out!'

Adam Bial certainly looked appreciative when he greeted her in the music hall foyer. As he ushered her to one of the fenced-off tables, he said: 'I can't help feeling I'm going to enjoy this – even if we are gonna wind up with more people looking at you than at the acts I'm paying good money for!'

Chilled champagne was waiting beside their table. 'You can have dinner here if ya like, Miss Casanova, but I don't recommend it. One cannot say of K and B's that *le patron mange ici*!'

Settling herself in her seat, Lottie began to enjoy herself. She gave Bial a big smile and said: 'If you treat all your lady artistes like this, Mr Bial, you must be snowed under with return engagements.'

He shook his head. 'This is the first time ever, as far as I recall. But then, it's the first time ever I had a serio-comic turn up all the way from England, on her own, one Saturday noon just to try out the acoustics!' He handed her a playbill. 'It's years since I saw an English music hall programme. Dunno how they compare nowadays, but that'll give you some idea of the way we do things.'

On paper, it was much like a London bill, offering about fourteen acts, with the headliners clustered in the middle, after the interval, and minor turns opening and closing the show.

'Oh, you have chairmen, too,' said Lottie, studying the bill. 'I could have sworn someone told me you never saw them over here.'

'We didn't until this guy came along. He's a comic genius, and what started as a little bitta stage business to round off his act has turned into the act itself. It's an accident, but he's wound up doing just what your chairman does.'

His name was James J. Morton and he started off the evening with his original act – the one which had evolved into the MC routine. For this, his partner was Maude Ravel, a buxom blonde with a bright smile and a good voice. Maude, apparently the star, came on, followed by the tall, cadaverous Morton, who proceeded to make agonised attempts to help her with her songs, failing dismally, getting in the way, never smiling, always apologising, and quickly reducing the audience to helpless laughter. Eventually, Maude stalked off, declaring she could no longer work with such an imbecile, and he

169

shambled around the stage, mumbling appallingly tuneless songs of his own, starting on monologues and losing track of the story, and generally holding everybody breathlessly poised between anguish and mirth as they awaited his next blunder. Gradually he began to reflect on the other acts on the bill, and managed to lead seamlessly out of his own routine and into an introduction for the next artiste.

Lottie was overwhelmed by his performance. 'What a pro!' she told Bial. 'My God, if they're all up to his standard I may as well go home now.'

Bial only smiled. 'Don't worry – they ain't. There's a coupla damned good acts, but Morton's one a' the best. He's only first on the bill because he introduces the whole thing.'

He was right about some of the other turns. There was an appalling child singer of the 'Give me a ticket to Heaven' variety. It was a routine that had never appealed to Lottie anyway, but well executed, it could move an audience to floods of tears. This child had a relentless toughness that convinced her the brat would have bought a round trip ticket and gone home again after prodding her dead daddy with a cattle goad.

'Laura's Last Ball', a short melodrama played with full Henry Irving histrionics but without any of the great actor's talent, was a minor disaster. Morton's brilliant clowning reclaimed the audience's attention after each rough interlude, aided by the better acts on the bill. And there were plenty.

One delightful double act featured a man and a girl, doing a fast cross-talk routine the like of which Lottie had never seen on the English stage. At one point the girl danced offstage for a quick change and returned, dressed in a vast, unalluring fur coat in a bilious shade of off-yellow, which reached down to her ankles.

'What d'ya call that?' asked her partner.

'I don't. I whistle and it comes to me.'

'It that the way you got it?'

'Naw – it was given to me. Everybody likes to give things to me . . . I once got $35,000 for a kiss.'

'WHAT?'

'Well, it wasn't really the kiss itself – it was what it led up to . . .' Whereupon the girl sauntered downstage to the footlights, flung open the vast coat and revealed the rest of her costume – a pair of beribboned drawers and nothing else.

The lights were killed in seconds and the act ended to uproar from the audience. The timing was perfect. When the lights came up again, man and girl were out taking their bow, the girl now wearing a perfectly respectable loose white frock.

'Great God almighty!' Lottie muttered to Adam Bial. 'You've been playing that one all week and no one got arrested?'

Bial grinned and shook his head. 'That bastard Hearst nearly got us closed down with his newspaper crusade last time some of our girls were thrown in the slammer. This was strictly kosher until tonight – she played it in pink tights and showed them off when the house lights came up again to prove she wasn't naked. We saved this little stunt for their last performance – tonight. That way they don't get in trouble, and we get talked about enough so's trade improves the following week. We always try to introduce a bit of spice like that. But ya gotta keep it unpredictable.'

The evening wore on, with Lottie enjoying every minute. Even the mediocre and bad acts were sufficiently different from their English equivalents to keep her interested. The much talked-about Eva Tanguay was topping the bill, and after twenty minutes' exposure to her iron lungs and leering *doubles entendres*, Lottie wondered how on earth American managers could claim they were cleaning up vaudeville. 'How the hell does she get to play in front of mixed audiences?' she asked Bial.

He shrugged. 'I think the puritans are scared witless of her. Every routine I've ever seen her do has been bluer than the Pacific.'

Lottie was glad to see the back of her – particularly as the remaining three acts were the best supporting routines she had seen anywhere.

The first was a novelty act – a legmania trio called the Majiltons, billed as 'A Study In Points'. They possessed a nightmarish quality, but one that fascinated. The act occupied a full stage set, with a central grand staircase. As the orchestra struck up a theme with a steady metronome beat, the fan-curtain parted and two men and a woman appeared at the top of the staircase. All were made up with satanically pointed eyebrows, three-pointed wigs and artificially pointed ear lobes. The men had sharp goatee beards, and their coat-tails, lapels and waistcoat bottoms echoed the point theme. All three wore black tights and long, pointed dancing shoes. The routine was practically a cross between dance and contortion. They advanced down the stairs together, the men lifting their legs almost casually over the head of the woman who walked between them, strictly in time to the musical beat. At the foot of the stairs, they went into a murderously difficult routine of splits and more effort-less looking high kicks, which built into a grotesque adagio-style dance. It was the mesmeric slowness and ease of the act which gave it its unique quality, and once the trio were started, it was impossible to look away from them.

The audience, many of whom had kept up a stream of chatter during Tanguay's performance, watched with rapt attention until the odd group left the stage. Then the applause was deafening.

'They're sensational,' said Lottie. 'Give 'em a couple of years and they'll be topping bills all over the world.'

'That's where you're wrong,' said Bial. 'I've booked them twice in five years, and they bring the house down – for a week. After that, nothing. There's something about them that gets under people's skin, and it'll always stop them making the big time. They've been around, ooh, ten, fifteen years now. Can't have many more seasons left in 'em. If they've got any sense they'll quit soon and put their savings into a gym or dancing school.'

'Maybe they don't have any savings.'

'If they don't, they must flush the dollar bills down the toilet. I've never known any of 'em go out on the town, or heard of them gambling, or womanising. Nothing. They should be loaded by now – and they should be wise enough to know when to quit. You loved 'em tonight, but I'll bet if you were sharing a bill with them next week, after the first coupla nights, you'd see to it you weren't in the wings while their routine was on.'

The next act had plenty of mystic trimmings, but in the conventional music hall manner, without the macabre feel of the Majiltons. It was a

Chinese illusionist, Ching Ling Foo, who offered clever but standard tricks, with two breathtaking exceptions. He appeared onstage in full Chinese robes, and displayed the original inscrutable Eastern facial expression as he twirled aside the silk brocade to reveal a dustbin-sized container full of fresh milk. Just to ensure the audience knew it was the real thing, he dipped out cups full of it and had them passed round to the front tables. Moments later another, opposite, flick of the robe revealed an even bigger can, this time containing a dozen or more live ducks, which disembarked irritably from their prison and waddled around the stage for the rest of the act.

'I can't even see how he gets onstage with all that up his frock, but he's brilliant,' said Lottie.

Bial replied: 'It knocks me out that we get guys of that quality year after year. They make good money for a while, then they just fade away. Beats me how they ever learn to be that brilliant in return for such small beans. The next act's the same.'

This was the spot that finished the show, always some sort of jolly instrumental or rough-and-tumble which would effectively drown the chaotic noise as much of the audience prepared to leave. In the business such routines were universally known as alley-oops.

Tonight's was spectacular – Hassan Ben Ali and his troupe of Arabian acrobats. 'Never saw an American troupe could touch 'em,' said Bial. 'They don't seem to think about it, just do it as casual as you or I'd walk down the street.'

They certainly slowed down the departing patrons, who hesitated to watch one stunt and gradually became hypnotised by the act. They tumbled around the stage with a reckless disregard for personal safety, somehow all converging on the leader, who managed to raise all eleven of them aloft on his head, shoulders and arms. As the applause began, he let out a loud whoop, and the entire troupe took off like birds, apparently leaping into thin air as they bounded off the stage and the fan screen closed behind them.

When it was all over, and the remaining patrons had settled over their drinks and private flirtations, Bial started to show Lottie out. 'Well, I hope you enjoyed your first look at vaudeville. What d'ya think?'

'I think I'd better practise bloody hard all day tomorrow if I'm to compete with that lot. My God, Mr Bial, once you cut out the dead wood, the standard is high.'

He smiled. 'Course it is. With Albee and Tony Pastor putting on them nice-as-apple-pie family shows, we got the pick o' the pros who hate that kinda hall.' Then his expression became morose. 'Trouble is, they'll all go that way in the end . . . whole business is getting prim and proper . . . hope I'm long dead by then. Vaudeville's about dumps an' honky tonks, not marble halls.'

'Hear, hear! I wouldn't like it any other way.' As she said it, Lottie wondered to herself how long it would be before decency and family programmes destroyed the raffish charm of the London halls.

She had not been flattering Adam Bial when she praised the standard of the majority of his acts. It had taken her by surprise and now she was shamefaced at the prejudice. With the effortless superiority of the Londoner, she had assumed that New York fell far short of the top English shows. But in one evening she had seen three acts, any one of which could have topped the bill at the Oxford or the Alhambra. Lottie began to feel nervous about her own offering. It was good material, certainly, but how would her slap-dash rehearsal programme stand up to the demanding audience that awaited her next week? She shivered at the prospect. Two badly received performances, and she was out, jobless and penniless, either marooned here with no prospects, or forced to return home steerage and humble herself to Ulick Farrell merely to get a roof over her head again. Long-suppressed memories of her room in Camden and the awful events that took her out of it sharpened her resolve. Sunday was to be no day of rest for her – she intended to rehearse until she dropped.

She was preoccupied with her thoughts as Bial steered her through the late-night throng in the foyer, on the way to find her a cab, and for a moment she was only half aware that he had paused to speak to someone who barred their way. Hence she missed the stranger's opening remarks, and surfaced only in time to hear Bial saying: 'Think again, Tony. She's due on stage here Monday afternoon and I know your way with women!'

'Really, Adam, you are a distrustful old thing. All I had in mind was a spot of supper.'

'That's all you ever have in mind, you bum. Now geddoudahere!' But Bial was smiling as he spoke and it was plain that the two men were old friends.

'Adam's the salt of the earth, but something of a rough diamond, if I may mix a couple of metaphors.' Now the new arrival was talking directly to Lottie and it was all she could do not to blush.

Misunderstanding her reserve, he said: 'Oh, forgive me – he hasn't introduced us, has he? I'm Antony St John Wilde – no relation to Oscar. And you?'

'Lottie Casanova – no relation to Giovanni! If I didn't know better, Mr Wilde, I'd almost take you for an Englishman.'

Bial exploded into laughter and slapped Wilde on the back. 'And I wuz worried about leaving her in your hands! Something tells me she's seen off your type before, Tony old bean!'

Lottie turned her most innocent smile on him. 'Of course I have, Mr Bial. What d'you think we have instead of men in London, curates?'

'Well, my dear, I gotta get back to work. The choice is yours. Do I see ya to yer cab, or leave you ta Wilde's tender mercies?'

She made a point of blatantly looking Wilde over from top to toe before saying: 'Oh, I think you can trust me with him, Mr Bial. I'm a very punctual girl, you know.'

He switched off the smile, 'You better be, Miss Casanova, because believe me, when you're the other side a' them footlights, I'm not the fella you see before you tonight. Ya gotta be sharp and ya gotta deliver the goods. Okay, off you go . . . and remember, Tony, the girl's living depends on her being here Monday.'

Wilde touched the silver head of his cane to the brim of his silk hat. 'Adam, my friend, did I ever let you down?'

'D'ya wanna list? Show her a good time, ya bum. G'night.' He turned away and the crowd closed the gap behind him.

CHAPTER NINETEEN

Antony Wilde was just what Lottie needed after her first evening. She was excited by the city, but nervous too, and the prospect of going home to bed immediately was unthinkable. She knew he found her attractive, but was almost as sure that she would not have to fight him off. This was a man who would flirt with her and try to seduce her with words, but who would never force himself on her and risk the shame of rejection. He was a man whose self-esteem surrounded him like a cloud. He also seemed to love music hall, and she badly wanted to talk shop after all she had seen at Koster and Bial's.

'After such a spectacular introduction to the city, supper should also be appropriately exotic,' he said. 'But in New York most of the really interesting places are strictly stag . . . you have a Chinatown of your own, in London, I think?'

Lottie was faintly puzzled. 'Yes, but what's that got to do with here and now? Limehouse is where you go if opium's your thing, but otherwise you keep well away, man or woman, both the same.'

'Well I'll be damned!' He chuckled, surprised at what she had said. 'I was reluctant to show you our Chinatown because I thought it was sure to be old hat. Clearly I was wrong.' He tapped the roof of the cab with his cane. 'Driver – Mott Street, please, Chinese Delmonico's.'

'Nowhere can be called that!'

'But it is. Don't look for false sophistication where it's unnecessary. Delmonico's is an excellent restaurant. The Chinese entrepreneur who set up the establishment we're about to visit knew he was going to start a good restaurant. What if he'd called it the Jade Garden or the Lotus House? He might have starved while he waited for fashionable society to find him. There are countless Jade Gardens in New York.

'So he called it Chinese Delmonico's and the *ton* all laughed, it's true, but they also thought it would be rather a good joke to say they'd visited the place. They did, and what do you know? It *was* a sort of Delmonico's *à la chinoise*. The enterprising Chinaman made his fortune and another good eating house was established on the New York scene. On my bad days, I sometimes think I should seek out that Chinaman and make him my business manager.'

Lottie had been studying him as he spoke. 'Which reminds me: what do you do for a living?'

'This and that. Have you made any guesses yet?'

'You're a bit of an enigma. I'd have sworn you were a rich boy who didn't work at very much and hung around the theatre for amusement. But here's something else . . . I'm sure you work, I just can't guess at a profession.'

His stare was penetrating. 'If I may say so, Miss Casanova, you, too, are something of an enigma. I've yet to meet a vaudeville artiste who uses words as you do. Just where do you spring from?'

'You shouldn't need to ask, with a name like mine. The London version of Little Italy, of course.'

'And my name is Eleanora Duse. Don't insult my intelligence.'

'Very well, you've uncovered my dark secret. My mother, a beautiful English duchess, bore me at dead of night in a remote castle and had me smuggled out by her faithful old nurse. I was brought up by simple shepherd folk and when they were struck by lightning, I went to London to make my fortune. How about that one?'

'Checkmate! I'll find out about you one day, Lottie, but for the moment I'm prepared to give up. I have to say you're very close in your guess about me. I do have enough to lead a life of leisure if I want it, and that's how I discovered vaudeville. But I got hooked, and for the past five years or so I've been writing songs – lyrics and music. Maybe one day I shall even graduate to a Broadway musical!'

Her heart plummeted. A whole city to choose from and she fled there from the clutches of one songwriter, straight into the arms of another. That was one more reason why Antony Wilde must remain a friend and nothing more. She retreated to less intimate ground. 'Will we be there soon, and will they still serve us supper? In London, it tends to be only the theatrical places in the West End that keep these sort of hours.'

'Oh, I don't think Chinatown ever closes, and it certainly doesn't turn seedy this time of night, either. You'll find women there who would regard it as social ruin to show their faces at this end of town in the daytime. Perfectly reputable at this hour, though . . . it's fashionable slumming, you see.'

She caught the contempt in his voice and said: 'It doesn't sound as if you like them very much.'

'I detest them! Why d'you think I hang around with people like Adam Bial? Because they're vigorous and lively, and when they're going to tread on you they usually give you fair warning. That bunch would slide a stiletto between your ribs and pretend it was nothing to do with them.'

'I know just how you feel.'

His grin was triumphant. 'Got you! Your origins are showing. Come on, tell me.'

She blushed deeply but refused to elaborate on her slip. 'It was a silly thing to say. No point in pursuing it – it's ancient history. I'll make you a promise, though. If I come back to New York some day as a big star, I'll tell all. There – that'll give you something to look forward to when you're being painfully bored by those society idiots.' After that she turned resolutely to superficial chatter about New York.

Chinese Delmonico's was up a staircase over a shop. It offered a prospect of glorious vulgarity which instantly appealed to Lottie. The long, open room was punctuated by decorative arches, where fearsome dragons wound their serpentine bodies through cascades of gilded wood. The ceilings were as elaborately coffered as any Jacobean great hall, and elegant Chinese paintings and calligraphy adorned the walls. The tables were innocent of cloths, with highly lacquered surfaces laid with the strangest tableware Lottie had ever seen. Beyond the eating area, a spotless kitchen was in full view of the diners.

The latter were a very mixed bag, ranging from the rich slummers and tourists Wilde had already mentioned, to ordinary Chinese who sat quietly around the corners of the room, eating with chopsticks from bowls held up close to their mouths. Between these ill-assorted groups was a scattering of Bowery youngsters, out for the cheapest palatable food in the area, great steaming bowls of the stew made of duck, chicken giblets, beanshoots and celery which they called chop suey.

Lottie pulled a face as they passed two diners feasting off the dish, and Wilde said: 'Don't worry – the Chinese invented that for Americans. No self-respecting Chinaman would touch it and neither will we.'

Wilde led Lottie through the intricacies of birds' nest soup, shark fin, steamed pigeons, pineapple chips and fresh lychees. It was all accompanied by fragrant jasmine tea served in exquisite little bowls of paper-thin porcelain.

The dinner cost Wilde rather more than Lottie was paying for a week's board at Ada Scully's. 'Christ!' she said, as she saw what he put on the plate. 'How on earth do those boys from the Bowery afford to eat here?'

'By avoiding the *carte*, of course. That chop suey mess probably costs them fifteen cents. You don't pay through the nose until you get a taste for shark's fin – and can you blame them? Mr Ling is probably the all-American Robin Hood, robbing the rich to put chop suey on the plates of the poor.' He laughed. 'The really crazy thing is that we smart types nudge each other in the ribs and feel superior because we know better than to order westernised slop. The Bowery kids reap the benefits.'

Lottie was still toying with her empty tea bowl. 'This is one of the prettiest things I ever saw,' she said.

'Then I insist we take you a memento of your first New York restaurant meal.' He said something in a low voice to the waiter, and when they left a few minutes later, the man handed them a small package. Wilde gave him a few dollars.

'There you are,' he said, 'the makings of your own tea shop. A porcelain tea service for two and a pack of jasmine tea.' He gave her an exaggeratedly moonstruck look and said: 'Who knows? Some day you may permit me to use the other cup.'

'Not this trip, old son! Although I may let you through my front door for another reason.'

'Name it, dear lady.'

'Having seen Bial's bill of fare, I'm terrified at the standard of the competition. As you're sort of in the business, d'you think you could come and help me rehearse tomorrow? Unless you have some pressing social engagement, that is,' she added hastily.

'Nothing to compare with enjoying your company. When should I arrive?'

'As early as you can, after breakfast. You could even come for breakfast, if you like. Mrs Scully is a very generous cook.'

'I think not. Coffee and a cigarette are my limit before eleven.'

'All right, after breakfast. Mrs Scully has an attic she sets aside for her boarders to practise in. Will you come and put me through my paces?'

'I can hardly wait. Do I get the pleasure of seeing you in tights?'

'I don't even appear on stage in those – unless pantomime has come to New York. Expect me in skirt and shirtwaist.'

He made a mock salute. 'Yes, ma'am! What time do I report for duty?'

'Coffee at eleven-thirty, start at noon, all right?'

'As I said, I can hardly wait.'

He put her in a cab and she clattered off back to Mrs Scully's.

Long after the carriage had disappeared, Wilde stood at the edge of Chatham Square, gazing after it. 'Where are you going to, my pretty maid?' he said, and then, in passable imitation of Lottie's gravelly cockney-Italian, ' "I'm going out beyond the stars, sir," she said.' He turned and strolled away northward, half looking for another cab.

After they had been in the attic for three hours, Ada Scully took pity on them and knocked on the door. 'Miss Casanova,' she said, 'I gotta tray fulla cold cuts an' potato chips an' pickles downstairs, and if your gentleman friend cares to come an' get it, he's welcome.'

'Oh, thank you! If I had to do another twirl I think I'd collapse,' Lottie told her.

She sat down with Antony and tackled her meal, along with a large glass of beer which Mrs Scully had sent up without mentioning it. Wilde was voluble about the food and about vaudeville in general, but had said nothing so far about her act. Eventually, Lottie could no longer resist the temptation. 'Well, what do you think?' she said.

He regarded her neutrally. 'Do you really want an opinion, or just compliments?'

'I'd like it to be the same thing.'

'Sadly, dear girl, it isn't. You're good — very good. But you're still on your way. Don't worry. Adam will be well pleased.'

She gave him a wrathful look. 'Well pleased? Bloody well pleased? I'm not three yards of worsted suiting! I'm an artiste. What am I doing wrong?'

'I knew you wouldn't like the truth . . . Lottie, there's nothing wrong. You have a perfectly acceptable act. One day you'll have something far beyond that. Don't expect the moon, yet, that's all. You're still getting started.'

'That's plain nonsense. You either have it or you don't, and I do. If there's something missing, it'll improve with practice. Come on, we've got work to do.' She jumped up and went to take up her position again as energetically as if she had barely stopped for breath, and had not just eaten a substantial meal.

He returned to the piano with a resigned sigh. 'It's no good, Lottie,' he murmured, more to himself than to her. 'You still need a little something extra to kindle the spark.'

CHAPTER TWENTY

Lottie was locking the attic door after Wilde had left, when she heard a noise behind her. Turning, she confronted an odd-looking trio: a man in shirtsleeves, tight black trousers, broad braces and a pork pie hat, accompanied by a woman who cradled a baby in her arms.

The man gave her a hesitant smile and started forward. 'Uh – you all finished up here now, Miss? 'cos if you are, Miz Scully says we can have the key and go through our act in there.'

'Yes, certainly. I hope I haven't kept you – I know I've been ages – but don't you want to get your baby off to bed first? I'll leave the room unlocked if you do.'

His smile dissolved into a laugh. 'Hell, no! He's part of the act – part that needs most practice, too.'

Lottie was aghast. The child was dressed to look as young as possible, and momentarily she had assumed he was an infant. Now she realised he was about three or four years old and deliberately disguised as a baby; but he was still impossibly young to be rehearsing for a stage act.

'Wh-what does he do?' she asked faintly.

'Oh, this'n that,' said the man. 'And this!' At that point he snapped his fingers and simultaneously turned sharply towards his wife. In one fluid movement she dislodged the child from his position against her shoulder and hurled him head-first towards the man. He flew through the air at alarming speed, on a trajectory considerably higher than the man's head. It seemed inevitable that the child would be crushed against the far wall, but the man reached out, hooked an arm around him and gathered him against his chest. Lottie discovered she had been holding her breath and now let it go in an explosive yell.

'You bastards – you might have killed him!'

But it seemed nothing could destroy the man's good humour. 'Hey, it worked, then! That's just how we figure the audience will feel.'

'You do that to him on stage? What if you misjudge?'

'Oh, we do, we do! Babies is much more rubbery than men an' women, though. Throw 'em and they roll natural . . . well, leastways, Buster always does. If Myra lets go too quick or I don't reach out fast enough, he hits the deck, rolls over an' sits up like he's been doing it from birth. Mind you, he practically has! Trouble is, we can't miss too often on stage, or the audience starts threaten-in' ta take us apart. So we need practice.'

'And you mean to tell me you're taking your own child in there at this hour, to throw him against a wall until you learn to catch him ten times out of ten?'

'Summin' like that, Miss, yes. Whatsamadda, you never seen child acrobats before?'

'Not when they're too young to express a preference for their means of earning a living, no.'

'Catch our act tomorrow, then. Miz Scully tells me yer on the same bill as us – Koster and Bial's.' His tone became confidential. 'Say, we're so nervous we're dropping the kid all over the place. Best hall we ever played yet. Until last year we wuz mostly workin' medicine shows. If we get this right, we're really be hitting the big time. How d'ya rate our chances?'

Lottie's indignation collapsed and she laughed helplessly. Where else would you hear a father expressing stage fright in terms of dropping his son on his head at frequent intervals? 'If you get it right, you'll bring the house down. I just hope I don't have to follow you, that's all. What's your name?'

'Keaton, Joe Keaton. Myra an' me appear as the Two Keatons, but if Buster here carries on the way he is, we'll soon need to change the billing to the Three Keatons.'

'If he survives that long!'

'Course he'll survive! Born in a theatre and weaned on grease-paint. 'tain't like throwing a normal kid around. Buster knows how ta bounce. Ya wanna come in an' watch?'

'I don't think my nerves are up to it, Mr Keaton, but good luck, anyway.' She touched the child's cheek. 'I'll pray for you, Buster. Goodnight, Mrs Keaton, Mr Keaton.' She handed over the attic key to Myra Keaton then made her way downstairs to her room.

Once she started going through her sheet music, she quickly forgot the interlude outside the practice room. Wilde had been reasonably enthusiastic about her performance, but certainly hadn't been bowled over. Lottie owed much of her success so far to a ruthless professionalism which had enabled her to see herself objectively and not merely as Ulick wished her to appear. Had she been dazzling, Wilde would have been dazzled. He wasn't. The act needed a lift.

It was well after midnight when she found it. It was a song fragment Ulick had dashed off for her three months before. He had completed it, but shortly afterwards had gone off on a drunken binge which had prevented them from rehearing the piece together and polishing it to fit Lottie's particular talents. For the first time as a music hall artiste, she was on her own in knocking material into shape. It worried her at first, but when she had been studying the song for a while, she realised that the polishing process had invariably amounted to Ulick moulding a combination of performer and song which reflected his personal view of Lottie Casanova's ideal stage image.

Until now, she had imagined he had stopped that when she refused to go on being the smooth young miss after her first few months on the stage. Now, with a shock, she realised he had never desisted, but had merely become more subtle about it. It began to dawn on Lottie that she might have a better grasp than Ulick of the persona that suited her best. She was back up in the practice attic before breakfast next morning, hammering out the catchy tune which was now imprinted on her mind, and trying an endless series of variations in delivery of the words.

It was almost ten o'clock when Mrs Scully knocked on the attic door and timidly poked her head into the room. 'I know I shouldn't disturb yer, Miss Casanova, but starvation never did a trouper no good and I ain't gonna have them saying my boarders wuz short a meal going onstage. Here's yer breakfast.'

'Mrs Scully, I don't suppose you play the piano?'

180

'If ya'd known my pa, yer wouldn't have to ask. He got religion, bad, and I had to play so he could lead the poor sinners in praising the Lord. Don't ask me ta read no music, but hum it an' I'll play like a church organist.'

As she spoke, she put down the laden tray on a small table. Now she sat at the piano and Lottie sang the verse and chorus a couple of times to give her an idea of tune and tempo. Three minutes later, Ada Scully was vamping out the verse and Lottie was giving her first performance of 'I Want To Go Where The Big Girls Go'. By the time they had run through it a couple of times, Lottie knew she was on to a winner. She might not bring the house down, but if they reacted the way Ada had, they'd certainly remember her.

Ada finished her accompaniment of the last chorus with a flourish of showy chords, then turned to Lottie, her eyes shining. 'When can I come an' see ya?' she said.

Flustered by her relief that she was not about to sink without trace, Lottie nevertheless held on to a sense of reality. 'Not until Wednesday at the earliest. Seeing you've helped make it possible, I want it to be right by the time you come. However well it goes down, I'll still be stumbling through it for the first couple of performances.' She reflected for a moment, then added: 'On second thoughts, you'd better come tonight. Bial's pulling me out on Tuesday if I haven't made good by then.'

Mrs Scully laughed. 'There's no fear a' that, honey. Yer'll be doing return engagements there in ten years' time if ya want to. I've seen solid gold before, and I know it when it hits me. Now, for my sake, eat some a' that food. Sausages an' pancakes ain't the best a' breakfasts when they're cold, but they're better than an empty stomach any day.'

Lottie removed the metal dish cover from her neglected breakfast and found it still almost as good as new. She wolfed the food, heart singing. Ada Scully watched her wonderingly. 'Beats me how ya eat like that an' manage ta keep that shape,' she said.

Lottie took a big gulp of coffee and grinned. 'Simple, I sweat it off, worrying about how soon they'll boot me out. You know, Mrs S, these pancakes are every bit as good luke-warm as hot.'

'Ada, honey, call me Ada. I feel as if I just delivered ya first baby.'

'I suppose in a way you did.' She fell silent for a moment and Mrs Scully thought she was going to cry. But then she uttered a deep sigh, shook her head as if clearing away unwelcome memories, and smiled again. 'Thanks for everything, Ada.'

As Lottie arrived at the 34th Street entrance shortly after noon, she heard faint strains of the orchestra inside the theatre playing 'The Entry Of The Gladiators'. She smiled faintly, half raised one arm in mimicry of the ancient salute, and said: *'Ave, Caesar, morituri te salutant.'*

'Now that, Lottie, is what I call class!' Antony Wilde was standing just inside the foyer, talking to Adam Bial, who merely muttered: 'What the hell's it mean?'

Smiling, Wilde translated: ' "Hail, Caesar, those about to die salute you." I fear our Miss Casanova has a grim opinion of New York audiences.'

'Jesus, these serio-comics get better educated every day. Dunno about being about to die; she's sure dressed up to kill though, I'll give her that.'

181

Lottie bowed slightly to Bial and said: 'Leave 'em gaping, Mr Bial, leave 'em gaping.' Then she swept past both men and into the theatre.

She had worn the most becoming outfit she had with her, and she needed the confidence it gave her. For the first time in her life, Lottie Casanova had stage fright badly enough to think she might dry on stage.

She shared a dressing room with the female half of a twelve-member trick cycling troupe, an ageing male impersonator and a French girl juggler. Fortunately for her sanity, the six lady cyclists departed for a last-minute run-through of their act – they were first on after Morton's MC routine. The impersonator was already a good way down a quart of whiskey, and the girl juggler looked as scared as Lottie felt.

Palms sweating, pulse racing, she sat in front of the fly-blown mirror and wondered why she was so terrified. 'It can't be not having Ulick along,' she muttered fiercely, 'it can't! I don't give a damn about him any more . . .' No, an inner voice added, but it's the first time you've really done any of it alone, isn't it? The Rose didn't count, not like this. Even a drunken friend is better than no friend at all, and here you are, about to make a fool of yourself in front of strangers.

Ada Scully's sausages and pancakes stirred uneasily in Lottie's stomach. I shall be sick, she thought. The orchestra'll get my breakfast all down their sheet music. The idea drew a hysterical giggle from her and earned her a forbidding look from the male impersonator, who clearly had troubles of her own. Lottie forced herself to calm down and went to check out her costume. Satisfied that it did not need ironing or running repairs, she hung it on the hook beside her mirror, then concentrated on applying her stage makeup. After that, she looked around for a copy of this week's bill. Until now she had avoided seeing it, afraid she would find herself next to an act as striking as the Two Keatons, but now she needed to know when she was to go on.

It was moderately reassuring. A male illusionist preceded her. No clash there, she thought. They'll be ready for a bit of glamour after the tricks . . . then it dawned on her that no one came after her. Bial was letting her close the first half. 'Christ!' she said aloud. 'Whatever possessed him to do that?'.

'Whatsamadda with you?' said the male impersonator, tipsy rather than unfriendly.

'I-it's just this bill . . . Mr Bial hasn't seen my act before, but he's closing the first half with me. There must be some mistake.'

'No mistake, dearie. If Bial decides you're rotten, he can just close the curtain on you and end the first half a bit early. His stage manager's got so good at it, half the blades never even notice the act has stopped before it's finished, if you take my meaning. Ya know Bial's motto? Be good, and if ya can't be good, be brief – or I'll see to it that you are.' She chuckled raucously. 'Don't you worry ya head about that spot being any sorta pinnacle. More like a slippery slope.'

'Thanks. That was all I needed to know.' Lottie eyed her reflection with disfavour and stood up to put on her costume.

She had barely finished when someone rapped on the door and bawled: 'Casanova – Lottie Casanova – she in there yet?'

Lottie went to open the door. 'Who wants to know?'

The stage hand stood back, studied her from head to toe, and let out a low, appreciative whistle. 'Me, for one, lady! But besides me, there's an entire orchestra out there, cutting up 'cos yer the only artiste hasn't run through her music yet.'

'Oh, Christ – I was so nervous I forgot about them!'

'Well they ain't forgot about you, and the conductor's getting edgy, so I'd get moving if I wuz you.'

In a flurry of petticoats, Lottie turned to grab her music. Each act did a quick Monday morning rehearsal onstage with full orchestra, but any who missed it still had to complete a run-through of their music before the first house started. She had skipped the rehearsal to practise alone at Ada Scully's, but now she had to do some sort of try-out. Hesitantly, Lottie approached the stage.

She had not fully thought out the sequence of her act, and that alone was unlike her. Normally, she and Ulick planned it like a military campaign. But this time she had been satisfied to get each song right and then make sure the dance routine went smoothly. If she had planned the sequence at all, she had done no more than vaguely assign her new song to the end of her act.

Apart from the new number, she had done the other two routines so often that they were as natural as breathing. The orchestra breezed through a handful of English music hall hits, a couple of them already well known in America. Then Lottie sang her new number. When she had finished, the orchestra leader gave her an amiable enough bow, but hardly seemed overwhelmed by her performance.

On her way back to the dressing room, she gave herself an angry little shake. Why should he have been? The mime routine that went with the song was what made it, as well as the minor high-speed costume change involved. She wouldn't be doing that until she appeared before the audience, so naturally he'd escaped the full impact. Why was she so worried?

Then realisation hit her and she stopped in her tracks. 'Oh, Lottie, you stupid cow!' she said. 'The first bloody lesson you learned and you've forgotten it already!'

Back in the dressing room, she laid out the sheet music and went over it all again. What had she been playing at? This wasn't a one-hour concert featuring her alone, building from modest beginnings to a grand climax. It was a fifteen-minute routine which had to grab the audience by the throat in the first thirty seconds or play to a chattering, distracted house. She had learned that the hard way at the Rose of Normandy the first time she sang professionally. And here she was, throwing away the best opportunity she ever had by saving the big number until last. Christ, Ulick had been more useful than she'd realised. Since he started managing her, she had never needed to use that sense of timing – he'd arranged it all for her. Well, onstage her timing was immaculate. It was about time she applied it to planning the act, too.

Lottie moved across to the screen where her extra costume for the new number was hanging on its hook. Of course this was the right way to do it. It even simplified the costume change. This way, she'd be taking off, not putting on and taking off, and there would be no need for her to flit offstage for a few seconds to fling on the extra clothes . . .

When the show opened, she was standing in the wings, palms wet, mouth dry, tortured by nerves as she had never been in London. What was it about this audience? The men out there were only the cousins of those she had played to hundreds of times at the Oxford or the Canterbury. Why did an American accent make so much difference? Her stomach lurched as the orchestra struck up a strident tune and Morton ended his comic introduction to the team of cyclists. Next came a troupe of knockabout acrobats. Their act put Lottie vaguely in mind of the Keatons, and she sighed with relief at the thought that they were appearing towards the end of the second half. She couldn't have endured the suspense of wondering about Buster's chances of surviving the afternoon of top of her own nervousness.

The first half acts seemed to drag on forever. Morton's patter, so brilliant on Saturday night, fell leaden on her ears today. Lottie had sent a note to the orchestra leader, instructing him that she was moving the new song to the beginning of her act. Now all she had to do was wait, and study the extra costume which was hanging on a rail beside her. She had no intention of putting it on until the last minute, otherwise it would crush the elaborate knee-length satin gown with its endless flounced petticoats, which was her costume for the bulk of the act.

Then the illusionist who preceded her on the bill was doing his big routine, drawing a hoop along the shapely length of the female assistant he had suspended horizontally three feet above the stage. Lottie turned away from the act and started putting on her extra costume. It comprised a child's doll, a giant muff and tam o'shanter hat of the sort worn by aristocratic little girls of the day, and a long coat, again of childish cut, fastened from throat to ankles. She had ordered it from Stinchcombe's months before her American trip, with a vague idea of putting together just such a song as the one she would sing tonight. But Ulick had not liked the idea and the coat had stayed in the back of the cupboard. Only defiance had made her pack it with her other stage costumes before coming to New York. Once it was on, Lottie looked like a devilish parody of a child, her flamboyant looks and garish stage makeup exaggerating the impact of the simple clothing.

She barely had time to tuck the doll under her arm, jab her hands deep inside the muff, assume an expression of angelic innocence, feel the pit of her stomach tumbling away from her into limbo, and then the orchestra was playing the introduction to Ulick's half-finished song. She was on.

Sauntering childishly, gazing wide-eyed up towards a promenade made invisible to her by the incandescent limelight, she began to sing in a piping voice:

> 'Nursey says I have to play with Dolly.
> Mother says I mustn't play with boys.
> But I just think it would be very jolly
> To leave behind these childish joys . . .'

At this point she flung aside hat, doll and muff, turning her saunter into a rippling stride, and came downstage into the full glare of the footlights. As she moved, she raised her hand to the coat collar and in one long, sweeping motion, undid the concealed front fastening from neck to hem, singing.

184

'. . . Because, you see . . .
I want to go where the big girls go,
I want to do the things they do.
I want to learn all the things they know –
And I want to learn them all with you!'

As she tore into the chorus, her entire personality seemed to change from baby to rip-roaring seductress, and when she did it in the right costume, with the boost an audience gave her as always fuelling her talent, the effect was electrifying. So was the contrast of her indecently tight-fitting red satin gown with the quiet grey of the coat she had just discarded. She turned her back on the audience, whose undivided attention was on her now, and wiggled back upstage, picking up the muff as she went. She turned again, pranced back to the footlights and sang the chorus once more, peeping seductively over the top of the furry muff. As she came to the last line of the chorus, she tossed aside the muff again, gestured forward over the orchestra pit towards a point in the front row of tables, assumed her most dazzling smile and purred:

'And I want to learn it all with you –'

Her pointing finger moved to the left, punctuating each repeated phrase.

'And you . . . And you . . .'

Every man in the front row of tables was convinced Lottie had fallen for him. Still blinded by the glaring lights, she knew what was happening out there without the need to see. Her nerves had vanished. They were men, weren't they? Give 'em the right come-on and they'd eat out of your hand. Why had she worried for a moment?

Lottie knew when to stop. It was a major reason why she had come so far, so fast, in English music hall. The second chorus was the end of 'I Want To Go Where The Big Girls Go'. Time to give them something else.

The something else was a short, witty rendering of 'She Was Only A Bird In A Gilded Cage', which Lottie performed as half parlour ballad, half dance routine. It was hilarious, and always went over well in London. Here, it appealed to the American tendency to regard the English as milksops, and her parody succeeded even more because it bolstered the audience's prejudice.

After that, she traded on her spurious cockney-Italian ancestry, and gave them 'Giuseppe, Play-a Da Organ, And Give-a Da Monkey Da Nuts'. By now, they were enchanted by the combination of jaunty humour and blatant sex appeal. Feeling the waves of pleasure rising from them, she thought, Christ, I could end with 'Abide With Me' and they'd probably join in! Instead, she performed one of her favourite songs, a number she seldom sang in England for the same reason her idol, Nellie, had usually avoided it. Other, better-known, English artistes had made it their own. It was still the all-time great music hall woman's song – 'The Boy I Love Is Up In The Gallery'. For this, she cast aside all flippancy and sensuality and went straight for the

185

heart-strings, assuming her brave-cockney-sparrow face. It was an unbeatable coda. Rivet them with the child-into-tart routine, make them laugh, then make them cry, and love you as a tough little girl with a heart of gold . . .

As she reached the lines

'There he is – can you see 'im? –
Waving of his 'andkerchief'

She heard the susurrus of masculine suiting against seat as half the audience turned and peered up at the promenade, instinctively seeking the man who had won her heart. Now *that* was a successful act!

Antony Wilde and Adam Bial were both waiting for her when she came offstage. Not that she really noticed. Half her brain had been calculating every move she made. The other half had been making love to the audience, responding to its surges of passion and drowning in the fulfilment of its desire. She was drenched in sweat and relaxed as nothing else but a successful stage appearance could make her.

Watching her approach, Bial murmured to Wilde: 'Hell, she looks as if she's just tumbled outa bed with the biggest stud in New York!'

Wilde smiled at him. 'She has, Adam. Haven't you realised that, after all these years in vaudeville?'

But Bial was not listening. He was greeting his new discovery. Beaming, he embraced Lottie. 'Well done, baby. From now on, it's Lottie and Adam, okay?'

She smiled dreamily. 'Thanks, Mr Bi . . . Adam . . . Look, d'you mind giving me ten minutes or so before we talk? I'm never much use when I come offstage.'

They let her go. Bial said: 'She'll bring the house down tonight, Tony. Why didn't ya tell me she was this good?'

'I didn't know, dammit! I spent nine hours putting her through her paces in that wretched attic yesterday, and I didn't see a trace of it.'

Bial stared at him. 'You losing your touch or summin'?' I'd a' seen her blazing out a hundred miles away.'

'Adam, I swear to God it wasn't there yesterday. That opening song was a stroke of genius, and she wasn't using it then. But it wasn't that – it was the whole act. She's a different woman in front of a full house. I think she needs an audience to seduce before she comes to life.'

'Hmm, I always thought Tanguay raped her audiences, but I'll admit this one is new to me.'

'You like it, though.'

'Love it! When she started that "You and you and you" business, I was ready to leap onstage with her, and I've seen it all. God knows what it'll do to the blades tonight.'

It did all they had hoped. Lottie was a sensation. After the second act, Bial extended her booking from six weeks to eight. 'I'd give ya more, but two months is the longest my audiences will go without wanting a complete change,' he told her. 'If you want to do some more at the end of yer tour, though, just let me know. I'll jump at the chance.'

Lottie was on the point of departing with Antony Wilde to celebrate her success. 'It's the dates in between here and San Francisco I need help with, Adam. All suggestions gratefully received.'

He gestured dismissively. 'Aah – no need ta worry about that. They'll be standing in line to book you.'

But he was wrong. Vaudeville was in process of transforming itself from a stag diversion into respectable family entertainment and the all-powerful managers who controlled theatre chains nationwide were rabidly anti-sex and anti-foreigner. Two months later, after her triumph in New York, Lottie was still confronting three and a half months without a booking. Daily it became more obvious that if she was going to work at all before her San Francisco date, she would have to do it in burlesque.

CHAPTER TWENTY-ONE

Sometimes Lottie wondered if she would ever have done it without Ada Scully. Probably not. Ada not only made it bearable: some of it was positively fun. The landlady involved herself at the beginning of Lottie's last week at Koster and Bial's.

'If ever I seen a face lookin' fer a shoulder ta cry on, it's yours,' she said, putting down Lottie's breakfast tray and seating herself across the table. 'How about tellin' me?'

Lottie smiled wanly at her. 'Thanks, Ada, you're very kind. But what's the point in my boring you? There's nothing you can do to help.'

'Often helps jest ter talk,' said Ada. 'So why doncha go right ahead. I'll shut ya up if it gets too much.'

Lottie started poking at her breakfast and said: 'It's the onward bookings, Ada. They've come to nothing.'

'Who're you using?'

'No one professional . . . not professional agents, that is. Adam tried to get me one and they were all so stand-offish about an unknown English artiste he said I'd have just as much chance if he and Tony Wilde tried to place me. He was right, I think, even if they haven't had any luck. I went to see a couple of the agents who *were* prepared to represent me. We had a name for their sort in London and I'm sure you have one here.'

'I never heard a' no agent turning down the prospect of good cash because he didn't like the English,' said Ada. 'Are they playing you straight?'

'Oh, no doubt of that. It's not that the good agents don't like the English. As you say, they like money wherever it comes from. It's just that they know we're harder to place than we used to be, with Tony Pastor and the others trying to drag vaudeville uptown by its suspenders. All the circuits are interested in is respectable acts and All-American acts. Their beau ideal is respectable All-American.' She laughed sourly. 'You know I'm not American, and no one would *ever* call my act respectable!'

Ada Scully thought that over for a while and then nodded grudgingly. 'Yeah, s'pose yer right. And now yer gonna tell me Wilde an' Bial have had no more luck than the agents, fer the very same reasons.'

'Of course. Ada, what am I going to do? As from the end of the week, I'm unemployed.'

'What d'yer showbiz chums recommend?'

'They're divided right down the middle. Tony says I should bide my time and try to tone down the risqué bits of my act, and that eventually there'll be a craze for foreign artistes and the bookings will come in.'

'Hmm . . . makes sense ta me. Fashions change so fast in this city, he could be talking about a few weeks from now.'

'Yes, but I haven't enough money behind me to take the risk. For a start, without the naughtiness, my act wouldn't be me. And what if I did clean it up and the fashion never changed? I'd be unemployable and I wouldn't be able to pay my fare home or to San Francisco, let alone survive for long enough to get there.'

'So that's one man's advice. What does the other say?'

'Adam? Oh, that's impossible, really. Burlesque.'

'Adam Bial suggested *you* do burlesque?'

Lottie nodded, too mortified to speak.

'But in New York that'd be professional suicide.'

'He said,' "Listen kid, you an' me gotta lot in common. Both of us would do anything rather than starve. So do burlesque. It ain't starvation." I told him I'd rather work the pavements round the Tenderloin.'

Ada snorted with mirth. 'Good for you. What'd he say?'

'Said it was easier on the feet but a damned sight harder on the butt and the pay was worse.' At that point Lottie saw the funny side of her predicament and she, too, started laughing. 'Oh, Christ, Ada, if it wasn't for the damage it would do me in vaudeville, I'd try it like a shot. But I don't want to spoil New York for myself in the future.'

'Ya really wouldn't mind burlesque?'

'I can think of things I'd rather do, but the way I began in London was much the same.'

'Ever thought a' trying it outa town?'

Lottie gaped at her. 'No. Since you mention it, I haven't. But how could I hope to get started?'

Ada tapped her own scrawny bosom. 'Me, that's how. I'd come with ya as yer factotum.'

'Don't be ridiculous. You have a business to run.'

'Yeah, and I have a daughter and son-in-law with itchy feet ta get in here and start managing it for me.'

'But, Ada, even if you could get free in the next few days, what on earth would you be able to do to set up a tour?'

'Maybe more'n you think. Don't you remember me tellin' you my pa was a preacher-man?'

'Of course. I still don't understand.'

'Lottie, honey, the reason I'm nailed down in a New York boarding house is that I never had the same roof over my head for three nights together when I was a girl – often never had a roof at all, come ta that. I needed somethin' permanent. My pa ran a glorified medicine show, with God as the cure-all tonic. I knew every dead and alive hole in the Midwest before I was nine, and a lot of other parts a' this goddam' vast country by the time we finally parted company. Guess what my job wuz.'

'Passing out the hymn books?'

'Fat chance! Going on ahead ta the next town and drumming up interest in Daddy's act. Findin' a free hall or at a pinch a bitta open ground where the Gospel meeting could take place. I know howta set up a hick town for a celebrity better'n anyone else you're likely to meet.'

Lottie was gazing at her in wonder. 'And you'd come with me?'

190

'I think I'd *pay* ta come! Boarding houses is all very well for a few years. After that ya get ta miss the road.'

'Ada, get hold of your daughter. You're on!'

They had fun planning it, because neither of them really believed it would happen. Lottie had counted her money and decided she could risk taking a week off after she finished at Koster and Bial's. During that time, Ada would instruct her daughter in the management of the boarding house – the girl had been her helper there for five years before her marriage – and make plans with Lottie for their tour.

Both Tony Wilde and Adam Bial had already told the women they were mad. 'For God's sake, Lottie, if you won't consider your own interests, what about Ada's? Wake up to it! She's a star-struck middle-aged woman who'd say anything to get a first-hand taste of vaudeville, even if it means giving up her living. What if you come back with your tails between your legs two weeks after you start out, and her daughter won't relinquish the reins? What if – and I'd take bets on this – she really doesn't know one end of the job from another?'

'What if bloody pigs had wings? Do me a favour, Tony, and stop acting like an old washerwoman. Me an' Ada know what we're doing, and –' here she turned a threatening glare on Adam, who was also present '– Neither of you old pros has had much luck placing me in New York, have you?'

They looked away, and Bial made dismissive muttering noises before saying: 'You should have been more flexible, Lottie.'

'Flexible! Flexible, the man says. If I'd been more flexible I'd have fallen over backwards and they'd have carried me off in a basket. Face it, Adam, no one in cleaned-up vaudeville wants me, and I don't want New York burlesque. If I do the same thing in the sticks, no one'll ever know. I'll make enough to live and I'll get to California in time to do my Orpheum Circuit stint. What's so wrong with that?'

'Relying on some demented preacher's daughter to get yer bookings, that's what's wrong with it! Christ, you'd be better off with a medicine show huckster!'

Lottie grinned at him, triumph in her eyes. 'That's what I've got, you bloody fool! What would *you* call a travelling evangelist if not a mountebank?'

Bial's face turned a muted shade of purple. Tony Wilde burst out laughing and conceded defeat. 'Lottie, your roots are showing again. Adam wouldn't know what a mountebank was if he passed one in the street – and most days he does!'

At the beginning of Lottie's free week, she and Ada spread out a huge map of the USA on the table in her room, and began drawing lines. 'Too hot ta head south this time a year,' said Ada. 'Anyway, I'm familiar with Illinois and Wisconsin an' a coupla points further west, so let's look up there.'

They mapped a route which took them directly to the Midwest and allowed for a fairly long stay around the middle-sized settlements before heading for California. Ada was searching out places with sizeable populations but few big city airs: she did not want to call down an important newspaper on Lottie's head. The plan was to get her artiste across the country with decent earnings and minimal attention from the press.

The game plan was as straightforward as Ada's target towns. She would travel a couple of days ahead and use a large mainline station town as her base. Once she had found enough dates in the small-town halls of the region, she would meet Lottie at the station and they would travel on together to the first engagement. A few days before the end of that booking, Ada would move on to the next major stop on their route and repeat the process. With three such sweeps, they hoped to fill the time and finance the journey to San Francisco. Neither of them was thinking ahead of that.

Anthony Wilde gave Lottie dinner the night before she left. Ada had already been gone for three days. This time he took her to the original Delmonico's, not the Chinese version. 'As you're going out into the backwoods, I thought I'd better give you a last taste of civilisation before we lose you forever,' he said. 'Where do you intend starting?'

'That's in the hands of Ada and the hall managers,' said Lottie.

'You must have some idea – where are you going tomorrow, for instance?'

'A place called Toledo. Does it mean anything to you?'

'Toledo, Ohio?'

'Unless you think Ada Scully could have made it to Toledo, Spain, since Wednesday, yes.'

'Dear God, I didn't know they *had* vaudeville in Toledo, Ohio.'

'For all I know, they don't. We shan't be staying there; Ada says it's too big. She's using it as a base for a lot of smaller towns in Michigan.'

Wilde closed his eyes with exaggerated horror. 'Lottie, you're making your own bed of nails. What on earth do you expect to do there?'

'Stop showing off. You know damned well what I intend to do – exactly what I was doing at K&B's, but for less money, that's all.'

'Where are you going after Michigan?'

Lottie's eyes were sparkling. 'Wisconsin . . . Minnesota . . . Iowa . . . oh, Tony, the places have such wonderful names: Iron Mountain, Eau Claire, Sioux City . . .'

'Sioux City? They probably still have wild Indians there!'

'I shall get really cross with you in a minute. In case you hadn't noticed, we're practically in the twentieth century and your countrymen have been systematically wiping out the poor Indians for long enough to make the West safe for chorus girls.'

He decided he had debunked her venture too much, and turned to a more serious line of talk. 'How are you planning to manage financially?'

She shrugged. 'I don't expect to earn anything like what Adam was paying me, and I've saved as much of that as I could to tide us over the bad spells. But any of these little halls are bound to pay big money by local standards to get a competent entertainer – and my worst enemies would admit I'm competent.'

'Hmm, but how will Ada convince them of this without your lovely presence?'

'A combination of her evangelical skills and application of the Bial performance-on-approval method. She tempts them into giving me a try-out with a guaranteed wage if they like what they see. If they don't like it, they get two nights and I get one third of the week's fee. If they do, I stay for the full rate. Doing it like that, even if we strike bad luck, at least our board and lodging will be paid for the week.'

'Did you think of that, or was it Ada's idea?'

'Ada's, a hundred per cent. I told her about Bial's system and she adapted it for the trip. Bet it will work.'

'For your sake, I only hope the locals will refrain from using it as a cheap way of getting a split week out of you.'

Lottie's look was withering. 'Once a hall full o' them have seen me on stage, I defy any shyster manager to try getting rid of me after two performances. They'd lynch him!'

'So nice to hear one so young and modest about her talent,' murmured Wilde.

'If you don't shut up, I'll make you come with me.'

'No, please! Anything but that!'

The old show business world of slabs, dives and honky-tonks was dying: had already died in Chicago, New York and San Francisco. Most vaudes welcomed the change. Nowadays they enjoyed better wages, more comfortable dressing rooms and refined audiences whose social pretensions stopped them throwing heavy objects if they disapproved of an act. But the occasional maverick lamented the transformation.

There were acts the length and breadth of America who had adored the cold, damp, ill-lit halls with their appalling backstage conditions and crowd of baying men out front. They made themselves respectable for long enough to reap the benefits of modern vaudeville, but now and then went off the rails, either fading completely from the scene or resurfacing around one-horse country towns, playing anything from medicine shows and state fairs to boom town bar rooms and outdated run-down theatres.

This was the world into which Ada Scully led Lottie, and she took to it like a duck to water.

Ada met her at Toledo with the news that she was booked in Ashtabula Harbor for one week and Saginaw, Michigan, for the second. 'When ya hear what they're payin', yer'll see why I didn't hang around lookin' for more work after them two,' Ada said gloomily.

'How much?'

'I hacked fifty dollars outa the guy in Saginaw, but Ashtabula was even worse. Forty was their limit.'

'Was it worth playing for that?'

'There has to be some good news, dearie. I got us a decent room in a private house for twelve dollars – full board fer the two of us. We'll make some sorta profit on the week, don't worry.'

That reassured Lottie a little. 'Well, to paraphrase Adam Bial, it pays better than the Tenderloin – just!'

It was an odd introduction to the American hinterland. Overnight, Lottie saw the opposite of what had impressed her so on arrival in New York. The brash sophistication of the city was replaced by a brand of small-town life she had never seen in England. She rapidly decided the whole experience was so entertaining that perhaps she should have been paying them.

When she saw the little hall at Ashtabula Harbor, she found it hard to believe it was used as a theatre. It was called the Melodion, and had started its commercial existence not as a music hall but as a dyeworks. 'It looks as if it still is one,' said Lottie, eyeing the structure with disfavour as the manager showed her around.

He had heard it all before. 'If we hadn't took the dyeworks, wouldn't a' been no theatre here at all,' he said. 'So I reckon it's not such a bad deal. Now, are ya gonna let me hear ya or not?' She did a couple of her standard numbers, explaining she had a novelty turn that depended on the costume for its effect, and he confirmed her booking for the week on the strength of what he had seen.

The bill was as old-fashioned as the area, with an afterpiece to close the show after the variety turns were complete. This consisted of a little drama, heavy on sentimentality and light on credibility, but had the advantage of featuring the exceptional talents of a young banjo player, Ben Rowland, who had appeared on the main programme.

Whoever converted the Melodion had done so as cheaply as possible, and a door at the rear of the stage still opened into the building's original toilet, a grand if noisome two-seater affair. Edward Husking, the manager, found various uses for the door, with a range of backcloths painted around it to transform it to town store, country mansion or humble log cabin. In every case, the players used the door as an entry-point to the stage, but as the only way to and from the toilet was the stage entrance, anyone coming on from there had to wait inside until his cue. Huskings had devised a self-closing mechanism for the door consisting of a heavy stone and a length of rope, which stretched over a pulley behind the scenes.

For the week of Lottie's engagement, Huskings, an old trouper himself, had written a sentimental sketch about an old freed slave – the virtuoso banjo player in blackface – returning to die on the plantation where he had spent his confined but nevertheless idyllic youth.

The old slave was supposed to maunder around the stage, plucking magical notes from a dilapidated banjo he found under a bush, until, as he collapsed in his final illness, his old master – Huskings – emerged from the toilet door, tonight masquerading as the old plantation mansion, and discovered him outside.

As the Southern aristocrat cradled the dying Darkie in his arms, the assembled cast backstage were supposed to provide a collective rendering of 'Sweet Bye And Bye'. Before they had the opportunity, the door, inefficiently closed, swung open to reveal the two-seater toilet. The property man in the wings, unaware of the catastrophe, ignited a shovel full of Red Fire to add a dramatic sunset tint to the sketch's closing moments, and the crimson light played over the exposed sanitary fittings, making the toilet the brightest point on set.

One of the hayseeds in the front row, carried away by the drama of the moment, yelled out: 'Jesus, the privy's on fire!'

Someone had the wit to lower the curtain and as it hit the stage Huskings, in a frenzy, screamed: 'Who took the fucking brick off that privy?'

Lottie, still in costume and make-up, turned and looked steadily back at Ada. 'I'm so glad I've done my act,' she said. 'How could anyone hope to follow that?'

The flaming privy turned out to be the highlight of the week in Ashtabula. 'I suppose we couldn't expect any better,' said Lottie as they boarded the Saginaw train. 'There can't be many women in vaudeville who've seen an afterpiece like that one.'

Saginaw gave them an unexpected opportunity to stretch their funds. It was a small town, and still predominantly a stag house, so Lottie had no reservations about doing her saucy 'I Want To Do What The Big Girls Do' routine. The

194

audience were appreciative and she really let herself go for the Wednesday night show. Afterwards, a well-dressed stranger was waiting for her backstage.

Lottie gave him a kindly but dismissive smile. 'Sorry, Mr, er . . . but I don't keep company with gentlemen from the audience after my act. Now, if you don't mind . . .'

She was already edging the man expertly towards the door when Ada fluttered between them, looking positively subservient. 'Miss Casanova, just a minute . . . I think you made a mistake. This gentleman ain't a – an admirer. He's in the business.'

Lottie stopped short. 'Then why didn't you say so?'

The newcomer smiled. 'You scarcely gave me chance to draw breath before I was out of the door, Miss Casanova. I caught your act tonight and I'm interested in booking you. We're a much bigger concern than this one.'

'Where?'

'Chicago. They don't come much bigger than that out here.'

Ada, how could you? Lottie thought. The very place I don't want to do burlesque . . . someone important might notice . . . But Ada was radiant. What was going on?

'My name's John Kowalski. I'm the manager of the American Music Hall. We've lost a good European act this week through illness and I'd like to take yours on to fill in. You're actually a lot better than the act you'd be filling in for, but I'm contracted to take her back when she's over this bug. It's only a week, but your dresser here says you have that long between here and your next engagement. How would you like to play the American?'

Lottie fought down a jubilant shriek and gave him an impassive look. 'What are you offering?'

Kowalski looked around the shabby dressing room and laughed. 'Oh, that shouldn't be a problem. Two hundred dollars for the week.'

'Mr Kowalski, you have yourself a serio-comic.'

The American was wonderful. The audience there were used to the slightly risqué tone of some European acts and they loved it. The clean-up campaign had yet to arrive in Chicago. It was like the first couple of nights at Koster and Bial's all over again, and at first Lottie wished she could stay for a month, then move on triumphantly to San Francisco.

By the end of the week, though, she felt differently about it. On Saturday evening, Ada caught her sliding an appreciative hand over the smooth surface of the dressing table in her well-appointed dressing room. 'Sad to be off, I'll bet,' she said.

'Not as much as I expected,' said Lottie. She smiled at Ada in the mirror. 'To tell the truth, those two weeks in Ohio and Michigan were so wonderfully awful that I'm quite looking forward to the next lot. After all, if it was only money that interested me, I'd have stayed in Wiltshire.'

'What's that yer sayin'? Wiltshire, where's Wiltshire?' But Lottie was already bustling about collecting her belongings in preparation to depart for their hotel.

In fact the Chicago engagement stretched two days into a second week, as the originally booked French singer was still unfit. Ada left Lottie in the city on the Monday and headed westward again in search of further work. John Kowalski

195

had supplied a couple of likely names for her to look up along the way.

He came to see Lottie the day before her departure. 'I hate to lose such a good act,' he said, 'but I'm booked right up to my budget for at least a month. I don't suppose you can arrange to come back here then? It would mean three or four weeks work for you.'

'I really wish I could, but that would take me too close to my San Francisco booking, and I don't want to miss that.'

'Yeah, sure.' He began to depart, then turned back. 'I have to say it – you have the damnedest way of getting bookings. How come a girl in your class is crossing the country on her own doing burlesque spots?'

Lottie gave him a brilliant smile. 'At least it keeps me off the streets, Mr Kowalski.'

When she got off the train at Omaha, Ada embraced her like a daughter and said: 'Honey, I hope yer ready fer this. Not sure I am . . . I got us three weeks, but Jeez, they're colourful places!'

Lottie was delighted. 'If it's work and the money is enough, I'm happy. How much?'

'Not what I'd like, but it'll get us by. *Ninety* dollars a week for the two-week booking in Sioux City, *fifty* for the single week in Laramie.'

'Well, the fifty could be a bit better, but I wasn't expecting anyone to go above a hundred out here. It's better than Ashtabula Harbor.'

'Wait'll ya see this place and yer'll know why. Ya may wanna back out. It's a sorta cat-house . . .'

'If a cat-house is what I think it is, indeed I may. At least, if they expect the artistes to participate in the off-bill entertainment!'

'Nah – not at your level, at any rate. The wine girls do, though. They do the chorus routines an' then go fer a little bitta slap and tickle with the customers afterwards.'

'In the theatre?' Lottie's eyebrows had risen somewhere in the region of her hairline.

'Good as. They got these little boxes each side a the balcony; look just like boxes in a regular theatre, except they got lace curtains they can roll right down. The manager says they can still see the acts through the lace, but the acts can't see them.' She sniffed. 'Jest as well, if you ask me.'

The River Palace was prominent among the cluster of buildings on the east bank of the Missouri River which formed Sioux City. In fact, it and the handful of other places of entertainment were the only buildings of real prominence. Danny May was the owner-manager of the Palace and he prided himself on giving his customers just what they wanted. The minute he saw Lottie Casanova, he decided she was it. Lottie shook hands with him warily. He was about forty, big, muscular and tough-looking, with a complexion that said he probably liked his whiskey too much. Judging by the look he was giving her now, he also liked women more than was good for him – or them.

'You've agreed to pay me a high salary for a place of this size, Mr May. Why?'

He smiled winningly. Aren't we just the innocent little boy, she thought. 'Mrs Scully described your talents so rosily that I couldn't say no,' he said. 'And now I've seen you for myself, I'm sure I did the right thing.'

196

'Nonsense! No one can spot talent until it's performing in front of him.'

'And aren't you doing just that, Miss Casanova?'

Lottie forced her temper to stay battened down. 'Not until I start my act, no. What you see before you is the off-duty me, and she's not available – for *any* engagements.'

'Well, we'll see about that. Why don't you take a look around the old place, starting with your rooms, of course.'

This was slipped in with the blandest of smiles, but Lottie stopped in her tracks. 'Surely, Mr May, you were not under the impression that Mrs Scully and I would live here during my engagement?' God, he should be on the stage himself, she thought, the way he's running through the theatrical expressions.

Now he was manifesting injured innocence. 'But of course. It's what all our young ladies do.'

'I'm not your young lady, Mr May – or anyone's, and I think that goes for Mrs Scully too. Now, I have a better suggestion. You tell me where we can hire some transport for half an hour or so, and we'll go looking for respectable lodgings. When we've found some, we'll be back to look around the River Palace. Any objections to that?'

'None at all. Of course you must use my rig. It'd be a pleasure. But remember, if you're unlucky, there's always space here.'

She turned towards the door. 'Never in a thousand years, Mr May.'

He offered to take them around the town but Lottie preferred to drive herself. 'I can't see them fighting to give us house room with him as our guide, can you?' she asked Ada.

Ada looked dubious. 'Don't know as it makes much difference, Lottie. Folks round here are bound to ask why yer in town – you hardly look like the new schoolteacher. Once they know, I wonder if any o' the respectable ones'll give us house room on any terms?'

They wouldn't. On the outskirts of town, a few attractive older houses had discreet signs in the windows offering rooms and board for respectable people. They made it clear that did not include Lottie and Ada. After half an hour of thankless enquiries, Lottie got into the rig and drove off without bothering with the last house in the tree-shaded road. 'No point in that,' she said. 'It'll be more of the same and I'll hit the next woman who treats me like Jezebel. There's bound to be an hotel in town. As long as May doesn't own it, we'll stay there.'

Not only was there an hotel, but it had a suite of two bedrooms and a connecting sitting room. There was even a bathroom across the landing from it. Lottie bargained like a cockney market trader and beat the clerk down on the price for a two-week stay.

Emerging triumphantly ten minutes later, she said: 'There! It might cost more than I intended of Dan May's money, but anything would be better than another of those sour old hens looking down at me and saying they wouldn't rent me a couple of rooms. Now for Danny Boy!'

Dan May was very proud of the River Palace. It had swallowed a lot of his winnings as a professional gambler and worse, but now it was repaying him a thousandfold in other people's weaknesses. The theatre admission charge

197

was minimal – between twenty-five and fifty cents. Even on busy Saturday nights there were never more than a few hundred tickets sold. There was no admission charge for high-spending regulars. Barmen and wine-room girls kept them supplied with complimentary tickets with the approval of May. His profits came from the sale of food and wine and running the gambling games.

The place was not strictly a brothel, but if any of the wine-room girls wished to boost their wages by taking customers back to their rooms, Dan was the last man to stop them. Outside the main entrance of the palace, facing the river front, was a hanging sign which said:

YOUR PLEASURE IS OUR BUSINESS

Dan meant every word of it.

The Palace opened around lunchtime, but it never ran a matinee. There was an opulent lunch counter which sold excellent cooked food – pie, oysters, fried chicken and enormous sandwiches – at ruinous prices. But it was the best food in the area and May's place attracted the sort of men who had money to pay top prices.

The stage entertainment never started before ten at night and continued as long as there were enough customers buying expensive drinks. Until the show started, they could amuse themselves in the gaming room at faro, roulette, spindles and eight-die cases.

Spindles involved betting a dollar a time on the spin of an arrow in the centre of a square table. The player won whatever prize it pointed to when it came to rest. The big lure was usually a pile of silver dollars, but as the arrow operator controlled where it stopped by a squeeze mechanism concealed at the corner of the table, few ever left the table richer than they arrived.

A square shallow case with a glass top housed the eight-die game. Under the glass was more money, ranged in amounts from fifty cents to a hundred dollar bill. Each little hoard carried a note of the number which must be thrown to win it. The player paid his dollar, then tossed the eight dice from a box across the glass surface. But the operator supervised the reckoning and most players found counting the total thrown on eight dice too complex after he had been at May's rotgut liquor for any length of time.

The Palace had a certain overblown glamour which relied heavily on fat plaster cupids, padded velvet banquettes and lavish gilding. In a region which was short on big cities, it seemed the last word in sophistication. The stage show offered a wide range of acts of startling contrast. Some were barely competent, others were performers with a high degree of skill who preferred to pursue their careers in the raffish surroundings of the Palace than to fit themselves into the straitlaced fashions developing in the East and far West.

The wine-room girls were not performers, although they flounced through a debased variant of the Can-Can at the beginning of the show to give the customers an idea of what they were offering apart from wine. After that, they worked on a drink percentage basis. A dollar bottle of beer earned them ten cents. Individual fancy drinks raised them five cents a time and a four-dollar bottle of champagne was every girl's target with its fifty cents commission.

The champagne was Danny's pride and joy. It came in beautifully labelled

198

bottles and was made up of carbonated pear cider which he bought for sixty-four cents a bottle in case lots. He kept a reasonable stock of the real thing, too. There were plenty of local politicians, cattle kings and mine owners he liked to keep sweet, and he had a taste for good wine himself.

He showed Lottie around it all, glowing with the pride of the self-made tycoon. 'Ten years ago there was no entertainment in this town worthy of the name,' he said. 'Now, look at it. Everything a man could want.'

'Depends on your man, I suppose,' murmured Lottie, then added more generously, 'You're right, Mr May, it's quite an achievement. Now, d'you want me to go through my act, or are you going to take Mrs Scully's word that I'm good?'

Then he turned from a potential adversary into a man she liked. 'Think I'd rather risk you being no good and see you for the first time the way my customers do,' he said. 'I always did like a few surprises in my life. Oh, and if it don't offend your sense of propriety, how about calling me Danny?'

'Okay, Danny. What time am I on?'

He laughed. 'It'd be some trick if I could tell you that. You never played this sorta place before?'

Lottie took in the Palace with one sweeping glance. 'I shouldn't think there *is* another place like this!'

'Well, when the acts get going is more or less up to the audience. If they like it, the act'll keep on 'til they've had enough. If it dies, the next turn is on in a few seconds. Be here for eleven o'clock and we'll put you in just before the first interval, okay?'

Ada Scully found Lottie in the wings shortly before 11.30 that night. She was sitting on an upturned packing case, chin cupped in the palm of her hand, watching a painfully violent knockabout acrobatic act which was going down very well with the all-male audience. The coat and muff for her opening transformation number were hanging on a hook close by.

'Why d'ya do it, Lottie? A lovely girl like you, what's the draw of hanging round a joint like this waiting for a bunch a thugs to beat each other ta death before you go on and throw in your ten cents' worth?'

Lottie said: 'I thought you were one of the ones I didn't need to explain that to, Ada. You feel the pull of it, too – enough to give up a good living in New York and traipse across the wilderness with me.'

'Nah – it ain't the same, you know. Told you why I do it. At heart I'm a gypsy and I been needing to wander awhile for years now. All it is with me is itchy feet. My likin' for vaudeville's separate from that. This time the two jest happened ta come together, that's all. It ain't itchy feet with you, though, is it?'

The acrobats performed a particularly bloody stunt and the crowd yelled their appreciation. Lottie gestured towards them. 'That's what does it. I'll tell you something, Ada; only two things in my life lived up to my dreams about them before I tried them. All the rest let me down. The first was champagne. Just as good as they all said. The second was a warm audience.

'I can't tell you why a bunch of roughnecks in a hick town should matter to me, but when I hear that roar and it's for me, they do. Something inside me says that will be there when I've lost everything else – and as long as I have that, none of the rest matters.'

'Doncha get lonely?'

199

'Not yet. But then, nineteen is a bit young to start getting lonely, isn't it? Come back and ask me again when I'm twenty-five.'

Ada's answer was lost in another great roar of applause, as Basco and Roberts executed their final horrendous bumps and ran offstage, grinning wolfishly over the success of their routine.

'Great audience out there tonight, babe,' Roberts boomed at Lottie as he passed. 'Go an' slay 'em!'

'I hope I know how,' she quavered, as the single great surge of nerves she always experienced gripped her throat and gut. Then she was into her child's coat and onstage, to groans of despair at the all-enveloping nature of her costume.

By the time Lottie left the stage that night, she was convinced she would never sing again. First she did her standard act – a brisk fifteen-minute routine starting with 'I Want To Do What The Big Girls Do' and running through the English music hall staples that had gone down so well at Koster and Bial's and later in Chicago. They greeted each song with mounting appreciation and by the time she had sung 'Up In The Gallery' she could see there was no chance of stopping there. She gave them 'Waiting At The Church', 'It's All Right In The Summertime' and 'Daisy Belle'.

By now she was sweating like a navvy and her throat felt dangerously relaxed, but still they were crying out for more. She came offstage and stood, breathing deeply to calm herself, while the audience bayed for her return. Danny May arrived from the front of the house and said: 'Lottie, why didn't I meet you years ago? They're busting a gut for you and by tomorrow we'll be packed to the rafters. Get back on and do some more, you angel!'

'Danny, I can't. If you want me working tomorrow night, it's got to be shorter than this. My voice won't carry it.'

'But they're tearing the place apart. Listen to 'em!'

Beyond the proscenium arch, the audience – more an enthusiastic mob now – were chanting: 'Lot-tie! Lot-tie! Give us more Lot-tie!'

'God help the poor bastard who's following me,' she murmured. 'Look, Danny, I'll make a deal. Double my money and add another twenty and I'll do two spots a night instead of one, but each spot to be no longer than twenty minutes. Deal?'

'Two hundred dollars a week? No one gets that outside Chicago! You're crazy.'

'Lot-tie! Lot-tie! Where's our Lot-tie?' hollered the crowd. There was a remote sound of splintering furniture.

'Okay, done!' said May. 'But you'll have to get back on now to calm 'em down.'

'No, I won't – it'll only make them worse. You go out there and tell them I'll do a second spot later – say, one-thirty, but only if they behave themselves.'

He eyed her reproachfully. 'I hope you know what you're doing'.

Lottie watched him edge gingerly onstage and murmured: 'So do I, old fruit – so do I!'

CHAPTER TWENTY-TWO

If Ed Maskell had not decided to take a long-overdue vacation from his San Francisco newspaper job and visit his brother's cattle ranch south of Sioux City, Lottie might have spent months entertaining the revellers at the River Palace. Ed was a city boy by adoption and his longing for wide-open spaces had been satisfied by the end of his first week at the Circle M Ranch. His brother Mike had sent his wife to New England for the summer and now he felt ready to show Ed that the Plains were not utterly devoid of lively diversion.

'A couple of my hands came home last week raving about some new girl entertainer they have up at Sioux City,' he told Ed at breakfast one morning. 'If what they say is true, she's a cross between the Queen of Sheba and Eva Tanguay. Even if she's a drunk's daydream, there's usually a good show at the Palace, and plenty of gambling.'

'I can't wait, Mike. Let's try it tonight.'

Maskell went back three times that week, first to wonder at Lottie's hypnotic hold over her audience, then to fall under her spell himself. It was as if all Lottie's earlier experience had been preparing her for the River Palace. Now she strode on stage for her second spot each night, a bawdy goddess in short skirt and black silk tights, and wrenched their attention from faro, fried chicken and ersatz champagne alike. They gazed transfixed as her lush body wove athletically through dance routines, gloried in the powerful, gravelly voice soaring through innuendo and sly joke to sentimentality and tragedy. They joined in choruses, yelled responses to questions and suggestions she hurled at them, and generally acted as if they would be happy to see her running Sioux City.

At the end of their first visit to the Palace, Ed told Mike he wanted to meet the new girl singer. 'So, our humble little dirt-pile has attractions for the big newspaperman after all,' said Mike with a grin. 'Shouldn't be too hard. I know Danny May, the owner, quite well. You wait here.'

Mike went and found the head barman, who in turn produced Danny May. Ten minutes later, May arrived at their table, flustered in a way Maskell had never seen him before.

'I hate to do this, Mike, 'specially to a good customer like you, but the lady won't come out.' He held up a hand to stem Maskell's instant protest. 'She ain't the regular sorta showgirl, Mike, and she don't take kindly to orders. To be frank with you, if I threatened to let her go unless she co-operated, she'd laugh in my face and clear out. Her act is getting me more customers than you'd believe. I don't plan to upset her. Look, let me buy you some champagne to make up for it . . . real thing, not perry,' he added in an undertone.

May joined them, and as they sipped their drinks, Mike Maskell started asking questions about Lottie. Danny was enthusiastic.

'Best chance I ever took,' he said. 'A few weeks ago this scrawny little piece called Scully turns up off the afternoon train from Omaha, says she's got a brilliant English vaude looking for a coupla fill-in bookings on her way to San Francisco. I look at her and think this is the cheapest con I ever saw. But there's summin' about the little biddy . . . she sure knew how to sell. In the end I said I'd try out this sensational artiste of hers and a few days later, this mouth-watering package walks into the Palace and nearly gives me heart failure.'

Ed Maskell's interest was more than casual now. 'You mean she really *was* on her way to San Francisco?'

May shrugged. 'Search me. Still may be for all I know. She was such a draw I doubled her salary and she cancelled her next onward booking to stay here a month longer. When it ends, I'm thinkin' a' kidnapping her if I have to. You wouldn't believe what the suckers are willing to spend after she's been onstage for twenty minutes. And when she comes on again for the late spot . . .'

'Poor old Ed, you look as if you found your perfect woman – and she doesn't want to know you!' Mike's words were lighthearted but he was surprised at the effect this female entertainer seemed to be having on his hard-bitten brother.

'I'll persevere. Faint heart never won fair lady!'

He was still persevering three days later and Lottie Casanova was still ignoring Danny's pleas that she should just take a drink with his influential customer's favourite brother.

'He's not *my* favourite brother, or my favourite anything, Danny,' she told him. 'If you don't think my act is enough, say the word and I'll move on. For all I know, that hall in Laramie may still be interested, even if I did let them down on Ada's original date.'

'No, no – don't do that. You're right; I'm just getting greedy. You go on packin' 'em in with your act, Lottie, and I won't ask for more than that, okay?'

'Okay, Danny.' She softened slightly and smiled at him. 'After all, if you look at it from my point of view, what could possibly be in it for me?'

'Yeah, you're right. He's only some hotshot reporter from a San Francisco newspaper. Ain't as if he has any say locally. If only his brother wasn't . . .'

'What did you say?'

'His brother. His brother's a big local cattleman.'

'No, idiot. Before that. About the man who has this urge to meet me. What does he do?'

'I said, he's a reporter or summin' on a paper in San Francisco. He's here on vacation . . . Lottie? What's wrong?'

Back in their hotel suite, Lottie was almost gibbering at Ada Scully. 'He's a newspaperman, Ada – a newspaperman from San Francisco! What am I going to do?'

'Stop over-actin', for a start,' said Ada. 'I never seen so much ham since my last cold buffet at the boarding house. What of it?'

'You know bloody well what of it! If they get wind in San Francisco of my appearances here, I'll never have a chance to fulfil my Orpheum booking. They'll drop me on the spot.'

'Crap! If you turn in a performance with this newspaper guy like you been givin' them suckers the past five weeks, you'll start in San Francisco as a headliner.'

Lottie managed a hollow laugh. 'And how, pray, would I do that?'

'You really have no idea what yer've done at this place, do yer?'

'Of course. I've made a success of my act and I'm earning a lot of money.'

'Yeah, but on top a' that. Yer blind if yer don't see it. Every night ya got close on a thousand men clamourin' for ya. The most ya ever take off is yer coat. That ain't burlesque. It's vaudeville. And it's headline vaudeville at that. Get this guy on yer side an' half San Francisco will know about it before ya get there. Not bad for an unknown, I'd a' thought.'

Lottie had been gazing at her steadily as she spoke. Now she said: 'What would I do without you, you cunning old devil? Christ – what if I've missed my chance and he doesn't come back?'

That made Ada laugh. 'I took a peek at him last night during yer second spot. He'll be back.'

He was, and this time Lottie went out front to meet him.

That alone nearly caused a riot. She had been singing at the River Palace for six weeks now, and the regulars had never seen her this side of the proscenium arch before. They almost mobbed her. Finally Danny May rescued her and put her in one of the notorious stage boxes with Mike and Ed Maskell.

He grinned cheekily as he left them to their drinks. 'Don't worry, Lottie, everyone'll know you're still a nice girl. The curtains ain't drawn!'

They had been chatting inconsequentially for some time when Ed Maskell said: 'You really are English!'

'Course I am, what did you imagine I'd be, Siamese?'

'No offence, but an awful lot of performers change nationalities overnight to get a little attention. I just thought you might be one of them.'

'With a name like Casanova? Come off it!'

'I don't follow . . .'

'Now, if I wasn't really English but pretending, why would I choose an Italian name? Doesn't make much sense, does it?'

'No, you're right. What about that name?'

She launched into a colourful tale of life back in Clerkenwell's Little Italy, almost believing it herself by the time she had finished adding touches of local colour. All the time, she was conscious of leading the newspaperman gently off down the path she had chosen for him. She spent more than an hour with the Maskell brothers and by the time she was due onstage again, she was willing to bet that Ed Maskell would come round from straightforward admiration to wanting to write about her.

As she slipped out of the box just before one o'clock to prepare for her second appearance, she said: 'Well, bye bye, boys, don't do anything I wouldn't do while I'm away.' She left them sighing after her just as she had intended, but she hoped Ed was simultaneously reaching for his pen and notebook.

It seemed he was. A few days later he was back in Sioux City. This time he came and asked for her at her hotel, and in spite of the clerk's raised eyebrows she invited him up to the suite.

He stood outside her door with his hands behind his back. 'Hello, stranger,' said Lottie. 'I thought I'd frightened you off the other night. Where have you been hiding?'

'Omaha. Went down there last night to pick something up off the Coronado as it came through. And . . . here . . . it . . . is!' Triumphantly he drew from behind his back a newspaper, already folded open at an inside page. There, blazoned across three top columns, heavy black type announced

CASANOVA STORMS SIOUX CITY
LOOK OUT, FRISCO, YOU'RE NEXT

The article was an inspired piece of promotional writing. Lottie could not have hoped for better had she bribed Maskell with her body and every penny she possessed.

'The paper's a day out of date,' he said. 'They'll have read that in San Francisco yesterday.' As though answering a cue, someone rapped on the door.

Outside was the boy from the local telegraph office. 'Miss Casanova? They said at the River Palace that I'd probably find ya here this time a' day. Cable for ya.' Lottie slashed open the envelope. The message inside read: WILL START YOU EXTENDED BOOKING ORPHEUM SOONEST DATE YOU ARE FREE STOP PLEASE CONFIRM TODAY STOP. It was signed by the Orpheum's manager.

Lottie gave a whoop of delight and threw cable and envelope in the air. 'Ada, where are you? Fetch us some champagne and three glasses! We've made it!' Then she flung her arms around Maskell's neck and gave him a smacking, totally unsensual kiss.

Ed Maskell had plenty of advice to offer about her move to San Francisco. 'Of course it's worth taking advantage of the publicity,' he said, 'you can see what it's done for you already. But don't think you have to drop everything to rush there before it goes cold. If they're eager enough when you get there, they'll revive the story and promote you with it when you open there. Time your arrival for the end of September when folks are getting more interested in what's on at the theatres.'

'What about the chance of extra work from them, though – a long extended booking would do me a lot of good.'

'Of course, but unless you've already got engagements in England when you go back, let them extend at the end of the existing run, not the beginning. That way you get the best out of this place and stretch them to their limit.'

She thought it over for a while. 'That suits me well. Danny May has been a decent employer and I don't want to run out on him without fair notice. And there's another thing . . . I don't suppose you know any songwriters in San Francisco?'

'Hell, no! Cops, crooks, nobs even – but no songwriters. One of the reasons they used my piece on you was that I don't normally cover a theatrical beat and they decided if you could get a hardboiled newsman like me going, you must be good.'

'Hmm, I was afraid you'd say that. You see, while I'm hidden away here with such a good audience, I'd love to break in a really first-class song ready for the city slickers. I just haven't got one.'

'Sorry, Lottie, that's your province. I can more or less guarantee a good press but songs are quite another matter. And now –' he sighed dramatically '– I suppose you'd rather like me to go.'

She favoured him with one of her brilliant smiles. 'Sorry, Ed, after all you've done for me, but yes. I either sleep or walk in the afternoons – something

204

quite away from what I do at night – and you're really part of what I do at night, aren't you?'

'If only I were!'

'Go on, hop it! You never know your luck in San Francisco.'

She tried to rest but she felt hot in the dusty late-summer afternoon and the noises of the street outside disturbed her. In the end she put on a loose cotton shirt and skirt and left the hotel by the back entrance.

Sioux City was still small enough for the buildings to peter out not far behind the main street. As Lottie strolled across a couple of deserted back lots, she heard banjo music and laughter in the distance and vaguely remembered one of the wine-room girls saying there was an old-style minstrel show in town that had been playing a couple of the rundown saloons. This sounded like them, but the music seemed to be coming from out of doors. She followed the intricate tinkle of the banjo and eventually found she had made a long half-circle to the rear of the River Palace.

Behind the straggling range of buildings which comprised the saloon, theatre, gaming rooms and accommodation block was a ramshackle yard, with seats made from old beer kegs and packing cases. There in the honey-gold afternoon sunlight, the cast of the minstrel show were staging their act for an audience of wine-room girls and off-duty whores from the local brothel. The men wore costume but had left off their blackface make-up and they looked worn and shabby in the intense afternoon light.

Their music was another matter. Each melody sprang sparkling fresh from the fingers of two superb banjo players. Lottie listened entranced for five or ten minutes before one of the wine-room girls saw her and made room for her on a packing case seat. As Lottie joined them, one of the minstrels started a fast, furious dance to a banjo tune which Lottie recognised as a speeded-up version of something more familiar. Why was it so irritatingly buried in her memory? Then she had it. Of course! She had been thinking of the wrong sort of music. Give or take a few notes, halve the tempo, and it was the operatic aria '*La Donna e Mobile*'.

The words were a different matter. This was rough, down-home entertainment designed for a stag audience with sensibilities so blunt they made the River Palace crowd look like aesthetes. The lyric of the song consisted of an unrepeatable series of salacious suggestions, each one culminating in the line: 'Tin-a-ling-a-boomderay!' The beat was compulsive and the other girls were as captivated as Lottie. One of them yelled out: 'Come on, Joe, teach it us! I wanna sing it after you've gone!'

He stopped his whirling dance and grinned at her. 'Okay, Cathy, but jest you remember to credit the Tuxedo Minstrel Show fer it.'

He repeated the routine three or four times and by then half the girls were dancing along in the afternoon heat. Eventually Lottie drifted away back to the hotel, the mad beat of the aria-that-wasn't still driving through her head.

It was still with her when she woke up next morning, having roared her way through a dozen different English music hall songs in the meantime. Why was that beat so insistent? She began wondering if she had found the seed of her new song.

*   *   *

205

Eventually Danny May recognised that all good things must come to an end and surrendered Lottie to the Union Pacific. She travelled on to San Francisco and her song tune was still beating in her head. She had cabled Ed Maskell to expect her and he met the train, escorting her and Ada to a small apartment he had engaged for them.

'I know you said hotel, Lottie, but this was cheaper and more pleasant than anything else so close to the theatre,' he said. 'And look – it's even got a piano.'

'D'you play, Ed?'

'Do I look like the kinda guy who plays the piano?'

'In England, it's not regarded as evidence of lack of masculinity.'

'Here neither – except among newspapermen. I'd never hold my head up again.'

'Well, I play and Ada plays. And you write.'

'So does the local schoolmarm. So what?'

'I need a songwriter, Ed.'

'No chance. I told you, with me, it's strictly police courts and eye witness accounts of sensational events.'

'Don't tell me you never wrote poetry.'

'All right, I won't,' he relented. 'Course I wrote poetry. But I stopped when I got over the age of twenty.'

'That's all I needed to know. Now's the time to start again.'

'Lottie, I adore you, but no – a thousand times no!'

'I've got a song, Ed, a lovely, haunting, mind-filling song. All it needs is words.'

'Hey, great idea! I gotta novel, gonna be the all time best seller. All it needs is a plot! Come on, Lottie, what d'ya take me for?'

'A writer. Now, sit down, relax, and listen to this.' She sat down by the piano and launched into a fair approximation of the banjo-player's tune, with lyric. By the time she had finished, Ada was giggling uncontrollably and Maskell had turned a deep shade of purple.

'If you sing that at the Orpheum they'll deport you,' he gasped.

'I know, silly! That's why I need some good substitute words. Forget the old lyric; listen to that tune. Isn't it wonderful? Ada, did you get it? Good – then sit down and play and I'll give you an idea of the dance that goes with it.'

Ada vamped out the melody and Lottie went spinning around the room in an abandoned caper that made the polka look sedate. Panting, she finally pulled up in front of Ed. 'I must have some good words, Ed. I'm not losing that song. How about it?'

The wild dance had finally kindled his enthusiasm. 'Okay, Lottie, you're on. But you may get something you don't like.'

'Why are you so sure?'

'Sitting there, I realised what it has to be. It has to start with a demure English Miss, terribly refined, saying quite slowly what a good girl she is, and then letting rip into the dance and chorus, taking everyone by surprise. I'm not at all sure I can get the right note of Englishness.'

She hugged him. 'That's my boy! You give it a try. I'll tell you if it isn't English enough. It sounds like a perfect idea.'

CHAPTER TWENTY-THREE

Lottie always remembered two things about San Francisco: it was the first place where she ever topped the bill at a major hall; and she broke her heart over a man there.

When she moved into the little apartment Ed had found them, and started working on her new song, she foresaw none of this. For the moment, the song came first. She had just over two weeks before she started at the Orpheum, and she would need every minute of it. She was confident that with a little prodding, Ed could come up with a satisfactory lyric for 'Tin-a-ling-a-Boomderay' but when it came to musical arrangement she was on her own.

Ada Scully told Lottie she would be crazy to carry on with her plan. 'Ya'll ruin a song that deserves better treatment, for a start, but think awhile what ya'll do to yer act,' said Ada. 'The audiences here ain't a bunch of skirt-crazy cattlemen. Well . . . skirt-crazy, maybe, but they got more choice a' skirts here. Ya can't jest walk on stage and flash yer legs to get a round of applause, Lottie.'

Lottie was furious. 'You were the one who thought I was so great in Sioux City, remember?'

'Ya were. That act'll get them standing hollering in the aisles here, too. But ya can't try out a half-cocked song on 'em like ya coulda done there, and expect ta get away with it, that's all I'm sayin'.'

The Orpheum had just told her she was topping the bill – taking the second spot after the interval. She almost felt it was the reward for being a good girl – for doing so well in what she still thought of as the Wild West. She wanted something spectacular to signify her arrival at the top, and the new song was to have been it. Now Ada was obstructing her.

Lottie stormed and sulked for a while, but she knew in the end that Ada was right. She was getting a try at the top, against all odds, earlier in her career than she could fairly have expected. She was getting it in a country where she had been cast loose only a few months earlier with nothing but her own stubborn temperament. She was pressing her luck too far to try launching a brand new song as well. In the end she settled down to polish the existing act, rehearsing it down to the smallest gesture.

Once she accepted Ada's good sense, she was cheerful again. 'Come on,' she said, 'we're going to celebrate. Put on your best clothes!'

Ada gave her a tolerant smile and shook her head. 'Ya want better-lookin' company than me if yer goin' celebrating. Ed Maskell said he'd be over this morning; think he's still hopin' ta persuade you not ta use his song yet. Won't he be the happy fella when he finds out you ain't? Take him instead, Lottie. Ya make a prettier couple.'

* * *

'I think I like this better than anywhere else I've seen so far.' Lottie was looking around appreciatively at the overblown splendours of the Palace Hotel's dining room.

'I'd have thought New York had a few more impressive places to offer than the Palace, much as I like the old place,' said Ed.

'No, silly, not the Palace – San Francisco.'

'Oh, now you're talking. I wouldn't change it for anywhere.'

'I can't think why I like it so much, though.'

'Nor can I. I thought you English always preferred everything dignified and proper. You can call San Francisco a lot of things, but not dignified or proper. It's a source of some distress to the ladies on Nob Hill.'

'That's it – why didn't I realise? It's a lovely vulgar place, as vulgar as me.'

'You *want* people to see you that way?'

'I've never wanted anything else, really. Ed, there's something stifling about refinement, particularly when you're surrounded by it all the time. I wonder why this place is so free of it?'

'The politicians would tell you it's because the Barbary Coast and the Tenderloin infect everything they touch. They'd like to cover up that side of the place, but somehow it never happens. Hope it never does.' He dropped his voice confidentially: 'Trouble is, some of the most expensive houses on Nob Hill have mistresses who started their careers as parlour girls. You don't get worse social snobs than them – unless it's their daughters – so if you ever find yourself in that society, you might cool off rapidly about this fine city of ours.'

But suddenly Lottie was only half listening to him. Across the room, sitting at a window table talking to another man, was Lottie's ideal lover – at least, in looks and bearing. His skin was lightly sunburned and his hair was raven black, like her own. He must be well over six feet tall, she mused, judging by his height seated. His long legs stretched across the space beneath the table, showing off the perfect cut of trousers and an extremely elegant pair of boots. The hand that toyed with a crystal wine glass was big and powerful, but with tapering fingers which added an indefinable grace to his idle play with the delicate stem. As she watched, his companion said something that amused him and he threw back his leonine head, letting out an unselfconscious roar of laughter that drew surprised glances from every table in the room. She did not catch his words, but his voice was a rich, purring baritone. Everything about him bespoke careless courage coupled with good taste and well-nigh perfect masculine beauty. Even at a distance, Lottie was already half in love.

'Who is *that*?' she murmured in an almost reverent tone.

Maskell put down his fork and glanced back over his shoulder. He chuckled when he saw who she was talking about. 'Oh, lady, you really have an eye for expensive baubles, don't you? That is the heir to the Johnstone Bank.'

'I'm supposed to be impressed?'

'You appear to be that already.'

'I am, but about him, not who he is.'

'In this case, I think *what* he is would be a more appropriate expression. When you're that big, you're corporate. He is real money, and what California regards as respectable money at that. I thought ladies in your line of work were uncommonly interested in that sort of asset.'

208

She grinned wickedly at him. 'You still have a lot to learn about me, Ed. First lesson is that I'm not like anyone else. I've always regarded money as a very over-rated commodity.'

'Then you've never been short of it.'

'Don't talk such nonsense!' she snapped. 'I've been sick and penniless in a slum before now, and—'

'Hey, calm down! I didn't mean to get you mad . . .'

'Well, you did. I know as much about poverty as anyone else, and don't you forget it . . . oh, how did this stupid subject crop up?'

'As I recall, because you were asking loaded questions about one of the heaviest wallets on the West Coast,' he said drily. What on earth was wrong with the girl? There were spots of burning colour in her cheeks and she seemed on the edge of indignant tears.

He had inadvertently touched Lottie's most sensitive spot. If she ever thought of Camden now, it was in terms of a valuable lesson about the toughness of life. Deep down, though, she knew that was a fraud. Joe, Larry and Ulick had rescued her from the horrors of poverty before she ever experienced them. She had known the terror of discovering herself without money, but before she needed to explore the reality and live on the few pounds she had left, they had stormed in and rescued her. She sensed she would never have any true idea of the day-to-day misery of penury and that therefore she had no real right to decry an interest in money. But it was hard to accept and impossible to admit. She suppressed the storm of inexplicable emotion and forced herself back to Ed's rundown on Grant Johnstone.

'The grandfather was a great brawling illiterate who got into railroads at the right time. At least he made his money riding horses along the track and helping to actually build the thing – an awful lot of our founding fathers did it from behind a counter. From the railroad, he diversified into banking. Once he made it, he got the usual culture-and-respectability bug and started buying bad art like it was going out of style. His son came in for the best of education in the East and arrived home ready to run the family business like a truly cultivated gentleman. Hey, ho, the best laid plans of mice, men and railway tycoons . . .'

'What happened?' Lottie had forgotten her discomfiture of a moment ago and was agog for details.

'Inevitably, he fell for the prettiest parlour whore in San Francisco. She was a bright girl as well as pretty. Didn't risk going up the hill to meet Father – she'd probably entertained him to milk and cookies in her professional capacity anyway – so she eloped with Junior, and didn't reappear till they were legally married.'

'In England that would mean instant disinheritance,' said Lottie, imagining how a newly respectable brewer or mill owner would have reacted.

'Here, too, maybe, if only Sonny-boy hadn't been the sole male heir. When you have Johnstone senior's dynastic drive, that's enough to make you forgive the girl her rough background. Anyhow, he probably saw reason and decided if he'd dragged himself up, so could she.'

'And did she?'

'Hell, yes. She wrote the book. We are, of course, referring to Grant's mother, now Mrs Theodore Johnstone, doyenne of Nob Hill society.'

209

'You're telling me to forget about Grant Johnstone.'

'Not necessarily. Depends on what you have in mind for him.'

'Surely it's a bit early for me to have *anything* in mind for him? I only saw him and thought he looked interesting.'

'Oh, dear, Lottie, if you express mere interest like that, I'd hate to be in the way when you get round to frank enthusiasm!'

'Oh, all right; I find it difficult to keep my eyes off him, and what you've said so far only makes me even more interested. You've told me about the family. What's the man himself like?'

'Much as you'd expect. Sent East to the best schools. Came back a couple of years ago and slid into the social swim here as if he was tailor-made for it – which, of course, he was. Since then he's been the quarry of every socially ambitious Mama but he's a husky runner and showing no signs of slowing down yet.'

'So he's not married.'

'Lottie, I don't believe this . . . let's talk about your act.'

'Pooh to my act! I have better fish to fry.'

'Only if you want to be his highly decorative floozy. You could have no place in the future they've lined up for that one.'

'I expect his grandfather thought that about his father.'

'Precisely. That's why they'll make sure history doesn't repeat itself. And this generation has one obvious advantage over the first: Mother Dear is still alive. The first Johnstone was a widower when his golden boy got taken.'

Lottie's eyes widened until they seemed about to swamp her face. 'Ed, what shall I do? H-he's coming over . . . he's staring at me . . .'

'As if that hadn't been what you had in mind all long,' murmured Ed. 'It so happens that I know the guy . . . and . . .' He broke off as Johnstone arrived at their table, already gazing at Lottie as fixedly as she had been regarding him.

'Ed, I just had to come and ask. Who is this lovely lady?' After that Maskell gave up and resigned himself to the role of go-between for two people who appeared to be drawn to each other by a magnet.

From then on, Lottie's days in San Francisco seemed to run beautifully and seamlessly together. Somehow her act was exactly right and the opening night approached without holding any threats for her. Grant Johnstone was the centre of her world and she had no intention of letting anything interfere with her pleasure.

At first she tried to tell herself it would be Ulick Farrell all over again – a fine promise of good looks and strength, backed by weakness and indecision and finished off by an inability to handle an assertive woman. It was not like that at all. He bore more than a passing physical resemblance to Farrell – exceptionally tall and muscular, with blue eyes and black hair – only his hair was a mass of small glossy curls where Farrell's had been straight. He was an entertaining talker and charming in pursuit of his goals, and to Lottie's delight she appeared to be one of them.

Ed Maskell made his excuses and disappeared soon after he had introduced them. Lottie and Johnstone drank coffee together, gazing at each other as if each had just discovered the secret of the universe. After a few minutes of small talk about the restaurant, Johnstone said, 'Don't tell me, let me guess.

210

You're starting some sort of charity drive and you were bribing Ed with a good lunch to publicise it in someone else's column.'

She smiled and shook her head. 'Do I look like the sort of girl who would run a charity drive?'

'Hardly, but I can't think what you'd be doing unchaperoned, with a guy who can't be your brother or your fiancé, in a place like the Palace.'

'Could it simply be that he's a friend of mine?'

His face fell. It was as unthinkable that a respectable unmarried girl should have men friends in San Francisco as in London. 'Don't tell me you're married!'

'Don't be absurd! Nothing could be further from my mind. Ed's an old friend. We met in Sioux City some time ago.'

'Ah, that explains it. You're a friend of his brother's family.'

She was teasing him now. 'His brother, yes. His brother's *family*, no!'

'If you keep this up you'll drive me mad.'

'Promise you won't walk out on me when I tell you.'

He managed an expression of mock horror, but she could see real apprehension under it. 'I'm on the stage, and Ed's given me some excellent publicity.'

'You're an actress?'

'Not quite. Try vaudeville.'

'Dear God.'

'Come now, it's hardly as bad as being a madam. Or is it?'

'Uh – forgive me, Miss Casanova. I really am being most rude. It's just that I didn't . . . couldn't imagine . . .'

Then she had a vision of herself as he had seen her. She was wearing one of her most restrained outfits, a beautifully cut mint-green linen suit, with a high-necked blouse of coarse cream lace under it, and a tiny hat of dark and light green silk flowers. Lottie burst out laughing. 'God almighty – you thought I was a lady!' Even as she said it, she felt a stab of regret that she was not. This is ridiculous, she thought, you've been disowning that for years. Why want it back now? Because, said a subversive voice, you'll only draw and hold this one if he sees you as a lady . . .

That made her overdo the cockney sparrow routine from sheer perversity. After a few moments' confusion, Johnstone's attitude changed subtly and he started treating her as a man-about-town would treat a vaudeville star. It was a world away from the manner he would have adopted with a woman he regarded as his social equal.

Impatiently Lottie told herself he was barely an acquaintance, that she might never see him again after this afternoon. Her emotions told her differently. As she chattered and flirted with him, she constantly caught herself wondering what it would be like to spend a long time with this man, to share his ambitions and to help him achieve them. There was a drive and an energy locked inside him that excited her and made her want to keep him at her side. And on top of his gut-wrenching attractiveness, there was the challenge. That dragon of a mother . . . all those pursuing West Coast debutantes . . . what a coup to pip them all to the post and walk off with the matrimonial catch of the decade! Almost since her first solo spot in music hall, Lottie had regarded being a woman as a profession, exactly as she saw being an artiste. To capture

211

Grant Johnstone would be the equivalent to starring simultaneously at the Tivoli and the Oxford.

An hour after sitting down with her, he still showed little interest in going anywhere else. Eventually, she said: 'I don't think we can stay here much longer without ordering afternoon tea, Mr Johnstone, and I've been here since before lunch.'

'Oh – do you have to go somewhere else? Can I see you again?'

'No, I'm quite free this afternoon. I just think we should move from here. Perhaps you have time to show me a little of the city?'

'I can think of nothing I'd rather do, Miss Casanova.'

'I'll let you call me Lottie if you let me call you Grant.' She saw him wince almost imperceptibly and wanted to bite her tongue off. He had been well on the way to forgetting she was a music hall singer and she had to remind him. No nice woman in Grant Johnstone's circle would be called Lottie.

But he recovered his poise almost instantly and she spent a blissful afternoon exploring San Francisco with him. From time to time she caught herself wondering why she wanted nothing more than to lean against his broad shoulder and stroke his curly black hair, but she was at a loss for an answer. She had seen plenty of men who looked as good as he did, most of them without the subtle 'don't touch me' feeling she got from him. But this was the man she wanted. By now she had forgotten how sharply the unseen mother and pursuing young ladies had fired her competitive spirit, and it never occurred to her that this was intensifying his allure.

When they left the Palace, an open carriage awaited them with a liveried coachman on the driving seat. Lottie was treated to a newcomer's tour of San Francisco in the second-best way possible. Johnstone said he was saving the hills for the day they had time to take a cable car.

The sun was making an impossibly showy leave-taking over the bay when he told the coachman to stop down on the waterfront and helped her out of the gig. 'You wait here, Stevens. We'll be at least half an hour. Are you ready for a walk, Lottie?'

She fought the desire to say with you, into the sunset? and only murmured polite assent. 'I don't really think you're dressed for it, but I have a little secret I'm bursting to tell someone, and you're just the sort of confidante I had in mind.'

The iron tub was out beyond the elegant lateen-rigged sailing boats of the immigrant Sicilian fishermen. After the natural grace of the smaller wooden vessels, her elephantine lines and rusty hull came as something of a shock. Johnstone stood aside to usher Lottie up the gangplank. 'We're going aboard this?' she asked dubiously.

'Beauty's only skin deep, remember. You're looking at my future.'

She gave a derisive laugh at that. 'From what I hear, your future is behind a big mahogany desk, counting piles of banknotes. What possible interest can you have in a rusty old boat?'

'More than you'd believe possible, my dear. Come on, and I'll tell you about it.' Once aboard, he glanced back and forth along the deck and then called: 'Joe – where are you, Joe?'

A face emerged from below, grinning broadly and topped by a mass of hair

212

as black and curly as Johnstone's own. 'Down here, Grant. You want me? I was just going ashore for summin' to eat.'

'No, that's fine. But have you got a bottle and a couple of glasses handy? I have a young lady here and we want to watch the sunset from on deck.'

Joe Sciccolone chuckled. 'Best time to be on deck here, eh, Grant? Can't see so mucha the rust patches then!' He disappeared and came back shortly with a newly opened bottle of red wine and two tumblers. 'See you later, then. I'll be a coupla hours.' And he was gone.

Lottie had been wandering along the companionway, fingering the flaking paint and eyeing the rust patches which even the failing light could not conceal. Finally, when he had seated her aft in a canvas chair, she asked Johnstone again about his unreasonable affection for such a heap of scrap iron.

'You may find this hard to believe, but I meant what I said when I called this my future,' he told her.

'I'll accept it as rich man's folly, but no more than that.'

He looked disappointed. 'You know, I decided to show you this on the spur of the moment, because for some reason I had a hunch you'd understand. I'm beginning to realise I was wrong.'

She felt a pang of shame. 'Oh, please don't take me seriously! I always let my mouth run ahead of my mind. Try me. I'll listen, and I promise I shan't think you foolish.'

'You have no idea how frustrating it is to grow up wanting to do something and knowing your grandfather and father did it all for you. For as long as I can remember, I've been trying to find an interest that would make me feel I had something to look forward to, and then it happened, when I was about eighteen.

'I came home for the summer and brought a couple of friends who were in love with boating. No one in my family had ever shown any interest in the sea, so it was new to me. I brought them down here – part of the tourist sights, you know – and fell in love with it myself. After that, I began to see something that would keep me occupied for life. But at first, I still couldn't work out a way of doing it for myself. Then I thought of something. It was cheating in a sense, but I couldn't see how to do it otherwise.

'My mother gave me blocks of stock as occasional presents when I was a kid.' He laughed, patently unamused. 'Other kids got a dog or a pony, I got a block of stocks. Couldn't blame her, I suppose. She'd known hard times. I never had. She was protecting me the only way she knew. I hated it, but then I thought, what if I convert that into my future?

'So I sold out what she'd given me – it was all safe-as-houses, low return stuff – and started playing the market through a college chum. He was really bright and helped me make a modest killing . . . which you're now sitting on.'

Lottie stared at him. 'You mean, you spent all your profits on . . . on this thing?'

'This thing is my freedom, Lottie. I got a little more, as it happens. I invested $150,000 in this and two small steamboats. I am going to found my own shipping line.'

She gazed at him in silence for a long moment, digesting what he had said and quickly coming to understand it. 'So although your mother staked you, in a way, after that it's all your doing, all your own success or failure. Good for you, Grant!'

'You see? I knew you'd understand when you realised what I'd been up to.'

She studied the ruinous vessel again. 'I understand, all right, but I'm not at all sure your investment will stay afloat long enough to make you any money.'

'I'm no longer troubled by that. The three boats are my assets. I own them outright and now I can raise loans on them. The loans will renovate them, the renovated vessels will make me a profit, and eventually the Grant Shipping Line will be known worldwide.'

'Why not Johnstone?'

'Surely you can guess that one? Even the name is something they made. Grant is starting afresh.'

'I envy you, Grant.'

'I can assure you riches are a mixed blessing.'

'Oh, I do know that – better than most.'

He looked at her sharply and she spoke again, hastily, to cover her blunder. 'I mean, you're so lucky to be born a man. Women can't free themselves by going into business like that. If you're female, you marry or you sell your flesh – six of one, half a dozen of the other, really. At least you men have some choice.'

'Less than you'd think . . . anyway, that's what I plan to do.'

'Will it give you so much pleasure just to come down here and look over your fleet, like a boy with a toy boat in the bath?'

'God, no! I'm a sucker for faraway places. As soon as the venture gets moving, I shall interfere like mad. I intend to sail as supercargo and see some of those magic harbours . . . Surabaya, Kandy, Shanghai . . . d'you think they're half as wonderful as they sound?'

She giggled. 'Each to his own. I hate to tell you this, but a couple of months ago I was sitting in Delmonico's in New York saying how romantic it would be to see Eau Claire, or Iron Mountain, or even Sioux City. Do you suppose there's a Chinaman somewhere having romantic dreams about Hackensack, New Jersey?'

'Shame on you for a cynic!'

'Don't worry, Grant. The laugh's really on me. Sioux City turned out to be every bit as exotic as I'd dreamed – just in a different way, that's all.'

'Then I needn't worry my head about the likelihood of cable cars in Surabaya?'

'No, I think I can safely guarantee that.'

They stayed aboard the *Californian Queen*, talking companionably, until the last of the afterglow had faded. Then he said: 'Come on, you'll be getting chilly. If you still feel like a little company, how about supper somewhere on the Embarcadero?'

They dined together and then wandered along the waterfront again, the lights of the city strung like crown jewels around them. Lottie gave a little shiver of pure joy. 'Oh, I do love this place, it's so vital, and so new!'

Johnstone stopped walking and gazed down at her. 'Just like you, my beautiful girl,' he said. 'I never met anyone like you before, and now I can't imagine ever not knowing you, even after just this one day. Don't go away, will you?'

214

Shaken by the intensity of his words, she tried to laugh. 'I have no intention of going away.'

'You know what I'm saying. I want you . . . want you with me like this . . . always . . .' and he bent, smothering her in a deep embrace which blotted out the twinkling lights, kissing her with a passion that awakened an answering need in her and stood her world on its head.

Moments later, stumbling slightly as she stood away from him, she said: 'You certainly know how to express your feelings.'

He did not answer immediately, first raising his long, elegant finger and drawing a line down her cheek. Then he held his hand up in front of her face. It was wet with her tears. 'So do you, my darling,' he murmured. She slipped back into his arms and it felt like coming home.

'Come on,' he murmured. 'We need to be alone. It's not much, but I keep a little cabin of my own aboard the *Queen*, in case I feel like staying sometimes.'

Lottie looked at him searchingly. 'Have you ever taken a woman there?'

Grant laughed. 'Good God, no! You're the first to share the *Queen* in all her ruined glory!'

'And the last, I hope.' She said it so quietly he could never be sure he had heard her properly.

The cabin was surprisingly well kept. White paint held the all-pervading rust at bay, there was a rug on the floor and engravings of sailing ships hung around the bulkhead. He had acquired an impossibly quaint country rocking chair from somewhere, and instead of crowding the small space, it seemed to fit in. Lottie glanced sidelong at the bunk, expecting the worst, and promptly had to stifle a flood of giggles.

Johnstone caught her reaction and said aggrievedly: 'I know it's nothing much, but I didn't expect you to find it funny.'

'Oh, Grant, really! You must see the joke . . . only someone from Nob Hill!' She bent to the bunk, and fingered the bedding. The sheets were of finest Irish linen, the pillowcases embroidered with swags of autumn fruit. 'Standard issue to all cabin boys, no doubt!'

Reluctantly, he grinned back at her. 'Well . . . I wanted something more than rough blankets to sleep in and I just grabbed something from the linen cupboard at home, that's all. Can I help it if my mother likes expensive things?'

'Mmm.' She fingered his lapel. 'I suspect Mother isn't the only one. This jacket is hardly rummage sale.'

He gazed down at her, unable to look away. 'I should feel it's impolite to comment on a gentleman's clothes, but somehow, everything you say seems to be all right . . .' He bent towards her and kissed her again. Lottie felt as she had on the dock. This time she let herself fold gracefully on to the narrow bunk.

Afterwards she wondered how they had managed it. The bunk was very small, they were big people, and explosively excited by each other. Just proves that love really does find a way, she thought.

At first it promised otherwise. Johnstone kissed her with mounting passion for a while, then she felt him drawing back. 'Grant? What's the matter?'

'I – I, nothing, really . . . perhaps it wasn't such a good idea to come down here.'

Lottie was bewildered. 'Why not?'

'God dammit – how do I undress you?'

She burst out laughing. 'Tell you what – I'll give you a special treat. Just sit back and watch – I'll do the rest.' And slowly, tantalisingly, she began to remove her elaborate clothing. Some considerable time later, she said: 'I'll need help with the corset . . . laces, you know . . .'

Johnstone leaped to his feet. 'I can't think of anything I'd enjoy more.'

'Not anything?' She regarded him archly over her shoulder as he untied the black silk laces which kept her waist murderously small.

He finished releasing her, turned her to face him, and said, 'Well, relatively speaking, of course . . .'

He drew her back towards the bunk. 'Just lie there and let me look at you,' he said. 'You're so lovely . . .' His fingers slid down her inner thigh. 'So soft, so smooth . . .' Then he bent and pressed his face against her slightly rounded belly. 'Everything so perfectly covered . . .' He moved up her body, finally brushing his lips across her breasts and then nuzzling at her nipples before starting to suck greedily at them.

Lottie pressed him ferociously against her, feeling the wonderful fit muscular frame bearing down on her body. 'Love me, Grant – love me quickly!' she said.

His mouth crushed down on hers and Lottie's desire for him surged up and took her over. Her thighs slid open and she felt him, pulsing, seeking her, thrusting down into her body. He possessed enormous physical power and it swamped her consciousness, concentrating the last shreds of her awareness on his body exploding into hers, taking it over, turning it into something else. His hands slid up and squeezed her breasts like great ripe fruit, and she felt her flesh overflowing to engulf him, the eternal male fertilising and fulfilling her eternal female. What was it she had wanted . . .? She no longer knew. Whatever it was, it hardly mattered any longer. What mattered was this beautiful stranger, possessing her, making her into something else, his whole hard rigid length stirring her to unbearable ecstasy.

He shuddered and was still, pinning her flat on the bunk. Her own climax came seconds after his, and she lay, breathless, expecting to faint at any moment and not really caring, such was her feeling of tranquillity.

Eventually, Johnstone raised himself on one elbow and looked down at her, his face full of wonder. 'I got lost,' he said.

'Glad to hear it. So did I . . . still not sure I'm found again.' She gave a little wriggle of pure pleasure and he laughed, the deep sound rumbling against her body.

'If you keep doing that, we might get lost again.'

'Is that a promise?'

'I'll have to see what I can manage . . .'

By the time she returned to the apartment, it was after midnight and Ada was working herself into a modest frenzy. 'Fer Chrissake, surely you haven't suddenly found young Maskell too wonderful to part with overnight? Where've you been?'

Lottie managed a happy simper. 'Nothing to do with Ed . . . Oh, Ada, I just met a man in a thousand!'

Ada slumped in her chair and took a stiff pull of the whisky she had been sipping to calm her nerves. 'Oh, Lord,' she said, 'Save me from men in a thousand!'

Only Lottie seemed unaware that the affair with Grant Johnstone was doomed. She began by assuring both Ada and Ed Maskell that she knew it was nothing more than a brief fling. They eyed each other pessimistically and privately agreed she was wrong. Her opening night drew closer and Lottie began getting more nervous about the impression it would make on Johnstone than her effect on her audience.

'Lottie, honey, yer crazy! Remember what ya told me? Only things that didn't disappoint ya was champagne and audiences? Johnstone ain't an audience. He's a rich boy out of his element. Stop foolin' yerself.'

'I'm not fooling myself, Ada, I'm in love, and it's wonderful. No wonder I said that – I'd never met anyone like Grant before.'

'No wonder you said that,' Ada mimicked, 'you was all o' nineteen years old – and in case yer'd forgot, yer only a coupla months older now.'

'Stop being stuffy. It will work out, you'll see.'

And for two weeks, it seemed to be doing just that. Much of what Grant Johnstone felt about his background matched what Lottie had felt long ago as Charlotte Cazenove. She understood just how bitter he must feel to know that all the high ground had been won for him, and was with him every step of the way in his fight to free himself of the family traditions. It formed a bond between them which both recognised without fully understanding. But she made the mistake of thinking they were too alike, and found herself before an insurmountable barrier.

The night before she opened at the Orpheum, Grant's parents were hosting a party at their mansion on Nob Hill. All San Francisco society was jostling to be seen there. Over lunch at the Palace, Grant invited Lottie.

She was nonplussed. 'Won't they all be furious?'

'Livid, I should think. But they might as well meet you now as later.'

'Why, Grant? In six weeks or so, I shall be gone from California. I may never be back.'

'Who says you're leaving?'

Her heart skipped and she had to force out the next words: 'I haven't heard anyone trying to stop me.'

'Well, hear it now. We'll have one hell of a battle about it with the family, but before we declare war, let's prepare the ground. How d'you feel about becoming Mrs Grant Johnstone?'

'You don't mean it.'

'I've been saying that to myself a hundred different ways, ever since we sat aboard the *Californian Queen* the other night and watched the sunset. But I do mean it, Lottie. Will you have me?'

'What about my career?'

He smiled and shook his head. 'No backing down. You're booked for a season at the Orpheum and you'll play it . But after that . . . well, I was rather hoping you'd want to help me with my little venture.'

Had she been less dazzled that might have sounded warning bells in Lottie's mind. Shipping, when she knew about song and dance routines? But her passion was on Johnstone's side. 'Oh, Grant, I do love you!' she said. 'Yes, of course I'll marry you, and give up the stage, and try winning over your parents. When do we start?'

He laughed. 'Hey, ease up a bit! I think the party might be a good time to let battle commence. Tomorrow, eight-thirty, dress formal. Bring Ed as your escort. Mother and Father will let him in the door – just!'

'Where does that leave me?'

'That, darling Lottie, is up to you.'

Ed Maskell was deeply dubious when Lottie passed on Johnstone's invitation. 'Lottie, you have no idea what these bashes are like. I'm damned sure nothing like them ever happened in England – at least, I hope it didn't.'

'But expensive parties must be the same anywhere.'

'This is all new money, showing itself off. You like vulgarity – you'll get it. I can't guarantee you'll be so keen on it after the ball is over!'

'But Ed . . . Grant and me – it's my chance to impress his parents.'

Maskell looked her over. 'Oh, you'll impress 'em all right. I'm laying odds on which one of them will take you aside before the end of the evening and try to buy you off – and how much they'll offer.'

'What a rotten thing to say!'

'Come on, Lottie, I told you what to expect. It's no insult to be found wanting by Grant's mother. Quite the reverse if you ask me. I'm not saying you'll lose the fight; just warning you it may turn a little nasty.'

'I know how to fight unfairly.'

'Do you? I wonder. I think your talents lie in quite another direction.' He studied her for a long time, his look frankly adoring, and Lottie began to get restive.

Finally she broke away and said: 'Well, will you take me or not?'

Maskell shrugged. 'If it's really what you want, Lottie. But I have a feeling it'll turn out to be a big mistake.'

As if fulfilling a theatrical cue, next morning a new evening gown was delivered to Lottie from the White House, one of the city's oldest-established department stores. She had chosen the fabric and style a few days before and ordered it to be made up for a celebration supper after her opening at the Orpheum. Now it was to serve a different purpose. Examining it, Lottie was silently thankful she had opted for something so shockingly simple.

Her intention had been to startle people who had seen her on stage by the contrast between abandoned hussy and demure lady. Now San Francisco could see the lady first and the hussy later. She began wondering whether there was any way of toning down her act before it did too much damage to her standing on Nob Hill.

The gown was a masterpiece in oyster-coloured satin, with a severe bodice, square neckline and big puff sleeves. It bore a strong resemblance to the refurbished garnet velvet gown she had brought so long ago in Stinchcombe's for her stage debut, but the cut was just sufficiently more refined to be acceptable in polite society. Lottie tried on the gown and Ada stood back with a gasp of admiration as she finished adjusting the long creamy kid gloves that went with it.

'Ya look jest like one a' them Russian grand duchesses,' she said. 'There won't be a girl in the place ter touch ya.' She picked up the exquisite fan which Lottie had chosen to go with the gown and handed it to her protégée. 'There! Honest, Lottie, lookin' at ya now, nobody'd ever know ya weren't from the top a' the tree.'

Lottie grinned at her. 'Wouldn't they be surprised if they knew the truth?'

'Mother, here's the English girl I've been telling you so much about. May I present Miss Casanova? Miss Casanova, my mother, Mrs Theodore Johnstone.'

Nicely done, my love, thought Lottie. Perfect manners and no mention of my common-as-muck first name. But not sufficiently nicely done for his mother, it seemed.

Mrs Johnstone smiled frostily. 'Casanova? That sounds an unlikely English name. More Italian, I would have thought.'

Lottie produced a self-confident smile and said: 'A well-travelled southern ancestor who settled in England . . . some time around the sixteenth century, I believe, Mrs Johnstone.'

Ed Maskell winced. Dear God! It was fast and smart, but Vera Johnstone would never forgive Lottie for asserting exalted ancient ancestry with such ease. It would be even worse when she found out it was a con.

Ed assumed that when Grant said he had told his mother a great deal about Lottie, he had not included her stage career. Carefully skirting her first name, as Grant had done, Ed said: 'Shall we get a glass of champagne, Miss Casanova?' Lottie bowed slightly, smiled at Mrs Johnstone and followed him across the room.

When they were out of earshot, he said: 'For Christ's sake, Lottie, don't antagonise the woman with your first words!'

Lottie turned innocent eyes on him. 'What d'you suppose she'd have said if I'd told her my father was a short order cook behind Hatton Garden? She'd have had me on toast!'

'She may yet do that if you're not careful,' said a voice behind them. It was Grant. 'What can we do with her, Ed?' he went on. 'I have to make Mother at least accept her. At this rate they'll never speak another word to each other.'

'That could be your safest bet,' said Maskell. He looked at the handsome pair in front of him. 'For what it's worth, my advice is you take a leaf from your father's book and run away together. If you think it's bad now, think what it will be like after Lottie opens tomorrow night.'

Grant's smile faded. 'I know. But it means a great deal to Lottie, doesn't it, darling? I can't ask her to give it up.'

She glanced up at him sharply. 'I didn't know you had any intention of doing so!'

'Well, no, I didn't, at first, but then I started wondering . . . perhaps it would make things easier for us. I'd see you didn't lose anything by it.'

'Grant, I hope I'm failing to understand what you mean.'

'Why? You know I could make it up to you, and you must realise how much damage it would do to our chances.'

'And *you* must realise how important that booking is to me. Ed does, and he's not in love with me.' She failed to see Maskell's expression as she uttered the words, turning a moment later and saying, 'Tell him, Ed.'

'She's right, Grant. Lottie's been working for something like this ever

219

since she went on the stage. Even if it all ends here, you must see she has to make that top-of-the-bill appearance.'

'Well, yes and no.' His tone told them that his own feelings were weighted heavily in favour of the 'no'. 'In normal circumstances, of course I'd understand, but now, with so much at stake?'

Lottie's expression had been growing colder as he spoke. 'This is the first time we've been together at a party given by your family, and you're already trying to change me purely because your mother made it plain she hadn't taken to me. I've yet to meet your father. You knew that would happen before you even invited me.'

'Lottie, please try to understand . . . somehow, it looks different now we're up the top of the Hill, doing it, instead of down at the bottom, just talking about it . . . look, Ed, give us a couple of minutes, will you?'

'Sure.' Maskell turned to Lottie. 'If you need me in a hurry I'll be out on the terrace. Just come and get me, all right?'

She nodded. 'Thanks, Ed. Don't go too far. It could be quite soon. Now, Grant, you were saying?'

Johnstone had been having second thoughts. 'Lottie, I've never felt like this about any woman. But I love you so much I thought it would be child's play to ride down my parents' objections. When I realised it wouldn't be, I just wanted to make it as easy as possible, that's all.'

'And my one ambition could be sacrificed without a thought for how much it means to me? Thank you. What if I'd suggested you abandon your boats?'

He glanced around, suddenly fearful. 'Hush! No one here knows about any of that!'

'Don't give me that old flannel! San Francisco society must be a village like any other. I bet they all know how much you paid for those boats down to the last penny. Your family are probably playing dumb because they think you'll grow out of it.'

'How dare you? You make me sound like some spoiled brat!'

'Well, aren't you? You know, Grant, you really impressed me because I thought you were a man who'd taken control of his own life in spite of being brought up in a gilded cage. I'm beginning to see how wrong I was.'

Lottie had gone on talking quietly, but Johnstone's voice was rising in step with his agitation. 'You don't know what you're talking about! You started from the bottom and you don't have the faintest idea of how hard it can be to do it the other way round—'

Heads were beginning to turn as people craned to catch both sides of the dispute. Mrs Johnstone, her face like a thundercloud, was moving through the crush towards them, her purpose obvious.

Lottie leaned close and said in a very low voice: 'You're wrong, Grant. My family were at the top when yours were scratching holes in dungheaps. I know better than you about starting up there and working your way down into the real world – and you're doing it all wrong.' She straightened up, gave him her most glacial smile and said in her normal voice: 'Now, Mr Johnstone, it's been a great pleasure, but if you'll excuse me, I'll find my escort and go. I have to make an early start tomorrow.'

Vera Johnstone had joined them as she finished speaking. Before the older woman could intervene, Lottie extended the smile to her and said: 'Mrs

Johnstone, such a pleasure to meet you. Thank you so much for inviting me. Perhaps next time I shall have the opportunity of staying long enough to meet your husband. Goodnight . . . so kind . . .' And she managed to separate herself from mother and son behind an eddy of people coming in from the terrace and to go and find Ed.

'Get me away from here this minute, before I start uprooting these disgusting bloody orchids they've got everywhere!' she snarled at him. Maskell asked no questions. He steered her along the terrace to the farthest set of french windows, where they could move through to the entrance hall without passing so many people. Within minutes they were out beneath the porte-cochère, where a uniformed manservant handed them into one of the dozen hired carriages which were ferrying guests to and from their homes that evening.

If Maskell had expected silence from Lottie, he was mistaken. All the way down the hill she raged at him about Johnstone's perfidy and his awful mother. When she finally ran out of abuse, he said: 'Should I take you straight home, or d'you want to let off a little more steam?'

She began to snap back at him, then took a deep breath and touched his arm gently. 'I'm sorry, Ed, I know I'm being a brat. Give me a couple of minutes.' She brooded awhile, then added: 'It would be rather silly to waste these lovely clothes, wouldn't it? How would you feel about giving me dinner at the Palace? I'll treat us out of my big star earnings – when I get them!' She managed a watery smile.

'Nonsense. You know I'd bankrupt myself for your company. Come on, you're on.'

Lottie forced herself to appear cheerful, but it was a dismal evening. She knew that however much she might despise Grant Johnstone's sudden change of heart, she still longed for him and still cherished a childish dream of sailing away with him on the elegant liner which would one day head his shipping line. She managed to maintain her light-hearted stance until Maskell took her home, but by then she was close to tears.

They were about to part outside her front door, when he said: 'I'm not letting you brood on all this. It'll wreck your first night at the Orpheum. Look, I've been working real hard on that song, and one of the guys at the paper gave me a few leads on musical arrangers. I've been putting something together. This big romance of yours stopped me telling you about it, but seeing how miserable that's made you, I'm going to bring the man and the music round tomorrow for you to try it.' She began to protest and he leaned forward, silencing her with a gentle kiss on the lips. 'Not another word. It's the only medicine to cure your blues. Now go to bed and think song, not love.'

He turned and started off down the path. As he reached the gate, she called after him: 'Ed, you're an unfeeling beast, I hate you, and thanks a million!'

He was right about her needing something to distract her from the fiasco of the party. Suppressed indignation carried her indoors and through her preparations for bed, but by the time she was lying between the cool sheets in the darkness, all she could think of was the misery of never feeling Grant's vital presence beside her again, and the emptiness of making plans for a future without him.

CHAPTER TWENTY-FOUR

Ed Maskell's attempt to distract Lottie from her broken romance worked in an unexpected way: The musician he brought along to play the newly arranged tune of 'Tin-a-ling-a-Boomderay' succeeded in showing her the deficiencies of the dance routine she had been working up to go with it. Instead of being pleased, she was furious at her own inadequacy. At first Maskell was worried, but he soon realised she was more easily distracted from her misery by anger than by mere professional interest.

On the morning of the day she opened at the Orpheum, she was standing beside the piano in a small practice studio they had rented behind a downtown drinking dive, listening for the third time to Karl Muttler's arrangement. Her expression was stormy.

'It's brilliant, Mr Muttler, but Christ, it makes me look like a dancing hippopotamus crashing around the stage . . . what I've been doing may be fast enough, but it's got to be light as well, dammit.'

'Looked pretty light to me, Miss Casanova,' said Muttler.

'Stop being gallant. You were peering at your music the whole time. You only saw the finishing flourish.'

He smiled sheepishly: 'It was a mighty fine finishing flourish, if I may say so.'

Lottie managed an indignant sniff. 'It'll need more than that to do justice to your arrangement. I'd have to be a bloody genius to get it light enough.'

Muttler was a shy man, a professional musician who played all sorts of engagements from seedy nightspots to stand-in engagements at classical concerts. Now he rustled a couple of sheets of music and some other papers on his lap, and looked faintly embarrassed.

Lottie regarded him closely and then said: 'You've got an idea, haven't you? Come on, out with it! I shan't be offended.' Why, she thought, the poor man's blushing!

Finally he nerved himself to speak. 'I – I have something that might interest you, Miss Casanova, but you will think I am a bad fellow for having it.'

Lottie was almost stamping her foot in impatience now. 'This is plain daft! I'm not standing here being called Miss Casanova by a maestro who's too shy to share a good idea. Look, my name's Lottie. Whether you like it or not, you're Karl from now on. All right then, let's see this thing that makes you a bad fellow.'

Still blushing, Muttler took out his wallet, and from one of the note pockets he drew a dog-eared photograph. Lottie glanced at it and then chortled. 'Oh, isn't she gorgeous? You old devil, I don't blame you for carrying around a little souvenir like this. I'd do the same if I were a bloke.'

223

She reflected momentarily on her own recent rehearsal and said gloomily. 'It'd beat having to watch me hoofing around here today.' Then she took another look. 'Hey, she must have been brilliant to hold that pose for long enough to photograph it!'

Muttler nodded. 'She was wonderful! Parisienne, of course. It was taken – oh, let me see – about 1890. Have you ever seen the Can-Can danced properly?'

'In London?' Lottie's scorn filled the studio. 'It looks interesting enough, but they massacre it. I saw a third-rate French troupe once do it at the Alhambra and even that wasn't bad. The real thing must be something special.'

'Believe me, it is – especially when performed by creatures as beautiful and talented as this one.'

The girl in the picture was small, curvy and rigidly corsetted. She wore what looked like a gloriously dishevelled pile of expensive underwear. Everything was frills and lace, all white, relieved by coloured ribbons threaded through border flounces. Her pose was what marked her out as a superb dancer. She stood rock-firm on one leg, while the other extended almost vertically into the air, her tiny foot pointing upward some way above her head, the stretched limb showing further wonderful flounces of lace and ribbon. 'My God, she must have held that pose for at least twenty seconds for the picture,' said Lottie.

Muttler nodded, smiling with a proprietorial air which suggested he had taught her the trick. 'If only she was available to teach you,' he said with a sigh.

'Paris is an awful long way from San Francisco, Karl. You must have a better idea than that.'

'Well, yes, I do. This Can-Can – I know it is not so new, but outside Paris it is seldom danced well. There are a handful of dancing teachers who understand it and who would help you work up your own routine using these steps. I have seen the best dancers doing it, Lottie. Believe me, your own solo arrangement would be just the thing to launch this song. With practice, I think you could dance it as well as Ghislaine.'

'But who the devil's going to teach me? I can't learn from a picture.'

'I may be able to arrange something. Just the other night, I thought of Ghislaine when I talking to a young man down at the Embarcadero, name of Shaw. He organises and trains dance troupes – an Australian, I think, but he has travelled in Europe. He knows and loves the Can-Can. If I could arrange a meeting . . . ?'

'Yes, a thousand times. Just tell me when.'

'I see Ed often these days. I will tell him. Now, you have heard my music. I think he has some words ready for you.'

Ed was almost shy about his efforts. 'I really don't know if this was what you wanted, Lottie. I told you, I'm no poet . . .'

'Neither are ninety per cent of music hall songwriters. Stop moaning and let's have a look.'

'Karl has been kind enough to write them into a musical notation. Here it is.' He assumed a timid country boy expression. 'And Lottie, please treat me gently – I'm a virgin!'

Muttler began the sedate, almost prissy verse accompaniment and Lottie absorbed the full degree of skill Ed had exercised just as she was drawing breath to launch into the verse. He had really come up trumps.

> 'A smart attractive girl you see
> The belle of high society
> Fond of fun as fond could be
> When nobody else can see.
> Not too young and not too old;
> Not too timid, not too bold,
> But just the very thing I'm told
> That in your arms you'd like to hold!'

As she sang, she was eyeing his simple treatment of the chorus and trying to work out why it had improved so immeasurably from the minstrel show ode she had heard a few weeks before. That was it – as you sang it, you felt the punch he'd put in. It was crying out for a shapely leg to be jabbed high in the air to emphasis it, and she was going to learn how to produce that effect if she had to hunt down the elegant Ghislaine herself. She launched for the first time into the chorus which was to be her immortality:

> 'Ta-ra-ra BOOM-de-ay,
> Ta-ra-ra boom-de-ay,
> Ta-ra-ra boom-de-ay,
> Ta-ra-ra boom-de-ay . . .'

She signalled to Karl to reprise the chorus and repeated it, raising the volume until the rafters shook and roaring out:

> 'Ta-ra-ra BOOM-de-ray,
> Ta-ra-ra boom-de-ay,
> Ta-ra-ra boom-de-ay,
> Ta-ra-ra boom-de-ay!'

She had been dancing as she sang to get the tempo, but had no ambitions to turn the steps she was using into a formal routine. As the music ended, she skidded to a halt and rushed across to Ed, flinging her arms around his neck.
'Liar – you told me you were no songwriter! With the right start you'd make more out of it than from newspapers.'
Ed chuckled and said: 'All for love, Lottie! This is going to be debut and swansong all in one. I couldn't stand the strain. But I'm glad you're pleased.'
'Pleased? I'm bowled over! We'd better stop now, because I have to get ready for the big entrance tonight. But I want both of you hunting down this man Shaw. The sooner we get a dance routine together, the better.'

I am topping the bill at a major music hall . . . Charlotte Cazenove is finally dead . . . God save Lottie Casanova. Lottie's mind was running on, freewheeling outside the perfectly tuned body which sat in the wings at the Orpheum, waiting to make its first top-of-the-bill appearance. The

225

surroundings were the same as they had been in halls right across America: a packing case as a seat; a rack to hold her coat, muff and tam o'shanter; stage hands ignoring her and concentrating on their next bit of offstage business.

The familiar last-minute hammer-blow of nerves wrenched her mind back into her body and she felt the sweat break out under armpits and behind kneecaps as the adrenalin cascaded through her muscles and powered her out in front of the flaring lights. As she minced childishly downstage for her opening song, she was thinking, what is it about this thing inside me that makes them respond the same from Stepney to San Francisco? Whatever it was, she was more grateful than she could ever begin to say that she possessed it. There could be no other thrill on this earth to touch the great surge of ecstatic power that went through her as an audience roared its appreciation.

It took her through the show, through the crowds of well-wishers who seemed to be everywhere backstage afterwards, congratulating her. It took her to the Palace with Ed Maskell in her gorgeous oyster satin – 'They must be getting sick o' this frock here, Ed, they've seen it almost as often as I have!' – and even down to Fisherman's Wharf for a final stroll at the feet of the city which had taken her to its heart tonight. Then she cried.

Maskell held her in silence and understood the tears. Eventually, when the sobs had tailed off into sniffles, he said: 'You ready to talk about it yet?'

'I don't know that I ever will be, Ed. What a damned fool I am about men. Every time I see that particular type, rich or poor, I fall for them and make a fool of myself. Every time, I know what's going to happen, but I go ahead anyway. And it always happens so quickly . . . one minute I'm in control, next thing I'm head over heels . . .'

He let her run on like this for a long while, until the words were calmer, less frenetic, then said: 'Lottie, if it's not a rude questions, how old are you?'

She smiled through the last of her tears. 'Nearly twenty, why?'

'Have you ever wondered if perhaps you're asking too much of yourself, too young? At your age, most girls are still getting crushes on the local doctor or sheriff, and singing in the church choir on Sundays. You're still no more than a girl yourself.'

'Yes, so Ada keeps telling me. I don't *feel* young, Ed, that's the trouble. I've been living like this for nearly five years now and I can't remember ever being a young girl in the sense you mean.'

'No need for you to try. All I'm saying is that it's natural you get these crushes on men. Just try not to take them so seriously and maybe they won't hurt you so much.'

'Do you mean you think Grant Johnstone was playing with me?'

'Anything but. I think he was caught just like you. For God's sake, the guy is barely twenty-four himself – hardly middle-aged! I think he was taken by surprise by the strength of what he felt for you and he had no way of handling it along with all the other threads of his life, so he tried tangling it all up together and made a mess of it.'

She looked as if she was about to cry again. He went on: 'Oh Lottie, Lottie – try and remember how short a time it was! A week to fall in love? Two weeks to decide on marriage? At your age that could be a fifty years' sentence. It's a lotta time to risk on two weeks of outings and kisses.'

'All right, what would you have done in his place?'

'You got me! I'd have run away with you and not let you out of my sight until we were married.'

As he spoke, the bantering tone had seeped away from his voice and now Lottie was staring at him, finally undeceived about his feelings. 'Oh, Ed, I'm so sorry! What a callous little bitch you must think I am, bleating about Grant all the time when all the time you . . .' She put her hand to her mouth to stifle the embarrassing words.

'I don't think bitches can bleat, dear Lottie, but I get the message and it's much appreciated. Come on, let's get a nightcap with Ada.'

The run in San Francisco was a triumph. The management kept up steady pressure on Lottie to extend her booking and she was about to do so, a week before the initial engagement ended, when she received a cable from Larry Nash, back in London after a year in South Africa and Australia. There was a pantomime vacancy if she wanted it – principal boy in *Aladdin* at Drury Lane. The Orpheum could offer no competition. She wired back: EXPECT ME EARLY DECEMBER STOP LOVE ALADDIN STOP.

The promised meeting with the genius choreographer had still not materialised. Each time she mentioned it to Ed, he said the young man was out of town. 'I don't know where he went, Lottie, but he can't be gone much longer. I know the troupe he manages are still in town so he has to come back.'

'Well, just as long as neither of you forget it when he comes. The minute you find him I want a meeting between you, me, Karl and him. This new song is itching to get out now, and I want it nice and polished when I set off for London.'

But it seemed she was doomed to disappointment. The following Monday, stickers went up over her name on Orpheum bills all over San Francisco:

POSITIVELY LAST WEEK BEFORE RETURN TO EUROPE!

It looked as if she would be heading home without her customised Can-Can. Then, just as she was leaving for the theatre on Friday evening for her last but one appearance, Karl Muttler's small son arrived at the apartment, out of breath and bearing a note from his father.

Dear Lottie
Shaw was out of town up in Sacramento for a few weeks but he got back today and says he will call to see you at the apartment tomorrow to find out if you can work something together before you leave. Hope this suits.

Karl

Well, well she thought, San Francisco might be unlucky in love for me, but it has its points for business! She left for the Orpheum feeling better than she had since the separation from Grant Johnstone.

When she came offstage from the most enthusiastic reception she had received to date, Johnstone was waiting in her dressing room.

Lottie was speaking over her shoulder to someone outside as she came in

227

through the door, and did not see him until she was inside the room. She expressed no surprise, merely stared at him impassively, and said: 'I assumed we had no more to say to each other.'

'You must know better than that! I've been trying to screw up the courage to come and see you . . . to apologise for putting you through that ordeal.'

Her eyes beamed hostility. 'Ordeal? You flatter yourself, my boy! All I recall is the unpleasant necessity of dealing with an extremely rude woman and a man who let me down. A disappointment, certainly. Hardly an ordeal.' She moved past him to her dressing table and added, almost casually: 'Have you seen my maid? She was here when I went onstage.'

'Er . . . yes . . . that is, I sent her out on an errand.'

'Ah, yes, of course! Perhaps you have a few things you'd like me to do for you, too?'

He had risen from the fragile gilt chair on which he had been sitting when she came in, and had stood awkwardly beside the door throughout the disagreeable exchange. Now he could stand it no longer and lunged across the dressing room, folding her clumsily into his arms. 'Lottie, stop this! You can't have changed so much in a few weeks!'

She stood stiffly in his embrace as though frozen there, and would not meet his eyes. 'Not a few weeks, Grant. Six, to be precise. Six weeks during which I've had a lot of time to wonder where you were and why you didn't come to see me.'

'You must have realised . . . realised how ashamed I was, how badly I wanted to make it up to you.'

She laughed at that. 'Of course I did! I'm developing a mind-reading act for next season, ain't I? Remote distances a speciality – all the way from the Orpheum to Nob Hill!' She switched off the exaggerated cockney she had assumed to provoke him and added: 'Why the hell should I have thought anything of the sort, you fool? It was fairly obvious that you'd simply abandoned me, and so far you've said nothing tonight to change my opinion.'

'But here I am! I wouldn't be here if I didn't want us to stay together.' As they argued, he had stepped back but had not released her from his grasp. Now he pulled her towards him again, pressing her head against his shoulder and stroking her hair.

The action worked better than a thousand persuasive words. He felt Lottie relax completely and heard the stifled sob as she buried her face against his broad chest. For long moments, he held her and talked to her as a parent would to a suffering child, making small half-nonsensical noises, continuing to stroke her hair, at one point raising her hand and kissing the palm. Finally she collected herself, stood back and said: 'Oh, Grant, I missed you so very much!'

'Me too,' he replied, scarcely above a whisper. 'Say, don't let's stay here any longer. Let's pay a farewell visit to the *Californian Queen*.'

'I can't, not like this! I'm all dolled up in my stage costume!'

'Yes you can. Put on that crazy coat over the top of it. Your profession meeting mine, in a way.'

She moved to obey him, then realised what he had just said. 'So you did come to see my act, after all.'

'Of course I did – I've been three times. I might not have had the nerve to try and make up with you before now, but I couldn't stay away from you completely.'

She struggled with the impulse to ask him what he had thought of her performance, and for the moment managed to suppress it. Something told her she would not want to hear his views. Minutes later, wrapped in the billowing grey coat, her stage makeup still garishly in place, she left the theatre with him and asked the stage doorman to see her maid had her possessions taken back to Ada at the apartment.

When they boarded the *Californian Queen*, it was obvious that Johnstone had prepared in advance to take her there. In the sheltered spot aft where they had watched the sunset weeks before, a table was set with a cold supper and champagne in an ice bucket. She clapped her hands in pleasure, but could not resist saying: 'What would you have done if I'd refused to come?'

He assumed an exaggerated scowl 'I'd have stormed down here all alone, eaten the food and got blasted on the champagne, that's what! But as I didn't, let's drink a toast . . .' He opened the bottle, then filled two delicate glass flutes with the bubbling golden wine. 'Here's to the future Mrs Grant Johnstone!'

Her enormous eyes regarded him doubtfully over the rim of the glass. She sipped the drink, but then said: 'On what terms, Grant?'

'No terms, only that I expect you to love me forever!'

'I offered you that weeks ago. Somehow it turned out not to be enough then.'

'Well it is now.'

She drank again, her mind nibbling at a host of questions which had suddenly arisen. Then an awful realisation began to dawn on her. She put down her glass and stood up, moving across to the ship's rail. When she spoke, her voice seemed to her to be coming from a thousand miles away. 'Grant, it was no coincidence, was it, that you left coming to see me until the end of the run?'

'I – I don't understand you. I told you, I was trying to screw up the courage.' He gave a forced laugh. 'In the end, it was only knowing you'd be gone in a few days that got me here.'

'No, I don't think that's quite true. What would you say if I told you I planned to appear on the stage right up until we got married?'

'I – well, you're not likely to, are you?'

'Would it make any difference?'

'There's no need, Lottie – surely you see that. You've had a triumphant run; you know how it feels to top the bill. Why not call it quits?' He turned a shaky smile on her. 'We can marry as soon as you like – I hate long engagements.'

'I'm not giving up the stage, Grant.'

'But you said – you said when you accepted my proposal – that you'd give up after the Orpheum run. What's changed?'

'Maybe I have. I'm damned sure you have!'

'I still don't understand you.'

'Really? You amaze me. I think *I* understand *you* all too well. I know, you couldn't live without me. But you couldn't live *with* me being in vaudeville, could you? So you put me through weeks of misery, staying away from me

229

while I was performing, when I'd have given anything to have you with me, and then when it was all over bar the shouting, you crept back, thinking "Ah, she'll give it all up for love now", and hoping to make me respectable for your dear Mama. Well, dearest, I'll tell you what you can do with your sodding proposal. You can stick it where the monkey stuck 'is nuts, along with this rusty old tub and your bloody parlour girl mother!'

Then she turned and stormed off the *Californian Queen* without looking back.

Shortly before noon on Saturday, a young man came to the apartment and Ada Scully let him in. She looked pale and harassed, and the living room was in a state of chaos. 'Aw, hell, Mr Shaw, I'm sorry ya come all this way fer nothing! I'm afraid there's been a change of plan. Miss Casanova won't be able ta work with ya after all,' she told him.

'Why not? Surely she can't have changed her mind so quickly?'

'Well, not straight out like that. It didn't really arise . . . Ya see, she ain't too well. Can't play her last turn at the Orpheum tonight. She decided she had ta get away somewhere quiet, so she's gone on back ta New York.'

'She's gone to New York for peace and quiet?'

'In a manner a' speakin', yeah. Left on the Coronado this morning. I'm only still here ta tidy up the loose ends an' do the packing.' She glanced across at him and one look at his face cut off her stream of explanations. 'Say, are you all right? Sit down a minute an' I'll getcha a drink. I could do with something myself.'

When she returned, he still looked as if the life had been knocked out of him. She handed him a hefty tumbler of whiskey and he swallowed half of it in one gulp. 'Now,' she said, 'would ya mind tellin' me why yer takin' this so hard? If ya must know, Miss Casanova was engaged to be married and it was all called off last night. She's very upset and she's headin' straight back ta England.'

Shaw nodded, then drank the rest of his whiskey. 'I might have known I'd be too late,' he said. 'My timing's always out with Lottie when it really matters. I know her from years ago in London. You wouldn't believe how much I wanted to see her again.'

Ada looked at him sceptically. 'Ah, come on – if it'd been that important, she'd a' remembered yer name. Tain't as if Shaw's like Smith or Jones.'

'My real name isn't Shaw – that's the stage name I took in Australia. It's Fanshaw – Tommy Fanshaw. I was her first dancing partner. You could say we grew up together.'

PART TWO

Prima Donna

CHAPTER TWENTY-FIVE

This time Lottie had no worries about the cost of a first-class steamship ticket. She travelled in one of the best staterooms abroad the *Teutonic*. The crew were treating her as a celebrity and she could only assume the British press had been making a fuss about her success in America. In barely half a year, she had made reality of the vague dream of stardom with which she had crossed the Atlantic. Why didn't it feel better than this?

Throughout the voyage, she repeatedly asked herself the same question and failed to come up with an answer. Perhaps she was missing Ada, who had intended coming on to England with her until she discovered her daughter was pregnant and would need her back at the boarding house. Maybe it was the abrupt disappearance of all the other friends she had made in America. None of these possibilities felt like the answer. She tried to dismiss from her mind the fact that she felt empty, but it kept creeping back each time she thought she had conquered it.

When the *Teutonic* docked at Liverpool, it grew worse. Passengers jostled at the rails, trying to catch sight of friends or loved ones in the crowd down on the waterfront. Lottie remained detached. There would be no one here for her – Larry Nash was meeting her off the train at Euston. All she had to do was whisk through Customs and let the porter instal her in a comfortable window seat aboard the train. She found her eyes straying almost enviously to the excited girl, about her own age but oh, so young, who was skipping about in excitement at the prospect of reunion with her English fiancé. As she went ashore, a young couple rushed past her to greet their middle-aged parents, who had travelled from New York in the stateroom next door to Lottie's. Everywhere were the sounds of heartfelt welcome. All her fellow passengers appeared to be on their way to a happy home.

And it's your own fault that you haven't a home yourself, she told herself crossly, so stop feeling miserable about it. She settled into her corner seat on the train and composed herself for the long journey to London.

'Lottie, you look wonderful! I'd swear you've grown two inches since I saw you last!' Larry Nash kissed her on both cheeks and took the small Gladstone bag she was carrying. 'The Hotel Cecil awaits you and I'm at your service. Not that I'm sure you need me . . . you seem to have done pretty well on your own account.'

'Oh, Larry, you're wrong – I shall be so glad to hand over the reins to you again!' Lottie walked along beside him in silence for a few moments, then said: 'I sometimes wonder if it might not have been better if you'd never made that trip abroad. If you'd been at home, I'd never have been taken in by that phoney American booker, you know.'

He laughed ruefully. 'I'm all too aware of that. It makes my blood run cold – if you hadn't taken such an appalling risk you certainly wouldn't be back here playing Aladdin at Drury Lane this Christmas.'

'I'm beginning to wonder just what it's all for . . . does it matter to anyone that I'm going to be a panto star?'

'Oh my, we are feeling down! I think a little violent shock treatment is called for. Are you too tired to go out tonight?'

'Good God, no! I did precious little but sleep and brood all the way across the Atlantic. Lead me to the bright lights! Where shall we go?'

'As if you need ask, after such a long and impressive absence. Romano's, of course! That's what I was thinking of when I mentioned a violent cure.'

'What are you talking about?'

'My lips are sealed until tonight. But if the right people are there, I think I can guarantee this will be the last time you indulge in Hamletish soliloquies.'

She failed to get any more out of him, and in the end, exasperated, she parted from him in the lobby of the Hotel Cecil and went upstairs to unpack.

Lottie had spent almost two weeks with Ada in New York before coming home, partly to try and compose herself after her conclusive rejection of Grant Johnstone, partly because she had realised for the first time that she had only one gown, the oyster satin, worthy of the star she intended to be from her first day back in England. A hastily arranged series of fittings with a first-rate dressmaker had put matters right, but the woman was unable to deliver gowns of the type Lottie wanted in less than ten days, hence the extended stay in New York.

Now, intrigued by Nash's hints of drama at Romano's, she was glad she had restocked her wardrobe. There were three splendid evening gowns and two formal day outfits. Those gowns were going to take some getting into and she hadn't yet engaged a personal maid. She decided she had better ask for the assistance of one of the hotel maids for tonight and then get someone permanent as soon as possible. It was amazing how quickly she had come to rely on Ada.

As if in answer to a prayer, the house telephone shrilled. 'Reception here, Miss Casanova. There's a person to see you. She gives her name as Lewis. Shall I send her up?'

'Lewis? I don't know anyone called Lewis. What does she want?'

There was a murmured exchange as the clerk turned from the mouthpiece to talk to the visitor. Then he said: 'The party says you will remember her better by her first name – Maud. Maud from Gower Street, Miss Casanova.'

The instantly conjured picture of Nellie Standish, attended by her treasure of a maid, was so strong that tears stung at the back of Lottie's eyes. 'Of course! Please send her up. And I'd like to order some tea in my suite, please. Yes, of course for two. As soon as possible.'

Maud looked more smartly dressed than when Lottie had last seen her five years ago, but otherwise she had not worn well. Lottie was hard put to understand why, then realised the woman had taken on a faded look, although she had not aged discernibly. Before she even set eyes on the maid, she remembered with a stab of regret that she had never made contact to find out about Nellie's death. The singer had made it clear she wanted no theatrical farewells and Ulick and Lottie had respected her request. Now Lottie wondered how much that had sprung from real delicacy and how much from a desire to pretend their beloved Nellie had not really died at all.

When Maud arrived at the suite, Lottie talked about herself for five or ten minutes before she could bring herself to ask about Nellie. Finally she blurted: 'You know how much I loved and admired her, don't you Maud? I wish she'd wanted me there at the end, but as she didn't . . .'

Maud reached out and pressed Lottie's hand sympathetically. 'Of course, dear. Anyway, it was better like that. It wasn't nice at the end. She timed it quite well, mind. Lasted just eight months after we went to France. Said she always liked the autumn and that was the best time for your final curtain.' She sniffed surreptitiously into a tiny lace-edged handkerchief. 'Oh, Gawd, Miss Lottie, I miss her so much! Nearly five years now and I feel as if she died yesterday!'

Lottie's own eyes were blurred with tears. She blinked them back and said: 'Was it just you and her at the end, Maud?'

'Oh, no. Tommy Fanshaw come an' stayed with us.'

Lottie stiffened. 'But th-that's impossible! He was . . . he went to jail.'

Maud laughed. 'What on earth give you that idea, Miss? O' course he didn't go to jail. He come out to us after that bit a' bother he had with Ulick Farrell. Said he'd have brought you, an' all, if Ulick hadn't sent you back home to your parents. I suppose you got tired of it after a while and came back to London, did you?'

Lottie was staring at her, completely perplexed. 'I don't understand any of this. I left home for good before I met Nellie and you – or Tommy, for that matter.'

'No, Miss, Tommy told us. You must remember. You did that first panto season, then there was that trouble for Tommy when Mr Farrell found Tommy and you . . . you know, together, like . . . then when Mr Farrell dropped the charges and Tommy come round to take you away, you'd been sent home to your parents. I know I was ever so surprised a year or so later to see your name on a bill for the Old Mo'. For a minute I thought it must be someone who'd pinched the stage name.'

As Maud spoke, Lottie had put down her cup and saucer with exaggerated care. 'Are you telling me Tommy didn't go to prison; that he came looking for me and I wasn't there?'

'Now you didn't think he'd leave you with that drunken Irish beast if he could of done anyfink to stop it, do you?' Maud was using the kindly tone she might have employed with a slow-witted child.

Lottie was almost afraid to ask the next question. 'What happened after he came to Wilson Street?'

'Oh, I think he was in a hell of a state. Said he walked round the streets in the Garden for hours, hardly knowin' where he was. In the end, he said, his feet just sorta took him back to Gower Street –' Lottie remembered her own half-involuntary pilgrimage to the house to lay ghosts of her own '– an' when he saw the blinds down and the "To Let" sign in the window, he knew what he wanted to do. He come and joined us in France.'

'But how on earth did he find you?'

'Well, I think Nellie was more concerned about Tommy managin' than you. After all, she really thought that Ulick would protect you. She knew he

235

an' Tommy would be at each other's throats in five minutes and she thought Tommy might need a leg up. So when she give 'im that money, the letter wiv it told him where her lawyer was, and said he could contact her through him if he was ever in real trouble. That's just what he did an' the lawyer told him the name of our hotel.'

She chuckled, remembering. 'If Tommy'd only hung on, he'd of given the lad a ticket, an' all, once he'd wired Nellie to make sure it was all right. But Tommy went off an' did that for himself with the money Nellie had given 'im. D'you know, I think Nellie hung on a good month longer – and happier – than she would of otherwise.'

'What happened . . . a-after?'

Maud said: 'Nellie could see how cut up the boy was about losing you, but she knew there was no point encouraging him to hope if you was back with your family. So she decided he had to make a fresh start. He liked that idea, an' all, because he was really terrified of Mr Farrell; thought he might have second thoughts about lettin' Tommy off and find some other way of gettin' at him if they ever met again. An' on top o' that, Nellie could never make him really believe Farrell was nothing important in Music Hall. Tommy thought he was one of the real big noises and that he'd never get nowhere if Farrell was around.'

'Then where did he go?'

'Australia. It was funny really. An old mate of Nellie's come to stay at the hotel. He'd been a small-time acrobat. He went off to Australia about ten years back, didn't make nuffink of his stage act, but he went as a gold miner when he couldn't get bookings. Made his fortune. He was in Europe spending some of it when we run into him. He painted this real pretty picture of a land flowing wiv milk an' honey for Nellie and Tommy, and next thing I knew, there was Nellie saying, "Go South, young Tom." He did, an' all.'

'You must have heard from him since he went.'

Maud shrugged and shook her head. 'Now how would I? I checked out of the hotel the same time as him, a week after Nellie passed away. I didn't have no idea where I was going to live, and Tommy certainly didn't. All he had was a cabin class ticket to Australia. I've never 'eard of him from that day to this. Long way off, Australia.'

Lottie's head was pounding and her sense of reality was slipping. Tommy, the lover and friend who had really understood her, gone and locked away for so long in the cupboard of her memory and now forcing open the door. But to what end? It only revived her misery at losing him, and what had come after. If he was lost to her forever, there was no point in reliving all this pain by learning, too late, how narrowly she had missed him.

With a start, she realised Maud was talking again. 'Please forgive me,' said Lottie. 'It's all so hard to take in . . . What did you say?'

'I said, when I saw it in the paper about you coming home a star, I decided I wasn't leaving it no longer. The *Post* said you was going to be living at the Cecil for a while, so I come here today, but not just to say hello.'

'What else?' Lottie wondered if the woman were in trouble over money, and whether she should offer to help, but Maud's clothes and shoes were of the best quality and almost new. Nothing impoverished there.

'Oh, you may think it's ever so silly, and you may get cross wiv me for even

236

asking – but I don't arf miss working for someone like my Nellie.' Before Lottie could respond, she went on: 'Don't mistake me. Nellie left me wiv enough so I'd never want. I was thinking of opening up a little boarding house or somefink like that. But it seemed ever so tame after life wiv Nellie. I been trying to kid myself I like being a lady of leisure for four years now, and it's time I admitted it doesn't work. Is there any way you could consider having me as your maid?'

'Maud, are you serious? I'd give my eye teeth to have you! When can you start?'

Maud, convinced in advance that Lottie would already have someone, was halfway into an explanation that she would work for very low wages, and took a few seconds to run out of steam. When she did, she said: 'You'll have me? Oh, Miss Lottie, that's wonderful – you'll never regret it, I promise! At home or at the theatre?'

'Could you possibly manage both? I'd see you weren't involved in any domestic work at home – just looking after my personal needs. At the theatre, of course, you'd be my dresser.'

'Oh, yes please!' Lottie wondered if she was imagining that Maud was already beginning to shed her faded look. 'When d'you want me to start?'

'How about ten minutes from now? I have a dinner engagement and a gown to put on that might have been devised by the Spanish Inquisition.'

All conversation ceased for a good twenty seconds when Larry Nash escorted Lottie Casanova to her table at Romano's that evening. Various papers had announced that she was arriving from America on the *Teutonic* this week; that she was being permitted to start rehearsals late for the title role in *Aladdin* because the management said only she would do for the part; that she had earned fabulous sums in America and had arranged her own tour programme in major halls right across the country.

'No wonder they're so bloody quiet – I'm pretty impressed myself,' Lottie hissed at Nash. He had brought the papers for her to see before they left the Cecil. 'Who told them this stuff? It's mostly pure make-believe. If you could have seen some of the places I played . . .'

Larry chuckled and touched her arm. 'But I can't, my dear, and neither can they, so let's not stint the story in the telling, eh?'

'One thing I will say: an injection of cash is going to be handy very soon,' said Lottie. 'Tearing back and forth across America at your own expense is damned pricey. I wouldn't be at the Cecil now if it weren't for putting the best face on things.'

'Have no fear, dear girl. The star gets rehearsal money at Drury Lane – half your wages, payable weekly from tomorrow. And your wages for the run of the Panto are very impressive indeed. How does a hundred and fifty pounds a week strike you?'

'How much? My God, at that rate I could buy the Cecil before too long!'

'There we are then. Say thank-you to your Uncle Larry for being a tough negotiator and stop scolding him for telling fibs about your American success. It worked, didn't it?'

'Larry darling, if it wouldn't cause talk I'd reach across and cover you with kisses this minute!'

'Mmm, I might take you up on that some other time . . . but right now, let's concentrate on business. I think your shock treatment just came in.'

Still laughing with pleasure at his cleverness, she turned to look at the door, and froze. Ulick Farrell had arrived, accompanied by a girl who at first glance might have been Lottie herself.

'Christ Almighty, if I wasn't sitting here I'd think that was me! Who the hell is she?'

'The pretty toy that enabled Farrell to convince himself you'd never gone away. Don't you know her? She claims to have met you – even says you shared a dressing room a long time ago.'

Still sick with a mixture of jealously and something she could not identify, Lottie looked again. Yes, the face was familiar. Now what was it about the resemblance? Why did she have the feeling this girl was a genuine version of what she herself pretended to be . . . ? Her heart lurched. Of course! The Clerkenwell ballet girl who had tried to bait her at Drury Lane the year of *Dick Whittington*. She'd had a real Italian name . . . that was it, Minoli – Christina Minoli.

'Yes, I know her,' she said to Larry, somehow managing to make her voice light and amused. 'How on earth did they run into each other?'

'I rather gather it was more a case of our Miss Minoli tripping over Ulick than running into him. He was pretty far gone at the time.'

'Larry, I must hear all about it, but what if they come over? I couldn't stand either being civil to her or having anything to do with Ulick at present. I have to get used to the idea.'

Nash grinned. 'Oh, dear, you have been away a long time! Cast your mind back. Have you ever known an aspiring artiste go and introduce herself to the star at Romano's when said star has just made a triumphal entrance? She'll descend on you some time, but not now, never fear.' He broke off to look after them. 'There, as I said. Ulick saw us and diverted her towards a table over at the far side. I've no doubt they'll be able to observe every move you make, but you won't have to acknowledge or even see them, so cheer up.'

Finally convinced she was secure from their direct attention, Lottie turned her fury on Nash. 'You bastard! Shock treatment, you said. You nearly gave me bloody heart failure! How could you? Think of all the things that might have gone wrong!'

'Rubbish! If you hadn't been capable of handling that, you certainly wouldn't have been able to handle *Aladdin*.'

Tacitly, Lottie acknowledged the compliment, took a deep breath and forced herself to approach the matter from another direction. 'I think perhaps I'd better ask how this got going. Ulick certainly doesn't look as if he's just got up from a gutter any longer.'

'My dear, she's done wonders for him . . . now before you fly off the handle, listen to me. I tried to tell Ulick what I'm going to say now; and I tried to approach it with you from a different angle. You didn't understand it and he wouldn't. Perhaps you'll see it now I've been proved right.'

'Stop hedging and try me.'

'Very well. Ulick couldn't live with your talent. The minute you began developing, he began drinking too much. He tried to deal with it by circumscribing what you could do on stage. I think the poor devil felt he would still

238

be in control then. But you were too good and you saw it would destroy you eventually. What you didn't see was that without that control, *you* would destroy *him*, without intending to do anything of the sort. Fortunately you split up before it quite came to that.'

'And what happened then? From what you said about the way he met this piece, I take it he dissolved into a puddle of his own making as soon as I'd gone.'

'You could put it that way. After you sailed for New York, he was drunk for at least two weeks. He was hanging around Oddenino's one afternoon, in too bad a state to get up from the table, when our Miss Minoli came in. According to him, she sat down beside him, gave him a smile that made him think you'd come back for a few seconds, and said: "You're Ulick Farrell, aren't you? I've always wanted to meet you." It went on from there.'

'How utterly banal!'

'Precisely. I think old Ulick was overdue for a little banality after you. Suddenly he was confronted with a female who looked very like you, but lacked the temperament and, far more important, the talent, to overshadow him. Within a couple of days he was sober. A few days longer and he looked respectable again. After two weeks he was writing songs and touting La Minoli around the halls at audition time.'

'And this was just after I left?'

'Yes. They appear never to have had a disagreement. He has regained most of his old regular newspaper commissions, he's writing the occasional passable music hall song and doing a reasonable job of managing Tina. I think you could call Ulick a modest success.'

'And you thought that would cure me of feeling lonely and unwanted!'

'Don't be childish, Lottie! I didn't think any such thing. I merely wanted to point out that if the right conditions could turn Farrell around from such a rigidly mapped road to destruction, you should have no trouble in recovering your own zest for the stage.'

'It does no such thing. All it does is make me feel even more of an outsider.'

'Lottie, this is me, Larry Nash, remember? I saw you performing in the Rose when you were just getting started. *We're* all the outsiders. There's one real world here – you and the stage, the audience. You're locked in there with a huge talent and if we ordinary types get between you and them, we get burned. I'm showing you your own uniqueness and trying to tell you it's time you appreciated it fully.'

She was silent for a long time, alternately drinking deeply from her glass and gazing morosely into its bubbling depths. Then she said: 'It's not enough for me, Larry.'

'Of course it is! You just get a bit nervous now and then and tell yourself you should be just like other people. But you're not. You may be many other things, but you are not like anyone else. You are Lottie Casanova, and you are a star. You will always be a star. Everything else is incidental.'

'Forever? That's a terribly lonely road, Larry.'

'I don't think it's more lonely than anyone else's, and my God, it has its compensations! All of us are left alone and friendless from time to time, but how many of us can claim that through it all there are hundreds – thousands – of people who live only for the sight and sound of us? There may be four or six in a generation, and you're one. Count your blessings.'

She thought about that for a long time, too, then gave him a regal smile. 'All right, I believe you. I think I'm going to get very drunk tonight. Then tomorrow I'm going to find somewhere to live, and after that I shall get used to being the greatest Aladdin ever. There's glory for you!'

He tried to discern her mood beneath the smooth smile, but she raised her glass to her lips again and turned her face away from him.

CHAPTER TWENTY-SIX

It was easier than Lottie would have believed possible a year earlier. On her first day in rehearsal, she was welcomed onstage like a princess. After the physical exertions of two spots nightly at the River Palace, she had developed a tolerance for hard work that would last her a lifetime. This seemed almost like play in comparison. It was also fun. As the rehearsals got underway, Lottie recaptured something of the family feeling she had experienced years before in Drury Lane pantomime. Oh, for a man who was in the business on the same footing as herself! These people all understood how it felt; she was beginning to think no one else would ever be able to live with it.

Now, though, she put romantic involvements out of her mind and concentrated on ensuring that *Aladdin* would fulfil all the expectations raised in the English audiences by Larry Nash's gossipy revelations to the Press. It was certainly a part that seemed made for such a task.

Lottie's costume for the main part of the pantomime comprised a fuchsia-coloured silk kimono which stopped at the hips, an automatic costume requirement for principal boys. Her legs were encased in fleshings, the heavy cotton tights which theatre managers hoped the League of Decency found less offensive than silk. Lottie did not mind. Her legs were so long and slender that even the unflattering cotton jersey looked good on them. Her marvellous black hair was braided into a pigtail which emphasised her long, straight back and ended precisely where her tunic did. As she moved about the stage, the pigtail bobbed provocatively on her shapely buttocks, ensuring no one forgot for a moment that this boy was really a girl.

The pigtail was topped by some costume designer's conception of a Chinese coolie hat, in this case an elegantly constructed flattened cone of Bangkok straw in a shade of pink that toned with the kimono – 'I didn't know they had kimonos in China', she had told the costumier, the same man who had clothed her a couple of years before for Dandini. 'Listen, lovey, for our audiences, anything east of Jerusalem and it's kimonos, all right?' he had said testily.

Like the pigtail, the hat bobbed jauntily when Lottie moved about. Adjusting it, the costumier stood back and studied his handiwork. 'Hmm,' he said, 'unless I'm very much mistaken, every little brat who sees you this year will want to give a fancy dress party and go as Aladdin.' His glare softened. 'You look wonderful, dear, a real credit to me. Wish they were all so easy . . .'

The transformation scene for *Aladdin* had to be the inside of the treasure cave, and Lottie watched in fascination as drab painted flats were shifted into position, looking monumentally unconvincing, only to leap to opulent life the second the stage lights were played on them. Some things never changed, and as always, tiny ballet girls were trained to be fairies, genies and jewel spirits while the older chorus girls looked on through the chaos.

The great difference for Lottie lay in being the star. Even in her second-principal role of Dandini, she had shared a dressing room. Now she occupied the room in which Marie Lloyd had talked to her the night before *Cinderella* opened. Next door, the other principal, Herbet Campbell, who played the wicked Abanazer, enjoyed similar status. It was like being queen of a kingdom of splendid seediness. Lottie knew she would thrive on it.

Then, with a fortnight to go before opening night, the Genie of the Lamp broke her leg. Chaos ensued. The part had been given to a girl because the producer insisted the light, airy dance routines they had worked up for the Genie and Aladdin would not work with a male dancer. Elsie Lambert, the chosen genie, was a young ballet dancer with ambitions for the serious stage. The broken bone was a nuisance to the theatre but a potential disaster to her. Lottie went to see her in hospital, and found the girl looking wan and neglected in an open ward that appeared to cater for every non-fatal ailment imaginable.

She eyed Elsie's fellow-patients with disfavour and said: 'What are they doing for you, then? Why d'you have to stay lying around here?'

The dancer was half-frantic with worry. 'Oh, Miss Casanova, it's terrible! They don't seem to know what they're doing with me and I'm so afraid my leg will heal crooked! I daren't ask to have it set and get sent home, because there's no one to see to me. But what if they mess it up and I can't dance again? I'll starve.'

'We'll soon see about that.' Lottie swished down the ward to the head nurse's office near the entrance. 'Where do I find Miss Lambert's doctor?' she asked the Sister who sat inside.

The woman looked her over and said, in a patronising tone: 'The doctors are not available at visitors' beck and call, you know. Are you a relative?'

'I'm a friend. The girl has no relatives. I want to know why she's been here two days and nothing seems to have been done.'

The nurse's glance slid away. 'There has been some . . . er . . . disagreement . . . over the best course of treatment. Miss Lambert has been seen by two competent junior physicians and they decided to await the consultant's visit tomorrow before a decision is made on treatment.'

'For God's sake, she's got a broken leg. Can't they just set it?'

'I must ask that you refrain from profanity, Miss, er . . .'

'Casanova. Lottie Casanova. Where does this consultant do business, then?'

The nurse was truly shocked. 'Oh, it's quite out of the question that you should trouble Mr McIntyre about the matter! He is not based here at the hospital.'

'I'm aware of the way medics operate, thanks very much. I'm talking about his availability to paying customers. You know, consultations. I want to talk to the top man, I want to do it today, and I'm fully prepared to go to his consulting rooms. All right?'

The sister, flustered now, went off to consult with someone else. Eventually she returned to announce that Mr McIntyre had been contacted on the telephone and would be happy to see Miss Casanova in his Harley Street consulting room in half an hour. 'Right,' said Lottie. 'In the meantime, don't do anything to that little girl except make her a bit more comfortable. I'll be back.'

'I'm sure you will, you dreadful woman,' muttered the nurse under her breath as she watched Lottie's elegant figure retreating down the corridor.

Within an hour, Elsie Lambert had been moved to a private room and the consultant had paid a special visit to see her. He examined the injured leg, pronounced that he could set it so that she would be dancing again as soon as the break was mended, and had her prepared for the operation, which was to be done under anaesthetic because the delay in treatment had ensured it would be extremely painful if undertaken on a conscious patient.

The following evening, Lottie was back, visiting a drowsy but grateful former Genie.

'You saved my leg,' Elsie told her, worship in her eyes.

'Don't talk so wet,' Lottie said. 'I may have helped save your career, but not your leg.'

'Yes you did, honestly. I heard one of the senior nurses going on at the young doctor who saw me when I first came in. She said if it had waited another day there was nothing Mr Wotsisname could have done but amputate. The doctor was blaming it all on his colleague, but he didn't say the nurse was wrong.'

'Well there you are, then. One day you may get a chance to save my leg – or my neck, judging from some of the scrapes I've got myself into before now. You just concentrate on getting better. The bills are all paid up here, and when you come out, we'll arrange for someone to see to you until you can manage. I don't want you undoing all that good work by using the leg too much before it's sound again.'

With that she said her goodbyes and departed. She had helped the girl from a mixture of outrage and sympathy. She was glad she had done it, but the effusive thanks were getting embarrassing. She wanted to be back in the cheerfully tough atmosphere of a theatre, not in this place that stank of cabbage, urine and disinfectant.

Lottie had spent long enough on the halls to know nothing was fair, and it all came down to the right break at the right time. Sometimes, though, she thought there must be a malign imp about who made sure good deeds were punished by a brisk blow with an invisible slapstick. They had not rehearsed the main Genie scene since Elsie's accident, instead doing those where the dancer made short appearances with one of the other small-part players temporarily standing in. While Lottie had been out and about arranging Elsie Lambert's medical care, Arthur Collins had been auditioning a replacement Genie. Two days after Elsie's operation, Lottie was introduced to her substitute, and almost stormed out of the theatre.

'Hello, Miss Casanova. What a surprise to be working with you!' The smile was pure poison. It was Tina Minoli, already wearing a new, larger, version of Elsie Lambert's wispy costume.

Lottie did not even dignify the other girl with a direct reply. She whirled on Arthur Collins and said: 'What the hell does this mean? You're not seriously offering this girl as a substitute for Elsie?'

Collins looked only slightly ruffled. He knew Tina was now living with Ulick Farrell and assumed Lottie was speaking from personal animosity.

There was a lot of it about in music hall, where partners constantly left each other for someone else in the same circle. 'Can't see why not, Lottie. She's a good little dancer and she can slip into the routine easy as you like. She's the best we've seen – apart from Elsie, of course.' He leaned closer, and said in a low voice: 'You can't let personal quarrels interfere with this business, you know.'

Lottie turned on him on fury. She did not lower her own voice. 'Don't be so bloody silly – I'd never dream of letting that sort of nonsense interfere. Look, I'll show you why it's damned daft!'

She stalked back across the stage to Tina, dragging off her elaborate hat as she went. Stopping close beside the other girl, she said: 'Right, what d'you see? Something about our heights?'

'All right, you've got a point. Tina's nearly as tall as you.'

'Exactly. And why did you cast a small, skinny girl instead of a male dancer as the Genie? To get someone I'd tower over in the dance routines. Now unless you suggest this one does them on her knees, I don't think that's possible, Arthur.'

'Well, perhaps now it isn't as important as I thought at first. You look very striking together.'

'I know, she could be my sister. Since when did the Genie of the Lamp look like Aladdin?'

Inadvertently, she appeared to have hit on the reason for Tina's selection. Seeing the slight change in Collins's expression, she moved back towards him. 'Don't tell me – that conniving bastard Farrell has been sweet-talking you, hasn't he?'

'Well, he did point out what a strong resemblance there was, and how much of a novelty it would be . . .'

'Enough of a novelty to make you scrap the original bright idea of some light little spirit? Nobody'd ever mistake that one for a spiritual type!'

The other members of the cast were watching gleefully, avid for the next act in the impromptu drama. Lottie was popular enough, but she had joined the company too late to have made any friends in the cast, and any principal as young as she would inevitably have provoked envy in more lowly performers. Lottie gritted her teeth and decided she could not afford to damage her standing with them by prolonging this row over a relatively minor player.

Using every ounce of her acting ability, she heaved a tolerant sigh and smiled forgivingly at Collins. 'Look, Arthur, this is all a bit silly, isn't it? Let's leave it for the moment, rehearse the other scenes we had down for today, and then you get Larry Nash and Miss – er – Minoli's agent together later to discuss it. If you decide this would do more good for the production, I'll go along with it. Otherwise, I suggest you have another look for a small, delicate Genie and put Miss Minoli in the chorus as compensation for not getting the part. Right, now shall we get on?'

The last words were uttered in an exaggerated sweetness-and-light tone that Collins knew well from other female stars caught in mid-tantrum. This one looked as though she could teach some of the great names a thing or two about theatrical temperament if he pushed her too far. He decided not to. 'Very well, Lottie. Let's do the Peking opening. I think everyone was ready for that because it's scheduled next anyway. Places, everyone. Miss Minoli, you'd better not hang on today. I'll sort it out with Ulick Farrell and Larry Nash later.'

And before the outraged newcomer could launch into her own version of a Lottie Casanova rant, Arthur Collins had turned away to set up the big opening scene.

Lottie's temper was not improved when Larry Nash laughed immoderately on hearing the news. 'You have to admit, Ulick has his moments,' he said. 'Since he pulled that off with Collins, I'll bet he's been waiting for you two to meet onstage like a kid preparing for Christmas.'

'I'm sure he has. Well, he must be very happy now, because I exploded. I am not sharing the stage with her, and that's final.'

Abruptly, Nash became serious. 'Careful, Lottie, it's all very well to be a prima donna, but you have a contract. It says nothing about you having control of casting, and if Collins thinks this girl is the best one for the part, you have to accept it. Look what you stand to lose: a very fat salary from Drury Lane until the end of February, and a devil of a knock to your reputation with other hall managers. It would take them years to forget this. No one walks out on Drury Lane panto, particularly when they've landed a star part so early in their career.'

He knew he had her. Lottie might sulk and carry on when she felt aggrieved, but she was a dedicated professional beneath the histrionics and would manage to tolerate this upstart player somehow. Nash hoped it would be unnecessary, because he was almost sure that fur would fly before the end of the run if the women had to work together. Still, better not tell Lottie that . . . 'After all,' he said aloud, 'apart from that big dance number, how many appearances do you make together?'

She pouted at him. 'About half a dozen. I admit only one of them is of any importance – the scene where the Genie is set free – and all the rest really only involve her marking time in the background, or snapping her fingers a bit to cast the odd spell. I still hate the idea, Larry.'

'All right, leave it to me. I won't promise anything, but we're in a reasonably strong position.'

Larry was meeting Collins and Ulick in the Café Royal, so Lottie knew there was little chance of running into Farrell or his protégée in the theatre. She had promised to go back there for a costume fitting. Her finale outfit was giving the costumier headaches and he wanted to see it on her again. As she emerged from the wardrobe room, she ran full tilt into Tina Minoli.

The girl had obviously been crying, because streaks of theatrical makeup were smeared down her cheeks. She stopped in her tracks and momentarily Lottie thought she would be physically attacked. Then Tina said: 'I mighta known you'd do everything you could to stop me. You always were a stuck-up cow, right from those first days in *Dick Whittington*.'

Lottie felt cold. Oh, dear God, she thought, don't let Ulick have told her about my background . . . it would finish me. But it seemed nothing was further from Tina's mind. 'I mighta known a tart from my own back yard would do for me if she got the chance, and you had to try, didn't you?'

'I confidently expect to have done more than just tried.' Lottie was all scorn to cover her own confusion.

245

'Well you haven't won yet. Ulick can charm the birds outa the trees – and it was a good idea, an' all!'

'Good for whom? How could it possibly benefit either of us for the audience to know we look like each other?'

'Oh, I mighta known you'd say that! Wouldn' be in *your* interests, you mean.'

'Nor would have been in yours, you silly little bitch. Look, I wouldn't like it because everyone would say, "Mmm, she's not so special after all, if she's got a double." But they'd forget as soon as the panto was over. But you! You'll be spending the next couple of years auditioning for theatre managers around London. In your shoes, I wouldn't want to draw their attention to my overpowering resemblance to one of the latest stars. They want variety – that's what this game's called, remember?' With that, she turned away, wondering whether what she had just said were true and hoping if it were that Tina would see it.

As she turned the corner at the end of the passage, the girl called after her: 'All this just because Ulick Farrell threw you over for me!' It took all Lottie's self-control to go on walking without a word of retaliation.

Her reward for such restraint was waiting outside her dressing room. It was one of the little ballet girls, a pretty, waif-like creature with auburn hair, still wearing her costume of opal fairy. 'Please Miss Casanova, I'm sorry to bother you when you're busy . . . but you went to see our Elsie, didn't you?'

'Our Elsie? If you mean Elsie Lambert, yes, but she told me she had no family.'

The girl giggled nervously. 'Yes, well she would. She 'ad an awful row with Father about . . . well about somefink. He said she couldn't ever come back. She didn't want to anyway. So now she lives on her own. But me an' Muvver misses her and I wondered – is she gonna be all right?'

Lottie gave her a big smile. 'Come on inside and sit down for a minute. You must be freezing out here in that skimpy costume. Yes, of course she'll be all right. A couple of weeks at the hospital, then home to rest with someone to help her and back on stage as soon as she likes.' Lottie studied the girl more closely in the brighter light of the dressing room. 'Tell me about yourself. How old are you – what's your name?'

She was fifteen and her name was Eugenie – ' 'cos Ma thought it was pretty, but they all call me Jean' – and she had been a ballet girl since she was nine.

'And do you want to do the same as Elsie?'

'Oh, yes, more than anything I can think of. That's why there was such a fuss. Father was mad enough about Elsie spending all her spare cash on proper ballet lessons, but when she started taking me an' all . . .'

'You can dance like Elsie?' Lottie hardly dared ask.

'Oh, yeah, sort of. Trouble is the teacher says I'm so light I'll blow away one a' these days.'

Lottie was up and at the door, yelling down the corridor: 'Maud – where are you? We need something to eat and an errand boy, quick!'

A surprised Maud popped her head out of a doorway a few feet away, where she had been gossiping with another dresser. 'All right, Miss Lottie, be there in a sec.'

Lottie went back to the ballet girl. 'Now, Eugenie, I want you to have a bite

246

to eat, because you may be staying on for a longish time. Not too much though – gotta stay light for what I have in mind.'

Eugenie was wide-eyed and nervous. 'But Muvver won't arf worry if I don't get home . . .'

'That won't arise. I'll get you a hansom. There's just someone I want to see you, and we're starting in Wardrobe.'

Within three-quarters of an hour, a messenger had taken a note to Larry Nash at the Café Royal and he returned to Drury Lane with Arthur Collins. Collins looked resentful, but had apparently acceded to Lottie's demand that Ulick should not come with them.

'What are you doing about your meeting?' she hissed at Larry as he arrived.

'Farrell's waiting for us to go back there.' Nash scowled at her. 'And, Lottie, this had better be good, because if it isn't, there'll be nothing I can do to make Collins pull that Minoli girl out of the show. He's furious.'

She merely gave him a cat-like smile. 'It'll be good, believe me.'

And it was. Not even Lottie could rustle up an orchestra at such short notice, but a pianist who had been rehearsing the ballet girls was still there. Now, beside a dimly lit stage, he played the tinkling chords of the introduction to the Genie's Dance, a beautiful little number that had been choreographed for the feather-light Elsie to perform immediately after Aladdin freed her from the lamp. A single spot tracked the tiny, ethereal figure as she appeared to flutter on rather than dancing. The occasional glint caught the gorgeous copper hair and her long legs, stick-thin but shapely, were white as snow. Jesus, thought Lottie, when did I ever see anything so beautiful? I'm gonna cry any minute . . .

She blinked hard and glanced along the row at Arthur Collins. He was sitting as entranced as she had been. It was a short routine – that added to its charm – but when it was over and the slender creature sank down beside the spot where Aladdin would be standing in the full performance, there was a stunned silence. Then Lottie saw a sight she had never thought possible. Arthur Collins, never known to say more than 'It'll do' or 'We'll be in touch' after an audition, was on his feet, applauding like a paying spectator and marching down the aisle towards the girl.

Lottie turned to Nash and flashed him the most predatory smile he had ever seen. 'And Miss Minoli goes to the chorus, I think.'

Somewhat to Lottie's surprise, the girl did just that. 'I'll give her full marks for guts,' she told Maud. 'That must have taken some doing.'

Maud snorted her disapproval. 'Not on your life! She's there because that Farrell told her she mustn't lose face. She's plotting behind your back, Miss Lottie. Just don't go down no dark corridors, that's all.'

'Oh, come now, it's hardly that bad!'

'If you think that, Mr Collins can't have told you about the lollipop he gave Tina to keep her quiet in the chorus. You now have an understudy.'

Lottie stared at her in the mirror. 'My God, I see what you mean about dark corridors. That should keep me healthy, shouldn't it?'

'Well, put it this way, lovey, we're going to see you stay wrapped up really warm this season. Don't want you catching a chill, do we?'

247

CHAPTER TWENTY-SEVEN

With such pressure on her to stay fit, it was inevitable that Lottie would fall sick. Early in February, she awoke one morning with the worst cold she had ever suffered. Maud took one look at her when she brought in the morning tea and said: 'Oh, Gawd, no *Aladdin* for you today by the look of it!'

'Nonsense,' said Lottie. 'You don't think I'm letting that Clerkenwell bitch take over, do you? It's only a cold.'

'You may say it's only a cold. I can just hear Arthur Collins's view of the matter now. It's not how you feel, Miss Lottie, it's how you look. An' you look terrible.'

Lottie groaned, but remained determined. 'Nothing a bit of makeup won't cure. Just you wait and see.' She sneezed, three times in succession.

'And I s'pose you'll play it with an 'ankie stuffed in the top o' your tights,' said Maud.

It was impossible. Lottie got as far as the theatre and put on costume and makeup. But within moments, her eyes and nose were streaming and grease-paint was smeared all over her cheeks. She thumped the dressing table in frustration. 'But I *feel* all right, dammit! I must be able to go on!'

'Oh no you can't,' said Collins when he saw her. 'It's up to you if you want to kill yourself, but my audiences have never had to watch a sneezing principal boy yet and I don't plan they should start with *Aladdin*. If you're sensible it'll only last a couple of days, anyway.' He was about to leave, when another thought struck him. 'Besides, whatever your feelings are about that Minoli girl, she deserves some sort of break after her disappointment. This one won't harm you and it'll make her feel a lot better . . . Go on now, home to bed.'

As the door closed behind him, Maud turned apprehensively towards Lottie, waiting for the explosion, but none was forthcoming. 'Yeah, he's right,' she said glumly. 'I'll never like the little cow, but it must have been rotten for her to get messed about like that, and I'll say one thing for her – she's never bothered me since she went back in the chorus. Go and see if she's around anywhere, Maud.'

Maud was back with Tina within five minutes. 'Have you talked to Collins yet?' Lottie asked her.

'No. Your dresser was bringing me back here when someone said he wanted to see me. I'm going to find him in a minute.' Her tone was sullen but Lottie saw the wild hope leap in the girl's eyes the minute she saw the star's sniffling state.

Lottie managed a watery smile. 'Well, you can guess what he's gonna tell you if you take a look at me, can't you? I'm out for a couple of days and you're going on as Aladdin. I just thought, as we hadn't hit it off before, it might be a good time to say let's be friends and good luck.'

Tina still looked suspicious. 'Why would you want to be so nice about it? You hated me enough to stop me getting the Genie part.'

Lottie sighed. 'No, I didn't. I thought the whole idea was stupid and it would have ruined that part of the panto, that's all. Look, you've got my good wishes anyway. I hope you do well out there tonight. D'you want to shake on it? Makes no odds to me if you don't.' She began to remove the mess of congealed eye makeup that marred her face.

'A-all right. Sorry to be so crotchety about it.' Tina moved forward, slightly shamefaced, and extended a stubby hand. Lottie grasped it firmly and said: 'Go on – show 'em you're ready for some nice music hall spots in your own right after this lot's over. I'd tell you to break a leg if it wasn't for what had happened to young Elsie Lambert.'

Tina was beaming now. 'Oh, Gawd, why am I hanging around? If I have to see Mr Collins and get changed as well, I shall be late!' Briefly she remembered her manners. 'Hope you feel better soon.' And she was gone.

'But not *too* soon, eh, little girl?' said Lottie to the closed door. Still sniffling, she began to take off her costume.

'How the devil did you know she'd make a hash of it?' asked Maud two days later. She had been sent to the Theatre Royal to see what sort of a performance Tina was giving.

Wide-eyed, Lottie said: 'I didn't, Maudie dear. What makes you say that?'

'Don't gimme that – I know you're an unselfish girl at times, but that Miss Sweetness and Light routine the other night just wasn't you.'

'Oh, but it was. I truly wanted to make the kid feel better about going on.' Then she chuckled. 'Mind you, I had a pretty good idea that if she hadn't got any further than pantomime fillers after about ten years on the boards and six months with a writer like Ulick to provide her material, she couldn't exactly be another Vesta Victoria.'

'You can say that again. She'll never get off the bottom o' the bill anywhere outside the smaller halls.'

'Mmm, that bad, eh? How did the audience behave?'

'Well, you know the Lane at panto time. I was at the matinée, too, remember. The kids are happy enough just to gasp at the Transformation Scene and boo Abanazer. And Herbert Campbell is really pulling out all the stops to make 'em forget Aladdin isn't as strong as they could wish . . . No, that audience will be all right with her. It won't be any use to her in getting music hall work after, though. No spark there, Lottie. None at all.'

'Poor girl.' Maud glanced at Lottie sharply to see if there was any irony in her expression. All she saw was sympathy. 'When you've got it yourself, and you hear that someone else hasn't, it's like being told they're blind or crippled,' Lottie explained, 'because to you it's as natural as breathing. Poor little cow. I hope Ulick has the sense to get her out of the business before it destroys her.'

She was back onstage after one matinée and three evening performances away. A trickle of feature performers came through her dressing room the first evening to say how much they had missed her and how happy they were to have her back. Tina certainly seems to have taught them to appreciate me, she thought.

She had been back for a few days and was alone in her dressing room one evening, having sent Maud off to get her something to eat. It was well after the performance had ended – for once she was not going on anywhere afterwards – and when someone knocked on the door she assumed it was a fellow performer and yelled, 'Come on in!' She froze as she glanced into the mirror and saw Ulick Farrell reflected there.

'What do you want?' she asked.

He managed a smile. 'Not to start a row, it's all right. You look wonderful, Lottie.'

Her own smile was as unsteady as his. 'You look pretty good yourself. Why are you here?'

'You'll probably think I'm a fool, but I came to thank you for being so kind to Tina when she took over from you.'

'She told you about that? I'd have thought she'd keep quiet about it in case it made you think I had a good side.'

'I think she only told me because it worried her. She couldn't see what was in it for you.'

'I hope you told her that sometimes people have other reasons than that for doing things.'

'I tried, but she's had a lifetime to learn that isn't true. I suspect she's still wondering.'

'You don't share her views, I hope.'

'Of course not! That's why I'm here. I know how hard it must have been, and I know it was genuine. I'd like to do something for you in return.'

'I think you already have, Ulick. You kept quiet about where I came from.' As she spoke, she could have bitten her tongue out. If he hadn't thought of it before, why put ideas into his head?

He saw the play of expression on her face and chuckled. 'Don't worry; my silence was deliberate. That's our secret, yours and mine, and no one will ever get it from me.'

'Then you've done all I could ever ask of you.'

'Very well, Lottie. I'll go now.' He turned to open the door.

'Ulick – wait! Are – are you happy now?'

His smile was weary. 'Yes, I think you could call it that. My life is in order. I no longer feel threatened . . .' He pondered. 'Perhaps "settled" describes it better than happy.'

'What an awful thing to say.'

'Sometimes, in the middle of the night, it's an awful thing to be.'

'We were never like that together, were we?'

'God, no! The opposite. But Larry warned me a long time ago and I couldn't accept it. You burn people out. You can't help it. I had some of my best moments with you, but I was destroying myself to have them. No one can go on long like that.'

'Perhaps I shall never make any man happy.'

'Oh, I think you will. The trouble is, he has to be as talented as you. That's a tall order.'

She nodded glumly, then her mind leap-frogged. 'Ulick, if it wouldn't cause you too much pain, how would you feel about doing a bit of work with me?'

'How much? I can't take on a permanent association. It would kill poor Tina.'

251

'One song. It's written, and the music arranged, but it all needs brushing up – and I've got to get hold of a Can-Can expert. Could you help with that?'

He was gazing at her and chuckling. 'Oh, Lottie, you're irresistible! Only you would go from disastrous love affairs to Can-Can experts in the space of one sentence! I think something might be arranged. Give me a few days and we'll see.'

'Ta-ra-ra-boom-de-ay' was Ulick Farrell's masterpiece. He insisted on it being registered in the names of Farrell, Maskell and Muttler, because he said the others had contributed at least as much as he. To hear him tell it, he had merely tweaked the lyrics a little, giving them a more thoroughly English sound. But he took Muttler's musical arrangement and altered it from a piece which could have been delivered by any competent singer to one which was Lottie's alone. She loved it. He also found the dance master of her dreams.

Marc Cambon had been brought over from Paris to coach the Gaiety chorus in a Can-Can routine. After a month with them, he was close to despair. 'Why are these girls so popular?' he asked. 'Why are the men always in line to take them home? They dance like cart-horses, and nothing will turn them into gazelles!'

'I don't think their dancing is what interests the men, Marc,' said Lottie. 'I hope you're not just as disappointed in me.'

He looked dubious. 'Ulick Farrell says I will not be. He says you dance like thistledown. But you are a big girl for fast dancing; that is part of the trouble with the Gaiety chorus, too. In Paris, it is only the small women who dance these fast dances – ah, I cannot think straight in your inches and feet, but they are, I think, only about five feet. You must be closer to six.'

'Give me a chance! I'm tall, but not quite that big. I'm five feet nine.'

'Precisely – that is six feet in those high shoes you wear. Some of my Parisienne dancers are only five feet with their shoes on.'

'All right, so I'm a giantess. Leave me to worry about that and teach me the technique, that's all I ask.'

She soon converted him. After two days of training to kick and hold the kick high for seconds at a time, she was provoking him to applause. 'I never thought I would say it, Lottie, but when I see your great long leg shoot up to the ceiling, it makes my little Parisiennes look like ponies beside a racing thoroughbred!'

'It had bloody better, with the agony this is costing me. D'you realise my maid is rubbing me down with liniment every night when I go home? Thoroughbred is right – my bedroom smells like a damned racing stable!'

It was worth it, though. Farrell and Cambon were the only two people allowed at her rehearsals. Larry Nash knew what was going on, and disapproved. 'There's a very fine dividing line between work and romance and you and Farrell have been on both sides of it,' he said. 'I don't like the thought of you slipping across it again – the complications were too painful last time.'

'Don't worry about that, Larry. This time it's strictly business. Both of us want it that way.'

'And what does Tina Minoli think of it?'

Lottie could not meet his eyes. 'She doesn't know. Ulick said she wouldn't understand.'

'Hmm, I'm not sure I do, either. Go carefully, Lottie, and let me know when the song is ready.'

The pantomime run finished at the end of February. No one was sad to move on. Christmas seemed an age away, and even the audiences had a somewhat shop-soiled look, except for the matinées where the children were as enthusiastic as ever. Lottie was itching to be gone. She had been booked to top the bill at the Tivoli, every artiste's dream of heaven. If she made a big impression there, with a triumphant panto season behind her too, all London would be at her feet. She was planning to launch her 'Ta-ra-ra-boom-de-ay' song and dance there.

To her delight, Eugenie Lambert had been booked in a good spot at the Old Mo' after the manager had seen her Genie Dance in the pantomime on a particularly inspired evening. 'I dunno how I'll ever be able thank you, Miss Casanova,' she said when she came to Lottie's dressing room with the news.

'I know someone in your family who must be itching to tear out my eyes for it,' said Lottie. 'Poor old Elsie really must feel she's missed the boat.'

Eugenie's face was radiant. 'No, she was tickled pink. Tell the truth, that Genie part was just to get hold o' some money for her ballet. Now she's rested and well again, that seems to be taking care of itself an' all. She's got a place in the corps de ballet in a proper serious dance company.'

'My God,' Lottie grimaced, 'rather her than me. Now that's what I *call* hard work!'

'Yes, but it's what she wants, and now she's on her way. I don't s'pose we'll ever be able to give you an 'elping 'and, Miss Casanova, but if we can, you know you only got to ask.'

Bloody hell, thought Lottie, I'm turning into a theatrical grande dame and I'm still short of my twenty-first birthday! At this rate it'll all be over before it's started. Aloud, she said: 'Thanks, Eugenie. I hope it goes well for you both. Off you go now, and give Elsie my best.'

There was no gap between the end of Drury Lane season and her booking at the Tivoli. One ended on Saturday, the other began on Monday. 'Are you sure you're ready with this song?' Larry asked her. 'If not, go with "I Want To Go Where The Big Girls Go" – it's a good song, it's new to London and you know it inside out.'

'But it's not new to me, Larry, and I need the fizz of a new song to put across. It gets the best out of me, you know that.'

'But I don't. That's one of the little myths you've built up in your head. I've only seen you do well-tried routines.'

'Well hold on to your hat, you're in for an education. Incidentally, I'm going to sing "I Want To Go . . ." as well. I'm opening the act with that.'

'All right. You obviously learned how to create your own routine when you were alone in America. I have to assume you can do it now.'

The night before she opened at the Tivoli, Lottie suffered a recurrent nightmare so vivid that she awoke still thinking it was reality. She was a member of the Majiltons, the weird legmania act she had seen in Koster and Bial's, only in the dream their 'Study in Points' was danced to the tune and tempo of 'Ta-ra-ra-boom-de-ay'. Even in sleep, the illusion of those terrific kicks performed at double-tempo polka beat was killing, and she woke up panting and moaning, the bedclothes churned up around her.

She peered blearily at the clock. It was barely seven. Lottie normally rose at nine. Dear God, was work beginning to spill over from the theatre? Perhaps Larry Nash was right and this number should be slipped in on a less important evening, when the Tivoli audience was less packed with music hall journalists . . . Then she was fully awake. 'For heaven's sake!' she said. 'They're only men, aren't they?' By the time Maud arrived with her tea, she was out of bed, doing the limbering-up exercises Cambon had recommended to make her supple for her dance routine.

Larry and Ulick came backstage before she went on. 'It's really weird seeing you two together,' she said. 'Just as if we were back a couple of years ago.'

'No, Lottie, not quite.' Ulick's dead expression told her he wished they were.

Nash broke it. 'If I didn't know you were nerveless, I wouldn't tell you this, Lottie. Everyone from the *Sporting Times* to the *Penguin* is out there, and hoping you'll either be brilliant or dreadful.'

'Oh, thank you so much! Who wants which?'

'You misunderstand. None of them minds which you are, as long as you're one or the other, and they can either confirm or debunk the American sensation. What they don't want is a nice ordinary act.'

'Good. Because what they're not going to get is a nice ordinary act. I've junked "I Want To Go . . ." by the way.'

'What? Why? It's your most successful number.'

'Because when I ran through it, there was no way of wearing the costume I wanted for the Can-Can and the underpinnings for the little girl as one and the same outfit. Now it's Can-Can or bust. The others are all nice safe songs.'

In fact she had put together a good range of music, starting with a couple of American songs to remind her audience of where she had made the big time, and then leading into 'Ta-ra-ra-boom-de-ay'. She was planning to follow up with a couple of good but run-of-the mill numbers which Ulick had written, but thought she might not even have to sing them once the audience had seen and heard the big one. She decided not to tell Nash that. He was already in too much of a state.

Lottie was wearing a theatrical costumier's idea of the sort of crinoline a Southern belle would choose down on the old plantation. It served a dual purpose, setting the right mood for the early, American songs, and effectively concealing the Can-Can dancer's petticoats in which she planned to belt out her big number.

Tonight was different from all other nights. The last-minute ball of nervousness in her stomach did not disappear as she went onstage. She would not be at ease until she had delivered her new routine. She was lucky. They were a good, receptive audience who did not need the main number to introduce the act. Lottie had deliberately placed the Can-Can well back because she knew she could not have gone through a complete stage routine after it. It was far too exhausting. For that reason, too, the Farrell numbers she had lined up to finish on were slow and dreamy.

Now, the last of the three American songs ended to a good reception. The

254

orchestra struck up a long, boisterous intro which had the gallery tapping its feet long before Lottie started to sing. As they launched into it, she slid offstage, where Maud was waiting with the big plumed head-dress she planned to wear. Maud attached the feathers as Lottie discarded her crinoline, then, with perfect timing, as the orchestra came to the last line of its intro she swirled back on, looking for all the world like a very expensive French dancer. Throughout the first verse, now in Ulick's anglicised version, she strutted only inches behind the footlights, twitching the gorgeous petticoats and singing:

'A smart and stylish girl you see,
The belle of high society,
Fond of fun as fond could be
When it's on the strict QT.
Not too young and not too old,
Not too timid, not too bold,
But just the very thing I'm told
That in your arms you'd like to hold!'

Then she took a deep breath and started the escalating series of high kicks Marc Cambon had taught her, a kick to a syllable, each rising higher than the one before it:

'Ta-ra-ra-boom-de-ay!
Ta-ra-ra-boom-de-ay!
Ta-ra-ra-boom-de-ay!
Ta-ra-ra-boom de-ay!'

The highest kick came on the 'Boom' syllable, and she held the pose with her leg higher than her plume of feathers for the rest of each line. When she repeated the chorus, she had no need to sing it, for the audience had caught it already and were singing themselves, compulsively,

'Taaa-raaa-ra-BOOM-de-ay!'

At the end of the chorus, the orchestra played a lightning-fast polka arrangement of the tune, and Lottie hurtled around the stage in a sequence of French dance steps which gave the impression she was performing non-stop cartwheels without putting her hands on the ground. In fact it was even more strenuous than a series of hand-assisted cartwheels and in the early days she had been all but spent when she completed this part of the dance. Not any longer, though. Marc Cambon was a tough teacher. The last airborne cartwheel brought her to the front of the stage again and she skipped upright and straight into another series of 'Ta-ra-ra-boom-de-ay' kicks. When the last line came, she leaped into the air on the penultimate 'ra' and landed in full splits.

The audience went wild. Lottie hastily remade her act, knowing there was not the remotest chance of her performing three more ballads after this routine. She managed to slide smoothly to her feet, gave them a pretty, but abbreviated, rendering of 'In the Shade of the Old Apple Tree', and ended the act. Her curtain calls took up almost all the time she had originally allocated for the songs she had cut. They pleaded, begged and cheered for more. Wondering if her legs and ribcage would take it, Lottie moved downstage, gestured at the orchestra leader, and they were off again in the mad gallop which was to be the hit of London music hall for two seasons and more.

As she flung herself around in a reprise of the cartwheel sequence, Nash stared at Ulick Farrell and said: 'You're letting her do this? It'll kill her in six months!'

Farrell eyed him sadly. 'Have you ever tried persuading Lottie not to do something she's set her mind on?'

CHAPTER TWENTY-EIGHT

Larry Nash stayed only briefly in Lottie's dressing room. 'I hope after that killing routine you're going straight home to hot milk and kind words from Maud,' he said. 'If you were in my charge, I think I'd already have you wrapped in a blanket massaging your hocks, or whatever it is they do to race-horses.'

Lottie laughed raucously. 'Any excuse to get your hands on my fair flesh, Mr Nash! Good grief, what d'you think I'm made of, glass? The act has to be shorter with that routine, but you've seen what it does to the audience. They go crazy.' She thought it over for a moment. 'In fact, when I get going on the cartwheels, I go a little crazy too.'

'That's what they love about it, Lottie, and it worries me. It – it's *frenzied*, somehow. It has a self destructive feel.'

'Of course it does! It's like watching a trapeze artist do a double somersault without a net – extra thrilling because there's a chance he'll kill himself.'

'Well I'm telling you, it's not healthy.'

'Neither are smoking or drinking, but you do both. Look, Larry, if you're going to be so gloomy, I suggest you buzz off home. Tonight I am definitely queening it at Romano's.'

He shrugged. 'Please yourself. I'll see you tomorrow. Oh, and don't mistake my disapproval for contempt. It's a magnificent act and it'll turn you into a music hall immortal – if it doesn't kill you first. Goodnight, Lottie.'

With a less than friendly glance at Ulick, who was lounging on Lottie's chaise longue and listening with undisguised amusement, Nash departed.

Lottie smiled at Farrell. 'Poor old Larry. He's a terrific agent-manager, but he has this unreasonable urge to make sure I live to see old age. How many real troupers have you known do that?'

'He has a point, Lottie. That routine really is a killer. Do you think you can keep it up every night? And what about multiple bookings?'

'I was talking to Marc Cambon at our last rehearsal yesterday. He said the Can-Can girls at some of those places in Paris do five and six sessions a night, with half-hour breaks in between and each session is two or three dances. Of course I can do it!'

'I've been to Paris and seen them, Lottie. He's right, but they're not soloists. Each girl has a special skill – those airborne cartwheels, say, or very high kicks repeated at double tempo. But they come forward and do a twenty or thirty second spot, then go back into the chorus and the chorus carries the non-stop dance. I can assure you that the main dance is nothing like as strenuous as what you're doing.'

'Of course not – I'm not doing it for six sessions of three dances a night, am I?'

'If I know anything about your greed for multiple bookings, you'll be getting close to it as soon as the word spreads . . . Listen, I'm not another Larry Nash. I think it's a brilliant routine and of course you should go on doing it. I'm simply trying to persuade you to take care not to overdo it, that's all.'

She had put down her hairbrush and was staring at him in her mirror, a habit he remembered with a jolt of nostalgia from their previous time together. 'Would it worry you if I overdid it?' she asked.

'Must I answer that?'

'Yes. All of a sudden it's very important.'

He rose from the chaise longue and moved across to stand behind her. 'Lottie, you exasperate me, you frighten me. Sometimes you make me feel more like a mouse than a man. But I've never stopped caring about you for a moment – never stopped loving you, either. Poor Tina! When I make love to her, in my mind it's really you. I just have to make sure she never realises it . . .'

Lottie stood up and turned to face him. 'I'm going to regret this, Ulick, but . . .' and she drifted into his arms, her head tilted to receive his kiss.

They emerged from the embrace breathless with the shock of the renewed contact, which was as potent as it had ever been. Lottie reached up and stroked his cheek. 'I think I'm ready to love you now,' she said. 'I wasn't, before, not really.'

She was wearing a heavy silk dressing gown which she had put on after Maud had removed her stage costume. Now Farrell drew her over to the chaise longue and began to unfasten the garment. 'What are you doing?' she said. 'Surely we're not . . . not here . . . you must come home with me . . .'

He opened the front of the dressing gown and began caressing her big, round breasts. As he moved to slip it right off her, he said with a grin: 'You wouldn't miss tonight at Romano's for the Prince of Wales, let alone a humble songwriter!'

'Ulick . . . what if someone comes in?'

'They'll feel madly jealous and leave hurriedly, I should think. Do you intend talking for the rest of the evening? If not . . .' He slid to his knees in front of her, and drew his hand lightly across the surface of her crisp, curling pubic hair. A delicious tremor ran through her and she swayed forward. Ulick embraced her thighs, pressing her buttocks and driving her pelvis forward against his face, nuzzling the fragrant, spicy-scented hair as he did so. She was moaning ecstatically now, her hands on his shoulders, begging him to go on.

He ran his tongue around the inner lips of her vulva and Lottie ground her nails into his shoulders. 'Ulick, you bastard, I can't stand any more, please . . . no – don't stop . . . I don't ever want you to stop again!'

He rested back on his knees for a moment, smiling up at her. 'I always liked a lady who made up her mind. Maybe if you just – came down –' he pulled her to the floor beside him ' – and joined me!'

She melted on to the rug, her robe in a colourful tangle beneath her, long, snowy limbs equally tangled around Farrell. She had not yet taken off her stage make-up, and now the kohl had smeared, widening her eyes to an impossible size that threatened to drown him in desire. Her hair had been loosely caught back in a makeshift bun after Maud had combed out the elaborate stage hairstyle, and now it was loose, cascading everywhere like a black waterfall. This woman is so beautiful that even looking at her brings a man to ecstasy, thought Farrell. No one would believe it if I described her . . . Then the fugitive thought melted away as the wide, perfect mouth engulfed his, and he tasted the sweetness of her tongue exploring his lips.

Her fingers were working frenziedly at his shirt front and she paused briefly to say 'Damn these stupid, stupid clothes!' Ulick managed to slip out of his jacket, but before he could remove anything more than his tie, she had unfastened his trousers and her hands slid inside, sinuous, demanding, endlessly exciting.

'L-lottie, now I can't stand it! I'm going to –'

'Not yet', she murmured against his neck. 'Not quite yet . . .'

She slid over him and sat up, her body engulfing him. Ulick thrust upward from the floor and the strong muscles inside her seized him, gripping, pulling, absorbing, until he felt he was being diffused through her whole body. She seemed quite unconscious of the motion; it was so regular, so compulsive as to seem a natural function like breathing. A vast sob of pleasure began forming itself in Ulick's lungs, pushing upward and outward in an uncontrollable drive to express his physical exaltation. As the great sound surged through him, her movement intensified. Her back arched and she leaned away from him for long seconds, hovering on the brink of some huge release of her own. As she let go, his yell finally escaped his lips, and Lottie collapsed across him, shaking with laughter. 'Talk about the mother and father of an explosion!' she gasped, when she finally managed to catch her breath.

More than an hour later, sitting with Ulick at the best table in Romano's, Lottie was sure half the customers must know what they had been up to, and she could not have cared less. Her body was singing with fulfilment and this felt like the happiest night of her life.

The first editions of the morning newspapers arrived not long after they ordered supper, and every music hall column reviewed Lottie Casanova's new song-and-dance routine. There was even a suitably outraged critique, headed THE DEVIL'S POLKA, which thrilled Lottie more than the rest because the scandal value would pack even more people in to see her. She sat and purred over the reviews.

Ulick watched her, his gaze unflickering. 'I'll never be able to compete with this, will I, Lottie?' he said.

'Don't be daft – you're responsible for it, remember?'

'I don't understand you.'

'Ulick, you were the one who knew me well enough to rearrange a nice workmanlike little number until it fitted me closer than my corset. Without knowing it, you'd already done the same in writing "I Want To Go Where The Big Girls Go". You're as talented as me – it's just a different sort of talent. Why should you feel the need to compete?'

He pressed her hand. 'Generous to a fault, as always. And with as little understanding as always, dear Lottie. It's not you I feel I have to compete with, I've tried to tell you often enough. It's your audience.'

Lottie gave an exasperated snort but her expression was loving. 'No one has ever been able to do what you did to me back there – nobody! Oh, I enjoy it all right, but with other men it'll never be quite as good as doing the last chorus of 'Ta-ra-ra-boom-de-ay' to a full house like the one we had tonight. With you, it's the same feeling, Ulick. I dunno how you do it, but then, I dunno how the audience does it, either. They're no threat to you, believe me.' She paused and reflected for a few seconds. '. . . P'raps it would be better for me if they were.'

'But that audience must be like an unending supply of caviare and foie gras.'

'Yeah, and once, that may have been all I wanted. Now I've reached the top, it's going to stay the same – unless I go downhill. Even foie gras gets boring if it's the only thing you ever eat.'

He tried a small joke: 'And I'd make a nice bit of scrag end for light relief, is that what you're saying?'

'Oh, my darling, please don't take it so seriously. No, of course not. It's a big fairy story that a star gets her thrills from the audience. Look around you. The big female names all have men in their lives, don't they? And plenty of them are strong enough.'

'Yes, and plenty are pathetic little shadows of their great ladies, too. I don't think I could survive that happening to me.'

Lottie was becoming indignant. 'This is silly. They were nobodies from the start. You're a big, brash, clever man with a marvellous education and a lot of talent. How could you ever become nondescript?'

'By failing to be a fifteen-hundred seat audience every time we were together, that's how.'

'If I hear the word audience again, I swear I shall walk out!' stormed Lottie, then abruptly transformed her expression to a regal smile as the first of an endless stream of well-wishers arrived.

'Wonderful what you did to that audience tonight, Lottie,' said the man, causing Ulick to choke on his champagne with mirth, 'wonderful. Not a man there who wouldn't have thrown up everything for you.'

As the man went back to his table, Ulick managed to keep smiling and said: 'See what I mean?'

But the resurgence of their desire for each other, and its delightful fulfilment in Lottie's dressing room, saved them at least temporarily from further argument. They drank champagne, chewed manfully through Romano's tough beefsteak, and paused frequently while Lottie graciously acknowledged her new pre-eminence. It was almost two o'clock when they took a hansom back to her house in Tite Street, Chelsea. Inside the cab, Lottie sat close to him and absorbed the warm, familiar smell of him, enjoying his nearness and resolutely keeping her mind empty. She was not going to spoil things now by thinking of Tina Minoli.

Maud treated Lottie just as she had Nellie Standish. During the day and at the theatre she fussed around in almost constant attendance, but once Lottie had gone out for the evening, Maud went to her room on the top floor and did not reappear unless Lottie summoned her with a bell rigged outside on the landing. In Maud's view, what financially independent women got up to after hours was no business of the rest of the household, servants or family.

Now Lottie and Ulick stood together, kissing, in the hall. 'Would you like a drink?' Lottie murmured indistinctly into his coat front.

'No, my darling, I'd just like you. You and a big, wide bed. Where is it?'

'Gentlemen leave their coats in the hall,' she admonished him, and helped him out of it. Then, almost skipping with pleasure, she led the way up to her bedroom.

One rosy-shaded lamp had been left burning at the bedside and the covers were turned back. Lottie gave a contented sigh at this well-ordered attention to her comfort, then began to work on her clothes. 'Allow me,' said Farrell. 'I'm going to enjoy this.'

As he busied himself unlacing her stays and removing layer after layer of petticoats, Lottie said: 'I can't help feeling that some day some bright girl will make a fortune by making clothes that are easy for women to put on instead of just fun for men to take off.'

'It'll never happen in our time, I'm delighted to say,' murmured Ulick, kneeling in front of her to roll down her black silk stockings.

This time their love-making was living up to all the confused girlish dreams which Lottie had created for herself back at Lyonesse. In their earlier relationship, when they made love, she had merely responded, following where Ulick led. Now she demanded as well as submitting. Physical desire and its satisfaction swept her away so completely that afterwards the whole experience was little more than a delightful jumble of impressions – her endless black river of hair twining around them both; his big, capable hand resting casually on the swell of her hipbone, containing it as easily as a piece of fruit; his mouth, laughing with her one moment, smothering her with delirious kisses the next. Everything was right about it, and it could not last.

For four days – and nights – Lottie's life was perfect. The audience at the Tivoli seemed to live only for her. Each time she went on stage the energy poured into her and she rushed out to meet her punishing dance routine with unquenchable zest. The newspapers continued to glorify her act, with the national daily press picking up where the specialist sporting and theatrical journals left off. Queues snaked down the pavement outside the Tivoli each day, waiting to see the phenomenon of the hour. And every evening Ulick – a new Ulick, not drunk, not in debt – awaited her backstage after her act.

Every night she cemented her triumph by an appearance at Romano's or the Café Royal; and every night she curled up in Ulick's arms after they had made love, and drifted into blissful sleep. She forbade herself to think of Tina Minoli. She refused to see anything but normality in Maud's face. Anyway, Maud was trained in a hard school to remain inscrutable when an employer did something of which she disapproved.

Then, on Friday of her first week at the Tivoli, Ulick sent a message to say he would not be with her that evening. The stage doorman handed her the envelope. 'From Mr Farrell, Miss Casanova. Came wiv these,' he said, producing with a flourish a vast bunch of roses and carnations.

The note simply said: 'A thousand pardons, my darling. I want to be with you but something urgent came up. Will be thinking about you every moment – not that you need my good wishes, of course! For ever yours, Ulick.'

Lottie liked to feel there were other things he had to do apart from lavishing attention on her – as long as they didn't drag him away too often. Now, assuming an irresistible journalistic assignment had come up without warning, she put aside the note, gave Maud the flowers to arrange, and placidly prepared herself for her act. Maud seemed to be behaving somewhat violently towards the poor carnations and roses, but Lottie put that down to a fit of temperament and did not try to draw her on the matter.

If anything, her barbaric dance went better than ever that evening, and when she came offstage the legendary Charles Morton, eighty-year-old manager of the Palace, was there to engage her for a two-week appearance at a fee that made the Tivoli look stingy. That evening she went home to her solitary bed without a second thought for what might be keeping Ulick away. A lesser ego would have turned jealously to visions of Tina Minoli; Lottie was far too sure of her hold on Ulick to consider the possibility.

Saturday matinées were something of an event at the Tivoli. This was the fashionable time for journalists, agents and managers to come along and look at what London's trend-setting hall had on offer, for rich stage door johnnies to enjoy a stage appearance by their latest pieces of feminine fancy; a time to exchange gossip and do deals. Most of them lingered around the promenade after the performance, and the artistes often went out to mingle with them. Lottie, intent on savouring the triumph of her first real week at the top, changed into a flamboyant dress and went out to mingle. She was the target of every piece of show business gossip in London that week, and most of the press were clustered in the promenade bar at the Tivoli, so she was unsurprised to hear her name on a dozen tongues as she made her grand entrance.

Most of those tongues were stilled as she swept in, but one unfortunate and particularly loud-mouthed journalist was standing with his back to her and carried on oblivious: 'Yes, they say he barely got back in time. She'd done a real botched job slashing her wrists. Farrell must have been frantic . . . lucky for him Charing Cross hospital was just a stone's throw . . .' Someone nudged him and he turned, his face flushing as he saw Lottie staring at him. 'Oh, Gawd,' he muttered, looking as if he was going to disappear inside his whisky glass.

Lottie had heard enough of what he said to understand what had happened. Her interest in the rest of the crowd was killed instantly. She turned aside to join the man, grim-faced. 'Something tells me that conversation involved me, Victor,' she said. 'Come on, spit it out – you might as well be the one to tell me, since you seem to be determined to tell everyone else in this bloody bar.'

'N-nothing, Lottie – it was nothing, really . . . just a rumour.'

'Look, mate, I've been around long enough to know rumour from gossip and gossip from God's honest truth. Let's have the unvarnished version quick, or I promise you it'll be bloody difficult for you to get inside this hall or practically any other one after tonight.'

'All right; you'll hear soon enough, anyway. You and Farrell back together, aren't you, since he did up this brilliant new song you opened with at the Tiv?'

'What of it?'

'Well, I think you 'eard the gist of the rest. That little girl he's got, Tina something . . . it seems she decided he wasn't coming home again. She tried taking some sorta sleeping draught on Thursday night in the early hours when he hadn't been home since Monday but it just sent her to sleep for about twelve hours. So when she woke up she decided to make sure this time, and she took his razor to 'er wrists. She'd have managed it, too, if she hadn't still been a bit dopey from the sleeping draught. As it was, she only got the artery on one wrist and she still had enough in 'er to save her when Farrell found her. He's been down Charing Cross Hospital with her ever since yesterday afternoon. Looks like she'll live, too. Course, whether she'll want to, without him, is another matter . . . Here, hang on, Lottie, you did ask . . . how'd you like to give me your side of it, you know, exclusive, for Monday's paper? Lottie . . . ?'

Moments later, Lottie swirled into her dressing room. 'Maud, quick, my cape and muff – and tell the doorman to get me a cab. I'll explain later . . . oh, what's that?'

Maud's face looked curiously pinched, and Lottie realised she must know at least some of what had happened. Now she was holding out an envelope to Lottie. 'It was delivered to the stage door by hand, five minutes ago, marked most urgent, Miss Lottie. I was just coming to find you. P'raps you'd better sit down.'

To Lottie's eternal shame, her first reaction was one of vaulting relief. She thought Tina Minoli had died. Then she opened the envelope and the real world intruded.

My dearest Lottie

You will not like what I have to say, but you have a generous heart and I pray you will understand it. Tina almost died yesterday because of the terrible cruelty you and I inflicted on her this week. Please do not misunderstand me: I know you are not to blame. I took responsibility for her, and I shall continue to do so.

In a sense, you were as innocent as she and I wish that you, too, did not have to be hurt. But I fear anything else is impossible. Although I found her in time, she remained inconsolable when she realised she was not going to die. She had no wish to hold me against my will. I did the only possible honourable thing in the circumstances. We were married at her bedside today by special licence.

I do not expect you to understand, though I pray you will. You should know by now that you will always be the only woman for me. All others are a pale imitation. I shall keep you always in my heart, as I hope you will keep me. I also hope that some day we shall be able to see each other again, to work together again, without pain. At least, in some unforeseen tomorrow, friendship remains a possibility.

Yours as ever, at least in spirit,

Ulick

Lottie slumped in her chair and let the letter flutter to the ground. Her head felt as if it were about to burst. 'I can't go on tonight, Maud,' she said. 'You'll have to tell them I'm ill.'

'If you want to say that, you'd better get someone else to do your dirty work,' said Maud.

That straightened Lottie's back. Her eyes snapped open and the woeful expression disappeared. 'How dare you? I told you, I can't go on! Isn't that good enough for you?'

'No, it isn't – and if you thought about who'd trained me, as well as you, you'd soon see why not.'

'Don't you try throwing Nellie up in my face!'

'Why not? If you ever fail to go on because of what some man has done to you, you're no professional, that's what Nellie always said.'

'But I already –' Lottie faltered, as she realised that if she ever told Maud about her flight before her final performance in California, the dresser would never respect her again.

Maud's face softened, but only minimally. 'Let me tell you a little story, Lottie. Nellie met the big love of her life a year or so before you came to London. She'd been around a lot, knew just what she wanted, and she was sure this was it. She tried to be cool and pretend he was just another masher, but it wasn't like that at all, really. Then she discovered he'd been deceiving her and she told 'im to sling his hook. Took it so bad she never really got over it.

'He didn't make it any easier for her, either. Kept begging her to come back to him, hanging around the stage door, showering her with presents and flowers, writing love letters . . . She never budged an inch. And she never missed a performance, either. Her dresser told me once, she'd cry nearly every evening before she went on, but after she got it out of her system she'd slap on the paint and go on and perform as well as ever – better, often as not.

'Her affair had been going on for six months or more, Lottie. You've only been back with Farrell a few days, and you can hardly call your previous experience with him a miracle of love, can you? Now, for Gawd's sake pull yourself together, if you've any understanding of what being a pro really means.'

She glared at Lottie for some time, then added: 'There, I've had my say. Now do as you like, but don't ask me to go an' tell lies to the manager for you.'

Lottie said: 'How did you know it was all over?'

'Do me a favour! What else would it have been to shake you like that – a religious conversion? Anyway, I got sharp eyes and ears. It's all over the Tiv this afternoon.'

'Including the wedding?'

'The what? Bloody hell, I'll say this for the bugger, he moves fast!'

Lottie picked up the letter and handed it to Maud. 'See for yourself.'

Maud read it and said: 'Well, at least for once he's done the decent thing. Must say I didn't think he had it in him.'

'But, Maud, he's ruined my life!'

'Rubbish! Stop trying it on. You've had a smashing week, wallowing in love's young dream, and now it's all over. Apart from the suffering that poor girl has gone through, it's the best thing that could have happened. If it had gone on any longer it would have got just like last time, only quicker and worse.'

'I don't believe you!'

'Then you still don't know yourself very well, my girl. You gotta be domineering and pushy, otherwise you'd be hopeless at what you do, and nobody could ever call you that. Farrell could never fit in with a woman like that in a thousand years, and at heart he knows it. That's the real reason he's run back to his Tina – he feels a bloody sight safer than he does with you.'

'Then it's true . . . I am going to be on my own for good.'

'You are behaving like a wet week! I said Farrell could never fit in with a woman like you. I didn't say the rest of the male human race couldn't either.'

'But they'll all see me the same way.'

'Course they won't, you silly! You've just gotta wait for a man who's so sure of himself he wouldn't care if you walked around everywhere with an escort of three hundred smitten suitors behind you. They do exist, you know, and just because you've survived twenty-one years without finding one, it's hardly cause to think you're on the shelf forever. Just don't fall for another Ulick Farrell, that's all I ask. Now, d'you wanna go back to Chelsea for a couple of hours, or have a little rest here? I think here would be better, myself.'

For the first time since she had come offstage that afternoon, Lottie started laughing. 'Oh, Maud, don't ever leave me! Ten minutes after you did, I'd drift up into Cloud Cuckoo Land for good.'

'Phew, that's a relief,' said Maud. 'Dunno about never leaving you – I didn't think I'd have a chance to stay after what I've just said. Come on, now, there's a good girl. Let's get your frock off, then I'll loosen your stays and you can lie down on the chaise longue. Much more restful than gallivanting over Chelsea an' back. I'll go an' rustle up a cuppa tea for you while you take your face off.'

She began to bustle away. As she did, Lottie said: 'Thanks, Maud. That helped. I *do* love him, you know.'

Instantly, Maud was back beside her, embracing her. 'I know, lovey, I know. But for you he's like takin' poison. Just try an' hold on to that. In a year or so it coulda been you full of laudanum and bleeding from the wrists. You know that deep down.'

CHAPTER TWENTY-NINE

Larry Nash was right about 'Ta-ra-ra-boom-de-ay' ensuring Lottie's music hall immortality. He was wrong about it killing her. Throughout 1900, the song was on everyone's lips. The sheet music was a bestseller and there were even special arrangements for stringed, brass and woodwind instruments. When Ed Maskell and Karl Muttler received their first royalty payments in America, they wrote effusive letters of thanks. Ed's was particularly adoring, with frequent references to 'when you come back to California'.

By April, she had so many multiple bookings around the central London halls that she asked Marc Cambon to choreograph a shorter, less strenuous version, and she performed it up to four times a night at the height of its popularity. It reached its zenith at Christmas, when the long version was written into the pantomime at the Grand Theatre, Islington, where Lottie was to play a cameo role in *Cinderella*. It was such a success that within a week the Tivoli had re-engaged her to perform it in the top-of-the-bill spot. The ultimate accolade arrived with a booking from the Gaiety, reviving their glamorised version of the traditional fairy tale, 'Cinder Ellen Up Too Late', to run concurrently with the other two. That was when she decided she had no more peaks to scale in English music hall.

Larry Nash lost his temper with her when she told him she planned to dance the original, longer, version at all three theatres. 'You won't survive the season, Lottie! For God's sake have more sense. I'd find it unreasonable if you intended doing two long versions and one shorter in a single evening, but three? That routine runs for ten minutes!'

'Oh, stop exaggerating, Larry. That includes a longish intro from the orchestra, and I'm standing around singing the verse for a couple of minutes. It's closer to five than ten.'

'Even if I accept that timing, which is doubtful, it's still too long, particularly with mad dashes across London in jolting cabs from hall to hall.'

'Across London? Do me a favour! The Tiv is all of two hundred yards from the Gaiety. On an energetic night I could probably run it quicker than a cab, and still have breath to go on.'

'Islington's a lot further, though, isn't it? I notice you don't mention that.'

'Once and for all, Larry, I'm doing it. Tell you what – I'll only guarantee the Tiv week by week, then if it proves too much, that one can go.'

He closed his eyes and turned away. 'You try and reason with her, Maud. I'm burned out.'

Maud made a face at Lottie behind Nash's back and said: 'Don't you think it's time you gave up trying to stop 'er doing what she wants to, Mr Nash? You know she always goes ahead anyway. You're just making grief for yourself.'

He sighed. 'You're as bad as her on the quiet, aren't you Maud? All right, Lottie. But don't blame me if you come out the other side with your health wrecked.'

'My health has stood up to more than three goes a night at "Ta-ra-ra-boom-de-ay", so don't lose any sleep over that.'

Lottie was right – just. When the pantomime season ended in February, she was exhausted and weighed nearly twenty pounds less than when it had started, in spite of eating twice as much as usual while the three runs were on. After her final, triumphant appearance to a full house at the Gaiety, she yielded to Maud's pleas and agreed to a short holiday. Two weeks of solitude in a Cornish fishing village restored much of the lost weight and brought her storming back to London half mad for excitement and bright lights. For the remainder of the spring and early summer, she performed her prodigy song only in its shortened version.

By now, she had tired of it anyway, and wanted to relegate it to an occasional piece in her repertoire before the audiences grew sick of it too. It had long ago achieved the status of the tune errand boys whistled until it drove the customers mad. Lottie had no intention of killing her popularity with an overdose of 'Ta-ra-ra-boom-de-ay'.

After the devastating blow of her final rupture from Ulick Farrell, she turned her attention away from men for a while. When she started taking an interest once more, it was with a completely different attitude. Now she used them much as a drinker uses alcohol, extracting the essential excitement from them and throwing them aside as the drinker might discard an empty gin bottle. Maud lost count of the different faces she saw waiting for Lottie backstage after performances. There were always expensive presents and extravagant little suppers. None of the men lasted more than a couple of weeks, and none remotely resembled a starving poet or artist. Lottie had decided that lust and wealth might lead to fewer tears than love and poverty.

At first she approached her new life with the vigour she applied to her stage act. She took most of her admirers as lovers, and occasionally wondered how soon she was likely to become pregnant, without giving any real thought to how she would react. But it never happened. Still short of her mid-twenties, she had not yet come to dread the prospect of a childless life. At present it was more a convenience than anything else.

Gradually, though, the sameness of her life began to pall. Whether it was true or not, Lottie always thought her greatest wish was to be loved, and whatever these admirers felt for her, love seldom had much to do with it. Her initial relief that deep emotion did not complicate matters turned slowly to disillusion with men in general, and as it did, her act began to reflect her cynicism.

Lottie had an unparalleled choice of good songs nowadays. Every successful writer in the West End wanted the Casanova seal of approval on his work, and she saw the best they had to offer. She always went unerringly for two types of material: the mocking, I've-been-around-since-Lilith-so-watch-your-step theme; and the variation of the wide-eyed young girl who turns into a brawling seductress at the drop of a wrap. Scatterbrained housewife types who talked almost exclusively in supposedly inadvertent *doubles entendres* were an occasional variation on the two-character theme.

It was an age when theatrical entrepreneurs like Oswald Stoll were building theatres for family audiences and presenting sanitised bills of polite
entertainment. Meanwhile, Lottie, dressed in a parody of everyday housewife's clothing, was asking a delighted and disreputable audience: 'Have You
Seen My Little Willie?' Even her rendering of 'She Was Poor But She Was
Honest' was reckoned too steamy to have passed muster with provincial
watch committees should she ever take her act outside London. As she had no
intention of ever doing so, this was nothing more than good publicity, but it
reflected a widespread reaction to her sort of act.

One of the reasons she continued to get away with it was her brilliant
dancing. It was often the dance routines which conveyed the salacity of the
numbers, rather than the songs themselves. She had Marc Cambon to thank
for most of this, and now Cambon was working for her almost exclusively.
He taught her a sly, suggestive slinking walk, which she generally used to
slide forward to the footlights at the beginning of her act, and which soon
became universally notorious as the Casanova Glide. Such was its power to
impress that East End mothers soon used the term as a furious criticism of
their fast daughters, while the daughters felt secretly complimented that their
attempts at imitation were at least recognisable.

Larry Nash kept a steady stream of bookings coming Lottie's way and most of
the time refrained from interference with her act. Nevertheless, early in 1902
he attempted to make her alter course.

'No one knows better than me how well you handle naughty numbers,' he
said, 'but there's a new feeling in the air and I don't think it will be tolerated
much longer.'

Lottie was sceptical. 'They were saying that in New York nearly three
years ago. I can't see evidence that it's happened.'

'No, because you've been back here more than two years and you know as
well as I do that we only get America's headline news in this country. That
sort of thing takes place in the small print. I'm talking about London, Lottie.
Good God – Marie Lloyd's been called to the Lord Chamberlain's office
three times and she's Miss Purity compared with you. Do you realise that
Stoll has notices backstage saying that artistes who swear will be dismissed?

'No – for a simple reason. I never play Stoll theatres.'

'In case you failed to notice, in future *all* theatres will probably be owned
by Stoll and his ilk.'

'Nonsense. The gallery would never stand for it.'

'Put together total takings for the gallery in a Stoll theatre and they don't
add up to six rows of stalls or dress circle. That's Stoll's market.'

For the first time, Lottie received a dim inkling that he might be right. She
stared at him, perplexed.

'I don't know how to do anything else, Larry.'

'Now you're the one who's talking nonsense! I never saw you doing that
Street Urchin Dance you started off with, but it was obviously something
special, and quite different from what you do now.'

'But that was years ago, before . . .' she had been going to say before life
touched me, but thought better of it '. . . before I grew up.'

'Of course. I wasn't suggesting a bogus little girl act. But remember when you unburdened yourself about not wanting to be limited by Ulick's vision of you? It seems to me that these days you limit yourself. Basically you only ever play three roles – knowing good-time girl, erotic child-nymph and lower class imbecile. There must be more faces.'

'You bastard – I'm never that crude.'

'Oh, come on, Lottie. I'm your most enthusiastic follower. I'm summing up the types you play, not offering a critical analysis.'

'Well, all right then. But you get close to being offensive at times. I don't know . . . can't think of anything else that appeals to me at present.'

'Have you ever thought about the fact that there's a war on?'

'It's hard not to, on the halls, innit?'

'Oh dear. That remark tells me you're not going to like what comes next.'

'That hasn't stopped you so far.'

Nash took a deep breath. 'Nothing goes over better with the gallery than a good patriotic war song.'

'I think I'm gonna faint.'

'Am I to take it that you don't fully agree with me?'

'Larry, I read the papers every morning. Even with the imperialist horse-shit they spread about, it's fairly obvious that our glorious empire is devoting its entire might to crushing a bunch of Dutch immigrant farmers. Worse still, the farmers are giving us a run for our money.'

'The gallery doesn't see it like that.'

'No. Nor does His Majesty's Government, more's the pity! That doesn't mean I have to agree.'

'Lottie . . .'

She adopted a reverential pose: 'I have the body of a weak and feeble woman . . .' her tone changed '. . . and, thank God, the mind of a realist. I'd rather stick to sex on stage, thanks. It's cleaner.'

'Couldn't you see your way to a little patriotic—'

' "Jolly Good Luck To The Girl Who Loves A Sailor"? Up your kilt, Larry love. I'm too honest.'

'You've never talked politics with me.'

'You and all the rest of the male half of humanity. Guess why? One: I'm female. I may earn more than you, but my sex means I'm silly, emotional and illogical. Two: I apply that silly little mind to world issues, and you know what? Straight off, I decide I have no wish for the vote if it only gives me the right to elect the sort of men that want to govern me.'

She watched him, smiling at his bemused expression. 'Look, Larry, I'm prepared to leave politics and patriotism and things to clever chaps like you and Mr Balfour who know how the world turns. But so long as I'm willing to do that, please try not to make a fool of me with patriotic tunes for the gallery, okay? Like I said, sex is cleaner, any day.'

He never discussed either the South African War or politics with her again. The night they announced the signing of a peace treaty in South Africa, and every theatre in London was en fête, he noted that the Tivoli management was forced to say that Miss Casanova could not join in the celebrations due to a temporary indisposition.

Larry's drive to make her a patriot and the encroachments of the Oswald Stoll brand of theatrical decency combined to foster a growing dissatisfaction in Lottie. She knew her act needed to change and develop, but inborn obstinacy stopped her from voluntarily taking a new path. Where there was opposition, it was worth sticking to the old ways.

She went on coasting on the surface of popular adulation until the middle of 1903. By now she had gone through a full year, including a pantomime season, without using 'Ta-ra-ra-boom-de-ay' as anything more than an infrequent filler. But stubbornness still prevented her from making radical changes to her act, and she was beginning to taste its staleness. Some day soon, so would the audience.

One summer morning she swept into Larry Nash's York Road offices. 'Larry, I have an idea. How about Australia?'

He gazed at her owlishly, his mind still on the problems of the touring company manager in the inner office who was auditioning chorus and bit players for an autumn production.

'Australia? I've been there myself, remember? Gold miners, ex-convicts and kangaroos. Not for you, Lottie.'

'Rubbish. I am being browbeaten by a golden-skinned giant with a fortune in sapphires to share his life in some place called – let me see, yes, that's it – Wagga Wagga.'

'You cannot mean that.'

'What, share 'is life? He does, but 'course I don't, you bloody fool. But d'you realise? He'd never *heard* of "Ta-ra-ra-boom-de-ay" until he saw me at the Old Mo' the other night!'

'No, Lottie, please. It's a very long way off . . .'

'Precisely! No Oswald bloody Stoll. No emaciated chorus girls all shaking their skinny little legs in strict mechanical time. Just big brawny lasses with an appetite for men, kicking up their legs and enjoying themselves.'

'And you're prepared to go there?'

Lottie struck a military attitude.

> 'We don't want to fight,
> But, by jingo, if we do,
> We've got the ships, we've got the men,
> We've got the money, too!'

'Larry – if the gallery wants that sorta shit, the sooner I go off to the Antipodes and leave 'em to it, the better.'

He took his time in studying her perfect caricature of a military posture, then said: 'Would it make any difference if I told you I loved you?'

Her face softened, but with pity, not with shared passion. 'Oh, Larry! Not you an' all?'

He nodded. 'How else could I have endured your absurd conceit for the past few years?'

'B-but you always told Ulick . . .'

The cutting edge of his laugh was sharp enough to cause physical pain. 'Oh, yes, I always told *Ulick*. I wonder what my motives were?'

Lottie went on staring at him. 'Oh, Larry, poor Larry.'

'My own fault. Self-righteousness was never very attractive.'

'You're not self-righteous.'

271

'Not attractive, either, it seems.'

'But you always moved away.'

Another bitter laugh. 'Lottie, I was the one who told other men you were the flame and they were the moths. After that I could hardly throw off my chrysalis and join them, could I?'

She had moved closer. Her scent rose from the warm flesh and engulfed his reason. 'Why not, Larry?'

'Because . . . because . . .'

'Because it should mean something more than the thrill the gallery gets? Rubbish! It's all the same in the end.' She drew long, cool fingers down his burning cheek. 'I'm sure your partner could finish up with the touring company auditions. Why don't you an' me go home and discuss the problems of Empire for a while? Maud said something about spending the rest of the day down Bermondsey . . .'

He was a tender, satisfying lover, and Lottie dallied with him happily for the remainder of the summer, but only after firmly instructing him to start setting up introductions for her in Australia. She sailed from Liverpool on Christmas Day. This time she had a companion – Maud Lewis.

PART THREE

Entr' Acte

CHAPTER THIRTY

It was two years before Lottie finally tired of Australia. At first she loved it. There seemed no danger here of the voices of decorum tidying up the glorious brawling vulgarity of music hall. With two or three appearances, Lottie shot to the top and from then on she always played to packed houses of cheering, ribald men and women. Backstage, she sat in the wings and watched delightedly as acts appeared, the like of which had ceased to exist in England ten years before. Many of them would have graced establishments like Dan May's River Palace.

Through it all a part of her could see there must be entertainment like this as long as there were people who spent their days in rough, harsh conditions without losing their sense of humour or their ability to endure. Music hall was a distorting mirror which reassured them, showed them the funny side of their life; assured them there was glamour in it; persuaded them with mawkish sentimentality that in the end everything would be all right. Maybe much of the reassurance was untrue, but it gave the audiences pleasure and relief every bit as intense as that a London highbrow might achieve from Mozart or Shakespeare.

In the end it was not the nature of the halls which persuaded Lottie to move on. It was the vast emptiness of Australia. Wherever she went, she always felt part of a tiny colony clinging by its fingertips to an uncharted wilderness. She was not drawn to wildernesses. She liked people, organised entertainment and an endless choice of diversions. This new country did not offer her enough of them. In 1905, towards the end of the Australian winter, she sailed for America.

They were halfway to San Francisco, and Maud was dressing Lottie for dinner aboard ship one evening, when she said: 'You still haven't said why you want to go to California again. The way you've always talked about it, I thought it was the last place you'd be seen dead in!'

'You're quite right, Maud, but I feel differently about New York. I want to go there for a while before we go home, and the best way is through San Francisco. Believe me, I have no intention of seeing *anyone* there I once knew!'

She kept her word, too, with one exception. She had written ahead to tell Ed Maskell she was coming, and he met them at the dock. The encounter came as a shock to Lottie. Ed had probably been the first respectable young man who fell sufficiently in love with her to want to marry her and take her into his own circle. Although she had refused, his subsequent attentions, his letters expressing yearning passion for her, had continued to flatter her.

Since her light-hearted departure from Lyonesse, Lottie had been through a hard school, and she had learned a lot, but she was still capable of shattering naivety. Now, staring at her former suitor as he stood on the pier to welcome her, accompanied by wife and child, was such a moment.

'What the hell's he playing at?' she muttered furiously to Maud as they stood together at the taffrail. 'You are looking at a man who swore eternal devotion to me not six years ago. Does he look like that to you now?'

Maud seemed more interested in Lottie than in the family tableau on the dock. After giving her employer a long, cool look, she said: 'Yeah, as a matter of fact, that's *just* what he looks like.'

Lottie whipped round and glared at her. 'Explain yourself.'

Maud sighed heavily. 'How old are you now, twenty-five, goin' on twenty-six? S'pose I might have expected it. Our Nellie was just about dead at that age, and she was still about as daft as you. Other people change, Lottie. I dunno why, but it's somefink a star never seems to realise. You go on developing new routines, seeing different places, taking new lovers. The people who say they'll love you forever mean it, and they keep to it. But they have ordinary lives to live, with a lot of dull bits in among the excitement that you get every day. They go on loving you, of course they do, but they've gotta go on living an' all.

'So they get married and have children. Unless they went into monasteries, they'd have to get married and have kids in the end, wouldn't they? One thing's as sure as death – they're never gonna wake up married to the likes of you.'

Lottie sniffed. 'Some love!'

'Yeah, some love . . . look at 'is wife, Lottie. Tall, broad shoulders, black hair, good posture . . . Could be you, in a bad light, couldn't it? Remember Tina Minoli? She was your double even in limelight, an' look who wound up married to her.'

'How many times do I have to tell you I don't want to discuss Ulick?'

'Forget bloody Ulick, he don't matter. It's you that matters, and at your age I think it's about time you started sorting out what you really want. There ain't much joy in being an old, retired, music hall star, livin' on memories and too crippled wiv rheumatism to get her kicks from an audience any more.'

Lottie's expression was stricken. 'Is that what you see ahead for me, Maudie?'

'It will be if you're not careful, dear.'

'But I don't understand . . . when I say I love a man, I mean exactly that. I want him with me all the time. Nothing else matters . . . why is it different for them?'

Maud laughed. 'It ain't. You're just not honest wiv yourself, that's all.'

'But I am!'

'Oh, for some things, you're the most honest woman I know. You stand up for what you believe in and make a damned good argument for it. But then you get to men and the blinds come down. If you're ever gonna be happy, Lottie, you gotta learn – really learn, mind – that nobody ever gets it all. Your trouble is you still think you can.'

Her meeting with Ed backed up everything that Maud had told her. He introduced her to his wife with breathless enthusiasm, picked the baby out of his bassinet and proudly showed him off to Lottie, then led her and Maud off to an enormous motor car which he had left just beyond the pier entrance.

Everything in his attitude shouted his pride that this was the famous star he had once been in love with, the woman he had helped launch to immortality with a song-writing exercise and a promotional newspaper article. He was out to impress his wife, and he succeeded. But she was the woman to whom he would go home that night, and every night. Lottie realised with a pang that she had become no more than a beautiful dream.

Lottie and Maud were booked in at the Palace. When they got there, Ed's wife, Margaret, said: 'I'll take the car, Ed. You be as long as you want. See you later.' She gave Lottie a smile of pure friendship. 'It was wonderful meeting you, Miss Casanova. Mind you look after Ed. Goodbye.' And she drove off, young, happy, competent, secure in the permanence of her relationship with a man Lottie had thought hers forever.

Ed had a few drinks in the bar while Lottie bathed and changed for their dinner engagement. 'You will join us, won't you, Maud?' she said as the older woman helped her into her evening gown.

'Gawd, no, Miss Lottie. I know we're friends, more than anything else. You don't have to take me along as chaperone to prove the point. I'll eat up here – it's roomy enough for me to entertain me whole family if I had 'em here. I'd be happier if you just took a bit of advice from me, though.'

'What would that be?'

'This chap's clever wiv words, ain't he? Gives a little extra thought, p'raps, to why he does things?'

'I think so, yes.'

'Well, I think you should have a serious talk with him about you.' She twinkled with a splinter of friendly malice: 'Heaven knows it's your favourite subject! Have a little word wiv him about what I've been saying to you. See what he thinks about staying in love forever wiv a woman as far away as you usually are.'

'Why would you want me to torment myself like that?'

'I don't, you silly goose. I want you to see – really see – what your life will always be if you decide you want to stay a stage star forever, more than anything else. There's no reason why you shouldn't, but I hate the thought of you doing it if you don't really understand what you'll be giving up.'

She eyed Lottie's stricken face and said: 'You don't have to talk about it *all* evening, you know. You're allowed a little bit of fun an' all!'

Lottie hugged her, straightened her gown, and went off to join Ed Maskell for dinner.

Ed continued to show signs of being the happiest man Lottie had ever met. When she pressed him about it, instead of turning sheepish, he heaped praise on Margaret, extolling her virtues as wife, mother and, discreetly, lover.

Lottie felt deeply envious, so her tone carried considerable asperity when she said: 'Remarkable! And all so soon after you said there could never be anyone but me!'

To her consternation, he burst out laughing. 'Of course, and I meant it – still do. You're the most sensational female I've ever seen. I could never forget you.'

'Well?'

'Well what?' Then her meaning began to dawn on him. 'Oh, my dear! I knew I never had a chance with you! Maybe the first couple of times I saw you in Sioux City . . . but in the nicest possible way, you made it plain from the start that you weren't interested, and that was that. But you'll turn my knees to water as long as I have knees to turn!'

A hundred warring emotions pounced on Lottie and she was at a loss to identify any one of them. She only knew she felt wretched. Eventually she managed to say: 'D-do you think every man who falls for me as you did . . . that is, that he feels the same way?'

Still blissfully ignorant of the chaos he was causing, Maskell said: 'Of course. You're such an exceptional woman, how many men would ever seriously hope to start something beyond a flirtation with you? Naturally, I'm talking about the stage Lottie Casanova, not the private one. Once you're back in your private world, I can see you get tied up with men the same as any other girl, and I expect when you decide to marry, it'll be someone you know from that part of your life.'

'But, Ed, there is no "that part" of my life.'

'Now it's my turn not to understand.'

'Because everything I do, I do as a star. I don't think I exist at all otherwise.'

'But that's ridiculous. You're the most beautiful woman I ever saw.'

'And when did you ever see me with a man?'

'Most of the time you were in San Francisco, that's when! I refuse to believe you've forgotten Grant Johnstone.'

'Of course not – but that ended in misery.'

'So what? Name me one human being, except the rich types whose parents arrange it all, who hasn't been through a couple of broken romances. That doesn't mean nothing will ever work for them. My God, if it did, the whole human race would have given up before now.'

Lottie was gaping at him. Finally she managed to say: 'But all the time, I thought you wanted to marry me.'

'I did, but I knew I never would, and I knew I was too young then. So when you left, I went through exquisite misery, and about a year later, I met the girl of my dreams – Margaret.'

Longing to break down into uncontrollable sobs, Lottie nevertheless managed to appear calm. 'I'm so pleased things worked out for you, Ed,' she said, the false smile stretching across her cheekbones. 'Now, let's hear the rest of the news. What's been happening to everyone?'

Maskell chattered on happily about his own doings, about Karl Muttler, who had used his earnings from Lottie's big song as the deposit on a winery, and had gone back to the land like his Austrian forebears; of Grant Johnstone, who had eventually married an East Coast heiress and now lived in genteel misery on Nob Hill; and of the vaudeville business in general. To Lottie, now, it seemed like someone else's world.

Eventually, quite late, she said: 'Really, dear man, I mustn't keep you from your family any longer. You get a cab and slip off home. I'm going to bed.'

'We must get together again. I know Margaret would just love to know you better. How about tomorrow?'

'Oh, you mean I hadn't mentioned it?' She was acting superbly, as she had thought of the plan only seconds before. 'This is only an overnight stop for us. We're off to New York tomorrow, on the Coronado. Alas, poor us, I fear it's the last we shall see of each other for some time.'

At Reception on the way to her suite, she remembered to tell the clerk she and Maud would be checking out next day, and to ask him to make train reservations for them the moment the Union Pacific office opened in the morning. Then she went upstairs and cried herself to sleep.

She had written to Larry Nash before she left Australia, asking him to contact her poste restante in New York. A letter awaited her, proposing various engagements in America, including the starring role in an All-British touring company which was being assembled to do a one-year tour across the continent and back. Lottie read it and wondered why the adrenalin did not start to race at the very thought of it. Instead, her emotions remained stubbornly dormant.

She felt much brighter when she got back from a walk down Broadway to discover that her old friend Antony Wilde had left a message. If she was free, he wanted to take her to dinner and the theatre that night. She tried to telephone him with her acceptance, but he was not at home. Never mind; she would see him at seven. Perhaps he would have changed less than everything else.

Another shock remained before she met Wilde. Still restless and with hours to kill before she prepared for the evening, she went to find Maud. 'Come on,' she said, 'I'll show you where I made my American debut.'

Only a year after returning to England, she had read with sadness of Adam Bial's death, and that his son had taken over the theatre. She had heard no more news of Koster and Bial's. When she alighted from the cab at the corner of 34th and Broadway, momentarily she thought they had been dropped at the wrong place. Then, with mounting horror, she realised what had happened. There remained no trace of the music hall. In its place reared a vast department store, which looked as if it had always occupied the site. A sign on its façade announced that it was called Macy's.

'Enough!' said Lottie. 'The whole damned world is falling down around my ears. Maudie, I'm going back to the hotel, then I shall have several large drinks to soothe my nerves. After that, I may get ready for Tony Wilde, or I may have several *more* large drinks. Now, let's get away from this hell-hole.' And she marched off northwards.

Maud followed, looking over her shoulder with considerable regret. 'I wouldn't 'ave minded looking around inside that shop,' she said plaintively.

In the end, Lottie remembered her manners and stayed sober. She decided that if her admirers were scattering like dead leaves in autumn, she had better make a special effort to retain Wilde's homage. As she recalled, he had always been fairly detached in his admiration in any case.

She chose one of her favourite gowns, a sleek piece of heavy silk jersey completely covered in jet beads and black, midnight blue and bottle green sequins. It fitted her like a glove and appeared to move like perfectly co-ordinated muscles when she changed position and the light reflected off the beadwork. In the current fashion for evening dress, it left her shoulders bare, then followed the lines of her magnificent body to mid-thigh level before flaring into wide gores that swept to the ground. With it, she wore her favourite ultra-long black kid gloves, and a cluster of blue-black feathers fastened with a sapphire ornament in her hair.

279

She looked like some fabulous mermaid, and in this outfit displayed none of the cheery vulgarity of the music hall. She could have been a duchess's wayward daughter, the wife of a millionaire, or a great courtesan, but no one would ever have identified her as a singer of ribald popular songs.

It would have been impossible to put on the gown, let alone fasten it, without help, and as Maud hooked her into it she positively skipped around Lottie, purring with pleasure at its effect. 'I hope this geezer appreciates a beautiful woman,' she said when they had finished their joint preparations. 'I've never seen you look better, Miss Lottie. You should be going out with an emperor in that lot, not just another ordinary man.'

'Oh, I'd hardly call Tony Wilde just another man. He's attractive, cultivated . . . comes from a good family, too. I think. And he looks marvellous in evening clothes, if I recall correctly, so I don't think he'll let us down, Maud.'

Lottie was pleasantly surprised when Antony Wilde called for her at seven o'clock. He had improved during the years since she had seen him – and he had been elegant enough before. Now, although still in his early thirties, he had intriguing flecks of pure silver in his dark hair, and a summer spent sailing off the New England coast had tanned his skin a vigorous deep gold. His tall figure showed off the faultless evening clothes and cape to perfection. As Maud watched them depart along the hotel corridor together, she fought an impulse to repeat the satisfied purring she had indulged in earlier.

'I've been talking non-stop about myself. What have you been doing for such a long time?' Lottie had given him a run-down on her Australian tour and swift passage through San Francisco. Now she was itching to know what had been happening in New York.

'Well, for a start, I no longer seem to be connected with the theatre except as a member of the audience.'

'I don't believe that, Tony! You told me a long time ago in Chinatown that it was one of the few pursuits that never bored you.'

'Ah yes, but times change.'

'You're telling me they do! I nearly passed out when I saw that damned great store today where Koster and Bial's used to be.'

Wilde nodded sadly. 'In a way, it was Adam's death that made me start easing back. The business was getting chock-full of puritans. I hardly recognised it any more, even as early as 1901.'

'Oh, no! I've been trying to tell my agent back in London that it couldn't happen in New York and won't happen in London.'

'Well, I fear it has, and it will. I was planning to take you to a vaudeville show tonight, as it happens.'

Her eyes sparkled. 'Splendid! I'll never forget that first Saturday night show Adam took me to at K&B's. I saw some acts that night I've never seen bettered anywhere.'

But Wilde still looked glum. 'I'm afraid this will be a disappointment to you. I wanted to take you more as an awful warning than anything.'

'Oh, dear, that sounds more like school than entertainment.'

'Perhaps it is. I was unsure whether you planned to take on any engagements while you're in New York.'

'Wish I knew myself, Tony. To tell the truth, I'm thoroughly confused. Everything seems to be running haywire at present.'

'Hmm, you're one of the old-style troupers, that's why. In a way, it's a pity you weren't born twenty years earlier. I have a feeling the new vaudeville – or should I say variety – isn't for you.' He considered the prospect in silence for a moment, then shrugged. 'Still, from what I remember of your talent once you had an audience to play to, if your heart's in it, you can adapt your material to suit anything.'

'I wouldn't bank on it, Tony. I loathe gentility more than almost anything else, and that's really what they're asking for, isn't it?'

'Afraid so, my dear. Never mind, let's go and take a look. The show is at Proctor's 23rd Street Theatre, and guess who's playing?' She shrugged. 'The celebrated Miss Lillian Russell.'

'Dear God!' said Lottie. 'She must be nearly a hundred.'

'Now, dear, let's not exaggerate. Shall we say ninety-five? Actually, she's still middle-aged, it's just that she's been around so long it feels like aeons. Sounds like it, too, I'm afraid. Whatever voice she had left her years ago, except in some very limited registers. I think we had better regard tonight's performance as an academic exercise rather than entertainment, don't you? Oh – one thing that might interest you, though, if you do care to consider cleaning up your act. They are paying La Russell $3,000 a week.'

'Christ, I'd sing hymns for that!'

'Thought it might excite your interest. Come on, let's go.'

When they left the theatre more than two hours later, Lottie was gibbering with indignation. 'How *dare* they do that to vaudeville?' she stormed, as they stepped on to the pavement. 'I wouldn't work in rubbish like that for a hundred thousand, let alone three.'

'My sentiments entirely,' said Wilde. 'As you can imagine, I very seldom go even to watch, now, and I certainly don't participate. I went on dabbling for a while, writing songs for musical comedy, but my heart wasn't in it . . . in the end I actually began to find the family business less dull.'

Lottie stopped and burst out laughing. 'Oh, lord, Tony, how terrible when a black sheep returns to the fold out of sheer boredom!'

He was smiling too, now. 'I know. Pathetic, isn't it? New York doesn't seem to be such fun any more. Although I will say it improved considerably when I knew you were back.'

She made a little bow. 'Lovely seeing you too, dear boy. Now let's go somewhere for a little more food and drink to wash away the bad taste of all that garbage, shall we?'

At a corner table in Delmonico's, with a lavish supply of champagne, Wilde said: 'Now I'm going to insist you keep a promise you made me a long time ago – you may even have forgotten it, but I shall hold you to it none the less.'

'I never make promises.'

'Well, you made me one, and this is pay day. When I told you that I didn't believe you were what you seemed, you promised that next time you came to New York, you would tell me the truth – the whole truth, remember – and as far as I know, this is your first return trip.'

'So I did.' Lottie sat back in her chair, a faraway expression on her face. After a while, she said: 'Very well, you shall have it. I hardly think you'll ever tell anyone else without my permission, but if you do I'll probably kill you.' And she told him the story of her life, from her childhood at Lyonesse to her rescue from Camden by Joe, Larry and Ulick, without omission or embroidery. Eventually she drained her glass, smiled at him and said: 'The rest you know. I think that earns me another bottle of fizz.'

'It most certainly does! Lottie, I think you could do worse than turn your hand to writing. An autobiography would earn you enough never to have to work again.'

She laughed. 'My talents are all face to face. Give me pen and paper and I turn into a bore. You may have a point, though. The way the business is going, I shall have to find something else. I'll be forgotten in five years if what we saw tonight is the new generation's vaudeville. Hell, imagine being a has-been before you're thirty!'

'There are worse fates, as long as you aren't starving. Anyway, enough of that. What you just told me is the most fascinating story I ever heard. Did your parents never come looking for you?'

'Oh, they could never have endured the disgrace of finding me. Long after it had happened, Ulick told me Papa had sent one of the cousins to make tactful enquiries. But when Ulick heard what they planned to do with me if I went back, he sent the chap away with a dreadful yarn about me running off with a salesman, and that put a stop to any further prying.'

'What *did* they plan to do with you?'

'Pack me off to the outer reaches of Scotland with my father's dreadful unmarried sister. I suppose after a while they'd have told everyone I'd been suffering from brain fever and brought me home again. Ugh!'

'Do you ever feel any regret?'

'For Lyonesse? Never! Mind you, I've learned some sharp lessons about the value of money and things like that. At the beginning, I despised it all. Now, I just loathe the way my parents used it.'

'I confess, all that limp-wristed culture does sound pretty terrible. I spend my money on horses and boats and parties and travelling abroad.'

'Now that sounds more like it!' Abruptly she got a glimmer of what he might mean, and was silent. He made no move to continue the thread of conversation, and after a while changed the subject.

'I remember when you were here in the nineties, having to explain to poor old Adam that you caught fire when you had an audience to please. Did that ever change?'

'Oh, no, Tony. That never alters. I think it's the thing that frightens me when I consider being eased out of the business. I never get scared that I shall fail – only that I'll lose my audience.'

He laughed. 'There are others ways of drawing an audience and keeping it enslaved – and other audiences than vaudeville.'

'What, legit theatre, you mean? I thought of that, and I'm fairly sure I could do it. But there's always a sense in which the theatre audience is there for the play, not for the individual actor, however good. You only get that – that worship, in vaudeville. As long as you're on that stage, they're all yours.'

'I wasn't thinking of theatre. We'll talk about it some other time. Look, Lottie, it's getting late. I'll take you back to the hotel now. Why not enjoy a holiday in New York – not even think of work for a couple of weeks? From what you say, you earned a king's ransom in Australia and there was precious little to spend it on.'

'That's true enough. I certainly could relax for a while.'

'In that case, may I be your devoted companion and guide? I've had no fun since my summer vacation and I have very little planned for the near future. How about it?'

'What about your new, earnest, working self?'

'One of the chief pleasures of being a dilettante is that one can drop everything when one chooses, and no one can complain when one returns.' He smiled wickedly. 'Particularly when one owns the business!'

When he proposed to her, Lottie was ready; she was less prepared for what he offered.

They were together in the sitting room of her hotel suite, quite late, having been to the theatre. 'I might have known *Floradora* wouldn't be your thing,' he said. 'No steel under the sugar and spice.'

'Is that how you see me, Tony, sugar and spice over steel?'

'Hmm, more or less. But it's not simply the ingredients – it's the unbeatable quality.' He leaned across and kissed her, not sensually but lightly, as if bestowing an affectionate compliment.

'What's that?' she asked. 'An expression of brotherly love?'

He gave her a sphinx-like smile. 'I'm saving the rest . . . I have a feeling we have a lot of time ahead of us.'

'You obviously haven't seen the anguished pleas poor old Larry Nash is sending me. He's going demented; says the All-English touring company will go without me if I don't decide by Thursday, and furthermore, I'm leaving it too late for him to make serious arrangements for the panto season on my behalf if I decide against the tour.'

'To hell with the panto season, whatever that may be. And to hell with the All-English touring company. It sounds like a raree show!'

'Which is approximately what I told him myself, give or take a few ripe old English phrases. I still don't know what I want to do though.'

'Will you take a suggestion from me?'

'Maybe, as long as it doesn't involve doing a Lillian Russell.'

'Hardly. I would be greatly honoured if you were to consent to be Mrs Antony Wilde.'

The silence lengthened, and she stared at him, speechless now, although she had suspected something like this might happen soon. Somehow the reality still dropped like a bombshell.

Before she recovered her wits, he was speaking again. 'Don't rush into an answer. Just sit there and listen to me. I think I can offer you more fun than any audience which may still be waiting out there. Wouldn't you enjoy playing a great lady, and taking in the best part of East Coast society?'

'Have you been drinking more than I thought you were having?'

'No. I'm sober and I love you. I love you so much I've come up with a diversion that might keep you interested for half a lifetime . . . go back to being Charlotte Cazenove – well, anyway, Charlotte Cazenove Wilde – and let everyone from the Daughters of the American Revolution to the

Rockefellers spend the next twenty years trying to unravel your past!'

'Now I *know* you're drunk.'

'Only with passion, Lottie, I assure you. Ever since we met again, I've been trying to think of a way of making you stay with me – and a practical joke that lasts a whole marriage seems as good as any. Plus, of course, my undying love and considerable fortune.'

'You mean this, don't you?'

'I do.'

'Well, before we get in touch with the funny farm, perhaps you'd care to tell me about it.'

'Lottie, other girls from music hall have married New York fortunes before. And other society matrons have swooped like vultures to demolish the fake pedigrees the newcomers put together to hide their disreputable origins. But don't you see, you're unique? You started at the top and worked down. If they pry into your origins, they'll find Lottie Casanova all right, but under her they'll find Lady Charlotte Cazenove. It will drive them demented! Oh, I *am* going to enjoy this.'

'Don't be absurd. That's the stupidest reason I ever heard for anyone getting married.'

He was no longer smiling. 'Oh, Lottie, believe me, that's not my reason for getting married. You are the first woman I have met since I was a boy who didn't bore me to tears within the first week of our acquaintance. I have a feeling I could be with you a thousand years and still wake up each morning to learn something new about you. I'm sure you'll exasperate me, hurt me and enrage me at times, but you'll never disappoint me, and I don't think you'd know how to lie to me. The practical joke is a sweetener to try and make you more interested in the challenge, that's all. I just want to marry you.'

Lottie stood up and moved across to the side table where she had left her glass. When she picked it up her hand was shaking. 'I-I don't . . . it's not that I didn't expect you to propose. I did, in a way. I'm just surprised it's taking me like this.'

He stood up and came across to join her. 'Like what? Perhaps like: maybe it would be fun?' He reached out and took her glass, putting it down on the table and turning her to face him. 'I think it would be lots of fun.'

This time his kiss was sensual and passionate. There was nothing companionable in it, but very much else. His hands moved to her throat and slid outward across her shoulders, then down the length of her arms. He touched his fingertips to hers, then clasped one of her hands, lifted it to his mouth, and slowly, deliberately, ran his tongue over the palm. Lottie gave a little moan and moved closer, pressing her body against his. As his arms went round her, he smiled and said: 'Why, you naughty girl, you're not wearing a corset!'

She returned the grin. 'I haven't worn one all this week, Tony.'

He let out a great roar of laughter. 'You mean I've been leading up to my grand seduction and you've been sitting around tapping your fingers and wondering why I didn't pounce?'

'Something like that, yes.'

'Now you'll have to marry me. I'm not letting a woman as rare as you out of my sight ever again.'

284

She gave him a modest curtsey. 'I'll think about it. Now, can we please go to bed? I have other plans for this evening than discussing marriage proposals.'

She was alone when Maud arrived with coffee the next morning. The maid drew the heavy curtains and wheeled a trolley up beside the high bed to take the tray. Then she stood back and studied Lottie closely.

'Someone looks like the cat who swallowed the canary,' she said.

Lottie gave her a beaming smile and stretched luxuriously before sitting forward for Maud to plump up pillows behind her. 'Come on, Maud, bring your cup and have some coffee with me. I need a bit of advice.'

Maud did as she was told, poured her coffee and perched at the end of the bed. Then she said: 'In my experience, girls who look like you do this morning don't usually need advice. They want to announce something.'

'Well, this time you're wrong. I mean it.'

She told Maud about the proposal. 'It would mean giving up the stage, of course. What shall I do?'

'You didn't ask anybody that when that chap, wotsisname? – Johnstone? – proposed, did you? You turned 'im down because he wanted you to give it up. This one doesn't seem to have asked you any such thing and you're more than arf willing to do it. I'd say that's a fair pointer to the answer.'

But Lottie shook her head. 'No, it's not quite that. I don't know, Maud . . . Oddly enough, in a way it's the other way round. I never thought I'd say it, but the stage isn't the same any more. I'm not enjoying it the way I used to. I already felt like that when Tony proposed. Now I'm afraid I'm only considering marrying him as a way out of music hall.'

Maud gave a contemptuous snort. 'I'd like to see anyone get you to do something you didn't want in that line! If you're prepared even to consider it, he's the man for you.'

'It's no use, you just won't understand . . . and there's another thing. I love Tony. I think I could live happily enough with him. But what about him? He's going to marry Lottie Casanova, music hall star, and wake up next morning with Charlotte Cazenove Wilde, English lady. What if he finds he doesn't like the exchange?'

'Lottie my love, whatever you're callin' yourself, you'll always be the finest dish o' greens a man could hope to lay hands on. He's not gonna care if you ask him to address you as your royal highness once he's got hold of you!'

'There's one final thing. Then I promise I shall make up my mind. I love him, and he's a very attractive man. But if I were never to see him again, I'd survive. I wouldn't find life unthinkable without him.'

Now Maud's gaze was openly sceptical. 'My dear Lottie, if every young woman in this world waited until the man of her dreams came along, the human race would have died out centuries ago. Thank your lucky stars he's rich and handsome and you're fond of him, and grab him quick before some other girl does.'

She paused, seeking something to drive home her argument, then said: 'Listen, love. What do you want to be doing ten years from now? You think hard about it, and if the answer is that you want to be standing in the wings in some draughty theatre, waiting to go an' waggle your backside at a thousand tipsy men, send Wilde packing. But if you got anything else in mind, marry him.'

Maudie was right, as usual, Lottie reflected after the maid had left. She had never thought she would go stale on music hall – wouldn't have done if it had been allowed to remain as it had been when she clawed her way to stardom. But this new stuff? Stomp up and down singing 'hooray for England' sort of songs for Sir Oswald Stoll's genteel audiences, or, just as bad, dress up in half the silk and feathers of five continents to warble sentimental ballads off-key in an over-heated New York theatre? Better out to grass than any of that . . .

She cried a little after a while, but only a little. It had been coming for a long time. She had heard the first warning bells long before she sailed off to Australia. Well, that had given her a bit of a reprieve, and she'd had a good time there, too. But elsewhere, her day onstage was almost done. They were doing away with the gallery. Lottie Casanova could not exist without the gallery.

'No,' she said aloud, 'and she can't exist without any audience at all, either – and Tony's not a bad audience!'

The thought made her feel a lot better. Yes, she would marry Tony . . . Her mind started ranging at random back through the last decade. What an eventful time it had been! Just as well she hadn't really settled permanently with Ulick. That would have ended in tears, no doubt about it. Beyond question, Tony was the man for her.

There was another, though, wasn't there, Lottie? The small thought swam unbidden into her mind. Another, with a cheeky grin and an embrace that radiated affection and made you want to laugh all the time, and then go out and conquer the world . . . go out and conquer the world together, though. Not just Lottie Casanova alone. Lottie Casanova and Tommy Fanshaw. Tommy Fanshaw and Lottie Casanova . . .

Lottie screwed up her eyes to force back the storm of weeping which suddenly threatened to overwhelm her. 'Oh, get out of my head, Tommy! I lost you, dammit, and there's no going back – leave me in peace, can't you?' She flung herself back on the bed and abandoned herself to tears. No going back . . . but if only there were . . .

THE SPORTING TIMES
Saturday, December 12, 1905

QUEEN OF MUSIC HALL WEDS MILLIONAIRE

The cream of music hall society gathered at St Paul's Church, Covent Garden, on Friday, for the marriage of Lottie Casanova, undisputed queen of the saucy song, for her marriage to American tycoon Antony St John Wilde. Miss Casanova, who was orphaned in early childhood, was given away by her agent, Mr Larry Nash.

The bride wore an exquisite gown of white satin, perfectly plain, with a four-yard train and the high corsage sparingly trimmed with point lace. Her attendants, the sisters Elsie and Eugenie Lambert, respectively eminent solo dancers in the ballet and on the music hall stage, wore gowns of gold silk with bodices of embroidered mousseline de soie and veils of gold tulle fastened with white feather aigrettes.

After a reception at the Café Royal, Mr and Mrs Wilde left for their honeymoon cruising the Mediterranean and in Egypt. They will live in New York.

Late on Friday afternoon, the boat train pulled away from Victoria station, where the last revellers still strewed train and platform with rice and flowers. Lottie turned away from the window, flung herself down on the seat and fanned herself with a glove. 'Phew!' she said, 'Now the main act really begins!'

CHAPTER THIRTY-ONE

Tony Wilde was a gambler by instinct. Born into a rich, long-established family, educated at the best schools, slotted into the family business in a manner that made no heavier demands on his time than a gentleman might reasonably countenance, he had never known the reality of deprivation. Insecurity was merely a word in Webster's Dictionary. From a very early age, the lack of it bored him.

So he had set out to seek risk. At Harvard, he had acquired a reputation as a rackety type who was always just one jump ahead of serious trouble. Let loose in New York a few years later, he had avoided his own set to cultivate the friendship of the likes of Adam Bial, as well as a vivid cross section of the city's low life. He played poker with the sort of men who were in it for keeps, and early in his career he indulged in financial speculations which would have made his conventional father and grandfather shudder with horror. But it was all done to taste adventure, not to accumulate more money. To one of Wilde's background and inclination, money had little meaning save in terms of possessions and comfort. The thrill of risking it was all.

His desire to court danger had been a major element in falling in love with his wife. When he heard her story, he realised he had found the one human being who had put into full, terrifying practice the inclinations that he had merely toyed with. He had to have her. Even at the time, it had also occurred to him that her volatile temperament and the proposed jokey deception of his society acquaintances about her, might give further colour to his charmed existence.

Reality had proved somewhat different. His wife was, above all, an actress. When she married Tony, and returned from her honeymoon as Charlotte Wilde, Lottie Casanova effectively ceased to exist. In her place there was a ravishing, self-assured society woman, equipped by the training of twenty generations of English aristocrats to quell any assaults from the social luminaries of New York or East Hampton. Charlotte rode to hounds, attended charitable functions, went to the theatre and gave brilliant parties, all with the same verve she had devoted to her music hall career.

At first, Wilde found it amusingly novel. And anyway, he was in love with Charlotte and found her exotic beauty endlessly arousing. But eventually the excitement he had anticipated in this lifetime's joke against his peers faded. His wife was simply too good at playing her part.

It turned out not to matter too much, because Tony found the ultimate risk in an area he was only beginning to explore when he married Charlotte: business. Not the business of his grandfather and his father, though – the soft, slightly rotten underbelly of Wall Street finance was what pulled him like a magnet, because suddenly he had realised it was the biggest gambling game in town.

For Tony, a gamble had to have the whiff of Russian roulette about it or it was not really a gamble. Risk was what made him indulge – risk of losing all, not of gaining more, which was what drove other men. In 1907 he came close enough to taste the blood in his mouth.

For some time he had been associating with a group of buccaneering capitalists who filled most conservative bankers with dread. His main contact was a fast-moving son of Brooklyn called F. Augustus Heinze, who had gone to Montana and made millions cheating the mining companies, then returned in triumph to New York in search of further profit. Gus Heinze was big, handsome and glamorous. Wilde enjoyed being seen with him; he had the right raffish image. Some of Heinze's associates were less amusing, but they fascinated Tony almost as much because of the truly horrendous risks they ran with their own and other people's money. He watched in something approaching awe as Heinze and his main partner, a New Englander called Charles Morse, set up bank after bank on completely fictitious collateral, breaking every law of sound finance that Wilde had ever been taught.

Starting with cash loans raised in all sorts of suspicious ways, the men bought controlling shares in a single bank. They then used the shares as collateral to buy into another bank, and so on, until each had set up a chain of non-existent security to cover very real borrowings. At the height of his naivety, Wilde asked Gus Heinze: 'But why do you want all those banks?'

Heinze stared at him for a moment and roared with laughter. 'Tony, you of all people should know what they keep in banks: money. Other – people's – money. If you're gonna speculate, you have to speculate big, and that means millions.'

'You mean you risk the depositors' funds on the money markets?' To one of Tony's background, that was like telling a Catholic priest you had spat in the communion chalice.

Heinze nodded slowly, like one explaining a simple trick to a child. 'And then, when you make your killing, you put the money back in the safe and everyone goes home happy.'

It took Wilde's breath away. 'Do you realise the state of the markets? The Bank of England has stopped advancing funds to New York. World capital is tighter than it's ever been. And you're dipping in the till?'

'Couldn't be done in any other conditions. Hey, don't take it so seriously – you old banking families get to regard the money like it was your own.'

'That is precisely what we are taught.'

'Well, this is a different world. You should come on in. The water's fine!'

Nothing more was said at the time, but later, Wilde thought about it again. To operate on that sort of razor's edge . . . now that really beat any poker game he could think of. After a few days he telephoned Gus Heinze and told him he wanted to buy in.

Fortunately, he had barely dipped a toe into the water when disaster struck. He made some large investments in the Trust Company of America, a concern the Wilde Bank would normally not have touched, and agreed to serve on the company's board. Then the Heinze–Morse partnership attempted a coup. When share prices in United Copper started rising unexpectedly on Monday October 14, 1907, they decided they had cornered the market and called in share certificates for delivery by the following afternoon.

But they had not cornered the market. Brokers who had made short purchases on their behalf were able to cover themselves and buy from hitherto inactive shareholders, and Heinze and Morse found themselves selling everything they had to cover their losses. It would have ended there if they had not already been in banking to cover their speculation. Now their main bank, Mercantile National, went to the wall. The newspapers had a field day, with financial news replacing everything else on front pages for days on end.

Tony watched all this with bated breath, part of him wishing he was in there, balancing on the tightrope with them, the rest of him supremely thankful the debacle had come before he was in any deeper. But within a few days it began to look as if he might be.

Heinze, Morse and their associates were stripped of all their bank directorships as a condition of the New York Clearing House Committee's offering help. Once that had happened, the Clearing House announced it was ready to back any trust companies who needed aid. But the damage had been done. Small depositors everywhere began reading headlines which said several banks were participating in one way or another in a speculation which had involved hands dipping into the cash register. Individuals and corporations alike began preparing to draw their deposits out of trust companies on which the slightest suspicion fell.

The weekend came, and with it an apparent move towards sanity. The guarantee of the Clearing House finally seemed to be taking effect. But the Clearing House Committee was just getting started. They were already investigating the giant Knickerbocker Trust Company, which had lent a large sum to Charles Morse. That was enough for the big bankers. The Knickerbocker might be above board, but in the interests of clearing out the speculators, it would have to be sacrificed. After the close of banking hours on Monday, the Committee announced that the National Bank of Commerce, which until now had cleared Knickerbocker cheques, would no longer do so; and that they were demanding the resignation of the Knickerbocker's chairman, Charles T. Barney.

Tony was taking Charlotte out to dine with friends at Sherry's restaurant on Fifth Avenue that evening. He sat at the circular table, proudly surveying Charlotte's beauty, the grace of his friends, the luxury of the setting. And beneath it all, the extra, secret spice of a gambler's nerve holding up under pressure made it all even better. What if the whole thing sprang open? Old family bank or not, his fortune would be swept away with the rest . . . none of this would exist for him any more . . . It gave fuller savour to the filet mignon and added bouquet to the claret.

His reverie had blunted Tony's awareness of what was going on around him. Now he became conscious that people were whispering and glancing around curiously. Here and there, men he had known for years were buttonholing waiters and murmuring secretively at them. The women in the room appeared interested but mystified. Too many men looked openly apprehensive.

'What on earth is going on?' he asked Charlotte. 'I was miles away for a minute or two, and in the meantime the world seems to have gone mad.'

She laughed at the overstatement. 'Hardly that, darling, but it is quite exciting. Didn't you hear Mark just now? Those idiots at the Knickerbocker Trust Company have decided to hold a disaster meeting tonight – here, of all places, in a private room upstairs.'

His heart lurched. They must be crazy. Half fashionable New York was here tonight. Tony's own connection with the Knickerbocker was closer than he cared to contemplate. The unfortunate Charles Barney was a director of the Trust Company of America, Wilde's own questionable investment, so he was well aware they had advanced Barney nearly $200,000. He felt slightly sick. 'Wonder if Mark will find out what's going on,' he said.

Mark Cutler was talking confidentially to their waiter, and when the man has gone, Wilde moved round the table to his guest. 'What did he say, Mark?'

Cutler shook his head. 'You're not going to believe this. They're up there discussing the future of the goddamned company and they don't even have anyone guarding the door. I gather a dozen or so people from down here have slipped up there to eavesdrop already.'

'And you?' Tony's heart was fluttering unpleasantly now.

'I was just about to tiptoe up for a listen. Coming?'

'No, you go ahead. I've nothing tied up in the Knickerbocker.' Except my whole professional reputation, his mind gibbered at him.

The rest of the evening was like watching the roulette wheel slowing down and wondering where the ball would land, when your last few dollars were riding on the result.

There was an all-night bank on Fifth Avenue, and Tony finally decided the Knickerbocker was doomed when diners started going out, always men, and always to return a little later and finish their dinner, relief written large on their faces. They were withdrawing their cash from the Knickerbocker. None of them believed it would be honouring cheques tomorrow.

On Tuesday, the Clearing House stood by and watched the Knickerbocker being wiped out. At nine o'clock in the morning, the lines of depositors started forming at the main uptown branch of the Knickerbocker Trust Company opposite the Waldorf-Astoria. By ten, carriages and automobiles lined the kerb, waiting to pick up depositors who had hurried there on hearing rumours of disaster. Crowds of spectators gathered on the opposite pavement. Throughout the morning, the pressure grew, and shortly after noon the Knickerbocker was forced to suspend payments.

Tony Wilde was sitting in his library at the family house on West Fifty-third Street, wondering whether to take Charlotte and as much cash as he could and make a dash for Europe, or stay and take the final, suicidal risk that the American Trust Company would not be next. Finally he decided to stay. No use leaving the table when the wheel was still spinning.

The next morning the *New York Times* and the *Sun* both reported a statement from a partner in the House of Morgan – the main force in the Clearing House operation – which said a settlement might now be in sight, with the backing of the US Treasury and the big banks. At present the chief sore point, he said, was the Trust Company of America.

Reading the *Times* report as he sat alone at the breakfast table, Wilde said: 'Thank you very much, J. Pierpont Morgan . . . I'll pick up my barrel at the door and over Niagara we go!'

Sure enough, the financial district awoke to a tremendous run on the Trust

Company of America. It began to look like a carbon copy of the previous day's scenes outside the Knickerbocker. Behind the scenes, a Clearing House team was examining the books. Out front, the tellers continued to pay out vast sums, wondering when the cash to refill their drawers would run out. Then, only minutes before breaking point, the big banks agreed a million dollar loan to the beleaguered trust company. In one day's business, thirteen and a half million dollars had been paid out to panic-stricken depositors.

It was all over. Wilde replaced the telephone on its hook and sat, staring at the wall, for a full minute. It was all over and his name was intact, his bank still solvent, his prominent role in the Trust Company of America unexplored by a muck-raking Press. Never again, he thought. Not ever again. By the standards of the House of Morgan, the Wilde bank was a small fish. But it had kept his family in considerable style for generations, and now it would continue to do so. For one appalling afternoon, Tony had seen a vision of his bank being the only one of the old-established, 'safe' financial institutions to have gone under. He had finally discovered an unacceptable level of risk. Or so he thought at the time.

After the lesson of 1907, Tony went back to poker for excitement. It failed to produce the killing frisson of semi-legal financial speculation, but it was the next best thing. Nevertheless, time dims all memories. Within five years, he was nibbling at the edge of speculation once again. It was much better than poker. As time passed, all the intricacies of shady financial dealing unfolded in their twisted glamour. He played, won, lost, won again. Almost without realising it, he became a professional gambler, but his casinos were the Stock Exchange and the brokerage houses.

Tony's father had died when he was still a baby, when he caught polio after a summer swim in an infected lake. His mother, always frail, had survived only until he was in his early twenties. It had ensured their son always had a clear field of play for his latest prank. No New York society mama would have let him marry Lottie Casanova. No Wall Street papa would have countenanced his reckless financial dealings. But he had no family brakes, so he careered downhill in whatever direction his impulses drove him.

Once he got the hang of things, he was amazed how easy it was to use the bank to cover much of his activity. The Wilde name stayed respectable, because the bank was still absolutely safe. But Tony's personal holdings gradually dwindled as he capitalised his original hundred per cent ownership to finance his Wall Street junketing.

A lot of the time, he won at least as much as he lost, but a couple of major setbacks soon corrected that balance. In spite of a highly profitable war, by the early 1920s he was substantially worse off than he had been when he married in 1905. Occasionally, Wilde found himself blaming Charlotte. He tried not to, because he had once been a tolerant and fair-minded man. All she was guilty of was conforming too perfectly to what he had suggested. Sometimes he looked at her and wondered whether she had ever stalked the music hall stage in red satin and black silk tights. Nowadays she was so much the ideal fashionable society wife and mother that anyone told of her past would have refused to believe it.

They had been childless until 1916, and Charlotte had given up hope of a

293

family, sometimes sobbing against Wilde's shoulder in the small hours because they would never have babies. Then, out of the blue, she had conceived. Their daughter Cordelia was a perfect replica of Charlotte herself, and from then on Charlotte appeared to have achieved all she wanted. If he ever felt faintly guilty at jeopardising the financial security of his wife and child, Wilde dismissed it on the grounds that it was his only opportunity of a little escape from connubial dullness.

Throughout 1924 and well into 1925, he recouped much of what he had lost by buying and selling land in Florida early in the resort property boom. Tony was well into middle age by now. He was not a stupid man, and in his more introspective moments he recognised his addiction and tried to work out ways of cutting it off. He never succeeded. He made two million dollars out of Florida. It cleared up all his bad investments and left him close to the position he had been in when he married Charlotte – except that now he was little more than a token name at his own bank. The difference that made to his real wealth made his latest speculative winnings look like pocket money. He tried to laugh it off by telling himself it was an old and respectable tradition that in all the grandest dynasties, the third generation gracefully squandered the riches carefully accumulated by the first and second. It was then left to the fourth to revive the family fortunes. But it was a thin joke, and at times he wondered whether there would be any family fortune left when his daughter reached womanhood.

He was still trying to make a fresh start when he was swept away on the crest of the great bull market of 1928 and '29. This was a gamble with a difference. This time, it seemed, all America was crowded on the roller coaster with him, and they were all going to be winners.

Occasionally during that manic eighteen-month period, he felt a pang of guilt, because Charlotte was blissfully ignorant that he had ever played the market. She had never taken an interest in financial matters and he could hardly accuse her of indifference when he himself had always airily assured her that he was richer than Croesus. Now, throughout the mad inflationary boom, as the financial news once again surged on to the front pages of every newspaper and stayed there, his wife occasionally made pitying remarks about the naivety of those who gambled on such illusory riches.

One morning she threw down the *New York Times* with a snort and said: 'Really, you could inscribe my stock market knowledge on a pinhead, but even I can see that this lot will collapse under its own weight sooner or later. Can you understand what drives them, darling?'

He could not quite meet her eyes as he joined her condemnation of such mindless speculation. Two hours later he was downtown, telephoning a list of purchases and sales to his broker.

Wilde lost himself beyond recall to speculation in the spring of 1928. In January, it seemed certain the market would collapse. With the conservative financiers prophesying Armageddon with gloomy satisfaction, he took the last of his Florida profits and spread them over the most unlikely companies. On March 3, General Motors, one of his heaviest investments, rocketed. The following day it was the turn of Radio stocks, another of his favourites. After that, everything went through the roof. Tony Wilde decided he would die a billionaire.

294

That year and for much of the next, millions of other Americans shared his dream and put up their life savings to prove it. Tony was out for blood now – even if it was his own. He had sufficient financial acumen to know it probably would be. Until the beginning of 1929, he was, at least, gambling with cash. But from January that year, he found the ultimate risk irresistible and began trading on margin. Once he was only paying an instalment on each block of stock, with the balance to come from the profit it would make as the price inevitably rose, the volume of his dealings increased tenfold. So did his indebtedness should anything go wrong.

Charlotte would have been blind had she now failed to notice he was up to something. Like any other sort of addict, his first thought each morning and his last at night was for his drug. At first she left him to it. For some time they had been pursuing friendly but largely detached lives. But then, one May morning when he was particularly jumpy as he studied the papers, she said: 'Are you in it for a great deal?'

Her question surprised him so much that he jumped violently as if she had caught him kissing a maid or robbing Cordelia's moneybox. 'Why – er – no, of course not . . . just interested because of a flutter I had after one of the bank clients tipped me.'

'Why would a flutter interest you, Tony? I'd have thought that for someone with your resources, that sort of gamble would be a crashing bore.'

'Oh, anything but! It's not the money, it's the risk. It's pitting yourself against chance and . . .' He caught her astonished gaze and his voice faded '. . . just a bit of good fun, that's all,' he finished lamely.

She continued to eye him for a while, then shook her head as if abandoning an insoluble puzzle, and went back to her own paper. After that, he sometimes felt her watching him if he displayed an excess of interest in the financial papers, but she never spoke of it again and generally he was careful to check out his speculations when she was not there.

The market had broken three times in the year or so that Tony had been most deeply involved: in June and December 1928, and more seriously, in March 1929. But the recoveries then – particularly in March when thousands of speculators had been ruined – encouraged everyone to think there was no end to economic progress. When a few prices started tumbling in the autumn of 1929, everyone thought it was another hiccup. Prices broke twice in September, only to recover quite quickly, although never to early September levels. But in October the decline began again, with a European financial scandal fuelling the unease of investors. By Wednesday October 23, the wise money was saying something worse was ahead. More than six million shares changed hands that day and dealing was so intensive that the ticker was nearly two hours late in transmitting details of transactions.

Tony Wilde was one of the speculators who decided this was the best time to buy – the culmination of the worst break since the beginning of the Bull Market. Already well down thanks to the previous week's losses, he bought with every cent of credit he could raise.

Next day the Stock Market crashed.

Radio, one of Wilde's favourite stocks, opened at almost $69 a share. Within three frenzied hours it was selling at $44. Tony owned ten thousand shares. By midday the ticker was running so far behind it was useless in

295

dealings. The Stock Exchange telephone system was hopelessly jammed. Wall Street had reverted to the jungle.

Tony's broker was an old college friend. They sat in his inner office for half an hour, listening to the mayhem outside. Eventually, having read a message which had just been brought from the Exchange, the broker crumpled the paper, flicked it against the opposite wall and stood up. 'Well, Tony, that just about sees me off,' he said. 'According to my reckoning, you went under about two hours ago. I'm going home to make plans. You might as well do the same. Nothing else that happens down here today will help either of us – we're dead.' He turned stiffly and walked out of the room, into a maelstrom of investors begging for news.

Tony sat in his Rolls-Royce and watched the crowds which milled along the pavements. All looked strained and white-faced. Many of them were directly involved, ordinary people who had flung their savings into the vast bran tub of Wall Street in the hope of a prize. Most of them were cheaply dressed, the women with hard permanent waves and garish cosmetics, the men with baggy, ill-cut trousers and jackets that sagged across the back. Wilde studied the lush interior of his car and thought: As from now, they're all better off than me. They have jobs, even if their security is gone. I have a limousine, until it's repossessed. I have a town house and a country house, until they're sold off to satisfy my creditors. I have no means of earning a living. Probably I no longer own the clothes I'm wearing.

It was barely three o'clock when he got back to the house. Charlotte would be out – she always had something on at this time of day. He removed his alpaca overcoat with exaggerated care and handed it to his butler, Hedley. As he began to head for the library, Hedley opened the door again. Maud Lewis came in with Cordelia.

'Daddy – what are you doing home at this hour? How lovely to see you!' Cordelia dashed across the hall and flung herself on him. Instinctively he picked her up and swung her round in the air.

'Hey, you're getting far too tall for this sort of thing. You'll be swinging me around soon!' he said, putting her down again. 'Anyway, what are you doing home? I thought you were safely banished to school until Christmas!'

She gave him an exaggerated scowl and he was reminded compulsively of the first time he had seen her mother. 'Dentist,' she said. 'You know how fussy Mama is about that man we always use. I'm going back in the morning.'

'Well, if it eases the pain of the jawbreaker, it's wonderful to see my favourite female. Off you go, now. I think Maud has plans for you.' He had sensed rather than seen Maud's disapproving expression as he called Cordelia his favourite female. Sour-faced old bitch, he thought. We can't all regard Lady Charlotte as the pinnacle of womanhood.

But then all such minor considerations faded as he entered his library and looked around at what he had lost. Not a bad run, really, he thought. How many other gamblers could lay claim to twenty-two years of straight wins? Well, perhaps that was an exaggeration. After all, the bank had gone, in all but name. He tried not to remember that there had been more than twenty million dollars equity in that, once upon a time, all his. And of course, the houses both had mortgages now. His father would have been most displeased at that . . . well, the smug bastard had always looked pretty disapproving in that portrait at the East Hampton house. Give him something to chew on for a change.

Almost casually, he wandered over to the walnut desk between the two tall windows, and opened the central drawer. Inside reposed a lethal bauble – a lady's pearl-handled pistol made in England in the previous century, and given to him by Charlotte on their first wedding anniversary with a bantering note that said something about 'a lady-killer for a lady killer'. He always kept it in perfect condition and there was a plentiful supply of ammunition in the little box beside it. For a while he stood contemplating the weapon. Then he closed the drawer and opened another, taking out pen, ink and paper. He sat down to write to Charlotte.

She had been to some charity ball committee downtown and had gone on to tea at Sherry's with two friends. As the ladies ate small sandwiches and cakes and discussed fund-raising, a black fog of disaster seemed to take over the tea room. News was spreading of what was going on in the financial district.

There were abrupt departures from several groups like their own, and eventually Charlotte, her curiosity piqued, called the waiter. 'Jacques, I'm beginning to think Central Park is on fire. What on earth is going on?'

'Haven't you heard, ma'am? Half the staff here are slipping out for a few minutes, too, to see if they can get some news. They say the Market's gone bust.'

Charlotte had a momentary vision of Tony's face, death-pale except for burning patches of colour on the cheeks, as it had been too often this year. She was already on her feet as she said: 'Really bust, or another setback?'

'Oh, the real thing this time, Mrs Wilde. They say every telephone line to Wall Street is jammed.'

Charlotte turned to her companions. 'Ladies, forgive me. I think maybe my charitable efforts are going to be required elsewhere this afternoon.'

Tony had said what he had to say to Charlotte. A gracefully penned letter reposed in its hand-made envelope on the marble chimneypiece in the library. He was in his dressing room on the second floor. He had thought long and hard about what he should do, and now he had come to a decision. Any gambler could blow his brains out when he lost. He was going to do something different. He still had about a hundred dollars in cash. America was a vast place, and he had grown up on tales of adventure and derring-do. Having dressed himself appropriately, Antony St John Wilde was about to take to the road.

He was singing to himself, quite happy now his mind was made up:

'Jay Gould's daughter said before she died,
"Poppa, don't allow them bums to ride.
If ride they must, let 'em ride the rods,
And put their trust in the hand of God.
In the hand of God . . . in the hand of God . . . !" '

'And I suppose you're going to disappear into the sunset singing that, and seeing yourself as the last of the travelling men! You sodding coward!'

'Lottie!' inadvertently he had reverted to the name he had not used for her since they married. 'What are you doing here?'

'Spoiling your final curtain, it seems. What the devil do you think you're doing?'

'You – I – that is, I told Hedley there was something for you in the library. Didn't you . . . ?'

'Indeed I did.' She produced the sheet of paper he had finished composing only half an hour before. 'I was rather hoping it was your way of laughing off this whole catastrophe, and that I'd find you lurking in the drawing room with a whisky and a cigar. Clearly I was wrong.'

He collected himself with some difficulty. Her look was enough to shrivel a hero of ancient Rome. 'I thought, this way, parting would cause less pain.'

'Pull the other one! You thought this way you could slip away and leave me to shovel up the muck. Shame I came home early to comfort you, isn't it?'

'You don't understand.'

'Oh, but I do. I understand all too well. What should you estimate, a week, ten days, before the smoke clears? Then the creditors will be down on the Wilde Bank and on Antony Wilde's personal assets like carrion crows. How uncivilised to be left there to face it! Much better to leave the little woman in charge. After all, she knew nothing about it . . . they're bound to go a bit easier on her, left alone with a child and no visible means of support.' She moved nearer to him. 'Because that's what you've left us, isn't it, darling Tony? No visible means of support. Christ, you must be the biggest piece of shit that ever got dropped on Fifth Avenue.'

'Vulgarity will get you nowhere.'

'I know, but by Christ, it makes me feel better! You're not seriously planning to do what you threaten in this letter?'

'Take to the road? Yes. I think it's about time I learned how the dispossessed survive. After all, that's what I am now.'

Instead of assaulting him, which he was more than half expecting, Charlotte abruptly stood back, put her hands on her hips and laughed in his face. 'I should have known better than to ask, really, shouldn't I? I should have known you were serious. You're dressed head to foot in your best Abercrombie and Fitch explorer's outfit! Don't forget to pack the butterfly net and specimen box!'

He attempted to salvage some dignity. 'Since you choose to raise the matter, I'm wearing these clothes because they're the most practical things I have for what I imagine is ahead of me.'

'Oh, sure, I can just see you now, sharing a tin can of coffee with Box-car Willie in that outfit. Get it looking a bit worn and they'll be featuring you on the cover of *Bum's Vogue!*'

'I've taken enough of this. I'm going. I meant every word I said. I think this is my only chance of salvation.'

He moved forward, attempting to pass her. She was no longer laughing. 'And what about our salvation, mine and Cordelia's? You ruined us, without any need beyond your own weakness, and now you're leaving us to deal with it alone.'

'But, Charlotte, you're so strong. You can survive anything, I'm sure of that. I'm nothing but a broken reed.'

'And I'm the Queen of bloody Sheba! I never heard so much rubbish in my life! All right, then, go. If you're this spineless, there's little point in begging you to stay and fight. But don't you ever come back begging from me, because I'll kick your bloody Massachusetts Bay teeth straight down your throat if you do. Now get out – and don't you *dare* let Cordelia see you – the way you look now, she might die laughing.'

Wilde had already decided he would leave by the back entrance. Somehow it seemed appropriate to his new, ascetic existence. Besides, it would have been hard to explain to any acquaintances he met out on West 53rd Street why he was strolling in a fashionable section of the city at six o'clock on an autumn evening in tweeds he would normally have worn for a country walk.

After he left, Charlotte sat down on the bed and cried until there were no more tears. Then she undressed, went to the bathroom, took a shower, re-did her hair and makeup, and summoned Maud. 'Unless you have plans for this evening, Maudie, I'd like you to have supper in my small sitting room with me. I have a lot to discuss with you.'

'Anything to do with what happened down Wall Street this afternoon?' asked Maud. Then Charlotte noticed she had been crying, too.

'Maud, don't tell me *you* got misled by that get-rich-quick rubbish? I thought you had more sense.'

'So did I, Miss Lottie, but I didn't. I was cleaned out today, left wiv what I stand up in.'

'Join the club. You'd better have some good ideas this evening. Tomorrow they're selling us up.'

PART FOUR

Grand Finale

CHAPTER THIRTY-TWO

'Let's face it, Maud, when I get it wrong, I *really* get it wrong! I appear to have wasted the past twenty-four years.'

'Hardly wasted, Miss Lottie –' Maud was the only person who had never stopped calling her Lottie ' – what about Miss Cordelia?'

'Yes, you're right. I can't imagine life without Delia. Anyway, I'm being melodramatic as usual. On balance, I've enjoyed it. It's just that somehow, I never seem to have been the centre of anyone's world.'

'After being used to audiences clamouring for you everywhere, you wouldn't have felt that with any one man, Miss Lottie, and you know it.'

Charlotte's expression was enigmatic. 'Oh, yes. I think I might have, if things had been just a little different. Remember Tommy Fanshaw? That was the only one . . . couldn't call him a man, although he behaved with more manly grace than most I've met. I know, I haven't seen him since he was sixteen . . . he's probably bald and fat, or dead, by now.' She let her thoughts wander for a while. 'Anyway, this won't keep the bailiffs from the door. I'm all ears for advice, Maudie my love. Where do we go from here?'

'Well, Miss Lottie, you're only good for one thing, professionally speaking, so I can't see there's a lot of choice.'

Charlotte giggled. 'I'm forty-nine years old! I know I'm still in good shape, but can you see me sashaying down to the foot-lights and singing "I Want To Go Where The Big Girls Go"? They'd laugh me off the stage!'

'Others have done it. There's plenty of stars kept on a lot older than forty-nine.'

'Maud, be reasonable. The ones who did that never went away. I've been forgotten for years. The few who remember my name probably think I'm long dead.'

'They'll never forget "Ta-ra-ra-boom-de-ay".'

'Christ, neither will I! Every once in a while I still wake up with that damned song echoing in my ears. Sometimes I almost believe I married Tony to escape from it. Besides, even if I could convince the world I was still worth booking, you know as well as I do that vaudeville is on its knees.'

'Hmm, and I know there's hard times ahead. Me and Mr Tony wasn't the only investors who were wiped out yesterday. There'll be an awful lot of people need cheering up, without much cash to do it. That was how the halls held their audiences in the first place, remember.'

'It's a lovely idea, Maud, but it won't work. Lottie Casanova's a figure from another century, and whatever bread and circuses the people get, it won't include vaudeville now. Let's leave that for a while and concentrate on what we have to keep us afloat in the immediate future.'

She went to a wall safe concealed behind a picture frame, and removed a deed box. 'I never thought I'd be the sort of woman who'd squirrel away assets from her husband,' she said, 'but then, until a few months back I never dreamed Tony's money would run out, either.' She unlocked the box and opened it. 'God knows it isn't much, but it's better than nothing.'

When she married, Charlotte had invested her own money in Government bonds and in New York property, a midtown apartment building. Once the cash was tied up, she had promptly forgotten about it. Compared with Wilde's wealth in those days, it had been pin money. But about the time she had realised something of the level of his speculations, an office building developer had approached her with an inflated offer for the apartment block. She had been about to turn him down, but her mounting suspicions of Tony's financial position changed her mind and she sold out. The proceeds had been reinvested in Government bonds along with the existing ones.

Now she stacked the certificates neatly to one side. 'At least that takes care of Delia's education,' she said. 'She can go back to school tomorrow without any of this having to affect her.'

Maud looked up sharply. 'You're making a rod for your own back, Lottie. That child worships her father.'

Troubled, Charlotte said: 'I know, and I have no way of dealing with it. How can I tell a thirteen-year-old girl that her great hero has run off with the raggle-taggle gypsies and left us women to cope with the mess he left? For a start, I don't think she'd believe me, and if she did, think of how it would hurt her.'

'She'll be hurt whatever you do. You've gotta tell her now.'

'It's no good, Maud, I can't. It's Thanksgiving in a couple of weeks. I'll find some way then, while she's at home.'

'Well, I've told you what I think and I shan't change my mind. What are you gonna do about everything else?'

Involuntarily, both women looked around them at the luxuriously appointed room. Maud added: 'Maybe you'd be better taking her out of school and using the money to keep a roof over our heads.'

'Out of the question. That education is my investment in Delia's future. Anyway, it wouldn't buy us a tenth of this place.'

'Surely there'll be something left, when the dust settles?'

Charlotte sighed. 'I wish I thought so, but I'm sure there won't be. Tomorrow I'm off to see Tony's lawyer – if I can get anywhere near him through the chaos downtown. I fully expect to find that we own neither this place nor the house in East Hampton; that the bank is still his in name only; and that he's so overcommitted through trading on margin that he'll be bankrupt ten times over and still owe people.'

'That bad, huh?'

'Put it this way, Maud. If you ever want to ride in a Rolls-Royce again, I suggest you come to the attorney's office with me tomorrow, because after that I suspect we'll be using the subway.'

Her position was every bit as bad as she had anticipated. Harassed as he was, Tony's attorney had a soft spot for Charlotte Wilde, and he knew even before detailed examination of her husband's finances just what an appalling position she was in.

When they had been through everything, he said: 'All I can advise at this stage, Charlotte, is that you let the servants go, close both houses, sell the cars and move to the least expensive place you can find. It will take months to sort this thing out – there are so many others in the same position – but in any court action it will reflect well on you if you're seen to have battened down the hatches the minute you realised what was going on. Have you no assets of your own?'

She explained about the investment for Cordelia's education, and he nodded his approval. 'And I shan't be homeless, either, if I'm prepared to move from New York,' she said. 'Tony bought me a cottage up in Vermont, near Lake Champlain, because I fell in love with the place when we spent a holiday up there just before Cordelia was born. I still have it, though I don't go there more than three times a year and it's out in the back of beyond.'

'Anything else?'

'Yes. Some jewellery of my own – stuff I had before Tony ever came into my life. I can sell it, but you don't have to tell me it will fetch peanuts at a time like this. I'll put that off as long as I can.' She gave him a conspiratorial grin. 'I'm not entirely destitute, though. I have a terrible confession to make. When I realised what was going on, I started salting away cash. My personal shopping stopped dead and each month I cashed the cheques I'd normally have drawn on our joint account to settle my personal bills. I have between seven and eight thousand dollars. I've managed a long time on much less than that in my younger days.'

'Then put it on deposit somewhere safe as soon as you can, and just keep enough to live on, day to day. Don't attempt to settle any bills that come in for the household when Tony was in charge. That will all go into the same pot when he's declared bankrupt. At least there'll be no big scandal. Half the country is in a similar position. So where to, now, Charlotte? Will you go to Vermont immediately?'

'Good God, no! I'm going to have to find a job.'

He gaped at her. 'Do you have the remotest idea of what you're saying? As of Monday, half the population of New York is going to be out of work, the way things look now, and you think you have a chance of beating them to it? If I were you, I'd take off for Vermont and start trying to raise chickens and vegetables. You stand more chance of surviving that way!'

'My dear Sam, not only would I starve, but so would the chickens. I am an urban animal, and here I stay. There's bound to be the odd bargain apartment for rent with all these people jumping out of windows. I'm going to look for one while I still have the car. Take care of yourself, and don't invest in any shaky stocks!'

She found an apartment in Greenwich Village after following Sam Forsyth's instructions to close the houses and dismiss the staff. The only one she kept was Maud. The maid was in her early sixties now, and it was unthinkable for either woman to manage without the other. The apartment Charlotte found was big enough for them both and for Cordelia when she was home for holidays. It was on the second floor of an attractive brownstone building near Washington Square, and Charlotte loved it on sight.

Thanksgiving was on them before she had moved homes. The unpalatable task of telling Cordelia about her father's defection still loomed ahead. Charlotte mentioned putting it off until Christmas. 'If you do, you'll spend it without me,' said Maud. 'You got a responsibility to that child, and you're falling down on it.'

Finally Charlotte bowed to pressure from Maud and arranged for them to spend Thanksgiving in the Vermont cottage. She had sold the Rolls-Royce and their other big car, but for the time being was hanging on to the small runabout the servants had always used for errands. Now, on the damp, misty autumn morning a couple of days before the holiday, Charlotte drove over to Cordelia's school outside Boston, having left Maud up at the cottage making things festive.

She loved her daughter with a single-minded passion which sometimes frightened her, and remembering her stormy relations with her own mother, she tried neither to smother nor neglect the child. It was uncanny, she reflected, how exactly like her Cordelia was growing, and how much she herself now resembled Laura Cazenove. If photographs of the three had been placed side by side, a stranger would have assumed they depicted the same woman at different times of her life. As she drove towards Boston, Charlotte smiled ruefully to herself and said: 'I do hope she doesn't find some reason to hate me as much as I hated Mama!'

The trouble with Cordelia, Charlotte reflected, was that she had always been a Daddy's girl. That was all very well as long as Daddy was big, strong and invincible. When he was a spineless coward it could lead to all sorts of difficulties. She was a little surprised at Cordelia's reticence about the financial crash since her return to school. Half the girls in her class must have been affected as their family fortunes took a tumble in the wake of the stock market collapse, yet the one letter she had received since the child's return to Boston on Black Thursday had been no more than a stilted account of that week's class work and outings. More ominously, no letter had arrived from her for Tony. Charlotte did not like that. Normally Cordelia wrote to her father twice as often as to her mother, but this time there had been nothing. It was almost as if they shared some telepathic link . . .

When she arrived at the school she learned fairly quickly that the link was not telepathy but the US Mail. Once he was on the road, Tony had delivered his *coup de grâce* and had written to Cordelia. Charlotte collected a tight-lipped, furiously resentful girl who answered her in monosyllables, apart from an initial outburst in which she demanded to know why she could not remain at school for Thanksgiving.

Charlotte's temper was as volatile as that of her daughter, and something about Cordelia always made her lose it quickly. This time she managed to exercise more control, because it was obvious that something had upset the child very deeply. It was hard going, though. Her daughter seemed determined at first to explain nothing. In the end, after driving more than forty miles without eliciting a word from her, Charlotte pulled in at the side of the road, switched off the engine and turned to face Cordelia.

Forcing an even tone into her voice, she said: 'Darling, you must realise that all sorts of things have been happening at home. We have to talk to each other, openly and honestly, during the holiday, but I can't see any way of doing that if you refuse to speak at all, apart from saying yes and no. Please tell me what's happened to upset you.'

Cordelia took a deep breath and opened her mouth as though to pour out a

306

torrent of invective, then seemed to change her mind and instead thrust a hand in her coat pocket. She produced a dog-eared envelope, so scruffy it had clearly been folded and unfolded countless times. Not scruffy enough to conceal the original, telltale cream colouring, the confident black ink handwriting on the back . . . oh, God, he'd written to her.

'If you're so desperate to understand, you'd better read that. But I'm telling you now, the minute I'm old enough to live by myself, I'm going to find him and help him. How could you just let him go like that, and not even tell me? How could you?' Cordelia burst into tears and buried her face in her hands.

Charlotte tried to hold the girl, and comfort her, but she was inconsolable. She shook off her mother's hands and turned away towards the window. 'Just leave me alone and read his letter,' she mumbled between sobs.

It was, Charlotte reflected, about what she might have expected. Tony could never have faced admitting to the most important being in his world that he was an addictive gambler on such a scale that he had beggared them all. Instead, he had produced a graceful farewell note which implied that the financial crash had destroyed him, and that they would be better off realising what they could of his assets than having him around where creditors could get at him and take away even the roof over their heads. Tacitly, it suggested that Charlotte had made no move to hold him back, that maybe, just maybe, in such circumstances he would have stayed.

She knew without having to ask that he had written it after she had denounced him so furiously when she caught him about to desert her. Beneath the charming surface, Antony Wilde had a broad vengeful streak. There was no truth in the letter, but its stream of innuendo was more than enough to alienate a child who regarded him as a hero and her mother with considerable jealousy.

Briefly, Charlotte wanted to kill him, but when her initial rage wore off, she recognised that if she had bitten the bullet and broken the news immediately, as Maud had begged her, Cordelia would at least have had a true account of events at the beginning. As it was, she had been brooding on this pack of lies for days, and there was nothing her mother could do now to change her mind.

The holiday was ghastly. Cordelia hardly spoke, and Charlotte found the effort of keeping her temper so great that she was constantly on edge. Maud was determinedly cheerful, cooking vast meals which nobody ate, taking Cordelia out for long walks in which she took no interest, and generally ensuring that mayhem did not break out. Every time Cordelia went to her room, they heard her crying. When the time came for her to return to school, Charlotte heaved a huge sigh of relief.

This time Maud accompanied them, as they had closed the cottage and were going directly back to New York after dropping off Cordelia. She had sat stone-faced as Charlotte told her their houses, money and security were gone, asking only when she would have to leave school. When Charlotte said that was not going to happen, she received the news in silence, and Charlotte realised with exasperation that the girl thought her father had found some way of securing her place there.

When she and Maud finally set off back to New York, Charlotte sat in the driving seat with tears coursing down her cheeks. 'That was the hardest thing I've been through since long before I was married,' she said. 'I know I should have told her before, Maud, but God dammit, did I have to pay quite such a price for it?'

Maud reached across and pressed Charlotte's hand, which was locked, white-knuckled, on the steering wheel. 'We'd all be bloody clever if we always got everything right, wouldn't we?' she said. 'If it's any consolation, lovey, I thought she behaved like a right little cow. I'm still trying to make excuses for her, but it's hard. She's no stupider than you or me. She must be realising now that her dad couldn't be quite the White Knight she's making out.'

'But what do I do as long as she insists on pretending?'

Maud shrugged. 'Go along wiv it, I s'pose. Can't really do anything else, can you? Let's just pretend things have always been like this and pray she grows out of it by the time she finishes school.' She turned a suspiciously innocent face on Charlotte. 'And if she doesn't, all I can suggest is you revive your music hall act an' bugger off to Australia wiv it!'

Charlotte had developed a wide circle of friends and acquaintances over the years. Her music hall background had developed into an intense interest in theatre and, inevitably, among the people she knew there were one or two who earned their living from the New York stage. James and Amy Channing were a successful husband-and-wife team who specialised in writing light comedies. They were among the few people Charlotte did not avoid after Tony's departure.

Too many shared friends of Tony's and hers still had their money. Some of them were scandalised that he had run through such a substantial fortune with such relentless efficiency; others sighed with secret relief that they had not suffered a similar fate. In any case, Charlotte found it uncomfortable to be with them now, and preferred to stay in touch with those who had minimal dealings with the world of finance.

Now she was trying to push Cordelia's misery out of her mind by throwing herself into the move to Greenwich Village. Once she had started to settle in, she got in touch with the people she still wanted to see. The Channings were among the first who visited.

Amy Channing was incurably nosey, and insisted on padding around the apartment, peering into dark corners and closets. Charlotte's new home possessed three bedrooms, two living rooms, a bathroom and a kitchen. The main living room was already sorted out and that was where she was entertaining her guests; but the second, which was to be dining room-cum-library, was still littered with half-full packing cases of books and papers.

Amy was wandering about, flipping through some of the books and idly chatting to Charlotte as she did so. Abruptly she stopped and bent to pick up an ornate red album. 'Oh, what a gorgeous binding! It looks like something from the Naughty nineties!'

Charlotte smiled. 'That, my dear, is exactly what it is. Take a look if you're interested. It's ancient history now; not something I ever talked about when I moved in polite circles.'

Amy opened the heavy book and was confronted by a full-length shot of Lottie Casanova, frilly petticoats foaming around her, one impossibly long leg raised above her head in the highest of high kicks. Amy stared at the picture, unable to believe what she saw, then raised her eyes slowly to Charlotte. 'B-but . . . it's you!' she said lamely.

'A Wilde by any other name,' said Charlotte. 'Yes, it's me. Darling, I know you're ten or fifteen years younger than me, but surely your generation hasn't entirely forgotten vaudeville?'

'No, but . . . well, dammit, you *can't* be Lottie Casanova! Of course I've heard of her. But you . . . Oh, my God, what a story!' As she finished the disjointed sentence she whirled round and rushed back to the living room, yelling: 'Jim – Jim, you'll never believe this, not in a million years!'

After that there was only one topic of conversation throughout the evening. Charlotte gave them some account of her music hall career; Maud was wheeled in for further reminiscence. There seemed no end to their curiosity. Finally Maud left them, grumbling that someone had to produce the supper.

Charlotte said: 'I hate to break up this fascinating exploration of my colourful past, but it doesn't solve the problem I wanted to discuss with you. How the devil am I going to earn a living now the first panic is over?'

James Channing had found it impossible to put down the photograph album. 'I don't know why you even need to ask,' he said. 'I'm amazed you haven't started putting out feelers about going back on the stage.'

'Oh, really, Jim, not you too! You and Maud must read the same pulp romances. For the thousandth time, I'm a middle-aged woman from an obsolete branch of show business. No one would pay me a living wage for reviving Lottie Casanova.'

'Don't be stubborn. I know vaudeville is dead – has been for years, without knowing it, otherwise you'd never have managed to slip out of the public mind so easily. But if the range of characters you portray in this album is anything to go by, you're bound to have some sort of acting ability. It's time you capitalised on it.'

'I don't think "capitalise" is too tactful a word to use on me at present,' said Charlotte. 'You are kind, though, and thanks for trying to give me a boost. But we're back with the age thing again, aren't we? It's always been an overcrowded profession. Who, in their right mind, is going to want a middle-aged woman who hasn't been on a stage for nearly a quarter of a century, and never played a legit part in any case? What I had in mind was to ask you if you could put in a word with someone who might want a dance coach or something. I'm still pretty good at all that technical stuff, and I've kept myself fit over the years.'

Channing looked past her at his wife, who nodded almost imperceptibly. 'Charlotte, you as a dance mistress. It'd be like giving Ellen Terry a walk-on as a parlour maid. We just might have something much more suitable . . . We're working on a play right out of the run of our comedy material. The Crash gave us a shock and we wanted to change direction a little.'

'And? From what I've read in the papers lately, serious drama is dying as fast as vaudeville. They're all saying everyone needs lightness and good cheer to help the general recovery.'

'Uh-huh. I read it too. I've read very little else since the beginning of November. I believe it as much as I believe what the President is saying about recovery being just around the corner.'

309

'So what have you written?'

He laughed. 'I don't know how you'll take this . . . it's about a bunch of people who hang round a neighbourhood café-bar, who all think that the good times are coming soon, all except a middle-aged female has-been – a tramp who's seen much better times. The main characters are the original dewy eyed boy-and-girl-next-door types. They start out full of optimism that they can beat the world because Love Conquers All . . . While they're having the stars wiped out of their eyes, the older woman is doing a sort of running commentary, almost an elegy, for the times she's had and the dreams she's lost. We haven't really decided yet whether or not it all ends in tears. That rather depends on the performance we get from the middle-aged has-been.'

'Oh, that'll really hearten the discouraged, won't it? I must say, though, it sounds fascinating. Is it finished? When it is, I'd love to read it, even if I don't get further than that.'

'Done! We're still polishing – and with us and a play that can mean rewriting two acts – but we're pretty damn' smug about it right now. Yes, I'll drop a copy round to you tomorrow.'

There was only one topic of conversation over supper. It was bad enough while just the three of them were discussing the project, but when Maud served the food and was let into the secret, she practically had Charlotte learning lines within five minutes. 'Told you that's what you should be doing, Miss Lottie. When will you learn I usually know what I'm talking about?'

CHAPTER THIRTY-THREE

Charlotte fell in love with the script the minute she started reading it. James Channing had brought a copy for her as promised, but stressed that she would have to audition for the part if she wanted it, along with a number of noted character actresses.

Maud was in the room when Channing talked to Charlotte, and privately she braced herself to inspire self-confidence in her employer after he had gone. To her surprise, it proved unnecessary. When Maud returned from seeing Channing out, she found Charlotte deeply engrossed in the script.

Eyes shining, she looked up as she heard Maud come in. 'I'll walk away with it, Maudie. Parts like this exist in cinema, but I haven't seen one in the theatre yet. They won't know how to handle it.'

Maud's heart soared, but she kept her face impassive. 'And what makes you think you do?'

'She's a real woman, that's why – not theatrical. She's every tart and naughty girl and middle-aged housewife I ever took off in the halls. When have you ever seen a legit actress do that?'

'Nah, you're right,' said Maud. 'They always seem to feel they gotta put their little hearts an' souls into it, don't they?'

'Yes, and let's hope they go on doing it. My God, Maud, forget the money. I want this part!'

The auditions were scheduled for the week between Christmas and New Year. Cordelia came home for Christmas, with heavily exaggerated reluctance, gave minimal thanks for her presents, asked if her room could be painted a different colour, and on December 27 went off to stay with a school friend in Massachusetts until the end of the holidays. As Maud shut the front door behind her, she and Charlotte exchanged a long look of profound relief, then went back to rehearsing Charlotte for her audition.

As the big day approached, Amy and Jim Channing began to get nervous about ever having involved Charlotte in their play. They had written a part for a blowsy, tired, undisciplined female of uncertain years, who had lived too hard and taken too many disappointments. Charlotte looked ten years younger than her real age; she was shapely, tough and fit; and her recent economies on clothes meant she was still wearing the cropped skirts and flat-chested sweaters of the flapper era. Husband and wife were getting terrible visions of the director thinking Charlotte had arrived to audition the female junior lead instead of the washed-up whore Addie O'Brien.

They had reckoned without Charlotte's ten years in music hall. She had never set foot on stage for a straight drama, but she knew how to get inside a character and portray it in ten seconds, because she had never had longer to establish an identity. The auditions took place the day before New Year's

Eve. The theatre was cold and Jim and Amy were nervous because they had never done anything like this before. Charlotte's spot was last on the list. Each woman had to read the same section of the script – the end of the whore-singer's big soliloquy which could either be the climax of the play or its coda, depending on the approach of the selected actress.

They sat through five grandes dames, who throbbed with emotion and became ladies defiled and reborn as they recited the closing monologue. The director, who loved the play on the printed page and had happily cast a brace of rising stars as the young lovers, was shifting in his seat and groaning with impatience. As the fifth diva swept offstage, he turned to Amy and said: 'Give her an asp and she'd have been a perfect Cleopatra. But she's not Addie O'Brien. Have none of these broads heard of naturalism?'

Jim sunk deeper in his seat. He adored Charlotte Wilde, but any woman less likely to create a naturalistic ambience would be hard to imagine. He tried placating the Young Turk. 'Did any of those appeal at all, Eddie?' he asked.

Eddie Doyle sat up straight and turned with exaggerated delicacy to stare at Jim. 'One hopes that Sir is joshing,' he said, then slumped back into his seat and roared out: 'Next!'

Jim closed his eyes. He wished he could have blocked his ears, too. He knew what Eddie would be seeing now. A tall, elegant female with sleek hair and skirts short enough for an adolescent. The guy was going to explode . . .

But no outburst ensued, and eventually Jim took his hand away from his eyes. For a moment he thought someone else had come to the audition in Charlotte's place. In the downstage spotlight stood a well-trodden woman. Not used up, just well-trodden. She was a little bit too big. Not sloppy – anything but. A man in his forties could look at those curves and want to bury himself in them on a cold winter night . . . She probably washed her hair often – it was soft and fluffy – but there was too much of it for a neat, thin, modern woman. It spilled out in a big halo around her head and the bulk of it was knotted carelessly at the nape of her neck. The dress vaguely followed current tastes, but it was loose, because there were breasts and hips and a belly under there, and skin-tight jersey would have made them obscene. The shoes had very high heels – probably because the female was a little too heavy for modern tastes and was jacking herself up to make the shape thinner. He remembered Amy telling him that's what big women did to minimise their bulk. The shoes were a little over at the sides – just enough to tell you she had been wearing them too long at her weight. A lighter woman could have kept them sleeker. A richer woman could have bought new shoes. But this female was neither of those things, so she wore her high heels and looked sloppy because she pushed them over at the sides . . .

With a start, Jim jerked upright. What was he doing, wool-gathering? This was Charlotte Wilde . . . *this was Charlotte Wilde*? Dear God, how had she managed to change into this tired old thing in less than twenty-four hours?

She started to speak, low at first, so low he had to strain a little to hear, although afterwards he realised every syllable was clear. The monologue started to harden up, the nuances of its language hitting him between the eyes in ways he did not know he, as the writer, had ever put into the part. The woman explained that you always thought one day someone would understand your dream and help you to realise it . . . that as they betrayed

312

you, each of your seducers made you think this was the real thing.

This was no longer something he and Amy had written. This was a shriek from the tortured soul of the ruined woman on the stage, putting up a trembling hand to shield her myopic eyes from the brilliant lime. He could not tear his attention from Charlotte for long enough to see how Doyle was reacting. All he wanted was to drink Charlotte's performance forever, and then, maybe, to run away and write something else that she would transform into a message from God.

The monologue was coming to an end. With a surge of guilt, he realised the last sentence was something of an anticlimax. Maybe they should work on that last section before it went into production . . . but wait a minute, what was happening? This wasn't the script.

It was an irony universally sniffed at by New York's literati that someone had copyrighted a song called 'Happy Days Are Here Again' within two weeks of Black Thursday. By Christmas, it was the popular hit of the year, sung by bouncy young people with broad grins and perfect teeth. Now Jim discovered that Addie O'Brien had commandeered the song. But she was no ingénue and the song was no longer a preview of a bright future.

Charlotte/Addie finished the last line Jim and Amy had written, and slid forward towards the footlights with the feline swoop that had once been acclaimed as the Casanova Glide. And then, if it was possible for a sound to resemble barbed wire and velvet scrambled together, such a sound filled the theatre, slowly, with infinite sadness, the tone and expression completely reversing the meaning of the childishly optimistic words:

'Happy days are here again . . .'

Why hadn't he seen it before? It was the great tragic aria of their time. It wasn't in the script, but no one moved to stop Charlotte. The theatre was plunged into reverent silence. Everyone within earshot had stopped, frozen by the siren call of some profane angel.

Charlotte had introduced the song at a point where the young lovers clung together like beaten animals. Their hopes for the future, their trust in one another, everything in their world, had been destroyed. Now the young man was off to start looking for work and both of them, their optimism spread thin and bright over despair, were attempting to encourage one another about future prospects. The original, spoken script line with which Charlotte was to have finished the play, was intended to imply an 'Oh, yeah, tell me another' attitude. The song, its sugar turned to bitter irony, did a far better job:

'Happy days are here again,
The skies above are clear again.
Let us sing a song of cheer again,
Happy days are here again.

No more sighing, no more crying,
Clouds of grey are turned to blue.
Sorrow flying, cares denying,
All our rosy dreams have come true . . .'

313

Tears in her voice, Addie O'Brien – Charlotte Wilde had ceased to exist for the moment – raised her head with the defiant pride of the eternal loser and cried out the pain of a whole generation:

> 'All together, shout it now!
> There's no one who can doubt it now,
> So let's tell the world about it now—
> Happy days are here again.'

She finished the song, and stood, head bowed, in the spotlight. The silence lengthened to a small eternity, then finally Eddie Doyle said in a voice that suggested he had found the Grail: 'When can you start rehearsing, Mrs Wilde?'

Come To Dust opened on Broadway in March, to rave reviews. Every critic in New York wanted to know how a middle-aged woman with no history in theatre could suddenly spring to prominence and paralyse an audience in its seats night after night, but before posing the question they all uttered paeans of praise to Charlotte's talent.

The play's success was all the more remarkable considering the swing of taste away from either harsh realism of 'jazz baby' themes. Writing in the *New Yorker*, Robert Benchley said:

> I am now definitely ready to announce that Sex, as a theatrical property, is as tiresome as the Old Mortgage, and that I don't want to hear it mentioned ever again . . . I am sick of rebellious youth and I am sick of Victorian parents and I don't care if all the little girls in all sections of the United States get ruined or keep from getting ruined. All I ask is: don't write plays about it and ask me to sit through them.
>
> I feel much the same about seething dramas of urban deprivation. Heaven knows, the signs of it are so obvious in our daily lives that we have no further need of it on stage, too. There is one exception to all this: *Come To Dust*. See it. Tell your friends about it. See it again. It's a small American tragedy which sends you out into the night full of hope, as well as sorrow, as if a terrible infected wound has been cleaned. The surgeon who performs this miracle is one Addie O'Brien, played by Charlotte Wilde, amazingly, in her forties, a new face on Broadway. We shall see more of Mrs Wilde, and I, for one, can't wait for the next time . . .

All the reviews were equally flattering, and when the fuss they made had died down, Eddie Doyle produced the next instalment of the Charlotte Wilde saga. A born publicist, he had gone into transports of delight when Amy told him about Charlotte's earlier career as Lottie Casanova.

'I don't believe this,' he said, 'all my boats are coming in together on this production. Not only is she sensational in the part, but she's got the sort of life story that Hollywood stars pay publicists to invent for them. We'll sit on this until a week or so after the opening, then release it. It'll double our coverage.'

And it did. Old shots of Lottie kicking up her legs on stage in England and Australia were reproduced. Columnists interviewed her endlessly about the astonishing roller coaster of a life, from nobleman's daughter to music hall artiste to society wife within a decade . . . they had never had a story quite as rich in incident as this one. Charlotte's only reservation was about her reasons for taking up straight acting in middle age.

She would have been perfectly happy to pillory Tony Wilde, but there was Cordelia to consider. There could be no question of confessing how he had dumped them in the wake of his financial ruin, so she insisted that her marriage had broken down in the summer of 1929 and that they had gone their separate ways. The implication was that, come the Crash, there had been no more money for alimony, so she had set out to make her own living. A much more respectable story than reality, she felt, and better than Wilde deserved; but at least it would cause minimal pain to Delia.

Unexpectedly, Charlotte's new stage career did much to improve their relationship. Cordelia and a school friend came to see *Come To Dust* during the Easter vacation. They were to join her backstage after the performance. Charlotte was suffering worse nerves at the prospect of their visit than she had before going on for her first night appearance.

'Dear God, Maud, if she blamed me for not telling her about Tony, think what she'll have to say about my music hall days! She'll never speak to me again.'

'If you ask me, it's about time that child started growing up,' said Maud with a sniff. 'You know I bled for her when her father went, but she hasn't arf played on it ever since. Enough is enough.'

That failed to calm Charlotte's nerves. When Maud went to let the two girls into the dressing room, she glanced apprehensively in her mirror to see the expression on her daughter's face. It was radiant. Cordelia bustled into the room, embraced Charlotte voluntarily for the first time since Thanksgiving, kissed her and said: 'Mother, you were out of this world! How did you do it?'

Over her shoulder, Charlotte could see Maud's face, the astonished expression mirroring her own. She tried to cover her confusion with a joke: 'Oh, mud calling to mud, I suppose.'

Then she discovered at least part of the reason for her abrupt rehabilitation with her daughter. 'All the girls at school are dying to come and see you! You'll never believe how many of them have asked for your autograph! Oh, Mother, I'm so proud of you.'

Well, well, well, thought Maud, pigs sometimes fly after all. Let's hope nothing happens to upset all this new-found family bliss.

The girls had been given special permission to attend an evening performance instead of a matinée, with Amy Channing escorting them to see they came to no harm. Charlotte was taking them out to dinner afterwards and they were bubbling with excitement.

Cordelia's friend Elie kept peering closely at Charlotte, who eventually said: 'What is it, my dear? Have I got a fly on my nose?'

Elie blushed furiously. 'Oh, I do beg your pardon, Mrs Wilde, but it doesn't seem possible you're the same woman as the one we saw on stage. You're so . . . so much *younger*.'

Charlotte grinned at Cordelia. 'You can bring this one backstage as often as you like,' she said.

Come To Dust ran for a year and a half and won a Pulitzer prize for the Channings. In the wake of the announcement came a magical summons for Charlotte: Hollywood wanted her for a movie version.

'But the whole idea is absurd!' she told Amy Channing. 'Either it has to be filmed straight, so that cinema audiences see nothing more than a stage play put on the screen, or it's impossible to do at all. I know enough about movies to recognise that you have to be a hundred times more realistic than you do in theatre, and that the sort of effect that makes stage hits just looks phoney anywhere else.'

'I wouldn't let that worry you, darling,' said Amy. 'By the time they've rewritten it, the whole thing will be unrecognisable as our baby anyway. Jim and I made each other a promise when the film rights were sold, neither of us was going to work on the screenplay, and we're sticking to it. Movie scripts need a different sort of talent.'

'Perhaps movie actresses need a different sort of talent, too,' said Charlotte gloomily.

'I'm sure of that. You only have to look at some of the disastrous showings the big Broadway names have made. But you can only give it a try. Think how you'd feel if someone else put Addie O'Brien on screen. You'd scratch her eyes out.'

'I hadn't thought of that . . . dammit, you're right. I regard Addie as my personal property.' She smiled at Amy: 'At times I even resent you having anything to do with her!'

They made a superb job of adapting *Come To Dust* for the screen. Much of the play's main action remained intact, except for being spread around more locations than the three-scene format which the theatrical setting had dictated. The vital change, the big final scene, was handled with such brilliant simplicity that Charlotte was left wondering why she had not thought of it.

The young lovers said their farewells in the girl's shoddy rooming-house apartment. Their fragile optimism was barely silenced when the camera cut to the interior of the bar, where Addie O'Brien, too, was preparing to move on. Instead of delivering a solitary monologue, she now spoke her last couple of lines to the barman, then picked up the shabby cardboard suitcase that contained all she owned, turned and swayed off on her down-at-heel shoes, out of the bar and along a bleak New York waterfront street enlivened only by bars of sunlight, which broke through between buildings, briefly highlighting Addy's hair and features from time to time. The sequence lasted two or three minutes, and as she walked, her expression gradually transformed itself from despair to the beginnings of hope. All the while, on voice-over, she sang 'Happy Days Are Here Again', just as she had done it on stage.

The movie opened in mid-1934, and became the springboard of Charlotte's second international career in a way no stage play, however successful, could have done. It played to packed houses in America and in Europe broke box office records in five countries, including England. After that, Charlotte received so many offers she began to believe she would still be working on her hundredth birthday.

The film version of *Come To Dust* gave her endless pleasure, but she did not care for the mechanics of being a movie actress, and began to concentrate on theatre again.

There was another reason for staying with theatre: Cordelia was beginning to be interested on her own account. She had been taking piano and ballet lessons for years at school, but now she asked Charlotte about dramatic training, and getting a voice teacher in New York.

'Honestly, Maud, I don't know whether to encourage her or not,' said Charlotte, after the latest pleas for singing lessons.

'After my experience, it's hardly a life I'd recommend to anyone.'

Maud's look was deeply sceptical. 'Oh, I believe you – and I believe in fairies, an' all. You know as well as I do that you're a new woman since you've gone back to the stage.'

'Yes, but . . .'

'Yes but nothing.' Her face softened. 'Look, Miss Lottie, I know how you musta felt when you decided to marry Tony Wilde. You'd gone as far as you could at the time, you felt all neglected an' lonely, and at the time he looked a pretty good prospect. But Christ, what a come-down afterwards! I can't imagine you ever really being bored with anything, but you came closer in those years as a respectable woman than I've ever known you before or since. D'you see Miss Delia settling to it any easier?'

'No, perhaps you're right . . . well, if it has to be, let's use some unfair influence to get her started, eh? At least I can fix the best teachers for her.'

It was some time before Charlotte realised Cordelia's interest lay more in singing than acting. She was developing a more youthful version of Charlotte's own smoky voice, but with a vocal range that made her mother sound pedestrian. She agreed reluctantly to go to college, but Charlotte in turn rewarded her with a preliminary year in New York, working on her singing and studying movement and modern dance. It delighted her that she could practise with Delia. Indeed the girl welcomed it and turned to her for advice. Within a few months, Charlotte was fitter than she had been since her days in music hall. The study-dining room at the Greenwich Village apartment had been transformed into a small dance studio and Maud made frequent despairing demands that they should move to a bigger place.

'Oh, maybe later this year, when Delia goes to College,' said Charlotte, adopting what Maud privately called her deliberately vague look. 'You know how I love this apartment. I'd hate to part with it . . .'

Charlotte was scheming about something, and for once Maud found it impossible to guess what it might be. She seemed reluctant to commit herself to any work that involved a long run, and became daily more obstinate about moving to a bigger apartment. Otherwise there was no superficial change in her, but Maud sensed a shift as profound as the one she had begun noticing when Charlotte abruptly threw in her stage career for marriage to Tony Wilde. Maud was deeply disturbed about the whole thing.

CHAPTER THIRTY-FOUR

No doubt about it, good tailoring was hard to beat, Tony Wilde reflected as he flicked a fragment of lint off the sleeve of his jacket. It was the same Abercrombie and Fitch tweed he had put on more than five years ago to set out on his great adventure. It might be sagging and stained now, the lining might be adrift where that bastard railroad thug had dragged him out of the box-car that time, but considering he had worn it non-stop since 1929, it was a miracle of the outfitter's art.

Funny thing about great adventures. They never seemed quite as exciting when you were living them as when they appeared on the printed page. For the hundredth time that week, he wondered if he could decently go home now. Better give it a little longer . . . never knew what you might find . . . amazing how ungracious people could be when they'd had it soft while you were out there surviving all the hardship . . .

His latest meditations on the attractions of hearth and home had been precipitated by a glimpse of a headline in one of the newspapers:

PULITZER PLAY MOVIE WINS
OSCAR NOMINATION
FOR SOCIETY ACTRESS

There couldn't be two of them, he thought, and set off in haphazard pursuit of the man with the newspaper. Eventually it was discarded in a garbage can and he dipped in for it, afterwards going across the road to sit in a barren little park and read the full report.

It seemed Charlotte Wilde could do no wrong. The film version of her Broadway hit had broken box office records in the US and Europe, and now she looked all set to win the Oscar for Best Supporting Actress. God knew where they had got the 'supporting' bit. Even he had read enough about her in discarded papers to know she had carried the whole production. She must be rolling in cash. Those Hollywood studios were willing to pay anything for the right talent and they were still touchingly naive about the selling power of a Broadway name. She probably never needed to work again.

A mean little wind whipped round the corner and pinched at his ankles where the socks had long ago worn to nothing. With it came an echo of the old idea. Why not go back? Why not throw yourself on her mercy? After all, you left for her and Delia's good . . . you were trying to save their faces above all else.

He remained seated there for some time, warmed from within by the fantasy of a hot bath, a good meal and a bed with clean sheets. Eventually, though, he returned to reality. He couldn't blame Charlotte if she felt bitter towards him. There was no real reason for her to scoop him off the streets after he had left her to sink or swim alone. No, better forget it . . . It was a comforting dream more closely connected with the fact that he was sixty-two years old and close to starvation than with any objective reality. Perhaps it was time to take a walk. That usually kept fantasy at bay – simply keeping going was enough to fill the mind.

In Sixth Avenue there were men and women standing in line outside seedy buildings which announced they were employment agencies that placed staff free of charge. Once he might have taken a passing interest. Now he knew better. There were ten million unemployed in America right now, many of them young, smartly turned-out and able-bodied. He was old, sick and shabby. The workers who stood there wore decent clothes; clothes that had never come from Abercrombie and Fitch but which had never been subjected to five years non-stop wear, to rolling in damp ditches and lying in squalid gutters . . .

At present he was more interested in the sign which blossomed over a bar beside the Williams Employment Agency and announced:

FREE FREE FREE! GIANT BEER WITH
FRANKFURTER, FIVE CENTS!

Now, if only he had five cents, that could solve a whole lot of problem.

The thought of food pushed a little adrenalin into his system and he headed east, along Canal Street, moving slowly but steadily with the bum's shuffling walk that respectable people ascribed to drunkenness but more often meant starvation. Finally, a long time later, he was in the Bowery. The late afternoon sunlight reflected on a drunk who lay asleep in the doorway of the Sunshine Hotel. A battered sign announced rooms with electric light for thirty cents a night.

Who needed a room, thought Tony, when thirty cents would buy six FREE FREE FREE large beers with a frankfurter? Momentarily his mind cleared. Damned idiot, he thought. When was the last time you saw five cents, let alone thirty? And why are you down here? If there's any small change in these gutters, the bums who are lying on it will have picked it up long ago. He turned and began to shuffle north, towards the richer pickings of midtown Manhattan.

Somewhere along the line he got lucky. A man in a hurry got out of a taxicab and as he paid the driver, a flurry of small coins scattered. The fellow was obviously pushed for time. He made a half-hearted attempt to pick up some of the money, but then moved off. Tony and another lurking bum slipped in and scavenged the gutter. They left with forty cents apiece.

It was more money than Wilde had seen since he had staggered back into New York five weeks earlier. Almost singing with gratitude, he continued his shaky passage uptown. A little way further he passed a cheap restaurant and realised with a surge of joy that he could buy any dish on the menu. For long minutes he stood outside, salivating as he contemplated pigs' knuckles, snout or head at ten cents a time, roast veal, hamburgers or goulash at fifteen cents, or – joy of joys – sirloin steak at twenty-five cents. Better have the sirloin, he told himself, never know when you'll get the chance again.

He ate a bowl of soup, the steak, coffee and cake, and was left with five cents. 'But worth every cent,' he murmured to himself. 'Worth every goddamned cent!' For a while the food gave him a little strength, and now he struck westward along East Houston. He knew where Charlotte lived; he had stood across the road, watching the building, on two occasions since his return to New York. Why not go and take another peek? Just one last look, then he and his nickel would get on the road again.

After a while, Tony began to wonder if something was wrong. The food sat like lead in his belly, and far from speeding him up, it was making him drag his footsteps. Never could trust those greasy spoons. They'd probably poisoned him in exchange for his little hoard of dimes . . . never mind. He'd sit for a while in Washington Square. It was a pleasant evening. Unless the cops were keeping too close an eye on things, he might even manage to curl up and sleep there.

Charlotte's apartment was in a street just south-east of the square, and he told himself he had to pass through it to get to the park itself. But once he had the neat brownstone in view, his will was paralysed. By now he really felt quite sick, and the feverish dreams in his head cleared occasionally long enough for him to assure himself that his wife would never forgive him if he failed to enlist her help in such circumstances. At seven-thirty that evening, he pressed the doorbell of the Wilde apartment.

Charlotte was just putting the finishing touches on her appearance before leaving for a dinner engagement. Cordelia jumped up when the bell rang and called: 'Don't worry, Maudie, I'll get it!'

She flung open the front door, still halfway through a snatch of conversation with her mother, and froze as she saw the man outside. He smiled at her lopsidedly for a few seconds, said: 'Hello, dear Cordelia. I've come home.' Then he collapsed on the doormat.

The next hour was a blur in Cordelia's mind. She let out a scream – half shock at seeing her father, half horror at his collapse – and Charlotte came running. Cordelia stood back, aghast, as her mother took in the situation at a glance, bent over the man in the hallway and put her ear to his chest. Then she loosened his filthy collar, forced his mouth open and stuck her fingers down his throat to clear any obstruction. Cordelia thought she would throw up herself, although she realised Charlotte was trying to help him breathe.

She squatted back and started looking around for something to put under his head. 'The doctor, Delia – for pity's sake call Dr Crane!'

By the time Cordelia returned from the phone, Maud had joined her mother in the hallway and her father had been positioned comfortably. His colour was dreadful – a weird combination of bluish and yellow tones – and his breathing so faint as to be scarcely discernible. But he was still alive, and by now Cordelia had realised her mother had been trying to ensure he did not choke. The doctor lived little more than a block away, and he was there minutes later. He examined Wilde and then helped the women move him into Charlotte's bed.

'Not much point in getting him to the hospital right now,' he told Charlotte. 'By the look of him, it was a slight heart attack which wouldn't have given a fitter man more than a bit of nasty pain. But there's nothing of him to withstand it. I'm surprised he survived – in fact, if you hadn't waded in as you did, Mrs Wilde, he probably wouldn't have.'

Charlotte was gazing at the emaciated figure on the bed. 'I'm beginning to wonder why I did wade in,' she said, then clapped her hand over her mouth as Cordelia, who had heard her, turned and left the room. 'Anyway, Doctor, what should I do now?'

'Your guess is as good as mine. I'm still not sure how much of it is a heart condition and how much is old-fashioned starvation. Judging by the way he vomited out there, he'd had a meal for the first time in days. Probably made a pig of himself . . . always a mistake in these circumstances. Look, my dear, I'll be quite frank with you – I know you've been separated from the man for years – he looks to me to be worn right out. He may recover some of his health and live ten years, although he's never going to be strong again. On the other hand, he could snuff out within days.'

He prescribed various drugs and left, promising to come back next day. Cordelia went off to the pharmacy to fill the prescriptions, and Charlotte sat with Maud in the living room, both of them with large glasses of whisky.

'So what happens now?' Maud said eventually.

'God only knows . . . one thing's sure, though. I'm not supporting the bastard – once was enough to clear up his mess.'

'You are a strange girl, Lottie. You saved the bugger's life out there on the landing.'

Charlotte snorted her indignation. 'Think I'm not realising it? I could have kicked myself when I realised what I'd done! My brain is as tough as old boots, but my instincts are still a bloody sight too soft, and they were what saved him.'

'How are you going to kick him out, if he gets better? You saw how Miss Cordelia behaved.'

'Oh, yes, I did. I suppose there'd be only one way: I'd have to give the swine an allowance. Anything to keep him away from me.'

The apartment door slammed. Maud pressed a finger to her lips. 'Careful, here's Miss Delia now.'

When Antony Wilde awoke, it appeared he had achieved the fantasy of a clean, warm haven he had conjured for himself earlier that day. He held up his hands. Spotless, although the nails were still worn and ragged. Someone appeared to have found him a set of pyjamas, and the sheets that caressed his skin were fine cotton. Gradually, he remembered something of what had happened. He had the absurd notion that somewhere in all the confusion of being taken ill, Charlotte had embraced and caressed him. Surely that must have been a dream?

Abruptly, he realised he was not alone. Glancing sideways, he found his daughter was sitting by the bedside. Even in his present sorry state, he was able to appreciate what a beauty she had become. God, what a family! Had he not known better, he would have thought the nineteen-year-old Lottie Casanova was beside him.

'Darling girl! Oh, you'll never know how I missed you!' he said.

She remained silent. He resorted to an old joke they had shared – *King Lear*, the play from which Charlotte had chosen Cordelia's name. When she was a child, they had taken pride in learning snatches and throwing it back

322

and forth between themselves as a private piece of father and daughter patter. It had driven Charlotte mad because she always felt excluded. Now he drew on their favourite exchange, normally used when she had been cheeky to him: 'So young, and so untender?'

Unblinking, she returned the next line: 'So young, my lord, and true.'

He felt as if she had slapped him. 'But not to me, by your tone.'

She sighed, got up and moved away across the room, no longer looking at him. 'Oh, you had it all, at the beginning. I gave Mother a terrible time, blamed her for everything that happened in 1929. I hurt her terribly, and she didn't deserve it . . . pretended I thought she'd driven you away, when all the time I knew really she was going mad trying to salvage something for us.

'I never managed to make it up to her, either. She just thinks I was impressed when she made it on the stage, and forgave her for being rotten to you. That's not true, though I shall probably never screw up the courage to tell her. What really happened was that I grew up enough to see through you. Big brave daddies don't go off and leave wives and favourite daughters to the wolves. They stay and fight it out for them. You ran, Daddy.'

Now he turned his face away, and felt the hot tears of self-pity spill from his eyes as he pressed his face against the pillow. She was approaching the bed again. 'I love you. I'll always love you, but don't expect all of me. As you're still tied up in that *King Lear* game, you might as well have the next bit: "I return those duties back as are right fit." '

'And no more?'

'And no more. I find I've used all the rest up on Mother the past few years. In case you've forgotten, she was there when I needed someone. Goodnight, Daddy. Sleep well.' She left one cool kiss on his forehead and then went to find Charlotte.

Antony St John Wilde died of heart failure in his wife's bed at her apartment on the night of May 13, 1935. Charlotte and Cordelia Wilde and Maud Lewis were the only mourners at his funeral. No one wept.

'I feel guilty because I don't feel guilty, Mother. Does that sound too silly?'

Charlotte squeezed her daughter's hand. 'I'm too damned relieved to care,' she said. 'I know how much your father meant to you when you were a child, and I was terrified that this awful episode might turn you against me a second time.'

Cordelia blushed. 'Was I utterly dreadful?'

'Pretty bad, actually. But you were only thirteen years old and you didn't even know one side of it, let alone both. I wanted to tell you the truth, but I hated my own mother so much I was half convinced you'd end up feeling the same about me.'

'Why did you hate her?'

'D'you know, I often ask myself that? When I look back on it now, there seems no very good reason. The only one that springs to mind is that she was the most appalling hypocrite I ever met, and she was determined to turn me into a carbon copy.'

Cordelia laughed. 'Well she certainly failed at that! I've never met anyone as straight as you.'

Suddenly, Charlotte was crying. 'Oh, my dear, dear Delia! I love you so, you'll never know how much. If this dreadful business with poor Tony achieved nothing else, at least it brought us together properly.' She dried her eyes, got up and went to pour herself a drink. 'I've been thinking. Instead of dashing off to Vassar in the Autumn, how would you like a year or two in England?'

'Why, I – I don't know. I'd need to think about it. It certainly sounds like a great idea. But what brought this on? Surely not fleeing the awful memory of Daddy?'

'God, no! The poor man lacked even the power to drive me away at the very end. No, I've been offered a good part in London, and to tell the truth, I've been missing England for a long time now. So has old Maudie, come to that. I think she'd like to end her days on her native heath.'

'Have you ever been back since you married Daddy? I seem to recall when I was tiny, you took a trip one summer.'

Charlotte chuckled. 'Fancy you remembering that! You can't have been more than seven at the time, and I was gone less than a month.'

'You did go to England, though, didn't you?'

'Oh, I did indeed. And what I saw there made me come beetling back with no desire to pay a return visit for a long, long time.'

'Had it changed so much?'

'Well, perhaps, in some ways, but it wasn't that. You see, I went to take a look at my mother.'

'And you were reconciled?'

'I'll forgive you for that, as you have no way of even suspecting what Mama was like! I didn't say I went to *meet* her. I said I went to take a look at her.' She paused, vivid memories flooding back. 1924, summer, and she had seen a snippet in one of the English magazines which were mailed to her each month, about a resort with an aristocratic accent.

The article had referred to a small group of legendary Victorian figures who met for a week each year in Eastbourne's best hotel, to exchange family news, enjoy the sea air and play cards together. They were portrayed, affectionately, as the last survivors of an order which had passed away. Laura Cazenove, Lady Ilchester, was mentioned as a regular member of the group.

Charlotte experienced a pang of regret when she read the magazine. Her father had died, without her ever knowing! But then, what else could she expect? To the family, she herself had been dead for nearly thirty years. Even if they had wished to inform her, how could they have done so? She began to soften towards her mother, and that was when she decided to make the trip to England. The article had been about English resorts in general, an introductory piece published before the start of the summer season. The group of friends would not have taken their holiday yet . . . the feature even mentioned the dates they were normally in Eastbourne.

Three weeks later she was wondering why she had bothered. It was a grey, wet summer in England. The hotel was comfortable enough, but the guests were fractious because they were unable to go out as often as they wished, and a general air of discontent hung over the entire establishment. Charlotte had taken the precaution of registering at another hotel further along the sea front. She did not think her mother would recognise her after all those years, but it would be pushing her luck to share dining room and reception area with Laura.

When she first saw her, Charlotte was deeply relieved to be staying some-where else. She might have been looking at her own reflection, with a couple of decades added. Laura Cazenove was still in excellent shape, although her hair was iron grey now and there were lines around her lovely eyes. No one could have mistaken them for anything but mother and daughter, and Charlotte had a number of embarrassing moments as hotel staff glanced at her, then looked again, trying to work out where they had seen her before.

As it happened, she did not need to stay long. One afternoon tucked away in a quiet corner of the Palm Court was more than enough. Laura was at the other end of the room, playing cards with three of her clique from the old days. As Charlotte eavesdropped on the conversation, she began to feel she had been thrown back to the 1890s at Lyonesse. A world war, widowhood, and, presumably, a decline in her fortunes, had made not a jot of difference to Laura. She still called servants James. She still believed the world was at her beck and call. She still regretted, in a gentle voice tempered with steel, that other people lacked the cultivated standards of her group.

Charlotte sat, wretched, over her cooling pot of tea, wondering what on earth she had expected to find in this windswept seaside town. Laura Cazenove was being herself. In order to change, people had to believe there was something wrong with the way they were in the first place, Charlotte reminded herself, and Laura was always the first to acknowledge that she was perfect.

Furious with herself for letting it matter so much, Charlotte stood up and hurried out of the Palm Court, less careful than when she came in about being seen. Arthur Kemble, a lifelong admirer of Laura, glanced up as she passed some yards from their table.

'Good heavens, Laura!' he murmured, staring at Charlotte's retreating back. 'If you hadn't been sitting opposite me, I'd have said that was your spirit, from twenty years ago, come back to dazzle us!'

Laura glanced up, peevishly rejected all comparisons, then looked away. 'Really, Arthur, sometimes you amaze me! How could a woman with such an unutterably vulgar walk resemble me in any way?'

Cordelia was staring at her mother. 'You went all that way and only peered at her through a lot of palm trees? Why on earth did you bother?'

Charlotte shrugged. 'You tell me . . . guilt perhaps. Although I detested her when I was a girl, as I got older, I wondered if I'd misunderstood her, and I came to think that if I had, I'd put her through a hell she never deserved.'

'And how did you feel after the visit?'

Charlotte laughed grimly. 'She deserved all she got – but I'm sure my abrupt departure from Lyonesse gave her more pleasure than anything else. I always thought my mother was a twenty-four carat bitch, and when I saw her in old age it confirmed that feeling.'

'And yet you're talking now of going back to England. Seems to me you'd be happier if you kept an ocean between you.'

'Mmm, you're right. But Mama died three weeks ago. There was an announcement in the London *Times*. I got the paper a few days ago.'

'But you never said a word!'

'No reason why I should, surely, in the light of what I've just told you? I didn't say anything, but I've been doing a lot of thinking, and my main conclusion was that now she's gone, I should very much like to go back. As you've never seen England at all, I thought you might like it too.'

'You're right. I would.'

'The only thing that bothers me is what it will do to your ambitions for a career. I know you're nerving yourself to start looking for work.'

'Oh, that won't be a drawback! Here I'm just another pretty New Yorker. Over there, think of it, I'll be an American Jazz Baby! They should be falling over themselves to book me!'

Charlotte put her hands to her face in mock horror. 'With this family's record, I might have known there was something in it for you!'

CHAPTER THIRTY-FIVE

London was a dream come true. The welcome Charlotte got from the newspapers, in clubs and restaurants, and even from people she met in the street, showed her that Lottie Casanova was still fresh in the Englishman's memory. Her movie and stage appearances had provided the stimulus to thrust the old music hall favourite back to the forefront of popular consciousness, and now they could not get enough of her.

A big part of her new popularity stemmed from her refusal to go along with the artificial, slightly precious revival dubbed Old Time Music Hall by admirers who should have known better, which was flourishing as a cult at small theatres in central London and the bigger cities.

Charlotte wanted none of it. To her, the real thing was as outdated as last year's popular songs, and its only place in modern entertainment was in one-off revivals, not in regular, inaccurate, reconstructions. Instead she turned to West End theatre for her main work, and spiced it with occasional nightclub appearances. Her name was guaranteed to elicit the offer of bookings at such plum spots as the Café de Paris. Cordelia, now working her way up the ladder as Dee-Dee Wilde, singing blues in small clubs for even smaller fees, often joked that she would sell her parent into slavery to get the engagements for herself.

Charlotte's first theatrical role on her return to England was that of a matriarch, once a great beauty, who was coming to terms with the loss of looks and influence as her family grew up and left the nest. The main action centred around the three sons whose views of their mother shifted dramatically during the course of the play, but there was a good supporting ingénue role in the woman's daughter, a beautiful girl very like her mother, whom the mother resented because she saw her own looks fade as the younger woman blossomed into womanhood.

Charlotte found it impossible to resist the temptation to suggest Dee-Dee for the role. Cordelia herself was reticent about it. 'Mother, I'm no actress, and you know it. Some day I think I'll make a better singer than you ever were, but when it comes to the rest of it, you could act me off the stage – or dance me off, for that matter.'

'You'll be acting *with* me, not in competition, you little idiot,' said Charlotte, determined not to be thwarted. 'At least audition for it. The director is really keen.'

Reluctantly, Dee-Dee agreed. The two were so alike physically that she certainly looked the part. But she was right and Charlotte was wrong. On her lips, the daughter's lines refused to come to life. The director was polite but noncommittal. The startling mother-daughter resemblance was a big bonus, but unless they were desperate, he did not think it strong enough to overcome Dee-Dee's weakness as an actress.

327

Maud had come along to keep the women company. Now well into her seventies, she had resumed English theatrical life with relish, uncaring whether it was variety or legitimate theatre. 'The grease-paint and dust smells just as lovely either way,' she told Dee-Dee. 'I love being backstage, simple as that.'

Now she sat, like a theatrical mother, watching her two charges, Dee-Dee and Charlotte. Charlotte was on stage, cueing each actress who auditioned as the daughter in a scene with her. Dee-Dee sat down beside Maud and whispered: 'That was really humiliating. I do wish Mother hadn't insisted.'

'Couldn't agree more, love,' said Maud. 'You're a terrific little singer and you know it. Horses for courses, I say. Mind you, unless they find a real corker, you may get lumbered wiv it yet.'

'Heaven forbid! I think I'd have a nervous breakdown if I had to do that every night.'

But Maud was no longer listening. Her attention was riveted on the stage and she muttered, 'Jesus Christ All-bloody-mighty, I don't believe it!'

Dee-Dee followed her gaze and there, onstage, was a girl who could have been her sister. The actress's appearance seemed to have fazed Charlotte as much as Maud, for she glanced sharply backstage as though to reassure herself that Dee-Dee had not returned for a second crack at the part. Then she recovered her aplomb and cued the new arrival.

The girl acted like a dream. She was the epitome of the formerly biddable, sweet child, who begins to feel her power as she crosses the threshold to womanhood, and embarks on a female struggle with her mother every bit as ferocious as any male rite of passage.

The scene ended and the director said: 'Thank you, Miss . . .' he consulted his call-sheet '. . . Miss Farrell. Perhaps you'd care to stay behind afterwards. Next, please!'

As he read out the name, Charlotte swivelled to face Maud, her eyes round, her mouth a perfect 'O'. Her expression was so comical that Dee-Dee started laughing. 'What on earth's got into Mother?' she asked Maud.

Maud was grinning too, as she said: 'A slight touch o' the old Nemesis, I think.'

Charlotte's instant, thunderstruck guess was correct. The girl, Mary Farrell, was the daughter of Ulick Farrell and Tina Minoli. She looked almost as much like Dee-Dee as her mother had resembled Lottie at about that age.

'I think some Cazenove went philanderin' in Clerkenwell a coupla generations back,' said Maud. 'They couldn't look that similar unless they're related somewhere. My Gawd, your mother will be livid!'

But Charlotte was surprisingly equable about it. 'Of course she'll get the part,' she said, 'and much as I'd like you to have it, Dee-Dee, I have to admit the girl was born to act. She's brilliant.'

At the end to the session, the director auditioned Mary Farrell and another of the brighter hopefuls again. There was no real contest, and Mary was offered the part on the spot. Beaming with pleasure, she was turning to leave when Charlotte called after her: 'Miss Farrell! Just a minute . . . If you're not in too much of a hurry, would you care to come and have a celebratory drink?'

The girl turned back, confused. 'I – well, that is . . .' she glanced in some embarrassment at Dee-Dee, who promptly burst out laughing.

'Don't worry about offending me,' she said. 'My audition was mother's idea. I knew I never had a hope in hell.'

In a pub down the road from the theatre, Charlotte said: 'I'm going to be abominably nosey. Please tell me about yourself.'

Mary looked down at her hands, square and stubby as Charlotte remembered her mother's. 'I – I know about you, Mrs Wilde. Mum told me she didn't think I had a prayer of getting this role because of you . . .'

'Well I'm damned, the cheeky little cow!' Maud broke in, before Charlotte silenced her.

'Hardly surprising, really,' said Charlotte, quite unruffled. 'I didn't exactly help her own theatrical career, did I, Maudie?'

Maud glared at her rebelliously but Charlotte's expression willed her to keep to herself any comments about lack of talent, suicide attempts and blackmailing men into marriage.

'What about your father?' Now it was Charlotte's turn to sound hesitant.

Mary looked her straight in the eye. 'You knew him. You knew how he drank. He gave up for a long time, but he went back to it in the late twenties. He came out of the Café Royal one lunchtime, too plastered to see, and went straight under a car. Didn't even live to get to hospital.' There was no sentimentality in the voice. She had probably suffered enough as a child from Ulick's drinking to have precious little tenderness left for him now.

'And your mother? I hope she's all right.'

'Oh, yes, fine. The ironical thing is that once Dad was gone, the royalties off his songs kept her in much better style than she ever enjoyed while he was alive. It's the only thing that got me to theatrical school, I can tell you that now. I still live at home – Dad's old flat in Henrietta Street.'

Good God, how's that for a full circle? Charlotte thought. Beneath the shock at Ulick's savage end, she felt a twinge of relief. No room for regrets there . . . if she had been tempted to think in might-have-been terms about herself and Ulick instead of Tony Wilde, what she had just heard ended any such fantasy. Her tribulations were nothing compared to the prospect of a drunken husband and a life of scrimping. She smiled at Mary Farrell with genuine liking. 'Well, Mary, I'm sure you and I are going to get on famously. You're a splendid actress . . . so good, I don't think I'd care for you so much if we were the same age! Anyway, cheers, and let's hope *Growing Pains* is a big success.'

It was. Nothing could repeat the pile driver impact of Charlotte's first Broadway role, but *Growing Pains* did her proud. *The Times'* critic wrote: 'This is where Mrs Wilde proves she can be as effective in a quietly powerful role as in expressing emotional pyrotechnics. Her control and range speak volumes of a rigorous training in a harder theatrical school than the present generation will ever experience.'

'Now isn't that nice?' said Charlotte, setting aside the paper and getting back to her breakfast the morning after the first night. 'Maudie, I think as everyone's being so lovely to me, we might think about doing a bit of house-hunting and moving out of this hotel. I have a feeling we're going to be here quite some time.'

It was Dee-Dee who spotted the full page advertisement in that week's *Country Life*. Under the heading A RARE OPPORTUNITY, the advertisement announced the auction, prior to sale of the estate itself, of the contents of Lyonesse, Wiltshire, country seat of Lord Ilchester. Viewing would be on the two days preceding the sale, in just over a fortnight. Fortunately Cordelia did not see the impact of the auction announcement on her mother. She had left the magazine folded open at the appropriate page, with a note saying, 'House-hunters could do worse!' For some reason, it was something Charlotte preferred to contemplate alone.

She sat and stared at the photograph of the main drawing room at Lyonesse, frozen by the camera just as she remembered it all those years ago. She wondered if it was a contemporary picture from her mother's day. It was hard to believe the house still stood unaltered after so many years. She felt like Alice, up on the mantelpiece, about to step through the looking glass into another world. But where was her resentment? What had happened to her contempt for this monument to her mother's taste and her father's wealth, to the overweening pretentiousness of them both? Apparently gone without trace. She found herself looking at the photograph with something like affection.

She sat thinking about Lyonesse all morning, and finally came to a decision. She telephoned Enquiries at Paddington and discovered she could travel to Handford and back by early evening, so she would have no trouble in getting to the theatre in time. It would mean a return trip if she intended to do any bidding at the auction, but she had something in mind which might make that unnecessary. Charlotte studied the small print again: 'By direction of the Earl of Ilchester . . .' Was that Tristram, or his son? she wondered. And were they so impoverished they had to sell? It was hard to imagine even the Great War and the agricultural Depression draining all the resources of such a rich inheritance. Still, she would soon see.

It was a brilliant day in late spring when she got off the train at Handford Station. It was unchanged since the day of her inspired sprint after Ulick Farrell's train – how long? – heavens, forty years ago. The mass of flowers still crowded the tiny beds of the station master's garden. The big platform lamps were still gas-fuelled, the ticket barrier still a wicket gate. What a comfortable, welcoming little place it was, and how she had once longed to be out of it!

The station master, a kindly man clearly bursting with curiosity, told her the only cars available for hire in the village were those of the undertaker, so she would have to travel in style whether she wanted to or not. He would telephone Prout Brothers on her behalf and ask them to send along a vehicle. Where would Madam be wanting to go?

She explained she wished to view Lyonesse before the contents auction, but would like to speak with Lord Ilchester first, if the station master had any idea where she might find him. For the first time, it occurred to Charlotte that he might no longer live in the area. Now that could pose problems . . . but no, it was all right. His Lordship had moved to the Dower House after his mother died and they closed the big house.

Mother? Charlotte mused as Prout's black funeral limousine headed for the Lyonesse dower house. Then it must be Tristram . . . strange there was no mention of a wife.

A manservant opened the front door at the dower house, and Charlotte asked him to announce Mrs Wilde. Moments later, a grizzled figure hurried into the entrance hall. 'Charty! Charty, my dear girl, after all these years!' The man enveloped her in a bear hug and she fought an impulse to cry.

When he finally stood back, she looked into his face and said: 'It's not Tristram . . . Oh, Ivo darling! I thought – I assumed it would be Tris.'

Ivo Cazenove glanced at the stone-faced manservant and uttered a small chuckle. 'I say, I think we'd better go off and talk in the drawing room like polite people. Poor Hawkins doesn't think this is good form at all!' And he led the way to a sunny sitting room.

It was a sad story. Laura Cazenove had continued to dominate her family after her daughter's departure. Her social set and her attitudes remained unchanged, although society altered cataclysmically around them. When the Great War came, her sons were thirty and thirty-five. Tristram had been married three years, but was childless as yet. Ivo, who was the only one of the family to take a practical interest in running the estate, was still single and spent most of his time at Lyonesse.

'Of course, with Mama virtually waggling the cross of St George at us and crying "Excelsior!", we both felt we had to volunteer, although our ages alone would have kept us a reasonable way down the conscription list. When they examined me, they discovered I had some sort of congenital lung deformity . . . it never troubled me from that day to this, but it seems to have saved my life. Poor Tristram went to Flanders with the Grenadiers. He was killed within three months. Mother, of course, behaved as if every right-thinking woman should give at least one son for England. Papa went into a long, quiet decline, and just faded away, really. He died shortly after the War. By then, Mama seemed so dependent on me that I somehow never got round to striking out on me own . . . sounds pretty feeble, really, doesn't it?

It made Charlotte's flesh crawl, remembering the courageous younger brother who had always wanted to try new things and explore new pastures. Here he was, in his fifties, tied to the same bit of England he'd been born in, with no intimate memories beyond those created by their monstrous mother.

'But what happened about the estate?' she asked. 'I've come to view the place, after seeing the *Country Life* advertisement. Are times so bad you have to sell up?'

He had been looking gloomy, but this made him smile again. 'God, no! I'll never be short of a bob or two. But you must appreciate what it's like. I've been locked up in the place with Mama all my life, because it suited her, not me. Since she died, I've been rattling around in it on my own, hating it. So I finally decided, the hell with tradition! The name and title die with me. I'll sell up, keep the dower house, and get a nice place in town. Then I can enjoy London and the country as I please, and maybe go abroad a bit too.'

He leaned forward, almost as though confiding a secret. 'To tell the truth, I'm looking forward to it like mad. Talk about power without responsibility!'

'Oh, Ivo, I hope you'll be happy. God knows, you deserve it.' She studied him fondly for a moment, then said, hesitantly: 'Did you hate me for going off like that?'

He laughed. 'Quite the reverse, old thing! Mama was so furious for such a long time it was worth it for the show alone! I missed you like mad, but somehow I'd always felt you weren't meant to stay here.'

'And after I went? Did they ever find out about me?'

'In a manner of speaking. Papa tried to make tactful enquiries without alerting the world to your having gone off like that, but it came to nothing. Then Tris started becoming a man about town after he went up to the University, and that really put the cat among the pigeons. He went to that hall with two names . . . what was it? Old something? That's it – the Royal Standard, but he called it the Old Mo'. And my dear, there you were, hurling yourself around the stage in that astonishing dance of yours.

'I gather it almost gave poor Tristram heart failure. I'm afraid he turned into a real prig about some things. He came storming home and told all, and after that no one who valued their skin mentioned music hall in front of Mama and Papa. Tris discovered a deep-seated love for opera and Shakespeare and never strayed over the threshold of a palace of varieties again.'

'So they *did* know! I wonder what Mama made of it.'

Ivo gave a schoolboy chortle. 'To tell you the truth, I suspect she was jealous. You know Mama. Her idea of paradise was to be in permanent occupation of the limelight. And that was literally what you achieved. Of course, she must have known about you becoming famous all over again in the proper theatre, because it was all over the papers when you got the Oscar nomination. But she flatly refused to discuss it. I sometimes think that when she finally expired, it was pure outrage at having seen the poster for *Come To Dust* outside a cinema in Salisbury when I drove her there a few days before she died.'

Charlotte put her arms around him. 'Oh, darling, it's so lovely to see you again, and to know you don't mind about me – what I've been and so on. It *is* nice to find I still have a bit of a family!'

He produced a handkerchief and blew his nose, then started fussing about the room in embarrassment at his own emotion. 'Same here, old girl . . . we mustn't lose touch now.' With relief he seized on a safer subject. 'But what brought you down now, of all times? Did you mean what you said about the auction preview?'

Charlotte said: 'I find it difficult to believe myself, but after all these years, Lyonesse is drawing me like a magnet. I'm planning to settle back in England, and I'm seriously considering the possibility of buying the whole thing.'

'Oh, dear girl! I have an awful feeling you're too late!'

'Too late? I don't understand you. The auction isn't until tomorrow and the house has just gone on the market.'

'I know. This really is too much. A chap came along yesterday to view the furnishings, then his solicitor telephoned and said he wanted to make an offer for the lot – house and contents – and offered me a price which would be hard to beat at auction. Oh, Charty, I said yes this morning!' Then his gloomy expression lightened somewhat. 'As a matter of fact, the chap is up at the house now. Asked if it would be all right to come for another nose around and I said yes. He seems a decent enough type. Perhaps if you explained the circumstances, he might reconsider. You can but try.'

'I can indeed. I've no intention of being thwarted at the last minute after taking so long to come round to the view that home is where the heart is!' Charlotte started moving out into the hall.

Ivo followed her. 'Perhaps I should come with you, introduce you to the fellow if he's still there. The caretaker let him in an hour or so ago.'

'No, that's all right, Ivo. I'll beard him on my own. I don't want you feeling I've put unfair pressure on while you're in the middle of a deal.'

'As you wish. Now you're here, though, Charty, you must lunch with me. Bring His Nibs back, too, if you've settled something with him. His name's Shaw – Sir Thomas Shaw.'

'Hmm, not a brewer or car tycoon then?'

'Oh, no, but he's certainly NQOCD – made his reputation in some branch of theatre, actually . . . been back and forth to Australia for years. No, the title is one of those "for conspicuous achievement" things, colonial version.'

Charlotte shook her head and laughed. 'Ivo, I love you dearly, but you've turned into the most incorrigible old snob! I'm half expecting to encounter a clog-dancing sheep shearer with corks around his hat!'

'He's frightfully smart, actually – neat but not gaudy, as Nanny would have said. Now, off you go and see if the Cazenove charm is still up to scratch.'

She pulled a face at him. 'No more Laura, remember? Now it's the *Wilde* charm!'

Funny, she thought, I expected it to be smaller . . . it's every bit as big and grand as I remember it. By God, though, the old cow had good taste! It still looks wonderful. Charlotte wandered through the great drawing room, with its eight windows spilling primrose sunlight onto the blue and grey washed Chinese carpet. The furniture was from Sweden, elegant but sturdy beechwood, painted in the same soft grey as the carpet and decorated in a yellow that her mother must have known would echo the colour of the spring sunshine. Off beyond the house, she could just glimpse the orangery. Oh, dear, what a volume of romantic secrets that place must hold!

She moved out of the great room, along the gallery-hallway which ran the length of the ground floor, until eventually she stood at the door of the orangery. It was open . . . the mysterious Sir Thomas must be in here, looking around. No one would leave a conservatory door open this early in the year. Charlotte crossed the threshold and instantly stepped back into a Victorian world. Any minute now, she thought, one of Mama's suitors will step out from behind a palm tree and announce he's been lost in here since 1898. She moved along the stone-flagged paths, designed to twist and turn among the tropical plants and produce the effect of an exotic outdoor land-scape rather than an enclosed greenhouse.

Eventually the path widened into a seating area, furnished with ornate wrought iron benches. Why, this was where Mama had sat while Ulick attempted to seduce her with Swinburne . . . Charlotte wondered how long palms lived, and whether the one she was staring at was the same as the specimen behind which she had hidden to spy on the lovers.

Abruptly she grew tired of the stuffy claustrophobic place and hurried on to the double doors which separated the winter garden from the orangery proper. She had always preferred the scent of the orange trees to the humidity of the palm house. Inside the orangery, she strolled across to one of the tall, elegant windows which framed a perfect view of the park. Gazing down the rolling lawns towards the South Lake, she murmured: 'I could be really happy here, now.'

'Could you? Don't you think it's a bit big for just one person?'

Charlotte turned with a sharp gasp of surprise. 'Oh, you startled me – you must be the man my brother . . .' She was looking directly at him now and her words faltered and died. 'Sir Thomas Shaw . . . Sir Tommy Fanshaw – Tommy, tell me I'm making it up!'

'Can't tell you no lies, Lottie girl – wouldn't be right, would it?'

The voice which had startled her seconds before had been transformed from perfect unaccented English to broad cockney. The man before her was about six feet tall and broader in the shoulders than half-starved Tommy Fanshaw, but the mischievous bright grey eyes were Tommy's, although they now shone in a heavily suntanned face with lines around temples and mouth. The spiky brown hair was sleek and peppered with grey, but the brilliant even-toothed smile was pure Wilson Street. Charlotte found she was no longer able to move. All she could manage to say was 'Tommy. Oh, Tommy . . .'

He stepped forward, said: 'It's all right, now, Lottie – everything's all right, believe me.' And kissed her.

After a long time she stood back from his arms and said: 'I've been waiting forty years for that.'

His eyes searched her face. 'Are you sure? If I'd been sure, we would have caught up with each other before now.'

She was bewildered. 'How? I never had a breath of you. I thought that Ulick must have finished you for the stage, and I didn't know where to start looking sooner.'

Tommy laughed. 'Farrell didn't quite have the guts to shaft me all the way. He let me go and pretended you'd gone home to your family, so I never came looking for you. Once I'd lost you, I wanted to get shot of England and I went off to Australia to make my fortune. I did, too. I got bigger and bigger and it was pretty obvious I'd never make a living from dancing at this size, so I went over to the choreography and production side. Within a couple of years I was running about six companies of girl precision dancers in Australia, like John Tiller's choruses over here.

'I nearly caught up with you in San Francisco, when I was on tour there with my lead troupe. You wanted special coaching, remember?'

'Good God, yes – Tom Shaw! I'd quite forgotten. But if you knew then, why . . .'

'Your friend, agent – whatever you called her, I think her name was Scully. When I came for you and you'd gone, she told me you'd just had your heart broken.' He sighed. 'I thought, come on, Tommy lad, pull yourself together. You may be in love still, but not the lady. Too much has happened to her. So instead of running after you across the States, I picked up my dance troupe, finished the tour and then off we all went back to Australia. I even made her swear not to tell you I'd shown up and said who I really was. I think she was carried away by the star-crossed lovers bit – either that or she thought you had enough on your plate already without yet another broken love affair come home to roost.'

Lottie was staring at him, aghast. 'I loved Ada Scully better than my own mother, but if I had her here now, I'd break her neck for that! Oh, Tom, all those lost years! If I'd known then that you were looking for me . . . ' She snapped away from the awful loss, unable, now, to absorb its full significance. 'What did you do with yourself afterwards?'

Gradually his life took shape in Charlotte's imagination. Back in Sydney, Tommy had started investing his dance troupe profits in bricks and mortar. Within ten years he had a string of theatres in Australia's major cities. By then cinema was becoming a strong contender against variety, and he went into the movie house business too. By the 1920s he was ready to expand into Europe, and returned to London to start investing in British cinemas.

'Ever since then, I've been shuttling between Sydney and London,' he said. 'The only reason you haven't run into me until now was that I was reorganising my holdings over there because I'd decided to settle here more or less permanently.'

'What made you do that, the knighthood?'

'Don't be daft, Lottie! It was a long time ago, but you knew me well enough even then to realise something like that wouldn't matter much to me. It was you.'

'Me – after all these years?'

'There's never been anyone else. Oh, there've been women, lots of them. You can't be in my business with healthy appetites and avoid it. But never anyone permanent. I never met anyone to touch you, Lottie. And when you filmed *Come To Dust* . . .' his eyes were misty. 'I got my own special print, extra to the ones we had for the cinemas, and I used to run it over and over again. I probably know your lines better than you do.

'I was getting ready to come to New York and lay siege to you, and then, out of the blue, I read a newspaper story saying you were coming to act on the London stage. That was when I got moving to tie up the loose ends in Sydney and get back here sharpish.'

'You're here because of me?'

'Best reason I can imagine being here for.'

'But Tommy, I just said, it's nearly forty years . . .'

'And *I* just said, in all that time there's never been anyone to touch you. I don't think I ever really dared ask myself what you might remember of me. Should I ask now?'

Her eyes were dreamy. 'Oh, yes. You were never as far away from me as you thought. At first, it was easy to push you out, but later . . . later, when I realised I'd jumped into a very flat marriage on the strength of a good lay and a general dissatisfaction with my career, *then* you came back to me. Sometimes I wished you wouldn't. I'd dream I was a girl again – this was when I was married, with a little daughter, remember – and running home to you, up those stairs in Wilson Street, something I never really did at all. And you'd be waiting, and it would be warm and safe . . .'

She had become wildly animated as she told him this. Now she slumped a little. '. . . Then I'd wake, to my exquisitely tasteful bedroom, and my frightfully sophisticated husband, and wonder why I felt so sad. And half way through the morning, I'd remember I'd been dreaming of you again. Oh, Tommy, you never left me, whatever you may have thought. In fact, I'm almost afraid this is a dream!'

335

'Maybe it is.' But his easy smile belied his words. 'You weren't the only one who dreamed. But somehow, my dream cut me off from a lot of the realities of life. Yours seems to have let you go on with that.'

'You wouldn't be so sure if you had any idea what reality consisted of with Tony Wilde. It was more like playing twenty-odd years in Drury Lane panto than anything else.' She shivered. 'Sometimes I think of it now and wonder if I spent the time in mothballs. It's only my lovely Delia who brings me back down to earth. At least she's tangible proof I was alive all that time. I've precious little else to show for it.'

'Oh, Lottie, I wish I'd known this before – even a year ago, let alone all that time back. D'you know, when I arrived in England and saw *Growing Pains*, even after deciding what I was going to do, I started getting cold feet? I thought, what if we meet, and she doesn't want me – worse, doesn't even remember me? So I kept putting off the contact. And then I saw Lyonesse up for sale.

'I came here, you know, after Ulick split us up. He said they'd run me off if I showed my face, but I wasn't going to let that stop me. I came down, managed to slip inside the grounds, and took a good look around. Then I asked some questions, and it turned out you weren't there at all. The chap at the station said you'd gone off and he reckoned they'd brought you back on the quiet and sent you abroad. I was so green I believed every word . . . Anyway, when Lyonesse went up for sale, I decided if I couldn't have you, I'd have the house. I offered on it yesterday afternoon. To tell the truth, if you hadn't arrived today, I think eventually I'd have nerved myself to come and offer you the house on a plate – you know, to try and attract your attention . . .'

He stopped speaking. Charlotte continued to gaze at him. After a time he became uneasy. 'Come on, then, Lottie – say something.'

'Yes.'

'What?'

'Yes. I will marry you, and come and live in Lyonesse. Yes, yes, yes!'

'Hang on – when did I ask you?'

'Within the next thirty seconds, if you have any sense!'

'But you don't even know if I'm still the sort of fellow you'd like . . .'

'I ran away from home at five minutes notice when I was fifteen. If you imagine I've learned sufficient patience at the age of fifty-five to think carefully, you never knew me at all. Apart from anything else, at our age, one of us could die tomorrow. I'd rather be widowed after I'm married, if I have to be at all.'

He pulled her close to him again, wrapping her in his arms. 'I'm probably dreaming all this, but if I am, I prefer to sleep for ever. Lottie, I love you. Will you marry me?'

She looked up at him with a glint of mischief. 'Will you want me to give up the stage?'

'Christ, no! If you did that, I'd never know what you were getting up to!'

'All right, you're on. I think we'd better go and tell my brother Ivo. I do hope his heart's in good shape. Lesser shocks than this have been known to kill members of my family!'

CHAPTER THIRTY-SIX
London, 1942

It had been, Lottie reflected, a marriage made in heaven. It seemed that her fifteen-year-old instincts had been the wisest she ever had. They had told her she and Tommy Fanshaw were made for each other. From the summer of 1935, she got the chance to prove them right.

Superficially, much of her life remained unchanged. She continued to play heavyweight theatrical roles, leavening them with appearances in cabaret. The difference was that now she had Tommy Fanshaw to lean on, Tommy Fanshaw to confide in, Tommy Fanshaw to love.

When he took her home one evening after a nightclub appearance, she was giggling helplessly. 'What's got into you tonight?' he said. 'You're like a ten-year-old kid.'

'You didn't see the mad dowager who'd come with her husband and family to hear me,' said Lottie, through fresh gusts of laughter. 'I suppose she was about my age, and for a while she was preening herself about how young "we" – she meant her and me – were looking. Then my set finished and I came out and joined you at the table and we had a little cuddle . . . I thought she was going to come across and accuse me of a public sex display! I think in her world, little old ladies of over sixty go home to cocoa and an improving book at night. It was pretty obvious we were off to champagne and a quick how's-your-father!'

'Shame on you, Lady Fanshaw! A woman of your years and respectability!' said Tommy.

'You can watch it too,' she said. 'Age, yes. Respectability, never!'

'All right, I take it back. Come to think of it, you wouldn't know how to start being respectable.'

Lottie was doubly conscious of their great happiness because she knew the world was about to change catastrophically, and that everything might end even sooner than she had expected. In September 1939, Britain and France went to war with Germany. Her American friends wrote to her, stridently demanding to know why she was not already on her way back to New York. One morning, breakfasting in bed at Lyonesse, she read out a section of one such letter to Tommy.

When she finished, snorting with derision at its panic-stricken tone, Tommy said: 'She might have a point, you know. An awful lot of people are crossing the Atlantic. It's going to get a hell of a lot worse before it gets better.'

'Come on, Tommy, you know me better than that! I hate pretend patriotism.

I wouldn't go along with it during the Boer War and I was damned glad to be out of England when the Great War was on. But this one is different . . . this man Hitler is a third rate bully and I'm buggered if he's making me run!'

Tommy did not mention voluntary exile again. Secretly he was glad his wife was so contemptuous of those who did. One day, he said to her: 'You'd never go as long as the remnants of your boys in the gallery were still trapped over here, would you?'

She gave him a radiant smile. 'That's exactly why I won't, my darling. They've got to stay, so I choose to. Now, let's try to ignore the whole shooting match. I've got work to do.'

But what she dismissed as a shooting match would not go away so easily. She went on working, and by 1940, her popularity stood as high as it ever had in her days of music hall stardom. Various theatre managements had begged her to top the bill at variety concerts with a theme of Britannia ruling the waves, or Little England standing alone against all enemies. She turned them down flat. 'I loathe patriotism now as much as I did in 1900,' she told Maud. 'Why should I blow their bloody trumpets for 'em? I wouldn't mind helping with the war effort, but as long as I have to do it with the red, white and blue wrapped round me, they can take a running jump.'

She modified her views at the end of 1941, when Pearl Harbor abruptly brought America into the War. She still opposed the flaunting jingoism of shows which featured strings of numbers like 'We're Gonna Hang Out the Washing On The Siegfried Line', but she was beginning to believe she had a part to play in boosting the all-important sense of alliance between America and England. All sorts of theatrical revues were being staged in London to encourage the war effort. They generally involved chorus girls dressed in travesties of military uniform, marching about and singing martial songs. Lottie despised them as bad theatre, poor propaganda and feeble entertainment.

Early in 1942, she asked Tommy to organise a meeting to discuss mounting a high-gloss revue that would leave everyone who saw it full of enthusiasm about the family links between England and America, but without a string of insincere patriotic nonsense on their lips.

Charlie Fletcher, a top flight American musical director who had stayed in Britain when the War broke out while he had been working in London, was the first to debunk her suggestions.

'It's no good, Charlotte. I share your feelings about all these stars and stripes and Gallant Little England routines, but it's what people expect at a time like this – what they respond to.'

'God dammit, I shall lose my temper in a minute!' stormed Lottie. 'It's nothing of the sort – it's a bunch of theatrical types churning out what they think will appeal to people. I'm sick to death of hearing ordinary people sneering about all that "There'll always be an England" nonsense. They're right to sneer, though. They know *they're* the real England, just as their opposite numbers in Queens or the Bronx are the real USA. They don't care a stuff about flags and bunting, because the past has taught them it's all phoney. What they understand is the need to survive, and I'm damned sure there's entertaining music that will help them to do that.'

'Such as?' Fletcher's tone dripped scepticism.

'Such as . . . such as – I'll tell you such as what, Charlie! A long time ago, it dawned on me that ordinary people needed songs to reflect their ordinary lives. It was why music hall was a hit for so long. Nowadays it's why a certain sort of movie does the same sort of business. They identify with it.

'I can't think of many better ways to remind people of what they are, where they come from and what they stand for, than a succession of their everyday popular songs, from the turn of the century until the present. No patriotism – all popular, lightweight stuff, half British, half American. It would run for ever, and we could give people a real boost about what they're fighting to preserve. They won't even be aware that it's propaganda, and that's why it will work.'

Fletcher began to shake his head, then said: 'Oh, what the hell! Against my better judgement, I'd like you to be right. Okay, let's forget yet another reprise of 'Hands Across the Sea' and go for some gut popular entertainment.'

'That's more like it. Good lad! And now, we need the sort of venue that will drag 'em in from everywhere . . . Tommy, where d'you think you're going?'

He grinned, resignation all over his face. 'I had a feeling you might start trading on your privileged position with me, Lottie, and I was trying to save you the embarrassment.'

'Don't bother. You know I don't embarrass easily. Drury Lane is dark at the moment, innit? I'm sure you could find out how long it'll stay that way, and don't they owe you a little favour or three? With the right pressure, we could be in there, with the biggest Anglo-American schmaltz hit in variety history. Come on, Tommy, lad, give it a go.'

'Good grief, Lottie, for someone who hates patriotic displays, you don't half use the same lot of sentiments from time to time . . . all right, I'll do it. I hope you can come up with a hit, though. Right now anything without soldiers, sailors and airman or a song saying "Thanks, Yanks" seems to be doomed.'

'Not this one, dear boy, believe me.'

They called the show *They Were Singing*. It was divided into exactly half American and half British popular numbers, and it was to catch the public mood so perfectly that it played to full houses until forced to close to make room for the Theatre Royal's next scheduled production. By then, it had been offered transfers to three other West End theatres and had been acclaimed by every newspaper and magazine critic in London. By the end of the year, it had opened in New York, where the Broadway version was even more popular. And it was entirely Lottie Casanova's show . . .

A single spot played on the curtain. The overture ended, and suddenly, a long, elegant leg slid into the spotlight. Its owner was still concealed by the joined curtains, but as the audience savoured the shape of the leg, with its alluring sheath of black silk fishnet, a familiar growling voice came from nowhere:

> 'I'm Bert, you'll have heard of me;
> Bert, you'll have word of me . . .'

A silk top hat emerged, above the leg, followed by an arm, clad in an immaculate piece of man's suiting. Then the spot expanded, the curtain whisked apart momentarily, and the owner of arm, leg and hat stood revealed. She wore a perfectly tailored evening coat, with tails, a white dress shirt and white tie – the collar and tie slightly askew to denote Bert's genteel poverty – black tights and skin-tight shorts which stopped dead at the hip joint. Lottie Casanova stood before them in a variation of all her pre-1910 glory. The orchestra struck up a prowling, predatory refrain and she slunk around the stage, posing occasionally with the silver-headed cane she carried. As the orchestral introduction ended, she slapped the top hat on her head and turned to face the audience:

> 'I'm Burlington Bertie,
> I rise at ten-thirty
> And saunter along like a toff.
> I walk down the Strand with my gloves on my hand
> Then I walk down again wiv 'em off.
> I'm all airs and graces, correct easy paces,
> So long without food I forgot where my face is,
> I'm Bert, Bert, I haven't a shirt,
> But my people are well off you know,
> Nearly everyone knows me, from Smith to Lord Rosebery
> I'm Burlington Bertie from Bow!'

To one side of her, a troupe of dancers in expensive evening dress came on and performed a stilted waltz. At the other side, eight costers, in pearl button-covered costumes, executed a clog-dance routine in the same tempo which mocked every movement. Noses in air, the evening-dressed group waltzed off.

Charlotte sidled downstage and leaned confidentially towards the audience:

> 'The Prince of Wales' brother,
> Along with some other,
> Slaps me on the back and says
> "Come and meet Mother!"
> I'm Bert, Bert, royalty's hurt,
> When they ask me to dine I say no . . .
> I just had a banana with Lady Diana,
> I'm Burlington Bertie from Bow!'

Originally she had planned to do all her old routines, but one rehearsal had convinced her that however fit she might be, it would not work. Then the solution had occurred to her: Dee-Dee! No one would know the difference between the young Lottie and Cordelia – indeed, Cordelia resembled Lottie more closely now than Charlotte herself did. The girl was apprehensive but willing to try it, and she was sensational.

The revue took a long and idealised look at stage entertainment in England and America since the turn of the century. There was no overt mention of the present War, but the entire ambience of the evening was the common

340

inheritance of both countries and a celebration of the entertainments that would always link them.

Dee-Dee had opened the show with her version of Lottie's original big number: 'I Want To Go Where The Big Girls Go', with the full dress transformation routine. All her mother's more energetic hit songs followed, interspersed with Lottie doing her own version of evergreens that other stars had made famous. Between the English music hall numbers were equally famous pieces from American vaudeville and cabaret. Dee-Dee earned a standing ovation in her own name when she sang 'Brother, Can You Spare A Dime?' standing to the side of the stage, clad in a stark, plain white gown, while a troupe of male dancers drilled as First World War soldiers and then lined up at a soup kitchen for free food as her unique voice wept out:

'Once in khaki suits, didn't we look swell?
Full of Yankee doodle dum,
Half a million boots went slogging through hell
And I was the kid with the drum . . .

Say, do you remember? My name's Al;
It was Al – Al, all the time . . .
Say, do you remember? I'm your pal!
. . . Brother, can you spare a dime?'

Backstage, Maud was sitting in a puddle of nostalgia. 'I dunno what it's doin' to that audience,' she muttered to Tommy, 'but it's wringing me out. I've never seen nuffink to touch it.'

Tommy tended to agree, with one reservation. He had no desire to push Lottie beyond her capabilities, but he still felt wrong about Dee-Dee doing 'Ta-ra-ra-boom-de-ay.' He need not have worried. As the 'Burlington Bertie' routine came to an end, the audience rose like a single being and started chanting: 'Lot-tie! Lot-tie! Lot-tie! We want "Ta-ra-ra-boom-de-ay!" '

Charlotte and Dee-Dee had gauged the time right. This was where the song was scheduled – in the spot immediately before the finale. But now both women stared at each other, stricken by the thought of a disappointed audience's reaction if they did not get the woman who originally popularised the song. To crown it, the rhythmic repetition of her original stage name threw Charlotte straight back to the night at the River Palace in Sioux City, where she had first fully understood her power to sway an audience.

Dee-Dee was already in the black and red satin, about to don the nodding plumed headdress. Abruptly, Lottie said: 'Forget it, kid. They'd lynch you! I'm fit enough – let's risk it . . . come on, quick, get your frock off, I haven't got all night!'

And before her daughter's astounded eyes she began to undress. Dee-Dee spluttered a protest, but then Maud was in front of her. 'Come on, love,' she said, 'Over your head wiv it, quick – at least we don't have to unlace any stays!'

Then it was as if she was looking in a mirror. Her mother, a wonderful reincarnated Edwardian maenad, stood there in the barbaric splendour of lace, satin and feathers. Her face glistened with the light sweat she had worked up in the 'Burlington Bertie' routine, but she looked fresh and vital.

'You could do the short version, Lottie,' murmured Maud. 'I know the orchestra have got it.'

Lottie twinkled at her oldest friend. 'And how d'you know that, Maudie dear?'

'Because I know what a stubborn old bitch you are and I didn't believe for one minute that you'd let Miss Cordelia do this routine. I give it to 'em.'

'In that case, you'll also know I'd die rather than do the short version.'

'You probably *will* bloody die, an' all, if you do the full thing,' grumbled Maud. 'You're sixty-two this year, even if you don't look it.'

'We can but see – and anyway, what a way to go! . . . now, if I don't go on, they'll tear down the theatre. Maudie, my plume, please!'

Maud set the cluster of feathers in place, someone signalled to the orchestra leader and they were off in the mad romp that preceded the most killing solo dance routine ever seen on a stage.

Lottie was unaware of her age, her joints, the anxious faces backstage. This was pure magic . . . it was every first night she had ever done, all rolled into one. It was running away with Ulick Farrell; it was hearing 'Ting-a-ling-a-boomderay' for the first time on a back lot in Sioux City; it was topping the bill at the Orpheum in San Francisco and it was playing Aladdin at Drury Lane.

My God, she had spoken nothing but the truth! If she died during this number, it would be worth every second . . . the first chorus came to an end and the orchestra tipped over into the racing refrain. Up went her leg, way above her head, scattering a shower of scarlet petticoats. Her feathers bobbed and the kicks continued – one – and – kick – and – two – and – kick – and – three – and – kick – and into the airborne cartwheels.

Nothing existed now except the circle of stage in which she cavorted, a wild, liberated spirit of a dead age, an age which had no means of rebellion and expression apart from women like Lottie Casanova and men like Dan Leno . . . and spin-and-roll-and-spin-and-roll-and . . . hell, she was dizzy . . . had the bastards gone into a second reprise of that refrain, or was it her age? No, there was that little skip to warn her the penultimate cartwheel was coming up . . . she spun into it, arriving with perfect timing at centre front stage as the orchestra struck a huge chord and she leaped into the air accompanied by an audible mass intake of breath by the audience. And up, up, higher than she'd thought she could still jump . . . legs wide, and down, into a perfect Can-Can girl's splits . . . then a regal dip of the feathers (like a bloody camp Dying Swan, she thought) and it was all over. She slid to her feet as gracefully as a fifteen-year-old athlete. To her surprise, there were tears streaming down her cheeks. She wondered where and when they had started. She had not been conscious of them.

Suddenly, she staggered. Christ . . . was she going to get off the stage? Then there was a strong, steel-hard arm around her waist, unobtrusively supporting her from behind. She glanced up in surprised gratitude and to her infinite pleasure discovered Tommy at her side. She had been so blinkered by concentration on her routine that she had forgotten anyone else existed. Now she leaned on him gratefully, and he edged them both forward.

'Ladies and gentlemen,' he said 'Most of you won't recognise me – I'm the silent half of this theatrical partnership. But tonight I'm stepping into the limelight and going in for a bit o' self-indulgence. I'm exaggerating the time scale for the next number, but the sentiment's completely honest . . .'

He signalled at the conductor, who struck up one of the most familiar, hackneyed tunes in music hall. Lottie turned to him, fresh tears flowing, and said under her breath: 'You sentimental old bugger – I'll never let you live this down!' Then the intro ended and Tommy began to sing, looking at her as he had once done as a boy of sixteen in a back bedroom in Covent Garden:

> 'We've been together now for forty years,
> And it don't seem a day too much.
> There ain't a lady living in the land
> As I'd swap for me dear old dutch!'

And, unforgettably, the audience joined in, standing, applauding, blowing kisses at Lottie Casanova. In the wings, Dee-Dee and Maud clung to each other, crying unashamedly. Finally Dee-Dee managed to pull herself together sufficiently to tell the stage manager: 'Forget the finale – we couldn't touch this. Give it another chorus and then bring the curtain down. She won't stand much more.'

Maud patted her cheek. 'Like mother like daughter,' she murmured fondly. 'You're a pro to your fingertips!'